Alphabet

'It is a wonderful book, peculiar, intense, revealing, challenging and above all riveting . . . I kept saying to myself, how could she know this?'

Erwin James, *Guardian* columnist and author of *A Life Inside*

'Sometimes novelists go too far – and sometimes they manage to demonstrate that too far is the place they needed to go . . . a book which lets us see the humanity and vulnerability that accompany monstrous acts' Roz Caveny, *Time Out*

'Page throws hope into a mixed-up world where only fantasies and delusions dare to grow' Susan Musgrave, *Globe and Mail*

'Page has . . . been courageous in making a sympathetic character of a man who has abused and killed a woman. She knows him in his full complexity, and that self-knowledge has risks, but also brings hope' Kath Murphy, *Scotland on Sunday*

'A truly compelling read, right to the last page . . . an excellent book group choice' *New Books magazine*

'Page captures the oppressiveness of the closed institution, the violence that always seethes beneath the surface . . . The inmates . . . are individually well-drawn and collectively they help to make the story compelling . . . Page lifts the novel out of its didactic casing, through the subtlety of her treatment of the literacy theme' Sarah Curtis, *Times Literary Supplement*

The Story of My Face

'*The Story of My Face* is a marvellously well-crafted book, subtle and measured yet with the powerful, disconcerting tug of deep and dangerous water. I can't remember the last time I was so compelled, impressed and unsettled by the emotional world of a novel, as I was by this one' Sarah Waters

'Page's descriptions of the cold and silent Finnish landscape are incredibly evocative and haunting. You can almost smell the snow melting as Natalie examines every detail of one life in a bid to understand her own . . . *The Story of My Face* is quietly gripping. It keeps you reading, wanting to uncover both Natalie's past and that of Thomas Envall' Clare Heal, *Sunday Express*

'The novel has a tightly written, wonderful structure . . . Page has a talent for vivid invention and detail, and rarely rings a false note . . . it's a world that envelops you, taking you on a compelling and unpredictable journey'

Rebecca Caldwell, *Globe and Mail*

'An elegantly compelling story of how a young girl's obsession forever changes the lives of those around her . . . a disciplined exploration of the complexity of human motivation and our need for redemption' Lynne Van Luven, *Vancouver Sun*

'. . . a most impressive achievement'

Jessica Mann, *Daily Telegraph*

'A moving, absorbing story . . . Kathy Page writes beautifully'

Helen Dunmore

Kathy Page was born in London but is currently living on the west coast of Canada with her husband and two young children. Her fifth novel, *The Story of My Face*, was long-listed for the Orange Prize in 2002. She has worked as a writer in residence at a variety of universities and in other settings, including a Norfolk fishing village and, in 1992, a men's prison in the UK. Her website can be visited at www.KathyPage.info.

By Kathy Page

Back in the First Person
The Unborn Dreams of Clara Riley
Island Paradise
Frankie Styne and the Silver Man
As in Music
The Story of My Face
Alphabet

ALPHABET

KATHY PAGE

For Keith —
who has been there,
and could have
written it!
Kathy Page
Nanaimo 2006

PHOENIX

For Richard

A PHOENIX PAPERBACK

First published in Great Britain in 2004
by Weidenfeld & Nicolson
This paperback edition published in 2005
by Phoenix,
an imprint of Orion Books Ltd,
Orion House, 5 Upper St Martin's Lane,
London WC2H 9EA

1 3 5 7 9 10 8 6 4 2

A CIP catalogue record for this book
is available from the British Library.

ISBN 0 75381 861 2

Typeset at The Spartan Press Ltd,
Lymington, Hants
Printed and bound in Great Britain by
Clays Ltd, St Ives plc

www.orionbooks.co.uk

contents

B

1

There's no chair, even. The room is blue-grey, fluorescent-lit, like the rest.

'Property?' the man at the counter asks. They've already taken his real clothes: Simon's standing there in a striped shirt and a pair of thin jeans that won't stay up.

'Anything that might get nicked or trashed,' the man says, 'Give it here –' he's done this a thousand times, has the timing just so. 'We'll seal it up nice and tight . . . then we'll lose it for you good and proper . . . Ha! Seriously, there's no liability.' Oh, he's proud of himself, all right. His white shirt glows almost violet. The breast pocket is stretched over a pack of twenty Bensons. The top of his bald head shines in the light as he taps the side of his nose, leans forwards:

'What you got, then,' he says, 'Mummy's ashes? The bleedin' crown jewels? Spit it out, we haven't got all day.' There are six more behind me, Simon thinks, and there's fuck knows what ahead . . . In the end, it can't matter much what happens to these two particular items of his. Except that this way he doesn't have to look after them and if they really are lost, whatever this bald bastard says, it won't be his fault. And the sooner he gets through this then the sooner he might get to lie down and he could sleep on a bed of knives in an earthquake so long as he was lying down.

He grins back at the big-headed, fat-fingered man; he keeps his thoughts to himself and puts his goods on the counter. First, the envelope. It's a small, thin envelope with just his name, Simon Austen, on the outside.

'It's sealed,' he says. *Well*, says the slow look he gets back, *opening your sodding correspondence is the last thing on earth I'd do, because, like you, it'll be a piece of –*

Simon's too beat-up to react. His eyes are so sticky he can hear every blink, feel it too. He had the shower after the strip search, but it was cold and he can still smell his own sweat. He stares at the counter top, dirty oak edging with Formica inset, and remembers how the envelope was given him by a washed-out social worker who first checked his birth certificate and gave him a speech about not expecting too much. Then she watched him tear it open, unfold the single sheet inside. After that, she read it to him, all two lines of it: 'I am sorry. This is the way things had to be. I really hope things turn out well for you, Sharon.' That's what the woman said it amounted to. Then she asked him would he like some time to talk about his feelings for his mother and when he said no, she said he needed counselling and gave him a list of phone numbers as long as an arm; he was so fucked off with her that he nearly binned the letter, but in the end he smoothed it out and resealed the envelope, kept it for years in the lining pocket of his pilot jacket . . . Well, as a matter of fact things turned out just about as badly as they possibly could, and this lot can lose the fucking thing if they want to, he thinks. He's moving on. In.

'One watch,' fat-fingers observes.

'It's a Rolex,' Simon tells him. Though it's not. He got it with his first month's proper pay, from someone he met in a pub. It loses. He was ripped off. So, good riddance. He'll travel light: washing things, bedroll, plate, bowl, mug.

'That it?'

He does his squiggle with the pen. The joker opposite seals up his things, then pushes over an empty envelope: brown with black type, official looking.

'Your Free Letter.'

'What's it for?'

'Well, son, you can wipe your arse with it if you want!'

'Right, mate,' Simon spits back. 'Maybe I will.' His hands are fisted and he's woken right up now.

'Keep your head down,' the man says, pleased, turning

away. Simon shoves the envelope in his pocket, collects two sheets and a blanket, stuffs them in the pillowcase, moves on.

The man in front of him has a moustache, the one behind a full chin's worth of hair. He can hear the creak of both of their pairs of shoes, the rattle of their key chains, their breath, his own. They pass through the next pair of doors, solid, then barred, and the next, and the next, pausing each time to wait for the key to slip in and do its work, two openings, two closures. Nothing is said. He thinks how he could die here. Be killed. Start using drugs and do the job himself. Just get old . . . and all of a sudden, how badly he wants what he's not had, all of it, even not knowing what it is! How much he wants to throw the switch, dematerialise, reappear somewhere else or as someone else, anyone. His heart is already fighting to escape his chest when the last set of doors opens on to the wing and the stench and echo of captivity smashes into him. It's like the opening of a furnace door. A wall of heat. They have to push him through.

'Go on,' says the bearded man behind, 'go on now, son, this here is a one-way street.'

2

I'm no good at reading, he tells them when they ask about his needs. Because Education is under-resourced, Ted Kennet comes on the bus to help out, changing twice, week after week.

Smoke? Ted asks as he sits down the first time. Next time he brings a paper bag of assorted sweets, *sweets* for God's sake: A for aniseed, B for butterscotch, C for candy twist: it doesn't have to be apple, ball, cat. It can be anything you want and it doesn't even have to start at the beginning and march through to the end. 'Start where you want!' Ted says. 'You pick. I'm trying to make it easy for you.'

They work in the back of the Education staff room, sitting under some book shelves that haven't been put up straight. People keep coming in to get to the stationery cupboard, which has to be unlocked and locked again every time.

'Remember, you do want this, even if you sometimes think you don't,' says Ted. If he's not busy with his roll-up machine or his pencils and paper, he sits with his big square hands like dead weights on his knees. The veins in his nose and cheeks are all bust up, the wrinkles on his forehead go up as well as down, cutting it up into squares. His hair is cut short and neat, but most of it has long gone. Simon's never sat as close to someone so old before and every time Ted coughs, he can hear something bubbling in his chest. D for disgusting.

Sometimes he loses patience. A for aggro. B for bastard. C for cunt.

'G for get on with it. I don't give up easily,' Ted says. According to him, reading is one hand (he lifts it, shows the palm, carved by lines into an elaborate hieroglyph) and writing is the other. Without them you'd be having to open doors with your teeth and toes. 'You've got a mind,' he says. 'Use it.'

Simon notes that Ted isn't well, and they don't pay him. He's impressed, though he won't fool himself that Ted's kindness is entirely personal to him because he also knows he's lost his wife and doesn't want to stay in and mope. And then again, it's clear that Ted is of the type that needs to do good. He's already put in thirty years as a UCAAT shop steward. You should have joined, he says. Might have made a difference, who knows? He believes in the two Rs, Rights and Wrongs. Illiteracy is a wrong on a par with being cut off from the electricity.

'It keeps you out,' he says. Knowledge, which begins with a K, is power. Work is another right. 'Two million unemployed!' he spits, grinding his roll-up into the ash tray. 'How come Thatcher's still got a job?'

Simon doesn't remember anyone in his previous life actually explaining in detail how, for the most part, the letters stand for sounds, how you build up the words. They must have, but he certainly didn't take it in. He was at Burnside, and number 32, and with Iris and John Kingswell in their poxy bungalow with its brown carpet and drafty louvred window panes. He's got one big memory that does for all the schools he ever didn't attend – the smell of stew and sweat, the feeling of misery as he walked in and the bite of free air in his lungs as he slipped over the fence at half past ten, running free. So it's more than strange where he has ended up:

'Paradoxical.' It's from the Greek, Ted says. 'Goes both ways.'

He's got all the time in the world and it isn't like school at all. Simon remembers everything. Soon he's way beyond the alphabet and the short, sensible words like man, dog, hat. Aeroplane. Cough. Through. Enough. Paragraphs, punctuation, even a soup-song of French and scraps of Latin as required: *et cetera*, *per se*, *ergo*, *ad infinitum*, he's picking them all up. And as for Ted, Simon feels something about him he can't remember feeling before: I've got absolutely nothing against the man, he thinks, and that's a not-bad feeling at all.

Eighteen months later, he's functional and Ted is coming mainly to chat. They discuss the news, which is nearly always bad: unemployment, privatisation, the Falklands. Then there's a message saying Ted is sick. He doesn't turn up for three weeks. Simon writes to him in his best joined-up, but it turns out that he's died.

Ted gave him a trade: he writes letters. He sits cross-legged on the bed in his six-foot-by-nine cell with a hardboard offcut to lean on and writes to lazy solicitors, members of parliament, the Home Secretary, the Parole Board; to unfaithful girlfriends, reluctant wives, sad mothers. He charges by the side, and depending on how hard it is to do. He puts a lot into it. He has designed several kinds of handwriting to suit the different tasks. He listens to what the bloke is saying, and then he cuts out the rambles, or fuzzes over the bluntness, makes it sound better. He looks words up, finds better ones, checks legal points if he can. Standing there blushing and fumbling to get the right words out is one thing but with a letter you can hit the bull's eye first time: 'I get results,' he tells his prospects. Though not of course every time. He's seen a bloke crying over a letter he's received, then had a bear-hug from him a fortnight later. Seeing as he doesn't have his own post, he even throws in his *free envelope* now and then. Plus, the other thing he does, because he's clean as a whistle, is sell his piss when they're testing. It's not so bad, though he thinks a lot of Ted when the Iron Lady gets in again. *Landslide*.

He gets into education, big time. He cuts the letter-writing out and concentrates on coursework, assignments. He passes GCSE English, Maths, Sociology and Computers, plus RSA typing and the Certificate in Verbal Communication, before they stop him, half way through his first A level, and decide to move him here, where they say he's had too much education and has to get to the back of the queue. Any kind of activity is a plus and has to be shared out. A bit of kitchen work. A stint in the electronics shop, assembling recycled hi-fis. So now he's been over seven years inside, twelve months in the same cell with the same wanker next door.

They told me I'm bright, he reminds himself. There's definitely truth in it because when he was sent to casualty for an abscess on one of his back teeth, he was sitting there in agony, waiting for hours with a screw chained to each arm and then finally the doctor came in and asked: 'Which one of you is Simon?' A *doctor*, right?

I could eventually get a degree, he tells himself. It's not impossible.

3

The Portakabins smell of paint burning on radiators and whoever's been in here before. Someone moves next door, the floor shifts. There's no ventilation and probation's man of the moment, Barry, is always giving up but actually, he smokes, heavily at that.

'How's things, Simon?' he asks. He's got a soft Welsh burr to his speech, a boyish face, though he must be forty plus.

'Pretty standard,' Simon tells him, 'bored witless.' Barry leans back in his chair, puts his hands behind his head. The narrow window is behind him, high up, looks right onto the prison wall. Also, it's never been cleaned. So Simon has to look at Barry, looking back at him with his serious brown eyes, or else at his own hands. He keeps his hands clean and neat, so there's not much going on there either.

'I'm still working on Education,' Barry continues, 'but the system's so crowded. More cuts in the pipeline too. A shame. But all the same, there is plenty else for you to think about. Did you consider what we said last time?' At this point, he comes out of his leaning back position and checks his notes, to remind himself what was said four months ago. 'Simon,' he says, 'you appear to be very cynical.'

'You must be too,' Simon comes back at him.

'You're capable of insight,' Barry persists, 'but you're still in denial. You can't progress until you break out of it.'

'You'd know, of course,' Simon says. 'Been there, have you?'

'Listen, Simon. The reason I'm here,' Barry says, 'is that in my old job, I always wondered what happened afterwards.' Well, Simon thinks at him, this is it! This is what happens afterwards! He decides against saying it. There's a long silence. Outside the Portakabin, some screws walk past, key chains jangling, and there's a sudden, staccato burst of laughter, which blanks out as the B wing door closes behind them.

'Women are an issue for you, aren't they?' Barry throws this in casually, as if it was a matter of sugars in tea, not half the human race. 'I've got a set of cards here, it's a way of starting up a discussion.' He shows them: the cards have a statement written on them and you have to say your gut feeling as to whether you agree or disagree.

'Want to give it a try?' *Why should I care?* Simon thinks. What matters to him more is when is Barry going to get out his thermos flask, as he normally does about half way through, and give them both a cup of proper coffee.

Barry hands him the first card. It's typed very large, and covered in shiny plastic laminate.

'Women have smaller brains and are less intelligent than men,' it says.

'Pass,' Simon says, because he'd say the opposite except that some of them do spectacularly stupid things. Like: almost all of the men in here, cons and screws, even *Barry*, are married to someone or as good as. He takes the next card.

'Women are naturally more caring,' it says. *Naturally* is confusing.

'Pass,' he says again. 'I don't mind telling you what I think,' he says, 'if you'll only get the coffee out.' He watches Barry extract the flask from his bulging briefcase and pour: the steel cup for himself, the plastic liner for Simon. Sugar from a small glass jar. The strong, bitter smell of the coffee seems to come from half a life away. The caffeine kicks in after a sip or two.

'Women. Off the top of my head –' Simon tells Barry, 'One: They like to be looked at. They smell nice. Even the cross-sex-postings we have here. Two: They tend not to hit out. A woman may scare you in some way, the chances of her actually, physically hurting you are almost nil. Three: they give birth, or decide not to. Sometimes they have children without meaning to and sometimes they have them and then they don't want them –' at this point Barry tries to interrupt but Simon is in his stride: 'OK,' he concedes, 'men have something to do with it, but not much. All of us have been inside a woman's body. A lot of people spend a lot of time trying to get back inside one: I'm not one of them. I'd hate to be a woman. If I was one, I'd steer completely clear of men. I'd be a lesbian! And I certainly wouldn't have something grow inside me. And another thing,' Simon tells Barry, 'you have to use a woman's weaknesses to make her like you.' He's lost track of the numbers so he stops, and drinks down the rest of the coffee, which has cooled down to just right. He watches Barry writing down what he's said.

'There's an awful lot in there,' Barry tells him when he's finished, 'and, without being judgemental, because with your background it's not at all surprising, I'd say there were a lot of contradictions too . . .' He gives Simon a big smile, and takes a sip from his own cup. 'Well, Amanda liked you, didn't she?' he says. Simon just looks through him; no one's going to catch him that way.

'What scares you about women?' Barry asks after another long pause. 'What is it –'

'They have the say-so, don't they?' Simon says. 'Teachers. Thatcher. That Currie Woman. Madonna.'

'It's clear that you need to feel a very high level of control over your life,' Barry tells him. Simon recognises this as a direct quote from Dr Grice.

'Well, I'm in the right place, then, aren't I just!' he says, and cracks up, but Barry's lips don't even twitch; he says nothing for a bit, then fumbles in his bag for the Marlboros. Simon reaches out and takes one for trade. Barry lights up, then plays with the cigarette, tapping it into the white saucer he uses as an ashtray, even though it doesn't need doing yet.

'It's up to you, Simon,' he says eventually, and they spend the next ten minutes or so talking over the football.

Simon is angry when he gets back. It's true about women, but at the same time, he thinks, Barry is top to toe absolute purest bullshit. Up to me? Too right. So what are you and the other one paid for? Because here's his view: of course you can understand how a bicycle works, but you still have to find your actual, physical balance and learn to ride it. You could actually do that *without* the understanding. What you really need is first, a bicycle, second, time to practise. The resources available here, *vis-à-vis learning how to relate to women*, are limited, stretched to breaking point, to say the least: The screwesses, who don't count (rumour has it they may not be actual women), the chaplain's groupies, and four of the teachers in Education, where he is not allowed to go. Female members of the public are not exactly queuing up to give lessons, are they? Fair enough, he thinks, but if I want whatever it is, whatever is the opposite of here, I've got to find the way myself.

It's good to have an example. Jay Cartwell, Simon reminds himself, was only on B wing three days before he figured out how to make a noose out of plaited dental floss. He used what he had already got to get him where he wanted to go, and that, he thinks, is what I will do too.

4

First: in the adverts that you see, people put in their age, their looks, sometimes job, hobbies – all of it most probably lies, delusions or exaggeration. Then they put in what kind of person they want, size maybe, some characteristic, like lively, sensuous, sense of humour, blonde, whatever. But Simon thinks anything definite could stand against him as much as for, so he's going to keep it brief: *Man seeks woman to correspond with, any age.* Plus, second, he won't specify looks because surely that stuff can only matter if you've got to look at the person day in day out, and hear the actual sound of their voice, very likely driving you straight up the wall. And, third, he's not saying what he wants the correspondence to lead to, because he doesn't exactly know. But it seems to him that you could well get further and closer with a letter than with talk. Sometimes, people will communicate more when they think they are on their own, and can concentrate properly on what they want to say.

I'm doing this my way, he thinks. There'll be no asking for 'the Governor's permission if you wish to advertise for a pen friend', no putting 'the correct address at the top of each letter', still less having his letters and replies opened for enclosures and possibly read by the idiot censor . . . This will be his very own correspondence course. All of which means, since he doesn't get visits, that he'll have to buy in help getting the letters in and out. He needs someone who gets through cash fast: Teverson, on the threes. Aggravated Burglary and GBH, fancies himself. Normally he'd steer clear, but.

As per, Tev's wired. His sounds blast out good and loud while they talk, gobbling batteries. There's two empty Mars wrappers and a bowl of tinned peaches on the table, plus a full ash tray. His pad is papered with women, mainly from behind. Bums are his thing. Natural position of a woman, he tells Simon, face down. Back passage has a good grip to it and you don't need to worry about knocking her up.

'Well, why are you here, mate?' he says. He's in his gym kit, and sweating as if he was still in there. The smell of it comes off him in waves.

Visits? His missus comes, and his sister and her sister and his mum: 'If you want a woman,' he says, 'why not take one of them off my hands! Nothing but hassle. Or I could get you a nice girl, friend of the wife, to come and visit, if you want something tasty to look at and think about later on, right?'

'No.' Simon doesn't want something second hand. He's doing this his way. 'Thanks, mate. I want letters,' he tells Teverson.

'Well, she'd write them!' Tev says, 'If you told her to. Save us both a lot of trouble.'

'I want someone who *wants* to. Look, I'm doing this my way,' Simon tells Tev. 'I'll pay. I'm after a mule. She'll have to get the letter out at a visit, then take the reply at her address, change the envelope, bring it in to you. If she gets more than one reply, well, then you tell her to bring the thickest one, and bin the rest.'

He's collected a few fags, so he offers Teverson one. Tev takes it without a word, banging his head up and down to the beat. 'Risky,' he says. 'I don't want to kill the goose that lays my golden eggs, do I?' But then again, he's got a few of them.

'How much?' Simon asks. If you want something, drink, snout, junk, sex, letters, it's the same: you have to put out for it. But if the bloke has any sense, he won't charge you more than you can get hold of.

'Thirty,' Teverson says. He claps his arm round Simon's shoulders and gives a squeeze, then a slap between the shoulder blades.

'How long you done?' he asks. 'Eight? That's as long as I

reckon I'll serve,' he says, pleased with himself. 'Keep busy and it'll go in a flash. Everything'll be hunky-dory when I get out.'

Dear is how you begin letters, even if you don't know the person, even if you don't like them, and *Dear* is what they call you when they write back. I like that, Simon thinks, and he also likes the thought of someone making the effort to get out paper and pen, and maybe looking back over his last letter to see if there are any questions to answer or points to pick up, pausing for a while and then beginning to write. At any point they might stop or be interrupted. But the idea of him waiting to know what they have to say keeps them going until the end: *yours, best wishes, keep cheerful, take care, write soon, love* . . . He is not deserving of these words, but once, according to Dr Grice, he must have been. Well, perhaps he can have the ones he's owed from back then?

He's waiting, just waiting, here on his bed. To the right: door, sanitary unit, ahead: table, chair, books, pens. Fifteen years, minimum. Five minutes to lockdown. Eleven hours in. Four hours till there's any peace and quiet. Eight weeks, he figures, till he might get a reply: the ad lies around at the newspaper office for ten days or so. Then the paper comes out, then it flits around the house for a bit, nearly gets thrown out, and then late at night she's looking through it and thinks, well, yes, I might. Then she has to actually write the letter. Then she forgets she's done it then she doesn't have a stamp and forgets to post it for a week and nearly doesn't bother. Then she does and it gets to Teverson's wife's sister, and hides under the doormat. Sod's law, she finds it straight after a visit, or it's not her turn, so that's another fortnight gone.

It's all relative is the thing to remember, and what he finds helps is to breathe in very slowly, hold it a bit, then out the same way. Plus, he tries to direct his thoughts the way he wants them to go. Forward, not back. What could be, not what once was. He's thinking now how he will keep copies of the letters he writes in one half of the Adidas box that he got from the

Irishman, and the letters that he receives from her in their envelopes in the other half. He's thinking how meantime, he'll keep up with the hap-kid-do and the stretching exercises and of course the yogic breathing. He'll read, and develop his imagination. One way you do this is by asking yourself questions, like, what kind of place do you think Teverson has on the outside? Easy.

A big council maisonette, with peeling paint on the outside, and every mod con indoors. Tiger-stripe rug, big mirror, huge TV, Marantz sounds, fancy lighting. Tropical fish. Huge bed. Sawn-off shotgun under it. Steel front door, metal grille on the windows.

What will she be like? he thinks. I don't know.

Who will I become? Ditto. A leap in the dark.

5

It is only four days since Dickie Walters called Simon to his office. What's going on? he was thinking as he followed the officer into the Magnolia Zone, where the odour of stale food and bodily miseries ceases abruptly, replaced by the aroma of fresh coffee that floats out of the cubby hole at the end of the wing. Had they found out about the deal with Teverson? Had someone grassed him up about something as petty as this? Just the thought of it balled his hands into fists; at the same time his eyes drank in the deep red of the carpet and his ears adapted gratefully to the new, soft soundscape of low voices, typing and telephones, female laughter from behind doors left ajar.

Get on with it! he thought as fresh-faced Walters shook his hand then sat down and went through endless preliminaries. *Don't piss me about!*

'Well,' said Walters eventually, 'good news. After consideration, as a privilege, but not a right, I've decided to allow you access to your last F75 report –' *Why?*

'I don't want it,' Simon told him. 'Why would I? I never asked for it.'

'These days we are trying to be as transparent as we can,' Walters continued, regardless, light glinting from the smearless lenses of his glasses. 'We feel it could be of benefit for you to see these reports, as and when, of course, staffing levels make it feasible. Just put in a request to your Personal Officer.'

First he had a good laugh. Ask that bastard for something? *You must be joking!* Then he thought he was indifferent. Then he thought he'd hold out: wrong. He applied and here he is, seated at a metre-square formica table placed plumb in the centre of a windowless cube of a room, perfectly aligned beneath the rectangular fluorescent panel on the ceiling. Hoskins is propped against the wall two paces away, sucking his breath in through his teeth, checking his watch every other minute. The report is in its slide binder in front of him. It's about half an inch thick. He can see that it's a mistake to have come, but even so, he opens it.

'Austen has an arrogant attitude. He has made no effort to address any of his offending behaviour other than poor literacy, which can have had only a minor impact on the trajectory of the offence . . .' Walters himself. Where do they go to learn this stuff! On it goes, on and on. Five, six pages! He whisks through, almost tearing the typed sheets as he turns them: '. . . attended the anger-management course but said it was only to satisfy the institution and commented that he had already discovered most of the techniques for himself . . .' Well, yes, it's called put a lid on it, you fucking have to or you'd explode! He looks up at Hoskins, who is looking at the ceiling, cheeks bright with burst veins, dandruff on his shoulders, no doubt fantasising about retirement, likely to be dead within six months of it.

'Austen is deeply in denial . . .' These words, typed out by the woman in the acrylic knitwear suits who sits next to the governor-grade offices, clickety clack, makes him want to spit. Literally, he can feel his mouth fill up. *Remove the stimulus!* He turns over a few pages at once. *Time out,* right? The Personal Officer, at least he's done his with his own hand, pressing hard, making blobs with the biro ink: 'Good behaviour, but sarcastic and a loner. This man strikes me as a time-bom (sic) that could go off any day.'

He turns over another clump of pages. Dr Grice!

'Steady,' puffs Hoskins, pushing himself away from the wall for a moment in case action is required, then settling back again.

'Rather than confront his early experiences of abandonment and rejection, Simon has developed a strategy of using hostility to pre-empt further rejection. He shows no interest in exploring this and over six sessions he frequently used mockery to . . .'

And so now all at once he's as tense as he used to get in that apricot-white room of Grice's: nothing to do but look at the over-painted brickwork, the freckles on the backs of Grice's hands, the stray grey hairs in his nose, the bald patch, the weave of the cloth his jacket is made from, look and look and look until it's like some kind of hallucination, waiting for time to pass. Grice could ask a question, and wait twenty minutes for the answer to come, or not. Didn't seem to bother him. Whenever Simon looked up at his face, he was always looking back, not staring, just alertly looking, just as if something *had* just been said, and it was setting him off on a new and interesting train of thought. By the time he got out of that room, Simon's teeth would be jammed together and his whole back hurt and he'd want someone to lay into him, just for the release of it and so he could hit back. The one time it happened, in the showers, some idiot laughed at one of his tattoos and he got him on the ground in two seconds flat, smashing his head on the tiles, 'Don't you dare laugh at me.' Result: a lot of respect, plus five extra days for resisting the screws who pulled them apart, plus he had to do the anger-management course. That was the last time before this that he had to go to see Walters.

'Well,' Grice said at the end of the last 'meeting', as he called them, 'we can of course resume at a later date, should you change your mind . . .' Simon was thinking: *Is this some kind of joke, it must be, when are we both going to crack up laughing or have you never done it?* But at the same time he was standing there in front of Grice as if he'd been turned to stone, as if somehow he couldn't go, now that it was really over.

Hoskins clears his throat, which sounds as if it's full of half-cured cement with a handful or two of gravel thrown in. He's on at least forty a day, and clearly desperate to get out of this No Smoking room. 'Just a few minutes more,' he says, and

Simon could leave it there but just to spite Hoskins he flicks over some more pages at random: 'Austen is fit and attends well to personal cleanliness,' he discovers, courtesy of the Medical Officer. What a gem! So who, exactly, is the expert here? Am I right or am I not? But does it matter one little bit?

'Crap!' Simon barks at Hoskins.

'What's new?' Hoskins comments, smiling gratefully as he finally unsticks himself from the wall.

'Learn anything?' he wheezes, bent over to lock the door behind them. I could floor the fat bastard, Simon thinks, but for some reason it doesn't happen. 'Back to business?' Hoskins grins, reaching for his Embassy and gold-plated lighter. How many times has he done that in his lifetime? I could write your card, Simon thinks:

Hoskins uses nicotine, alcohol, spouse abuse and a mildly sarcastic manner to distance himself from his environment, colleagues and charges. His unusual hobby, photographing night scenes, especially firework displays, provides relief and satisfaction . . .

How can anyone here act normal, even remember what it is? Hoskins sighs as he lights up, and as an afterthought, offers Simon the packet. He takes two, puts one behind each ear.

Hoskins accompanies him to the toolshed, unlocks it, watches him pull on huge red rubber gloves, like udders, and extract wheelbarrow, dustpan, brush and so on. Then he's on his own for almost an hour. Despite his being a time-bomb, his new job requires him to be trustworthy and he gets a red band to wear on his arm while out of doors. Mornings, it's a matter of picking up the shit-parcels thrown from the cells of those not fortunate enough to have their own sanitary unit, along with the odd sandwich, sweet paper and so on. Afternoons, sweeping up dust. The job doesn't earn respect, not even much of a wage, but it gets him out of doors. He can walk behind the Education block and hear Marsden practising on the upright piano. He can inspect a larger bit of sky, feel scraps of wind on his face. And at some point, he can pass by the boiler sheds where Teverson works, shovelling coal. He does it stripped to the waist, dusty and sweating, like something in a picture book about the mines a hundred years ago. He only takes the job on to keep up his fitness, he says, and he's certainly winning there. The screw looks on, pot-bellied, smoking.

'Got mine?' Tev yells at Simon. 'A big, sticky one. No paper. Sorry, couldn't wrap it up, mate.'

'A rat ate it up,' Simon tells him. 'Then it died.'

'See ya!' Tev says, seemingly satisfied, and turns back to his work. Tev has been coming up to Simon two or three nights a week, on the scrounge. Hand on shoulder, like a ton of bricks from behind. Mostly, but not every time, Simon gives him some dark, gummy prison tobacco or a couple of real cigarettes, like the ones he's just got from Hoskins. Simon doesn't ever ask about his letter, not even when, as today, he knows Tev has just been visited, has sat out his half hour in that stuffy room where two worlds meet, where half of the other halves are blubbing, all the kids are screaming blue murder and everyone concerned would be better off not doing it, but they do.

His own last – only – personal visit was in remand. His ex-foster mother Iris Kingswell asked to come and he let her, just so as to get things clear.

'Simon,' she gasped, when they brought him in, 'it's ten years but you look just the same!' She didn't. She was bigger, softer and less distinct, like a shop-window reflection of what she used to be. Old. He hardly recognised her, which made it hard to say what he had to say, but he started out anyhow.

'I don't know why you wanted to come here –' He meant to go straight on, but at this point she leaned forward over the table, took hold of his arm.

'Because I care,' she said, frowning and looking into his face like there was something lost she might find there. 'I'm sorry to see you here,' she told him; her eyes teared up. 'I know it went wrong, Simon. And I'll admit it wasn't all your fault. Sometimes, I feel we really let you down. I was going through the change, you know.' A shame she didn't change into something better! He can still remember how she told him he was more trouble than she was paid for and now this woman she was hiding inside of wanted him to say how he had turned out wasn't her fault. Well, work it out for yourself.

'Whatever the rights and wrongs, you were with us a good few years.'

'I didn't want to be!' he told her, but she went on as if he hadn't spoken, talked right over him, it was all some sort of script she had learned by heart.

'However things turn out, I'd like to keep in touch: I've always wanted that.' Finally, she stopped.

'But I don't. I never have,' he told her. 'I never wanted all those birthday cards. I don't want you watching me sent down. I want nothing from you, nothing, understand? I'm going to get life. Then, I'll start over, once I'm properly inside. Look, Iris, the past, the whole fucking lot – just forget it!' They sat there opposite each other on the bolted-down chairs, her with the tears now running down her powdery cheeks, the round-edged plywood table, also bolted down, in the middle. Why, he thought, doesn't she just get up and go?

'It didn't work out before. It's not going to be any better now, is it?' he told her.

Finally she levered herself up out of the chair, pulled her cardigan tight around her.

'Nothing I could say would ever been good enough. You're a bad lot and that's the end of it!' she said. 'I shouldn't have come.' He stayed sitting down until she started to walk out.

'Goodbye, Iris,' he said then, and she turned round.

'Where on earth does that smile come from?' she said. 'It doesn't belong to you. You must of stole it off another little boy, going down the slide in the park.' He didn't even know what his lips were doing, until she said it and anyhow, that was the end of that.

Teverson's shovel scrapes along the ground, then the coals hit the side of the bunker and tumble down over the existing pile.

Simon takes off his gloves and throws them and his own shovel on top of the plastic sack of shit in his barrow, picks up the handles, swallows his frustration and begins the return journey to the bins. There's no point in hurrying. It's still better out of doors than behind them.

'Here, mate,' Tev calls out, just as he's about to turn the corner, 'see you later, eh? Drop by.'

Big T, Teverson likes to be called. Some creep has drawn a cartoon of him, all the muscles even bigger than they are, which makes him look just like the capital letter, and he's got it taped to his wall. Right now, he's on his bed, zonked, the magazine that was in his hand on the floor next to him. The bums on the wall behind look down like so many misshaped planets.

'Got any batteries?' he asks, his speech slurred. He turns onto his side to look at Simon standing in the door. One hand dangles down over the edge of the bed. Like some fucking Roman emperor or something, Simon thinks, is that what you think you are?

'No,' he says. Tev's either got the letter or he hasn't . . . Let's get there. Slowly, Tev sits, then pushes on the edge of the bed to get himself standing up.

'You got any of them wobblies that's going round?' There's one he's dropped on the floor, bright green, and Simon points it out to him.

'Look, T, I've paid up front,' he says.

'It was harder than I thought,' Tev tells him. 'I need something else. What can you get me?' Simon looks back at him, tries to keep his face in neutral. He notes the bulge of Tev's bright blue eyes, their red rims, the mixture of sunburn and freckles, a day's growth of ginger stubble, the neck twice as wide as his own, shoulders pretty much like the cartoon, a kind of anatomical joke. Tev looks steadily back.

'Not up to much, are you?' he says, breathing heavily. He's half way out of his tree and he's gonna try and go for me, Simon thinks. He loosens up his own hands, relaxes his knees, settles himself right on his feet so he can get out of the way or even flip him back on himself if there's room. After all this time putting up with Tev, you could say it's an opportunity – but then the bastard grins and says:

'No use to me, is it? Over there, under the *Sun*,' and all Simon has to do is take one step, check the door, pick up the envelope and get it inside his clothes.

'Cheers!'

Big T grunts, sits heavily down on his bed again, passes out.

'Body count! Back in your cells,' they're calling out on the landing, all of a sudden business-like, and blokes are shouting back at them.

'Come on!', 'Get lost!', 'Fuck off!', 'On the Roof!', because it's almost ten minutes early and the TV's been switched off.

'Hurry up. Get in. Lock down, now!' The metal landings shake with the weight of men legging it back. The bolts shoot home, quicker, harder than normal. Shouting and chanting start up. It'll be a long night, Simon thinks. He sits back to the wall, cross-legged on his bed, as he does every night. The envelope is waiting under his pillow. He rests his wrists on his knees, lets his hands open up to where the sky would be, were it accessible. He breathes in, a while later out and – as suggested in the book the tutor lent him, years ago – imagines that he is sitting at the bottom of a deep, green pond, thick, opaque water above and around him, the bubbles – images, memories, thought – slowly emerging from his nose and floating away.

6

There's a smell of hot dust and drains, uncollected shit-parcels. Simon is in his football shorts with the window open the entire three inches but it doesn't make any difference. The cell faces in; bricks hold the heat. Sod's law: the kangas decide to work to rule and the same day the temperature soars to 28 in the shade and stays there. Everyone's had enough of it. There are sudden, surprising moments of quiet that make you hold your breath, then the banging and yelling starts up again. Roger next door is singing hymns. Chip Butty two along lost it yesterday, got twenty days in the seg for trying to improve the ventilation. Niall likewise, for going for a screw when he was unlocked. But Simon's OK. He's got plenty to think about.

Dear Whoever-you-are, is how the letter begins. Her own name, Vivienne Anne Whilden, is embossed along with the address on the top of creamy-smooth writing paper, thick stuff that won't fold properly. As he reads, the noise turns into a kind of soup and then he doesn't hear it any more.

> Who am I? A maudlin, menopausal drunk who looks every inch of her age and is about to be unemployed. Currently off sick, which does not help. Bereaved three years ago, but I should have got over it by now. Yes, sir! I have never done this before. I probably won't send it . . .

The letter is eight pages long, partly due to the size of the writing. It tangos across the paper in huge italics that just don't give a toss whether you can read them or not, or maybe, even, they would rather you didn't. But Simon has been sitting on the bed with his back against the wall, hour after hour, reading it over and over until it's almost part of him.

> Hal and I lived together for twenty-seven years. No children – I regret it now. I am v. fond of my teenage niece. She is not allowed to visit me at the moment because, my saintly sister Laura says, I'm a bad example.

He's read the letter so many times now that he can actually hear her voice: someone who believes she has a right to exist, and to bend the rules if she wants. Loud. A bit sarcastic. On the out, it would annoy the hell out of him but, as he puts it to himself, we beggars aren't to chose and Vivienne Ann Whilden has cost the equivalent of twelve hundred quid, if you bump a week's wage in here up to what it would be on the out. He's got to make a go of it. Though it's not easy:

> It seems no one likes me much. I dare say you won't either. Even I can't think of much to recommend. Well, I'm not fat. I dress well. I speak my mind – though that's unpopular too. I should have been a man, really. But then I would have had to use the Gents. Too bad –

Where possible he adds two and two together: Hal was much older than her, an artist. She was one of his students at art school, moved in with him, ended up lecturing herself, *Art His-story*, so that he could sit around and drink and paint. This all happened before Simon was even born. The later years, Hal did quite well selling his pictures but he was falling to bits physically and pretty much gaga: Vivienne looked after him. They both drank. *Like bloody whales.* Right now, she's refusing to retire early, but off sick, due to the drink problem. The other teachers in the college are all young and *don't understand paint.* Last term, an American student on exchange made a complaint after she mislaid his work four times. But really, she once lost an essay of his when she left it outside and it was blown away in the night. As for the other times, he's an idiot:

Utterly inane. Virtually brain dead! She couldn't bear to read what he'd written or deal with him, so she just let the work slip to the bottom of the pile, then, when he asked her, she said the first thing that came into her head.

> Tomorrow I have to go in and be hauled over the coals about Nathan Goode. At nine a.m., Good God, why? Shall I stick to my story, or else suddenly find all his rotten little word-processed scripts and read them? Which is worse? What do you think, whoever you are? Still there?

Vivienne Anne Whilden does not bother with any kind of goodbyes. The signature is huge and sprawling, like she's thrown it down, and there's a messy sickle shape of what can only be red wine filling up the rest of the page. That big, empty house of hers, Simon thinks, must smell of empties and ash trays, a high note of oil paints and a good sprinkling of house dust thrown in. She's someone who will wake up with a thumping head, and not much idea of what she's said or written the night before. But she'll keep smart even though she's going down the drain, freshen up regularly, using some classy kind of soap and a splash of matching perfume. She'll slap on some lipstick and a bit of jewellery and sit in front of the Dean looking together enough, even though she's at least half mad . . .

He's pretty sure he can work with her, now he's got over the initial shock and disappointment. She's desperate and he understands desperation. It's a force, running through you head to toe. You can struggle to tame it, to resist, to drive it out, but it will probably win because the fight will drain you dry. Or, you use desperation's energy, to take you where you want: that's the clever thing to do, and that way the thing that frightened you becomes the thing you need most, and both of you have won.

What she wants is a feeling of someone on her side: an ear, a hand – but nothing too obvious. He can do that, once he's found the right way in.

★

When he stops in his readings of Vivienne Whilden's letter, the noise comes back and the heat pushes in, like it's some kind of *thing*, a monster you can't see. Sweat runs down his chest and back. He's on his feet before he knows it, going for the door with fists and feet:

'Sort your fucking selves out, won't you,' he yells at them. 'You dumb cunts! You stupid bastards! If you don't like the job someone else'll do it!' He yells it over and over, with variations: 'Get on yer bikes! Get those fat arses into gear! No one asks you to work in this shithole!' until his voice gives up, then he lies down again, his heart racing. Nothing happens.

It's one hour until supper, fifteen till breakfast. He's had the letter four days. He was twenty-nine last month. More numbers: he's served three thousand and eleven days (not counting remand), that is, more than eight years. If he keeps busy and gets tired out it's OK but that's a challenge in itself. When things are slack like this sometimes the bad dreams do come despite the breathing exercises and so on. Afterwards he doesn't want to get out of bed in the morning and says it's flu. If he told Barry, he'd get a brownie point, but then he'd have to go over and over it again in the daytime too.

The door took skin off his knuckles, but the plus side is he's tired now. He doesn't move a muscle when he hears the screw pause and look in, move on.

Six days he's had the letter by the time conditions return to normal, some promise or other made, and at last he gets to the library, where the same old posters, prisoners themselves, are up in the same old places, fading gradually in the fluorescent glare. A shelf of poetry. Thrillers. Sociology. Law. Romance. A picture of Shakespeare and another one of James Baldwin. The pen is mightier than the sword! Of course it is, hasn't he seen with his own eyes how a bloke can be stabbed in the kidneys with a ballpoint, and almost die of it? Not that he'd mention this to John Travers, the civvie librarian: if he's got a sense of humour he doesn't bring it to work, plus he leaves his bicycle clips on half the time.

'What else have you got on art?' Simon asks Travers. He already has the entire stock lined up: someone called Pendez, plus Picasso, Pre-Raphaelites, Rembrandt, Rodin – all oddly close together alphabetically, and all falling to bits. Some kind of job lot.

'Nothing,' Travers says. 'I don't get art in any more because people cut the pictures out. I can't be turning every page over to see if anything's missing. Or else there's this kind of thing.' He opens the book on Rodin and as it happens there's a photograph of sculpture called 'The Kiss', and someone's drawn in the hidden bits. He flicks through the others.

'These cost fifty quid a throw. I can get ten books on weight-lifting for one on Picasso and more people read them. It's the way of the world, I'm afraid.'

'I don't damage books,' Simon tells him.

'You probably don't,' Travers says. 'As ever, everyone has to suffer because of a few selfish people. Libraries are about sharing, so far as I'm concerned, but there you are.'

'What do you suggest, then?' Simon asks. All the while, he's kept his eyes on Travers's thin, shiny face, giving him nowhere to hide. Now he watches him get his pen out of his shirt pocket. He wears these little short-sleeved shirts in polyester, all of them roughly the same but in different checks. Because he forgets the cap and puts the pen in head down, most of them have blots at the bottom of the pocket.

'I don't mind sticking my neck out just once to see how it goes,' Travers says. The library screw is in the office having tea served to him by the orderly, but even so Travers looks over his shoulder when he says this, as if someone might be taking notes.

'Something general,' Simon suggests, 'about the Modern Period plus any of these you can find.' He hands over the list he copied from the back of the Picasso. Travers pulls a face.

'These'll have to come from Boston Spa,' he says. 'I'll see what I can do. Keep it under your hat and don't hassle me.' Travers has seen some of the Pre-Raphaelites, he says, in Birmingham and in the Tate in London. Dreadfully detailed, he says, must have been such a headache to do, but he doesn't like them, or only one, 'The Scapegoat' by Holman Hunt. He goes to show it to Simon in the book, but just as he said, it's been torn out. In the encyclopedia there's a tiny reproduction, about the size of a postage stamp.

Simon walks past the TV room on his way back, zonked-out bodies slumped in rows like it was the cinema, except the chairs are hard, there's a few hundred watts of fluorescent light picking out every line on every face and every speck of ash on the floor, and of course there's a screw instead of an usher watching from the doorway. Slack faces, soaking up soap before the switch gets thrown at eight-thirty. He thinks of a mushroom farm. He thinks: suckers. He's on to something better, doing something for himself.

He doesn't like Picasso, props Pendez open over the sink, so he can study a picture a day and make his mind up. Pendez lived 1889–1959, in Barcelona with his sister. Over half the pictures are of her, a plump girl with her hair up in a knot. They're roughly done, not trying to be exactly real. You can see the brush marks, and bits where he's gone over and over the same thing. Simon can't work out if they're actually any good, but that means they probably are, because normally he knows straight away when he dislikes someone or something.

A name comes to him in the middle of the night: Joseph Manderville. It suits the address: 3 Sandringham House, Mile Road, London SE22. In reality, it's a council estate, but since the number's low she need never guess. Joseph Manderville is very polite. He holds open doors for women. He uses cups and saucers, not mugs, and he's clean and tidy, competent around the house, without being fussy. He's forty-seven: Simon thinks Vivienne would like someone just a little but not too much younger than her. He reads a lot and has got a serious, lined sort of face and wears hand-made shirts open at the neck – Simon has seen adverts for the kind of shirt in the quality press. Also,

Joseph would use a fountain pen, but Simon will have to make do with a brand new fibre-tip.

He's wired up, high on the challenge and danger of the thing. It takes a week to do a short reply, looking things up, copying and recopying, checking the grammar, examining every word, thinking over how it makes him sound, what picture of Joseph she'll get in her head, running the lines over in his head as he is doing his rounds, or eating his bright yellow vegetable curry and welded-together rice. He's thinking about it all the time, even when showing respect to the tough guys, talking to some deluded idiot like Jones, who thinks a) that he is innocent, and b) that he can play guitar, or taking in the outside news.

It's not a race, he keeps reminding himself. Quality not quantity. He spends the maximum possible time in the library, not actually hassling Travers, but making sure he doesn't forget. There's nothing about Pendez or Hal Brodrick in the encyclopedia, but A for artists get quite a mention in general. Art is different from craft in that it doesn't have a practical purpose: you don't need to have a ceiling with God painted on it, whitewash would do. You don't need sixteen pictures of your sister when a camera would take the perfect likeness, plus you live with her anyway, so why? But still, they do it. Mainly, artists paint women. Women's faces, women's bodies, women with babies, women washing themselves, women asleep, women running along the beach with their arms in the air and two noses, even dead women, women with wings. The artist's mother, sister, lover. The women sit still and let themselves be painted. Just like I said to Brainy Barry, Simon thinks, they like to be looked at. Men don't. If you look at someone too long here, it's What you looking at? and a smashed face. Mind you, you can get one of those without doing anything. You've got to keep eyes in your back. Another good reason for having no visits and no home leaves is that no one thinks you've got anything in your arse worth ripping you to bits for . . . Plus, of course the canteen deals keep people sweet. Trade. The writing paper for Vivienne Whilden cost half an ounce of tobacco for thirty sheets from Jaycee in the print shop.

> Dear Vivienne,
> I imagine it would be far worse to read the essays. Hopefully the matter has by now been resolved in your favour?

As for presentation, his 'childish' style, for which he'd use a cheap biro and press really hard, put in a capital or a backwards letter now and then, is clearly no use. *Dead Normal*: upright, gently rounded, very even, is only good for official things, or where he doesn't know who he is writing to. He tries doing something slanted and bohemian, like hers. But in the end, he decides complimentary is better and he writes to Vivienne Anne Whilden in his scholar's hand, which is very small and low, like knotted string, but with confident down strokes and plenty of space around the words.

> I was fascinated to read that you lived with Hal Brodrick. What a rich and interesting life you have led. Did you continue your own work at all? What was it like to live with an artist? Did Hal ever paint your portrait?

Questions are good; they fill the other person's head up. It's herself, he guesses, that she's interested in right now. He apologises for his life being dull in comparison to hers. He tells her about his late mother's illnesses and how he looked after her because he couldn't bear for her to go into a home.

It's hard to do that bit, even though he's overheard people talking about such things many times in the past. For some reason it repeatedly puts him in mind of Hazel Brooks, Amanda's mother, who was always kind to him, and it's not good thinking of how things must be for her. Barry and Co., they want you to rake every last thing up, but they can't have a clue what that means. They haven't ever had to do it themselves, have they? It's good to be someone else.

We certainly share a love of painting, Simon writes. *Lately, I have developed a particular interest in an obscure Spanish painter called Pendez – do you know of him?*

As for alcohol, he's only got to look around. No preaching. He tells her many people have had drink problems and got rid of them, so no doubt she will too. Then he throws in that he recently visited Robin Hood's Bay, on the north-east coast, with a reference to the landscape putting him in mind of Holman Hunt's 'The Scapegoat'.

I am looking forward very much to hearing from you again if that is what you want. I am curious to know more about you, and hope you will reply.

It's just two pages long, but he feels as if he's written the phone book.

'To be honest, mate, I've been thinking it's not worth the risk,' Tev says. They're jogging, side by side at exercise, and for a moment Simon feels as if his legs have dropped off. Then they're going double time and it takes all Simon's got not to hit out, this fucker has already had everything he's got, result of several complex deals, selling ordinary canteen goods for smuggled-in cash at a hundred per cent mark-up to those who can't keep control of themselves and live within their official income . . . *I've got to stay cool,* he tells himself and finishes the circuit.

'What's up?' he asks, his face a careful blank, when Big T catches up. It turns out that Chas further down on the threes has nicked Tev's Walkman and now he wants Simon to get it back. I'm not stupid, Simon thinks, Tev's paid for something with that Walkman and now the stuff's gone he wants it back. Most likely outcome: I get the beating if Chas adds up and makes four, who wouldn't? And/or I get the rap, may be fourteen ADA, so much in the seg, whatever, if we're caught Offending Against Good Order And Discipline . . . Or, maybe Chas is especially riled, gets me with some kind of blade or another and

I bleed to death in the toilets, End of Story. Take your pick. But after all this, I want my letter out.

He goes in, finds the Walkman under the pillow, for God's sake! and stuffs it in his shirt. On the way back he bumps into Doggie, who's supposed to be lookout but he's pinned and not doing such a good job of it. Simon gives him a half roll-up, and he's just on a lucky streak and so is Doggie, because Chas shouts blue murder all night but the next morning, like magic, he's ghosted, so none of them have to pay, or not in the foreseeable.

'We're a team, mate. It'll go first class,' Big T says, stuffing the letter down his jeans. It doesn't bear thinking about where it'll have been before it gets to Vivienne.

There's nothing more he can do. He lies back in the nearest there is to dark and imagines: Vivienne, letting herself into the big hall of her house after a day's work. A glance in the mirror shows grey hair falling out of the knot on top, lipstick worn off, but at least wrinkles don't show too much indoors. Briefcase down, she kicks off her shoes. Picks the post off the mat. Hangs up a cardigan or a hat or something on the post at the bottom of the stairs, then straight to the kitchen to get a drink, cold white wine or G&T. Then she's back to the study at the front to put on some music. Classical. Pictures are everywhere. Portraits of her when she was young. She has a desk in the alcove by the chimney, covered in papers she ought to attend to. But instead, she sits in the antique easy chair, shuffles through the post and comes upon his envelope, because it's handwritten. She's forgotten all about answering that advert in the middle of the night and she wants to know what it is, wants something new – because, this is what Simon thinks, when people write letters to strangers, they're on the turn between one phase of their life and the next, like snakes struggling out of an old, too tight skin. They need to be free of themselves and of the memories of those who know them best.

Vivienne. It's a nice name, he decides.

*

Lunch was bad: vegeburger and chips, everything brown, even the lettuce that came with it. He's washing his hands when the door crashes open. Two of them plus dog come straight in, another one is waiting outside. They're in overalls, with a two-way radio and a tool belt, and look fitter than average. As for the dog it's got a wet, shiny nose, dribble dangling out of its mouth and the longest, pinkest tongue you ever saw, hair sticking up in a ridge on its back.

'Time for a spin. Got anything here you shouldn't have? Out on the landing, now.' They go for the bed first. Covers off, round the edges of the mattress, open up the pillow, turn the frame over, unscrew the legs. Ventilation grille next, nothing there. They shake the art books, losing all his markers, peer down the spines. They take the Adidas box off the table, turn it upside down, screw off another set of legs. Then they go back to the box, shake Viv's letter out of its envelope, shuffle through all the drafts of his that he's kept copies of, the lot.

'Dear Vivienne,' one of them reads aloud in a funny voice. He should've just learned them by heart, ripped them up and flushed them away. Or even eaten them first, then flushed them away, once the words had become part of him. But the point of a letter is that it is a thing. It doesn't vanish like conversation. People keep letters even when they'd be better off not to, in shoe boxes like he has, or slipped between books on the shelf, tied up with ribbon at the back of the wardrobe. Years later, there it is: not what you remember being said, but what was actually written down. You may feel different about them, but you won't so easily forget the people who have written to you, nor who you were, then, when you wrote to them because you wanted to, badly enough to write *Dear*, and then the name of someone you'd never met.

There being no dirty bits, the man in the boiler suit is not interested. He drops the pages back in the box and reaches for the radio, takes the back off, gives it a shake. The brand new sewing needle Simon has taped into the innards stays put.

Boiler suit dumps the radio on the ruined bed without putting it back together again. Number two boiler suit is busy with shoes and toiletries. The dog, by now, has sat down, panting. They bring Simon back in.

'Strip off, now. Pants too. Bend over. Socks –' They look underneath his feet, in case he's keeping something at the back of his toes. He's starting to smile, now.

'What about Big T, then?' the biggest boiler suit asks. 'What's taking you round there?'

'Training partners,' he tells them.

'We're watching you,' the one who was on the landing says. Not for letters, though; you don't keep those between your toes. Afterwards, he lies on the wrecked bed grinning, and almost wishes he had someone to tell it to.

It turns out that Teverson had his place turned over too, but he was warned beforehand. He's paying someone for that, thinks Simon, which means I am too. All they found was a hash pipe made out of a biro casing, and a bucket of hooch.

'Gone sour anyway,' Tev says. 'Would've killed anyone that drank it.'

Thank you for your kind, encouraging letter, Vivienne Whilden writes, and Simon, eventually, reads. She is clearly nearer to sober this time around, the writing still very large, but more carefully formed.

> I am ashamed to say I cannot remember much of what I wrote to you before. However, I am more on top of things now. I would not have begun this correspondence sober, but it is quite interesting to write to a stranger like this.

So far, he thinks so not quite so good. 'Quite interesting' is not as useful, from his point of view, as drunken despair and desperation . . . But it is a reply at least, and he has heard her that other way too; he knows it exists, underneath. Things can still work out.

I must say it's refreshing to encounter someone who actually likes painting. My view, *vis-à-vis* the pile of bricks and other such postmodernism, is that anyone not an utter moron can tell the emperor is naked. This is psychodrama or theory. Art, on the other hand, must engage with the world and not merely contemplate itself. This view has made me very unpopular here. I used to hope that they would come round, when they became bored of looking at nothing, but it has not happened yet . . .

What happened about Nathan Goode, he wants to know. She's not telling.

I enclose a bibliography for Pendez. There's not a lot, but the Russell Findlater is good. Until you mentioned him I hadn't actually looked at Pendez for a long while but I remembered admiring him. So I've been back to him and, as you say, the brushwork strikes a wonderful balance between spontaneity and control. Some of the glazes impress me very much too. Especially when you consider the use of colour, he must be counted as an expressionist, but at the same time he stands slightly outside the main trends. The compositions can be almost naive and all the emotionalism is in the intimacy of the brushwork, but it doesn't shout and there isn't any obvious stylisation, rather, a deep, but disciplined sensuality. In context, if you consider the build-up to the war, etc., it's absolutely heartbreaking. I think you might also like the work of Soutine? Am I correct?

No, he thinks, you're up the fucking gum tree! This second letter has an alternatively mind-numbing and enraging effect, similar to reading an F75 report. It fills his head up like so much knotted string to undo. It would take about three months just to work out exactly what she means. Talk about out of his depth! He skims through the rest: some clever-clever book someone wants her to help them with. Hopeless. There's only so much you can take. If he so much as tries to respond to this, he'll fuck up. Plus, not a single one of his books has come through, and he can't afford Teverson's escalating charges anyway. Simon tosses Vivienne's second letter in the shoe box with the other one. He goes over to the sink, takes Pendez down and closes him up with a snap. End of Story, he thinks. What next?

It's only a fortnight later, during exercise, that Big T pulls his arm up his back till it hurts, and tells him: 'You've got mail.' Simon says he can't have, but one look at the envelope and he knows it's her all right. What the fuck?

'I don't want it,' he says.

'You should've told her not to write, then. Don't mess me around, I can't have that.' Tev's voice is edgy, he's colouring up.

'I'm cleaned out,' Simon tells him.

'Then you owe me, right?'

Don't open it, he advises himself, not listening.

> A bit of a wild idea. I have been thinking about taking a holiday, and, after all our discussion about Pendez it strikes me that Barcelona would be very interesting. The flights aren't expensive right now. I do get low if I am too much alone and, especially as I am making a determined effort to curb my drinking, it would be good to have sober company, someone to talk over the galleries and share supper with. Of course, we needn't be in each other's pockets all the time. If you were agreeable, we could perhaps meet in London next month, say at the Tate, to see if we got on. If so, we could make the trip on a strictly friendly basis. Do give me a ring, if it seems . . .

Vivienne Anne Whilden wants Joseph Manderville to go away with her! And Simon Austen, former carpet-layer, a prisoner serving life and currently working as shit-parcel collector, sits in his cell, amazed. To his left is a lump in the wall where they say the treadmill used to be. The chipped paint on the walls and ceiling is hundreds of layers thick, which, if you think about it, must make the room even smaller than it was to begin with. He sits, letter in hand, facing the sanitary unit, which gleams like a god in the far right corner; meanwhile, in some other universe, Joseph Manderville and Vivienne Anne Whilden, companionably quiet, stand arm in arm in front of 'Julia With a Vase of Flowers' in a cool white room in Barcelona. It's hot, a ceiling fan whirring overhead. She looks at him and he looks back at her, not scared at all. Both of them smile and nod, then walk on to the next picture in its gold frame, while songbirds twitter outside. It's what you call a result.

7

Thirty minute wait, and now he's standing with his back to the rest of them, in a Perspex dome that's supposed to insulate against sound. Odd to be doing such an ordinary thing, after all this time. His hands are shaking a bit.

'Hello?' she says. 'Hello? Who is it?' It's the most amazing thing: Vivienne's voice is just exactly as he imagined it. 'Hello. Say who you are, please, or I shall hang up.'

Vivienne? It's Joseph. Lovely to hear your voice. Yes, it is a bit noisy. I've only got five minutes or so before either this card runs out or I get my arm broken. Also, someone is probably listening to every word. The thing is . . .

He can't do it, and hangs up just before she would have. Later, he trades in the rest of the phone card for some more good paper. He doesn't want to lose her. His thinking is that he'll try to come out with the facts slowly, bit by bit, hoping that just as her enthusiasm for painting rubbed off onto Joseph, so her liking for Joseph will rub off onto him, will cling like stardust, even when he is fully himself. If things change slowly enough.

> I'm afraid this will be brief; I'm laid low with Asian flu and have had to cancel everything. Vivienne, I have a confession to make. I told you I was forty-seven but I am in fact younger than that. A lot younger than you, and you see I thought you might prefer me to be closer to your own age: stupid, I know. It has been bothering me ever since I did it. I do hope you will forgive me! And perhaps I have been so interested in what you write that I have neglected to give you a proper picture of myself. I am for instance very

interested in social questions such as Education, Unemployment and the Penal System. Our prisons are bursting at the seams; prisoners are kept in crowded conditions with little or no access to the educational or social opportunities which might reform them. Out of sight out of mind, I'm afraid. I do feel something better should be done, don't you?

It's wonderful, Vivienne, to feel that you are there to talk to about the important things in life, and even though health concerns mean that I may not be able to come, I must thank you again for asking me to Barcelona.

Maybe it's just because he so much wants things to be fixed that he doesn't take as long on the letter as he should; maybe he doesn't read it back to himself because he knows it sounds barmy. In any case, he can't get it posted soon enough.

'On the slate?' Tev says. 'You'll pay the lot next time.'

When the answer comes a huge Rasta by the name of Leon is hanging out by Teverson's door and Simon can see straight away that Teverson has taped some paper over his observation panel.

'I'm owed,' the Rasta says. 'Give it me, white boy.' Simon doesn't believe him but when he puts his head round the door Tev says, 'Give it him,' so he hands the cash over then goes in to sort things out and pick up. Teverson is standing there, naked from the waist down, holding his cock. There's some reggae from two doors down, very loud.

'Can't stand that jungle music,' he says. 'If you want your love letter, stick that wedge under the door then pull 'em down and get on the floor, arse up.' Simon decides: I have what he wants. That's what matters. He's done it before, after all, at Burnside.

Simon hears Teverson spit. It hurts as he pushes in, then it's not so bad.

'You bitch' Teverson says to the back of Simon's head, 'you queer bastard, you.' Teverson's sweat drips on his neck and he breathes out with each thrust, hot and damp. Simon counts: forty-two, feels Teverson grab his shoulders and pull, like the other man's trying to push up through the top of his head. Neither of them makes a sound.

'Hurry!' Tev says as he gets up, staggering a bit. One thing's for sure, neither of them want to be seen. It's almost funny.

'I'm not bent, understand. But you, you really liked that, didn't you,' Tev says, into his track pants now, and lighting up.

'Under that magazine,' he says. 'Now fuck off.' There's a damp stain on the front of his pants, a sour grin on his face.

Simon is thinking of that stuff inside him and how he'll lay into Tev, come up quiet when he's not expecting it, get him where it hurts, stop him doing it again – at the same time he tells himself over and over it doesn't matter: just a different deal and not as if Tev touched *his* cock. He'll wash. Then, after lock-up, he'll open the letter.

It's one of the screwesses, Martine, tonight, and she calls out as she does the job: 'Sleep tight, boys.'

'I'm lonely, miss,' some joker always pipes up. 'Give us a kiss, miss.'

There's just one sheet of paper inside the envelope:

> I am uneasy at the turn this correspondence has taken and do not wish to continue it. Please, do not write again, or I will contact the police.

He needs to do something to steady his hands. Seeing as letters are out, it's got to be another kind of writing. So he inks up with biro on his upper arm, running down towards the elbow. If he could reach that far he'd go for a laugh and put it right where Tev was just now but he can't and he doesn't want anyone else doing this for him. He can work left-handed easily enough: it's just a matter of a letter at a time or else the ink dries too quick. He gets the sewing needle out of the radio, strikes a spark from his flint, lights a Marlboro and uses that to heat up the point till it glows red, waits, then pushes it in, again, again,

again as dense as possible. Rub in, wipe off when it's done. Doesn't hurt beyond what he can stand, it's more that after a while he feels like passing out, that's OK, and anyhow he never does. So – BITCH: it's on the right forearm, nicely balancing out, on the left arm, PRICK. So he's got the beginnings of a collection there on his arms, linking up to DUMB on the fingers of the left hand, CUNT, as in *you dumb cunt!*, on the right, which was told to him years ago in a police van when he asked if it could stop because he was going to throw up . . . Altogether he has a fair number of words on him now. There are things he has been called since he came inside, mostly bad: ARROGANT, WASTE OF SPACE, BASTARD, SHIT, and so on, he's got all those, plus one or two from before that stuck in his mind, like IMPOSSIBLE, WEIRDO, CARPET-FITTER, MURDERER, of course, along with A THREAT TO WOMEN, BRUTAL and COLD, which were the judge's words for him. BRIGHT, he was called when he was in Education and he had that one done properly, on his back.

The ink goes in under the skin and once the scab is off there you are, it's yours to keep. Some of them have turned out better than others and a couple of the older ones do have spelling mistakes, but even so no one laughs at him when he strips to shower because they know he'll go apeshit if they do, because this, he thinks, this is what I *am*.

8

The library books arrive, six of them, smelling of ink and weighing about a hundredweight; funny, really, very I for ironic. But at least it means there's something to talk to Barry about. Simon sits in the sweltering Portakabin – the air's so warm that just breathing makes him sweat – and passes on all his thoughts about A for art. He gives Barry an outline of the life of Pendez and his sister Julia, explains that their relationship was a criminal one and it went on until his death, so you could hardly call it accidental! Did the art that came out of it, 'Julia in a Man's Jacket', 'Julia Sleeping', 'Julia Alone', 'Julia Before the Mirror' – did all that A for art make it all right? And if so, suppose a murderer did paintings about murdering or wrote poems or a book about it, would people start to overlook the murder the same way they overlooked Pendez fucking his sister when he shouldn't have? You could say that they are both *taboos*, Simon points out. *Social conventions* . . . After this, he thinks, I'll never get out. So what?

'What do *you* think?' Barry asks, when he's finished taking notes.

'I'm asking you,' Simon says.

'I'd like to ask you something different,' Barry counters. 'Can you see a difference between killing someone and, as you put it, fucking them?'

'One of them's repeatable, the other isn't,' Simon says, fast and hard. Oh – throw away the key!

'Anything else?' When Barry is riled, his mouth puckers up: looks like an arse, Simon thinks.

'Not that I can think of right now,' he tells Barry, just for the hell of it. 'Pass.'

That's when he starts to cry.

'Sorry,' Barry says, finding the tissues and taking one himself as well, to mop his forehead. 'I overstepped the mark there. I'm pushing because I believe in you . . . Can you tell me what is happening now?' He asks, 'What's going on?' As if I was hidden from you, Simon thinks, under a blanket or something! I'm blubbing, aren't I? Everyone does it now and then, some more than others . . . though this is a different sort to the ordinary, it's not that kind of lonely, worn-out misery that's an almost physical kind of thing. And there's no frustration or anger in it at all. It's something else.

Barry fiddles with his cigarette lighter, opens his packet of Marlboro with the other hand, discovers that it's empty.

'Please, Simon, talk to me,' he says. But what can you say about it all, any of it? It's so complicated and joined up to itself, he'd just mess around and make things worse, plus the letters are illegal anyway . . . So he doesn't try; he shrugs and asks about the coffee and they have that and then Barry eventually changes tack and says he's going to leave the service in October, for health reasons, and will be handing over Simon's file to his successor. Congratulations! Simon tells him. They shake, and that's the end of another that.

At odd times the crying keeps coming back. Two days in a row, he looks bad enough to get off work, then he realises that only makes it worse. For Christ's sake, he tells himself, it was only some old cow I'd never even met! Yet all the same, it's like falling backwards into a black pit, and you've got to climb out or you'll be there for ever. Think positive! he tells himself. You're not the only one, he's reminding himself minutes later, because the fact is there's been another suicide, the fourth this year. Simon, collecting with his barrow and shovel, saw them load the dead man into a van on a stretcher, all wrapped up in sheets like something from Tutankamen's tomb. They drove him out; the gates closed behind Leon, the Rasta who was outside Tev's cell that night. There was a bright blue sky and a bit of a breeze tugging the blossom off the invisible chestnut trees outside, blowing it up and over the walls. The smell of diesel lingered, then vanished.

Not my style, he reminds himself. I'm still here, right? Desperation won't get the better of me. Use it. Ride it like a horse. Think. Find an angle . . . For example, let's say it wasn't a complete waste: I did get somewhere. She liked Joseph; I made him, I was *in* him, somewhere, wasn't I? And I understood her, up to a point. I started to like her. I definitely liked getting the letters. I want more. So – he lectures himself – don't repeat the mistakes that got you to here! Learn! Change! Don't be proud. Do different, better . . . Cheaper would be good too.

By the entrance to B wing, he puts the barrow down, piles in the shovel and gloves, then strips off his shirt and leans against the wall, feeling the fierce summer sun on his skin. See? he tells himself, his eyes closed, his head flooded with red light. See?

9

So: the prisoner number and prison address must be clearly at the top, the envelope is to be unsealed when handed in for post; it will be searched, looked over, and, possibly, read. The replies will be opened and likewise dealt with . . . All of which, in Simon's opinion, sucks, but, then again, think it through: what are they looking for? Witness nobbling, escape plans, drug deals, directions to hidden cash, threats . . . and besides, is it proven that anyone in the censor's office can actually *read*?

> In answer to your ad, I'm slim verging on thin but not scrawny, quite supple from practising yoga, aikido and keeping generally fit. Some tattooing, but no broken nose or facial scars, my ears are flat against the side of my head, etc. I look younger than I am (29) and always have done. Clean shaven, five eleven, thick blond hair that curls a bit if I let it grow, clear eyes, tidy eyebrows, firm jaw. One odd detail is that my left eye is brown and my right is blue-grey. I enjoy reading, fitness, and most sports to some degree. I don't smoke, have no personal bad habits to speak of. However, as you will have noticed from the address above, I am one of Her Majesty's guests (not that she visits much), currently serving life. Fair enough if this puts you off. If not, I would appreciate the opportunity . . .

Sod the censor if he decides he wants to read through this sort of thing (and sod Teverson, asking if he wants something posted, then, when he doesn't, suggesting an eighth of blow. I'm not interested, End of Story! Ask me one more time, and I'll stick you up).

*

So the letter goes out, legit, written in Dead Normal, to six different box numbers at once. Eleven days pass. Then his name is on the letter list stuck to the landing office window: four replies. Moira, Josephine, Shelley, Tasmin. He could keep them all but he's doing this by the book. Moira is very religious, so she's out, likewise Josephine: overweight, depressed and shy is not very inviting. Shelley is a single mum, twenty-four, two boys, likes running, mistrusts men . . . so *why?* Interesting. It's between her and Tasmin, seventeen, at college in London, who put her ad in as a joke, then forgot about it, but actually likes the sound of him and isn't afraid of what she calls *the heavy stuff*:

> I used to be really, really into clothes, clubs all that, but not any more. It's not meaningful. I like poetry. Everyone says I seem older than I am, maybe because of being an only child and always spending time with adults. Mum and Dad work in the media. There was always a nanny or an au-pair. But from when I was five I'd come down to their parties, so I've met famous people and I have travelled a lot but maybe all that gets in the way of understanding Life, which is what I need to do more than anything. So please, write again. I think you are very brave, Simon, to reach out like this. I appreciate your honesty. What is it like in there? What do you do all day? Is there something I can send you? Why are you there? What do you want? Are you guilty, or innocent? Please, tell me everything.

Do different. Don't be proud, Simon reminds himself, as he makes his way to the blessedly cool chapel, where all God's new wall lights are shining behind their plaster shades, and Cutler is in his full gear. He's a stickler, whereas the local vicar, David Marchmont, wears jeans and doesn't seem to care whether you believe or not. The elderly women who come to help Cutler are always very kind. They wear beige jumpers and a scarf round the neck and smell of lavender and talcum powder; they keep a box of HobNob biscuits in a cupboard in the dressing room, in exchange for one or two of which Simon is always willing to sweep God's already spotless parquet floor, or get things down from the higher shelves.

'Would you like some orange squash too?' they ask. In other circumstances they'd put a *Dear* on the end, but not here. Same as no one touches you, in case you think it's an invitation, or in case you haven't been touched in that many years that it blows your mind. It suits Simon just fine.

'All of the truth, always?' he asks the Reverend Cutler, leaning on his brush. 'Is that what you are saying the old man up there wants? Is that what you, personally, do?'

'That's what He wants,' Cutler says, conveniently, Simon thinks, not answering the second part.

'What counts?' he asks: what about not picking up the phone so as to avoid speaking to someone? Withholding facts to avoid trouble, or so as to get things your way? What about telling the truth if it hurts or upsets someone? What is the truth anyhow – are the bare bones enough, or have you got to go the whole way to make it count? Our conscience is there to guide us, Cutler says. What about a just war, Simon asks – they've discussed just wars on a previous occasion. Suppose you've been taken prisoner and are asked by the enemy to give information which would hurt the just cause? Something very basic, requiring just a yes or no answer: *Do you lot have much ammunition left?* No torture need be involved. There's a pause, during which he looks Cutler up and down and notices he has a shaving cut on the edge of his jaw and a stain, ketchup or some sort of sauce, on his cassock.

'You have plenty of philosophy,' Cutler says, 'but it's not what you need.' The biscuit Simon bites into, using one hand to catch the crumbs, tastes unexpectedly delicious.

'What about the example, though?'

'I would remain silent,' Cutler says. There is silence, as if he is proving the point. They look at each other, know that if they were both on the wing they'd be going for each other by now. Simon forces a laugh back. This week's lady, Dorothy, clears her throat.

'You have to be honest to someone or something, Simon,' she says in a watery, whispery voice. 'It can't be in the abstract. Be honest to God and you won't go far wrong.' She is sitting down to polish the cross, looking at him to see if her words have got through, and smiling, smiling – smiling, maybe, he thinks, so as to show how good it feels once you've handed over your brain.

He smiles quickly back, then asks Cutler, 'Can I give you a more specific example?'

'Welfare is probably the best place for that,' Cutler says. 'Dorothy and I have work to do.'

H is for honesty. You have to be prepared to try new things:

> I am here because I killed my girlfriend. I did it but pleaded not guilty on legal advice. Like any such story, it is a long one. I will leave it at that for now.
>
> As for what I am looking for, I don't have any family. Of course there's plenty of people around, this is not a private place, but they are like me or worse or else they are in charge of me. So I am really interested to make contact with people whose lives are not like mine. Especially women, because I have problems relating to them. Well, if you have need of a friend, or just information about how the other half lives, I am happy to do what I can. I envy you being at college. In the past I have studied for a variety of exams, from O levels to RSA typing, which I know is unusual for a man. I peaked at 60 w.p.m., but since then have not had access to a machine. I do have a radio. It has to run on batteries since there's no power supply in cells. I take daily exercise unless there is a staffing crisis. Every other week I get to a martial arts class. I also practise yoga exercises and breathing.

The reply comes quickly, almost too quickly. She must be answering as soon as she gets his, writing back the very same night.

Dearest Simon

Total openness is what I believe in, and anyway, I hope it won't put you off if I say that what I want is something deep: to find my other half and feel complete, like Plato says. If it does put you off, then it wasn't right to begin with. I have had a few of the other sort of purely physical relationship but I want something different now. I did use to do drugs at parties but a friend died, actually it was in all the papers, now I'm steering clear of that scene and only into natural highs. I believe there are always reasons for anything. We are all human beings. Also I believe that a person rebuilt from the ruins must be stronger than one that's never had much to deal with. There is good and bad mixed in everyone and in everything that happens. Do you know the Tarot? Even the hangman's card is a good one because an end is a beginning too. So please, tell me what happened. Everything. How else can I get to know you?

Does he want to be *known*? The letter, on softly flecked pale pink paper sits in its matching envelope, in the shoe box. At the same time it fills up the whole of his head. It's not long before he replies:

My probation officer who has just retired also wanted me to tell him everything. I never felt he would know what to do with it if I did. I believe it is more important to go forwards than to look back, particularly on dreadful things. Telling you everything would be difficult to do, for many reasons. It would take a very long time, pages and pages. Also, Tasmin, you cannot know quite what you're in for and you might regret asking. So – why not tell me some more about *you!*

That's just two reasons, not *many*. She might notice, or she might not. As for him: he can always not reply, and she can't come knocking on the door. So, it's just before 7 a.m. and he's sitting here, half-lotus, wrists on knees, hands upturned. The letter is addressed and stamped, first class. There's a nice soft slice of light beginning to come down through his window, and a feeling of possibility: he doesn't know what'll happen next, but it won't be that bad and it could even somehow be tending towards good . . . it's a feeling, almost, of luck.

'You've been writing letters,' Dickie Walters says as he waves Simon to a squat four-legged beast of a chair opposite his own state-of-the-art swiveller with suspension and padded arms. Despite the sudden lurch in his chest, Simon keeps his face in neutral, shrugs.

'So?' he says. 'It's allowed.' He notices Walters's office had been refitted since the last time he was there: fresh off-white paint, huge mahogany desk with framed photos (smiling wife, four children) propped for Walters to contemplate; Venetian blinds, big posters on the wall: a desert, a pod of whales, skyline of Manhattan. Behind the desk, certificates, photos of Walters himself, beaming from ear to ear while shaking hands with the Home Secretary.

'Your girlfriend, she must like those letters of yours,' Walters says, pulling a quick grin. 'Spicy, are they?'

'No,' Simon tells him, 'they're not.'

'Must be. Anyhow, she's sent you a parcel which contains a metal object. You'll have to make an application.'

'Parcel?' Simon says, bewildered.

'Make an application, and then a decision will be made as to whether you can have it or whether it will be kept for you, or returned to the sender,' Walters tell him.

'But what's in it?' Simon asks.

'A typewriter,' Walters tells him, just as the answer comes to him from inside. *Of course.* And now he wants that metal object, that typewriter, that gift, sent because of something he wrote in a letter, more than he can remember ever wanting anything before.

10

The vinyl case zips off from the base. Inside, the rows of keys, the hollow curve of the waiting letters on their long steel arms, a brittle-looking blue-grey shell. Space bar, carriage-return, caps lock, tab key, margin stops: all there. Plus a spare ribbon, still wrapped, a little packet of what turns out to be correction paper, ten sheets of Croxley Script with five envelopes . . . It's sitting on his table and it's like a spaceship has landed in the back garden, all blinking lights and soft little hissing and beeping noises, doors wide open but what's in there? If he goes in, will they ever let him out again?

I meant what I said, her note says. *What's the point otherwise? Perhaps this will help?*

The paper vibrates as he fumbles to feed it in, falls still as he snaps back the bar. He looks straight ahead at the wall, stops thinking, finds his fingers do indeed reach unbidden and remember well: *You cannot imagine*, he types and the noise of the keys picking themselves up and careening into the paper is almost wet. It's like rain on a tin roof. The space bar chugs along. There's a sharp ring, a tiny cranking sound, then the sudden freefall of the carriage-return, a crash as it hits base. *You cannot imagine what it is like for me to receive such a gift!*, he tells her, speeding up. *I was not hinting*, he tells her, *in what I wrote. But, spot on! Thank you, it will be very useful indeed . . . Still, it is very difficult for me to do what you want . . .*

Somehow, the air in the cell seems extra quiet when he pauses – as if perhaps it has been listening to the words as he typed them. So he finds himself listening to them too, and then imagining Tasmin, dark hair like a curtain, sitting on some low beanbag thing in a dark-coloured, complicatedly lit attic flat, hearing his voice in her head as she reads the letter he's working on. What she says back is, *Try. Aren't you going to try?*

Amanda, he types, this time slowly, watching the letters appear one by one until the word is complete. According to psychologists and probation officers, using a victim's name can help bring her or him properly back. Although that doesn't occur, he feels the name pulling at him to go on. So he types it again and again: Amanda, Amanda, Amanda.

She told him, he remembers, that Amanda is a Latin name; it means *worthy of love*. At the sports centre where she worked, Amanda sat all day in the glass box, issuing tickets, making bookings, answering the phone, opening the turnstile. He came in with Tim Briggs to fit new lino, acres of it, in a turquoise marble effect. She was bordering on dog, according to Tim: even though she couldn't be blamed for the tracksuit he could tell just from the glasses with thin gold frames and the scraped back hairdo and the naff make-up and cheap jewellery she wore that she had absolutely no style, not to speak of far too much flesh on her . . . But Simon liked shy girls and one time he saw her laughing with one of the others, they couldn't stop themselves, kept looking back at each other and starting up again, wobbling and spluttering into their Cokes and he liked that too. The first time Amanda came back to his place he knew she expected him to kiss her and he was very nervous. So when he sensed her waiting for it he just said to her instead: what does your hair look like undone? She had it in a pony tail, high on her head, and straight away she reached up and let it down.

'I like it like that,' he said, and gave her a smile. Despite the glasses, she was vain. And it seemed like she was very eager to please. But all that was before. Before Before, almost.

Amanda. Everything is there, waiting, in that one word. He takes the paper out and is putting in a fresh sheet when the bolts on his door shoot back and it lurches open, making him jump; he's completely forgotten to be listening.

'Grub!' shouts Miller.

He eats the vegetable pasta bake, thinking it's pretty good until he finds a long, grey hair in it that can only be from Dave Wellington. Then he sits all evening with the typewriter on the table, refusing to be ignored. Although he wanted it so badly a few days ago he sees now how he could grow to hate the thing. All these years, he has been confined, but at least he's never had to share for more than a week or two and there was a space around him that was almost his. Now, it's been occupied by this thing he asked for without meaning to, and there is nowhere else to go.

At the Kingswells', and after, when he used to bunk off school, the first thing he'd do was get some distance. Run, till his breath ran out, then walk. Jump on a bus, get thrown off, walk some more. Half an hour, an hour, more, moving on, not quite sure where he'd end up, which would be the result of opportunities thrown up, the 66 coming before the 45, as much as any decision made. Come eleven o'clock, he might be on a building site, picking up a bit of cash for getting teas or banging on miles of skirting board, or he might be shirt off in some park, or lying on his back by the outdoor pool, soaking up sun and listening to the muddle of other people's voices. Maybe he'd find some older lads kicking a ball, hang around, join in. Movement was the thing: pumping his legs and filling his lungs, the sheer relief of it. Being able to go, to get away, feel alive, look down on the world from up a tree or a tenth-floor window ledge. If he needed even more distance he'd jump the train and do the same things in a strange place. He was always found the next day or the day after, courtesy of his unusual eyes. He was never in serious trouble, partly out of luck but mainly because he didn't like the look of what drugs did and hated the thought of needing anything that bad, it was bound to let you down in the end. So he'd let them take him back; he knew he could go again.

Here, he thinks, I can pick the typewriter up and hurl it at the wall. I can do what Tasmin is asking me to do. Or I can just sit here like this – except that I can't, because the damn words have started to come into my head, whether I type them out or not.

11

Tasmin, I am going to try and do what you asked.

September 2nd 1979, Amanda and I ate in a fancy Chinese restaurant Amanda had heard about from a friend. We had won ton soup, crispy seaweed, then pork in black bean sauce with spring onions and ginger: peculiar, salty-sweet, slightly sticky things. Egg rice. Straw mushrooms. What do you mean when you say, *Tell me everything*? How much detail do you want? Those bright yellow chickens squashed flat, the brown ducks slowly turning on spits in the window, the bundles of lanterns, the little red candle in a glass bowl, the tiny waitress with heavy framed glasses who poured out wine for Amanda and water for me, Amanda's napkin smudged with lipstick, our smiles as we fumbled with our chopsticks, us pushing hand in hand through the crowds in Leicester Square to get back to where I'd parked the van in Frith Street?

Tasmin, I want to point out there's nothing I can do right here. Such as, when I use the word 'we'. You and I both know that Amanda and I are soon to be as separate as you can get. Her dead, me alive, that's what's coming along, via me doing it. All the same we were a couple of sorts. So everything I write will pull both ways and start to hurt your ears, like the weird music you get on Radio 3 when no one normal is listening.

Also, I'm putting into words something I know already even if I'd rather forget it. You – sitting up at night in a dim-lit room, jolted along in a tube-train fug or sipping breakfast coffee in some busy café – are taking in something you did not know before. Well, you may have started this, but you don't have to go on. As for me, it's all or nothing. I've lifted the lid, and I've got to go on until the box empties out, which is why I never wanted to do it in the first place, because if you let it, memory grows like weeds in here. Attached to each memory are another six and attached to each of those six more. If you've the patience you can unwind it all. And once you've got it, you can deliberately re-remember it as a whole, then call it up whenever you want. You pick pleasant memories if you've got any sense, but even those can connect up unexpectedly to bad ones, and lead you astray in the end. Which is why I always avoid those tangled lanes and try to live in the present, which is all there really is. The past doesn't actually exist. It's only some kind of story, in parts. The End. Before. Afterwards.

We're still just about in Before. I drive us back to my place, She's chattering and flicking through music stations on the way, roughly the same as we've been doing once a week for the last couple of months since we met at work. The pattern being, I drive to collect her from her parents' house up by Streatham Common: thirties semi, replacement windows, brand new pink Wilton throughout. Mr Brooks fitted it himself; did a good job. Though why? Everyone fits them for free.

'Do call me Hazel,' Mrs Brooks says, then starts on the third degree. 'Do you have brothers and sisters, Simon?' and there's the cake crumbling in my hand and the teacup and saucer and spoon and so on – too much. I try to take the initiative, ask rather than answer – difficult with Mrs Brooks, she being used to having her way in conversation. Mr Brooks just watches, smokes his pipe. 'Look after Mandy,' he says, grabbing my hand at the door. She's twenty, but still living at home, that same house all her life. They always seem glad for her to get out a bit.

We climb up the three flights of stairs. I'm fiddling to get the key in the lock in the dark on the landing, making a joke of it, feeling nervous but pretty good. We don't touch, except when I guide her in to the dark room: the main bulb's gone and the lamp's on the other side. She pours herself a glass of the fizz I always get in for her and then looks at me, so as to say, what next, Simon? Because the deal we've come to is that we go out and afterwards she comes back here, and we talk a bit about what we've done, or rather she talks, I ask: what did she think of the movie? What did she like about the food? She's good at talking. And she has a fantastic memory. Everything: people, names, places, her whole past is still there, all the Christmases and Easters and trips and holidays and long weekends she had taken with her mum and dad, Mr and Mrs Brooks, and brother, Alan, all the friends she'd ever played with in the street and the park, what game they'd played, individual programmes and episodes she'd seen on TV, toys and pets she's had, towns she'd visited, the location of the shops where she'd bought everything she'd ever bought and how much it'd cost. It's all there. So I get her talking.

Or sometimes I turn the TV on. We talk or she watches TV, and meanwhile, I watch her doing the things I've told her to do: take your top off, pull your skirt up a bit while you talk to me, put your hand in your pants. A big part of it is that she has to try and keep talking properly while she does it, though she can't really manage it of course. I sit there and watch her, she's right on the verge and breathing hard, beginning to sweat, looking back at me through her thick specs . . . and it gets me high as a kite, her too though sometimes it gets her laughing instead. She's good at that too: watching her watching a movie, you'd know from the set of her face almost exactly what was on the screen – grim, heart-warming, boring, difficult, funny. If it's even the smallest bit funny, she laughs out loud, no holding back, no being critical. She crumples up, shaking like a four-year-old. I like that too, but I don't always want her doing it, I talk her back until she's serious again, her faced flushed, her eyes deep.

'Aren't you going to do anything?' she asked me at the beginning, holding her tits, the way I'd told her to.

'This is the way I do it,' I said.

So I tell her: 'Take your things off, everything.' She's waiting for this. Looking forward to it, you could say.

She goes to the bathroom. I'm supposing it's just for a pee and I sit there, pleased with myself and the world, in the fancy reclining chair I got hold of shortly after we met. It and the lava lamp and the stereo and the TV are fine things in the otherwise pretty sordid bedsit, brown carpet, torn two-seater sofa, limp curtains blowing in a gritty bit of city breeze, sagging shelves and units with their doors long gone, whoosh, whoosh of the traffic on the New Cross Road. I flick through a couple of channels. She's gone a fair while. It's when she comes out that I realise things are going wrong. She's already completely naked as I've never seen her before. I notice that the hair on her is fairish, like her head hair was when she was a child, in the photo on the dresser in her parents' house. I notice how pink her skin is, I notice that the curves of her look better, more dignified somehow with absolutely nothing on. But I meant for her to undress in front of me, talking like usual. I had it planned. I'd have her put something in herself while I watched. Maybe she'd beg to have me in her instead, but I wouldn't, not yet, though don't get me wrong, I'm fully functional down there, I can prove it, but if the deal's not financial, if it's a 'relationship', then I think you need to be careful and know what you are getting into and who's in charge and be sure that it won't get out of hand. All the same, looking back, I'm the first to admit it could only have gone on so long like this. Perhaps I would've ditched her. Or her me, or maybe it would have been all right, somehow turned into a normal relationship. There's a chance. I think about it sometimes, that chance, that needle's eye that could have been gone through, if only she had kept on doing what she was told.

She's standing in front of me. I'm rattled, I can tell something is going wrong and going to get worse, actually, I'm shit scared.

We're getting to The End. She says my name: 'Simon', very softly, it makes the hairs stand up on my arms. And then I realise she doesn't have her glasses on. My heart starts to put out a steady beat as if I was running uphill.

'What do you think?' she says. She's got these green eyes, very clear, sparkling from what she wants and I start to want to hit her.

'I can't wear the hard ones but the technology's improved,' she's saying. 'These are extra soft. I can keep them in for three hours now.'

'They're fucking shite,' I tell her. 'Put your glasses on, or get back dressed again. Phone a cab. Go home, now!' She doesn't do any of it.

'What?' she almost laughs. 'What's the matter with you? I've always hated my glasses,' she says. Well, I knew that. We've all got things we hate about ourselves and that was one of hers: quite small on the scale of things. 'I look much better like this,' she says. 'Don't I?' She comes over, takes hold of me, squeezing, rubbing herself against me. 'Come on, now,' she says. She takes my hands and puts them on her hips. She slips her own hand up between my legs but there's nothing going on there by now and I push her away hard and she staggers into the coffee table, shrieks.

'Get off!' I tell her. I turn the TV on again and sit down again, act as if I'm watching it, the late news, though I'm too angry to take it in. She comes over, squats down in front of me, blocking the view. She's still stark naked, she puts her hands on my knees and looks into my face.

'Don't you ever do that again,' she says. 'Look, I don't mind doing the things you want, letting you watch, all that, it's been fun. But I won't lower myself. I won't wear glasses for you when I don't want to. That's the end of it . . . Listen, Simon Austen, I do know I've got nice eyes. I know because I've been told. And if this thing is going nowhere, well, let me tell you, I get offers. In fact, I've even been out with another bloke, once or twice – but we haven't done anything, really we haven't . . . I'm just saying this, because I'd much rather it was you, I really would.' Then she starts crying.

It's one of the gym instructors, she says, without me even asking. 'I've always fancied you,' she goes on. 'I don't mind going slow. I'm quite shy but I'm not a prude. But I'm beginning to wonder whether maybe you're just some kind of weirdo.'

I'm thinking, quicker than it takes to blink but at the same time so strongly that it fills me right up: *this has got well out of hand. It's upside down, the wrong way round. I can't have this,* and by that I don't mean her doing whatever she did or didn't do with the gym instructor or keeping things from me or even standing there naked and making me lose it completely, telling me I'm weird. I mean her not doing what I wanted, just exactly that, and trying to get me to do things her way. It makes me feel like I'm nothing and there's nowhere to go –

So then, *I just flipped*: that's the thing you say, and in due course, I said it. Is this what you wanted to know?

12

The lights went off two hours ago. If hours were people they would be thickset men with flat feet and asthma; eight more of them have to pass through every bit of the prison before the doors are unlocked. The typewriter is zipped in its case, the letter addressed, stamped; the flap of the envelope is open in case it is one that the censor selects to check for threats, accounts of escape plans, or plots . . . Simon lies on top of his bed, eyes wide. Vivienne asked the impossible. Tasmin asked him to do this, just very, very difficult. What he has written is hers, he reassures himself. On the way to breakfast, he will hand it over. He will feel better for just getting rid of it and then, when she actually reads it, it will become fully hers. She asked for it. She can decide what next.

If he makes it through until she answers, well, then he'll be able to cope with whatever comes next, but until then, there can be no more going back. He must be alert; he must concentrate, resist the sly approach of those sudden bursts of remembered sound, the waves of nausea and terrible intimate glimpses that seem to want to return, now that he has once let his guard down. He will keep busy. Seek out talk, effort, work of any kind. Of course, there will be the nights to deal with. He needs batteries for the radio and should have thought of that before he started out. So right now, the only thing is to keep his attention out, not in. For example, listen: an officer just walked across the courtyard, whistling through his teeth, and let himself in to A wing. If he tries really hard, he can just about make out the rumble of the occasional bit of haulage on the main road, a quarter of a mile beyond the wall. But in between, it's quiet, the very quietest time of night. Think of something pleasant, he tells himself, as he finally gets his heart rate under control, think of something simple and sweet, like ice cream.

13

The Canteen Officer, Richards, shiny with sweat, mops his face with a handkerchief and speaks through the circle of holes drilled into the Perspex grille:

'You are only allowed four at a time, but anyhow, we're out of them!' he repeats. 'They didn't have any at the Cash and Carry. It's not my fault.' The canteen is in the basement and the news echoes up the stairs.

'No batteries – bloody forgot them, didn't they!'

'No fucking batteries!?' It won't be long before everyone knows, but Simon's having trouble believing it. 'No batteries?' he asks again. His voice comes out thin and hoarse.

'You've got £8.90 credit. Do you require something else instead, Mr Austen, or are you going to move along?' Behind Richards are shelves on which sit the boxes of confectionery, Mars, Curly Wurly, Toffee Crisp, Murray Mints, Marathon, but no KitKat, Toblerone, Yorkie or Fruit 'n' Nut, nothing with foil; a crate of softening Golden Delicious apples and a few withering oranges but not any bananas – *Not my fault mate, some idiots dry out the skins and smoke them* – the dried milk, sugar, HobNobs, the Marlboros, Old Holborn and Hilton (less than half price), the special orders, vitamins, biscuits, washing powder, magazines, all bagged up and labelled on the top shelf, a box of Sure deodorant, Gillette shaving foam, disposables, but no batteries, not even the little ones that won't do that much damage when knotted into the end of a sock and used as a club, no batteries, not a sign of them.

'I mean it, Austen.'

'Tobacco then, I'll take it in tobacco, Old Holborn, and papers, and a Curly Wurly.'

'Plan on smoking a lot this week, do you? Three pence left in your account, sign here and let's pray we go back onto the pre-orders before I drop dead.' Simon scoops his purchases up, drops the cigarette papers, and, as he bends, finds the floor rushing up to meet him, the world whiting out. It doesn't last long enough. Minutes later, he's parked head in hands by the wall waiting until things come back solid. The queue has moved on.

'You all right?' asks a new bloke in dirty glasses he doesn't know the name of. The first thing he does is check his goods; it's a good thing none of the four packets of tobacco has gone missing.

'I need batteries,' he replies pushing himself upright.

It's not until evening Association that he gets them, supposedly brand new but probably just hotted up, one set for two packets, a deal. Plus four thrillers from the library; it's going to be harder than he thought, but she'll answer as soon as she can, he's pretty sure of that.

14

Blake in the landing office is a trim, shortish bloke who cultivates the Hitler look but without the manner; once he bought in a pot of E45 cream for a bloke with bad skin. Now, he weighs Simon's envelope in his hand like some odd vegetable he might or might not buy.

'This has come back. Too much,' he explains, throwing a sideways glance to check that Simon won't go apeshit, then lifting the unsealed flap so he can peek inside. 'Way too much!' Yards away, a door crashes shut.

'But I put seventy-five pence on there!' Simon hasn't slept since he wrote the letter. Also, he's having trouble with food, has to keep swallowing his saliva down, and noises bore right into him, he can feel them in his bones. His back has gone stiff, his hands too. He knows he needs to be careful, mustn't over react.

'Staff shortages. Too much for the censor to read, should he want to. *Too long*,' Blake informs him, brandishing a scrap of paper.

Simon disconnects, somehow, from his fury at this turn of events, but finds himself pushed by an older rage from that chair in the flat in New Cross Road. He's up, reaching for her, seeing her see him, her mouth loosen, gape . . .

He digs his fingernails into the palm of his hand to bring himself back: 'Two pages max at the moment unless it's legal,' Blake tells him. 'Take it, then. What's up with you?' Blake says, putting the letter in Simon's hand and folding the fingers over. 'Move along, or you'll miss exercise. You OK? Did you get your batteries?'

So what is he to do with the fucking thing? I don't want it, he thinks, not on me, not in my cell . . . Bin it? Flush it? Burn it and set the alarms off? Make it into paper planes, see if he can get it over the wall? No. It's Tasmin's; she asked for it. He could split it into five sections of two sides each, number them in sequence, unzip the infernal machine, type the address four more times, plus new covering letter to explain . . . What chance all five get there the same fortnight? Fucking lunatic rules. Fucking stupid woman putting him through this. He folds the letter in half and stuffs it in his front pocket. It digs into his groin with every step he takes.

Outside in the yard, it's turned chilly. He clenches himself against the cold, stamps his feet, does arm swinging with his sleeves pulled over hands, still not warming up. He's too low and stiff to run. Grey sky, spitty bits of rain in the air and no blood sugar doesn't help. Hardly anyone else is out: no blacks, just the fat-burgers and the nutters, and the glasses bloke, Dennis, who's now been found out: messing with kids – he won't last another day unless he gets himself on the Rule. Of course, Big T is always on hand to make bad things worse.

'What's up, android? Knockback?' he says, clasping Simon's shoulder, falling into step.

'Fuck off. I'm right on the edge. And I've got no tobacco.' I could do with one of those, Simon thinks, taking in the Chelsea bobble hat Tev's got on. Beneath it purplish white skin, a couple of days' worth of ginger stubble, two red-rimmed, ice-blue eyes swimming in water – looks as if he's being boiled:

'Listen to this,' Tev says, 'Straight after my appeal folds, she sends me a Dear John. Wants to live in Wales with the kids, get them a better life, new start, sorry, tara . . . Bitch!' he punches air with his right, then his left. 'Bitch. Not that they're my kids, I never believed it, everyone's been in that cunt! Who does she think she is?' Steamy breath streams out between the words. He grabs hold of Simon's arms, digs his fingers in. 'What about me in here? What about my visits, my supplies? I tell you, I'll fucking kill her –'

Call this a problem? But there he is, banging Tev on the back through his parka, telling him, 'Steady now. You don't need it. You're better off without,' even though he hates the bastard to kingdom come, and he's thinking, good luck to her, except why tell him where and Wales just isn't far enough and it rains too much, how about Australia or maybe the fucking Moon?

Teverson shakes his head like a wet dog then bangs Simon's back in return. 'Too right. You're solid, mate. Plenty of fish, eh? But the thing is, I've gotta look in the mirror and shave, haven't I? I'll make her pay for it.' He wipes his nose on his sleeve, laughs, a noise like something wooden breaking apart.

'Steady,' Simon tells him.

'You –' the screw barks at Simon as they line up. 'You, Austen, wait.'

'What about some manners?' Tev yells back. 'This is a mate of mine!'

'Oh, fuck off, Teverson,' Simon tells him. 'I don't have mates.'

In the Magnolia Zone they go on five doors past Dickie Walters's office and up to R. F. Grange, MSc.

'I've not been this far before,' Simon comments.

'You won't get much joy out of it,' the screw says as he knocks.

The office is double the size of Walters's. The desk alone seems to be the area of Simon's whole cell. There's a matching filing cabinet, both made out of some fancy grained wood and a computer on a separate stand close by. Grange, small and bald, very straight-backed, gestures at the empty chair.

'So,' he says, 'you have a pen friend.'

'Yes,' Simon tells him.

'You'll call me sir,' Grange says.

'Yes, sir.' Simon says. He doesn't at this point care. It's very quiet in here, he realises. There's no need to shout, even a whisper could be heard. At the same time, there's plenty of light from the high-up windows and the brass fittings mounted above the little paintings of horses and other livestock and it shows up flaws. He feels very shabby, in his layers of badly washed cotton and polyester, his underpants that have done three days, everything suddenly way too loose. Grange is in crisp, striped shirt sleeves, with the suit jacket over the back of his chair.

'So, Austen,' he says, 'who are you writing to at the moment?'

'Tasmin Rolls-Hamilton, sir.' Grange's lips twitch and his eyebrows shoot up, like he's suppressing a laugh.

'Tasmin Rolls-Hamilton,' Grange says. 'Tell me about Tasmin Rolls-Hamilton.'

'Nothing to tell,' Simon tells him. 'It's a new thing. She likes poetry.' If he wasn't so cold and tired, he'd be more worried and more angry.

'How old is she?' Grange asks. It seems a strange question and it takes a while to remember.

'Seventeen.' Grange studies Simon for a while, then reaches into his in-tray.

'I've had a letter too,' he says. He sends it skidding across the expanse of desk between them. It falls on the floor; Simon ducks down to pick it up.

> One of the inmates from your institution, Simon Austen, has been corresponding with my daughter, who is fourteen years old and in a vulnerable, distressed and possibly manic depressive condition. She is under care of the doctor at this moment.
>
> I am not prepared for these letters to continue and am writing to demand that Mr Austen terminate this correspondence immediately. Under the particular circumstances I think this would come better from him, rather than as a prohibition from us, her parents. Any further letters from Tasmin should be returned unopened. Should Mr Austen act otherwise, I will have no option but to lay the matter, via my solicitor, before the police. I trust this is clear.

Fourteen? Simon thinks. She did a good job! Or was he just being thick? The letter she was supposed to have by now stabs him in the leg as he reaches over to hand Mr Hamilton's ultimatum back. His hands have started to shake.

'You see?' Grange says. 'What do you think?' He thinks: no wonder she was so understanding, seeing as she's a sort of prisoner herself. Has her own censor too, plus also she's pretended to be someone else, just as he did to begin with . . . As if a switch had been flicked, Simon starts to be able to imagine her properly, whereas before the things she said and asked of him got in the way of that. She's got a plump face, skinny body, maybe she's got that starving disease, dark shadows under her eyes . . . he finds himself interested, in a way, more than he ever was before. A screwed-up kid. Rich parents, but otherwise, she's not so different to Danni and Suzette and the other girls in Burnside who cut themselves, nicked stuff, got knocked up, ran away.

'I didn't know,' he says. Grange lifts his hands briefly in a way that suggests it not being worth his while, absolutely beside the point, to decide whether Simon is lying or not. *You smug bastard.*

'Do you think a young, vulnerable girl should be corresponding with you?' What's the point, really, in answering?

'This bloke is asking me to lie for him,' Simon points out. 'And if she's already so screwed up, has he thought what will be the effect, now, of me pulling out of it?'

Grange flips the file on his desk shut, pushes it to one side.

'I'd avoid the moral high ground if I were you, Austen. Come to a decision as to whether you are going to co-operate or else make life difficult for everyone including yourself. Discuss it with probation, if you need the situation spelling out.'

'He's retired and the new one is already off sick,' Simon points out, as a matter of information, not because he actually wants to talk to anyone. But Grange is already on the phone.

'There's a man here needs to talk to you,' he says, and then, after a while: 'Nine tomorrow. Thanks, Bernie.'

*

Hours later his hands are still not steady as he prises off the back of the radio, slots in the last of the batteries and finds the ten o'clock news, a long item about a country he's never heard of called Latvia, then a medical phone-in: people describe their symptoms to a doctor – Doctor, Doctor, I've got blood in my piss, I've had a headache for three weeks, there's a lump in my gut – and then are told in a roundabout way to go and see their GP. It's quite good, almost makes him laugh and he's sorry when it gives way to some jazz, not the kind he likes, so he finds the World Service news and then an OU programme about statistics. Finally, he strikes gold with an hour or so of some Indian-sounding music, very fast, round and round the same thing over and over again but getting higher, a voice wailing away in gibberish. It almost sends him to sleep but then voice and drum come to an abrupt, simultaneous halt and catapult him into silence. He flicks round for a bit, the sound getting fuzzier all the time. He's got the thing pressed into his ear. By the time the farming news comes on he's more or less imagining what the words are and he abandons the radio, strips off and washes, tries a few sit-ups and stretches, then puts his old clothes back on. The letter to Tasmin is still in the pocket, softened up by a day's walking.

He gets the typewriter out, makes the best job he can of writing to her: he says that he has really appreciated and enjoyed their correspondence so far, but at the same time feels that he made a mistake starting it and it would be wrong of him to continue. She is a lovely person and he wishes her all the best. Would she like the typewriter back? It has been hard to write this but he knows she will understand it is too early for him to have a relationship again . . .

He types out a copy to Mr Grange. Only takes a minute or two despite his fingers feeling so cold.

Anyone touches me in that breakfast queue, he thinks, I'll explode. And I'm not seeing fucking probation.

15

Three steps up to the Portakabin door. Jackson knocks:

'Man for you, Bernie.'

'Send him in, please.' It's a woman.

'Bernadette Nightingale,' she says, as she gets out from behind the desk and comes over, holding out her hand to shake. She's about his own height, well-rounded with a plump face, pale, smooth-looking skin, dark eyes and thick, shiny hair, chestnut, fixed up in some kind of a knot at the back of her head.

'I don't really need this. I've only come –' he tells her, letting go of the offered hand. '– because I need to get out and work's cancelled. Staffing.'

'Uh-huh. Well, pleased to meet you, Simon. I just started here last month. We haven't met before, have we?' There's Irish in her voice, overlaid with a posh school, and Lord knows what else. 'Sorry it's so cold in here!' she says, rubbing her hands together. Her fingernails are neatly filed and polished, covered with rings, both hands, all fingers, plain, complex, old-fashioned, modern, ethnic – all different. How old is she? More than him. Getting on for forty, perhaps? 'The heating will come through soon,' she tells him. 'Then we'll bake!' Her skirt rustles as she moves back to her chair.

'So,' she says from behind her side of the desk, 'what is all this about letters and a teenage girl?'

'A mistake,' he tells her, flatly, so as to conceal his irritation. 'I didn't know she was so young. I've written and told her that I don't want to go on. I handed it in this morning.' He's too tired to be aware of expecting any particular response.

'Have you had a pen friend before? Are you going to look for someone else?' she asks.

'What's that to do with you?' he snaps.

'I just wondered,' she says, lifting the ringed fingers of her right hand slightly from the desk. 'What's the problem?' Her eyes seem to be looking right into his, but because of their darkness, he can't be sure.

'Listen, it's just a hobby,' he tells her, 'like painting eggs or binding books. Except it makes less clutter!'

She waits a little, then says, very softly. 'I expect it is more than that.' And it seems to take him for ever to decide what to do, whether to tear her off a strip (except that he has a ghost of a feeling it won't work) or to stop talking, to change the subject completely, or to leave.

'I haven't slept for five days,' he finally says and then everything seems to shift a gear.

'Are you going to tell me why?' she enquires. The small pause she leaves beforehand has a calming effect. It says, somehow: I know this will rile you, but all the same, I do have to ask.

'I don't know a blind thing about you,' he points out.

'No?' Her lips pull into a smile. 'But I expect you've made a few guesses,' she says, 'and they're probably right. And if there's something specific you want to know, you are perfectly free to ask.' She sits there waiting, her head tipped slightly to one side, a bit of a smile, her eyes glittering, bird-woman. But he can't think of anything at all to ask. Even if he could think of something, it strikes him that she would somehow end up learning more about him as a result of his asking it than he would learn about her.

'That won't last,' he tells her, pointing suddenly at the big spider plant in a blue pot that she must have brought in from home, 'there's no enough light in here.' She considers it a minute, shrugs, returns her eyes to his face and likewise his attention to the question she asked. Then she leans back in her chair, sighs, looks away. It's like a light being turned off. The place goes back to its dull and cold usual self. So as much as anything else, it's wanting her attention back that makes him do it.

'The fact is,' he says, 'I wrote to Tasmin about Amanda. I've opened the whole can of worms. That's why I can't sleep. OK?' He's staring at her like she must know what all this means, but of course she can't have read the file yet.

'Amanda?' she asks and her ignorance seems like an advantage, an invitation. There is just him and her, here and now . . . he can get rid of the damn thing at last, he can at least do that. Simon stands, pulls the letter out of his pocket and does what he can to flatten it. He can see how she's watching him carefully; he noticed when he came in the panic button fixed onto the right-hand side of the desk. She's well placed to reach it if she wants to. So he slows down his movements as he removes the letter from the envelope, keeps to his half of the room when he holds it out to her.

'You can have it,' he says, adding, 'the fact is it was only by sheer luck that it wasn't sent.' She stands up, also quite slowly, reaches over. He feels the most extraordinary sensation of relief as she takes the letter from him, sits down again, removes the pages from the envelope and puts them on her desk. She reads a little, glances at the clock on the wall, then looks back to him.

'It looks important,' she says. 'I'll need clear time for this.' *You can't do this to me*, he thinks, *just read it, will you?*

'Took all night to write but you could read it in about half an hour, I reckon,' he tells her, jauntily, though it's hard to keep the edge out of his voice.

'Well,' she says. 'I'll need to look up the background, make notes and so on; I want to take it on properly . . . So you see, I'd really much rather set clear time aside. Meanwhile –' Glaring at her doesn't work. When she looks back at him, bright and curious, his eyes stop glaring and slide away . . . he can see: a brown sheepskin jacket thrown over the chair, a set of Ford car keys and a pair of leather gloves on the table. Things from outside. Part of a life. This, his life, is just her job. What a job. Why do it? Why do people work here? 'Meanwhile, we can try and sort out your sleep problem. And then we can talk about this on Wednesday,' she tells him, tapping the letter with the fingers of her right hand. 'Do you understand?' she says. 'Depending on the exact content, I may have to take copies of what you've given me and show it to my manager. It's possible that certain things might follow on from this.' Might they? What things exactly? he should be asking, but his anger has suddenly twisted away from him, run off and left him there, stranded, with everything, even his own reaction, suddenly out of his hands. Why? It must be her voice: low, strong, blurred here and there, elsewhere oddly precise – the hidden spaces and sudden slopes in it, the way it can be so clear even when she lets it drop right down, the way it seems to add extra meaning to what she says, to widen and soften and explain it . . . At any rate, the fight has gone out of him and all he can do there is sit, watching Bernadette Nightingale talk. Then he lets his eyes close and for a moment all there is is darkness and a kind of woody scent, which could be her perfume, or just the smells of wherever she's come from, clinging to her clothes.

'Now then,' she is saying. 'You seem in a bad way, Simon. I could ring the medical centre and ask the Medical Officer to give you something that'll get you to sleep . . . Simon?' she asks. 'Shall I ring the doctor?' He opens his eyes again, nods, then watches her press out the numbers, push back her hair, pick up a pen, check him out periodically while she waits for a reply.

'He looks like he could pass out. Very anxious,' she says.

'Let's get you straight there,' she tells him when she hangs up. She hooks the sheepskin coat over her shoulders, making coins rattle in the pockets, and comes over to him. 'He is a bit of a stickler but I'm sure he'll say yes when he's seen the state of you. Just a day's worth at a time, you know.' She opens the door and lets in a rush of cold, damp air. 'Now, you'll be OK, won't you? Wednesday, first thing. Hang in there . . .' She chatters a bit about the weather as she walks him back to where Jackson is smoking in a patch of thin wintery sun, a little pile of butts on the ground beside him.

'OK?' she asks, beaming at him. Then she's gone and he is following Jackson towards a smell of antiseptic and the prospect of oblivion.

16

A two-hour wait. Then a three-minute examination: pulse, tongue, chest, torch in the eyes, piss test thrown in. Result: two red and white capsules to be taken with water after food. Lunch missed. Three hours, supper, pills, then thirty-nine more hours, the first eighteen lost, like falling into some kind of black hole; the rest spent climbing out of it. But now Simon is fully alert, showered, shaved, dressed in cleanish clothes. He wants to know what Bernadette is going to say and also he wants to know if he remembers her right. He walks out into the chill of the yard, past the well-raked, empty flower beds to the mud-coloured Portakabins. The sky is bright, cold blue with a curved slash of fresh jet stream running right across.

The room is completely different. Her desk has been pushed back and the two grey chairs are in the rest of the space, not quite facing each other, not quite next to each other either. Wearing a brown knitted dress and leather boots, she's there, sitting in the chair furthest away from the door.

She has Tasmin's letter on her lap, a briefcase to her side, his file on the floor by her feet. Her voice as she greets him is at any rate the same: low, strong, blurred here and there, elsewhere oddly precise.

He stands there, looking: from her neck hangs a heavy silver pendant in a shape like a smoothly melted O; the rings are still on her fingers. She doesn't bother with how he is and so on but he can see her checking him out. 'Take a seat,' she says. 'I've tried to make it a bit less formal in here.' He sits in the chair, making sure not to sprawl. All of this, just getting into the room seems to take a long time, as if it was happening underwater.

'It was painful to read. Very different from the statement you made at the time –' she gestures at the file '– but it feels true,' she says.

'It is,' he says. 'My brief went for the jealousy angle. From the start, he said it would be easier for people to understand that I flipped and went for her because she was messing me about . . . Then forensics turned up that she'd had it with the gym instructor – it was a gift, my brief said. And maybe I *was* jealous. But it wasn't why . . . It was how you've just read. Because she wouldn't take out the contact lenses . . . Same result, of course.' He looks straight at her. What he's talking about, what he wrote about, seems almost to belong to another life.

'What was it like to write this?' she asks.

'It was OK once I started,' he tells her, jauntily, 'but hard afterwards. I wouldn't say it has improved my quality of life.'

'Are you going to write more?' she asks, her head cocked to one side again as she waits for his reply. It's always the left side that she leans to, he notices. The shine of her eyes comes from them being such a very dark brown, and maybe there is some subtle kind of eye shadow on the lids, maybe not. Maybe she's just tired.

'I don't know,' he says. 'This was for Tasmin. What would be the point, now?' And for Christ's sake, he thinks, wasn't it enough? Though if she wants it, maybe I . . . then he catches himself: What the hell's going on here? The fact is he wants somehow to keep this thing going, he wants to please her, but that's ridiculous, because what is she going to be thinking when she looks at him? Strangler? Coward? Loser? You Sick Bastard? Nothing at all? He can't know, unless he asks – not even then, and he can't ask . . . But even so, he's smiling. Why? What possible good is a smile right now? All the same, it uselessly comes and to hide it, he looks down at his hands, the lettering there on his fingers, indelible blue: DUMB CUNT. I did the thing written down on that paper, he thinks. I did that . . . In the same life, he is now sitting next to Bernadette Nightingale and feeling like he's inside a washing machine, a cocktail shaker, on one of those rides at the fair . . . What is it about her? He looks across again. Bernadette is not smiling, but her mouth is plump, the corners upturned. Her eyes are still on him, but it doesn't feel like a stare as such, more like warm water pouring over his skin.

'I feel this is a beginning,' she's saying. 'You call it the end, but I feel this is really a beginning.' It's a shock to realise she is about to start giving him the exact same kind of jargon that Barry used to offer up and in almost the same words.

'You do, do you?' he says, the smile obliterated, his voice narrow: stop there. Don't make me go back.

'Yes,' she says; continues, impervious, her mouth still plump, the corners still upturned, 'This changes things. It makes the offence seem more complex than before . . .' she pauses, frowning slightly. 'But *also* –' her face opens, it's like the clouds have suddenly been swept away '– *also* it means you can move on. You can begin to feel the consequences of what you did that night. You can start to look at how you came to act that way, and that certainly wasn't an option before you admitted how it actually was . . .'

'Sounds like that will be one big bundle of fun,' he says. 'Enjoy it, would you? Like to watch?' This finally brings her up short, but immediately he feels grubby and says, 'Sorry'. She makes a quick gesture with her hand, so as to push all that aside.

'I take your point,' she says. *I take your point* – it's as if they're on a serious radio discussion, *Kaleidoscope* or the *PM* programme or something; it's just as if she expects him to have the same kind of mindset as her, bar a few superficial differences – 'The thing is, if you don't begin to look at all this, Simon, what then?' The thing is, he thinks, if I do, what are the chances I'll make it through? Life's a gamble, everyone knows that, even him. So far, he feels he has tended not to win . . . What does she know about all that? Even so, he takes in a breath, lets it straight out. Empty, he tells himself . . . empty. Then *go*: like making a jump or a catch.

'You may be right,' he says. He waits to see how having said such a thing feels: OK, good even, except for them being in this room, with other men's misery stuck to the walls and asbestos beneath the paint and lining paper. A window that opened would be something. Still, you can't have it all and now the smile is back and this time he lets it be.

'Yes,' Bernadette says, smiling too. She picks up the papers in her lap and looks across at him. 'I really do think you should keep on doing this.' She removes the paperclip she's put on it, and returns the original copy of Tasmin's letter to him. He puts it on the floor, and leans back in the chair.

'Unless you want me to, I won't say any more about it right now,' she says, 'except to make clear how much I admire you for having done this. I do think it is very courageous.'

'Oh,' he mumbles. 'Like I said, Tasmin wanted me to.' But her words, the sentence *I admire you*, the adjective *courageous*, sit in the room like some third person who has suddenly arrived by mysterious means. And, just like the typewriter, he never knew before that he wanted them, but now they are here he realises that he always did. Perhaps they too will be a curse as much as a blessing, but there's no point telling himself Fucking likely story! or pointing out that he doesn't deserve such words, because whether he does or not, they've already been snatched up. It's how it must be when a fix goes in: no, he never asked for it, but yes, he could want some more pretty soon and the shock of how it makes him feel means he only half hears Bernadette saying how she has been talking to her line manager.

'There will be a meeting in the next few weeks to discuss all this and the implications . . . Your new Home Probation Officer should be in touch any day now, but meantime, I'll certainly argue that you should be in a situation more suited to looking at all these issues . . .' *Issues?* Really, this can only be some kind of dream in which he has been turned inside out, become someone else like his former self only in that he is its opposite; whether this is good or bad Simon is not certain, but some time – soon, he supposes – he will wake up.

'Simon?' she prompts.

'It's been good talking to you,' he says, twisting across and offering his hand to shake. I've got to get out of here, he's thinking, as, overcoming her surprise, she grasps the offered right hand, the one with DUMB tattooed on the backs of the fingers, and gets to her feet. Her hand is hot and dry. Her hair is flying out at the edges of its cut. It's like she's two times alive.

'Same time next week?' he asks. 'What shall I write about next, then?'

He notices her hands lift themselves, the ringed fingers outspread in front of her – as if to catch something flying towards her.

'That's up to you,' she says.

17

'Ice cream?' Bernadette asks, with a short, perplexed laugh. This time she's wearing a soft-looking, maroon sweater and new denim jeans, along with a string of silver-mounted amber beads, earrings to match.

'I is for ice cream,' he tells her, grinning, 'which used to be my favourite food. Can't get it here, of course. It's a memory. Nothing to do with Amanda, I'm trying to steer clear of all that.' She glances at the single spaced page, ICE CREAM in capitals at the top, back at him, down again, as if to make sure nothing is concealed.

'Go on,' he says, 'it won't bite.'

Twenty-six years ago, Simon, aged nearly four, is sitting in his pushchair in a park, eating an ice cream cone. It's vanilla. Next to him, sitting on a wooden bench, is a woman with an almost hollow face, paper-white face, her hair scraped back into a pony tail: Sharon. He's taking his time with the ice cream – he'll be in a hurry later on, but right now it is just beginning to soften, yet still icy cold and perfect. He runs his tongue in careful circles, keeping the mound evenly pointed and smoothly round. He gives himself over to the cold, the sweetness, the way it shocks his tongue alive. Meanwhile, the thin woman stubs out one cigarette, lights another. Her hands are shaking. Her eyes scan the distance; he might as well not be there. He's used to this and doesn't much care, just goes on with the ice cream, sinks his lips down, pulls them up, presses them closed as he gets towards the top of the ice cream hill, twisting the cone, so as to ease off the very tip; he holds that right on the middle of his tongue, until it melts . . .

'Sharon – this is your mother?' Bernie asks, quickly looks up

– by now, she has had time to really study the file. He nods, smiles: the memory of ice cream came to him clear as day, like some kind of slow-moving movie projected onto the wall of B232, except that he was inside it too, tasting the lost taste of vanilla ice, and feeling the sun on his scabby little knees. Then it was gone and he was remembering it, so he could write it down.

And now, grown into a man, callous killer, cunt, prick, dick head, et cetera, he sits in the poky room haunted by Bernie's almost imperceptible, thoroughly complicated scent. He sits, straight-backed in his chair, hands on knees, watches as she reads these words of his about the vanished past, notices how she swallows a couple of times; thinks how she is perhaps a little older than he first thought, observes that she definitely does wear make-up: mascara, a bit of lipstick just darker than the skin beneath, perhaps other things he's not close enough to see. He doesn't mind it . . . At one point she frowns a little, then raises her brows as if she were talking to someone rather than just taking in typed words. Later, she smiles . . . It's a three-quarters view. Hanging from the lobe of her left ear is the string of tiny amber beads on their silver pin, absolutely motionless. If I was an A for artist, Simon thinks, I'd draw this. Woman Reading a Man's Memories. I'd draw it, so I could have her picture on my wall –

Bernie reads how four-year-old Simon was biting neat scallop shapes from the side of the cone, when Sharon suddenly turned and smiled at him as if someone had switched all the lights back on inside. 'I'll get you another one!' she said, picking up her bag. 'Wait right here, OK?'

'And she just never came back . . .' Bernie says, a moment later, putting the paper down in her lap. For a moment, her face has slipped, as if what had happened back then, to someone else, has physically shaken her. He finds himself trying to explain.

'She got distracted. You've surely seen how it is once someone gets hooked on that stuff? She met someone who had something for her, you see. Probably why we were in the park in the first place – I don't think she was a fan of fresh air. So Iris Kingswell collected me from the police station. She was fostering. Monthly visits, I think it was, but Sharon vanished pretty soon after this. Later, after she killed herself, they almost got me adopted, but it didn't work out. Too stroppy. Back to the Kingswells, but she was having the change of life and couldn't cope either. Anyway, this is the last I remember of Sharon –'

'Your mother,' Bernie says.

'As for him,' Simon leans back, interlocks his fingers in front of him, turns his hands palm out, stretches. 'Who knows! Could be some old lag in here, for all I know. Maybe it is. Maybe that's why I've turned out this way . . . Mind you,' he says, leaning forward, 'I didn't really want that second cone, though double-size to begin with would have been fine! When I was working, I used to have ice cream almost every lunchtime. Sometimes that *was* my lunch: a King Cone or a Choc Ice. Or both. Any kind, really, but those are what I used to like best. I reckon that's the first thing I'll do when I get out. I'll buy an ice cream.' The phrase 'when I get out', brings him up short and hangs between them in the room, glittering treacherously with what Bernie might call its 'implications'. Another thing, Simon thinks in the pause that follows, another thing is that by now, there must be kinds of ice cream he's never even dreamed of.

Bernie puts the typing to one side. She doesn't say anything about 'abandonment' or 'issues' or ask him to go into how he felt. Her face has composed itself again, a new picture, could he draw, and she's sitting there waiting, or thinking things over. It's hard to tell.

'Not what you expected?' he asks.

'Well, no!' she says.

'You did say *anything*. I'm not just what I did that night,' he points out, meaning *I'm not all bad, am I?* and immediately wishes he could press a button, explode himself out of the place. Where's the one-liner that would do that? It won't come, though it would have, without him even asking for it, were he talking to Barry or someone like that.

'No,' Bernadette says, again, smiling at him, 'you're not. Of course you're not. I'm sure you have many good qualities.'

Name them, he thinks at her, but it doesn't have any effect: she leaves him there on his own with this new kind of desperation: it's fucking pathetic, he thinks, wanting something from someone like this, some stupid words – give me my old kind of desperation any time! But the horse-to-be-ridden has galloped away, leaving not even a plume of dust, and he is stranded in this chair, in this flimsy room, with Bernadette Nightingale. Who are you? he thinks at her, half angry, What the hell are you doing here? Where do you live? What roads do you drive in that Ford of yours?

'Your Home Officer is still sick,' she's pointing out.

'Bad back,' he says. 'Carrying all those files, maybe.'

'Nice try,' she says. 'But I believe he had a mountain-climbing accident. Well, anyhow, we can continue like this.'

Thank you, Tasmin, and I hope you're doing OK. Thank *you*, even Mr R. F. Grange MSc, for not taking the infernal machine away . . . Simon's fingers dance over the keys and he misses exercise some days, to sit there typing out anything that comes to mind. Talk about a bottomless pit! For years the past has been a no-go zone, has become a kind of dull blur, a dimly lit, dank-smelling corridor in some place no one wants to go to, locked doors all along, like a premonition of where he has actually ended up. But now some lights are going on: memories, good, bad, all kinds. His boyhood bedroom at the Kingswells', the floral pattern of the old wallpaper showing through a meanly applied coat of pale blue. The Kingswells themselves: Iris as she used to be, plump and smooth-faced, always wanting to stop you or move you; John skinny and grey, in his overalls, ghost of the garage that came out intermittently for meals and to find fault; their 'real' kids, Susan, Elizabeth, Maria; the musty, chemical and tomato smell of the greenhouse out at the back where he sheltered when sent outside until he apologised . . . There are snatches of kids he took up with, odd incidents, places. Playgrounds. Building sites. Stations. There is the dog which belonged to the Murrays, Belinda and Nick, who eventually decided against the adoption: well, the only loss there was the dog, he really liked that dog, and so now he's got Tasmin's typewriter and he writes a whole page about the dog: the way the short brown fur lay smooth or pricked his hand if he stroked against the grain, the good, dirty smell of it, the pricked-up ears, the way it rolled over and over, panting, head flung back, tongue out, tussled with him in the weedless, intensely green grass of the Murray's town house, long before Before – a while to go, even, until they got fed up with him. Maybe Bernadette will like that one, the blond, curly-haired boy with mismatched eyes playing with the big dog, rolled together and parcelled up in a sweet musk of sweat and chlorophyll?

He manages not to mind too much when his appointment is cancelled, twice. He tells himself it's an opportunity to write more. Days pass pretty fast between work and the typing, which now, he is doing for Bernie. He can picture her waiting, with the silver and amber earrings on, her head to one side, her eyes looking without staring, as he types page after page. As for where she is while she waits, he's not quite sure. Some kind of out-of-the-ordinary place he can't quite imagine, a cottage in the woods, a houseboat, a castle on a cliff, a stately home with deer in the park. Not the Portakabin at any rate. He forgets how it began and what is supposed to be the point of it all, until, on a damp afternoon at around five o'clock, the visible scrap of late-afternoon sky dark violet against the electric light, he finds himself back where he does not want to be, the place where he left off.

He is sitting in the leather chair, with Amanda standing right there without her glasses, stark naked in front of him, even though he told her to take the lenses out and go away. She didn't. She still won't. She never will. All right, he tells her, and himself, as he pushes yet another sheet of paper into the roller, clips it down, cranks it up – all right. This is it.

It's December now and the Portakabin is completely in the

shadow of the block wall. Inside there's a fan heater whirring away as well as the radiator. Bernie has had her hair coloured a slightly deeper chestnut than before. She is wearing a thick, brown sweater, with a white pattern of diamond shapes around the yoke, a broad silver bracelet, plain but for the hinge and clasp. Does she buy these things herself? Does someone give them to her?

'I'm sorry – first the work to rule, then the flu. Well, at least they did give you the message,' she says.

'I do feel the cold,' she tells him as they move to the chairs.

'I guessed that,' he says. He's already too warm himself, could do with taking off his sweatshirt, but feels inhibited about doing it. 'Well, here you are!' he tells her as he hands over a couple of sheets of paper, impeccably typed as ever, the corners folded to keep them together. 'Mind, you'll want to take it away. It's heavy – more detail.' Bernie considers for a moment or two. DETAILS OF KILLING AMANDA, the header says. Simon's veins tighten up just seeing the shapes of the words. What's it going to do to her, reading this? Why didn't he bring the dog one instead?

'I do know this territory a little by now,' Bernie says, slowly. 'And you too. So why don't I read this now, if that's OK?' His heart is going at double its proper pace. He puts his fingers to his pulse and tries to think it down. Remember what happened to Joseph M., he reminds himself. Here, I'm doing different.

'OK, Bernie,' he says.

It's very quiet, with them just sitting there. He can't look at her while she reads about Amanda. The very end: how she's just given him that speech about not being a prude and is he a weirdo and he's springing out of the armchair. He pushes her onto the floor, gets on top.

'Gently, Simon!' she says, and opens her legs, getting it all wrong, not fighting back, which helps him to pin her down and get his hands to her neck.

Then she knows. She twists and bucks underneath, tries to get her arms out that he's got gripped with his legs, kicks on the floor with her heels like she thinks someone downstairs might hear her, but even if they did they wouldn't come. *What the hell am I doing?* He's started this and he's just too scared to go back. He's going to The End, because what the hell will happen if not? What will she do or say to him if he lets go? What could be between them? This way, she can't speak, argue, tell on him. He shuts his eyes to her face, his ears to the noise they make, his grunts, her breathing, the thuds and bumps of her struggles, and he keeps on, long after she's stopped moving, gone quiet and soft. His head is empty except for knowing that nothing will undo it now and he has got to open his eyes . . .

Bernadette reads this and she reads how when he did open his eyes, Amanda's face was swollen, her dead eyes looking at the ceiling. The lenses had come out, one of them was on her cheek.

I got to the toilet and threw up, took my jacket and wallet but I couldn't find the keys so I put the door on the latch and ran out down the stairs.

Simon hears Bernie sigh, the thin rustle of the pages as she puts them back together. Again it is hard to look, but when he eventually does, Bernie has changed. Her mouth still curves upwards, but it seems smaller, somehow lost in the spaces of her face. Her eyes are too bright, and her silence is unbearable.

'What are you thinking of me now, then?'

'Simon – the fact is, I'm thinking,' she tells him 'of what it must be like for her mother . . . Hazel?' He has to look away again. He folds up, holding his head in his hands. There's no word for it, this feeling of being unable to look at her, but wanting to stay there with her at the same time . . . In case, somehow, it turns out to be all right? So that she can sentence him afresh? Wipe it away? It's worse, even, than the dreams he's fought so hard not to have, dreams in which Amanda comes to him in his sleep walking down the landing, click-clack in medium heels, smart clothes. Heads turn. It's you, Simon Austen, isn't it? she says and walks right up to where he stands; she has grown older and more sure of herself, he hasn't. She comes so close that he can smell the real smell of her under her scent and see the tiny hairs on the top of her lip. Or else she comes to him as she really was at the end, bruised, bloodshot, broken, naked, blundering as she heaves herself up some huge, broad, circling staircase: she doesn't understand and she wants him to explain . . . This is worse than that. It goes on for who knows how long, for ever, and he is asking himself, What did I expect? Didn't I always know it would be like this?

He hears Bernadette get up, the friction of her boot soles on the floor. She squats down next to him. He doesn't look, but he can feel her there, hear her exhale. She touches him lightly on the shoulder.

'Simon,' she said, 'Can you sit up?' She keeps her hand on his shoulder until he has done it.

'There,' she says, and after a moment, resumes her seat.

'I stayed two nights in a B&B up in Whitby,' he tells her, looking at the wall opposite and remembering that other room: its sloping ceilings and the mansard window looking out onto other slate roofs, streets and courtyards. There was a sepia photograph of fishing boats and a broken barometer on the wall, a collection of old books in a glass-fronted case – not back then a lot of use to him, though he picked a couple up and wished, but not that hard, that he could make sense of them. There were model aeroplanes hanging on the ceiling, action man dolls propped up between the books and sitting in a row on the sofa. 'Julian does the decorating,' the man called Stuart said, 'He likes to have a theme . . . You can watch TV with us downstairs if you want.'

'I knew they'd find me,' he tells Bernie, 'but it was a kind of break. I was having a bit of someone else's life before my own came back. I sat up a while in the old leather armchair and listened to the sea churning about and the rain on the roof and despite what had happened I felt just fine. In the morning, they lent me boots and a rain jacket and I looked at the docks and the cliffs and the ruined monastery, had fish and chips. I didn't think of what I'd done to Amanda. I knew it, but I didn't think of it. When it got dark I went to the pub. There were old men with whiskers and a few couples. The beer was thick and bitter, salty, but that must have been the sea spray on my lips. As I got near the bottom of the glass I came back to being myself again – like I'd been spinning around and then stopped but the spinning went on in my head and then all of a sudden I was still as a stone. I thought: they're bound to come tomorrow, and once I thought that, I hadn't the heart to stay in the pub, and anyhow, I'd run out of cash . . . That's about it,' he says, turning his eyes, one blue, one brown, suddenly to where Bernie is – she's still there. 'The police turned up next morning. I told them I'd done it and then I was charged and cuffed up and sent in a van back to London. Well, you know it all now,' he tells her. You know more about me than any one else in the world, he thinks, and for a split second it is as if he is actually standing back there in the Portakabin bollock naked, bar the words pricked into his skin.

'You've really begun something,' Bernadette says, 'don't you think?'

'It feels different, all right,' he says. 'It's OK. But, like –' he gestures with a jerk of his head towards the wing behind them, 'I really don't want to go back in there. What next? Got any ideas, Bernie?'

'You need to be in a different, supportive environment, with specialist staff,' she says. 'I'm just hoping we get an answer to my report sooner rather than later. It's just so frustrating that, like everything else now, there's a queue –'

'I'm quite happy with this,' he tells her. 'You do an excellent job.'

'Thank you. Still – I do feel like I'm just holding the fort.' She goes over to the desk for her diary. The next date he gets is for after the holidays: no point in whining, it's the first available. And she deserves a break, doesn't she? How, he wonders, does she get rid of the things she's been told about, other people's lives and deaths, everything, all the details? How will she get rid of Amanda? She must be able to somehow, or she'd go crazy. Maybe she has a dog, takes it for a long walk.

But of course, these are not things she's done herself. It's different. Bernadette, Simon thinks suddenly, is the opposite of him. He looks Bernadette properly in the face, braces himself.

'So, are you going away at Christmas?' he asks: she told him he could ask things, didn't she? If she didn't mean it, then he doesn't know what he'll do. 'Are you going home?'

Her mother's house, she says, is in West Cork. A big old place, in beautiful country, but very wet. She has three younger sisters, and two older brothers. They'll all be there. She'll travel on the ferry – prefers it to the plane, even though it takes twice as long. She will be away for two weeks. Her voice grows more Irish as she talks of it. Then there's a knock on the door, and she glances at her watch.

'You'll suit one of those waxed jackets,' he says. 'Have a good time, then. Plenty of R&R.'

'The holidays must be rough here,' she says. He shrugs, drinking up the last seconds of the time. Drop me a line, he almost says.

Bernadette Nightingale, he thinks, pulling the fresh, chill air into his lungs as he follows the officer across the brief stretch of tarmac, What do you do when you get home of a night? Is there someone there? The wing door swings open, and he steps through.

18

'Twenty,' Simon says.

'Forty,' Alex immediately replies, running his hand over his recently shaved bald head, caressing the back of his neck. He sports a stud in one ear, an intricate celtic knot bracelet slithers its way around each well-developed bicep. He's wearing a sleeveless vest, very clean, his fingernails are evenly filed, a ring, to match the bracelets, is tattooed round the third finger of his left hand. 'Cost you four times that outside,' he points out. 'I sterilise my needle in bleach,' he adds.

'Haven't got it,' Simon says.

'Owe me – or why not say it shorter? What's wrong with *brave*? Nothing, *per se*. But it's just not what she said.

'I want the whole thing,' Simon tells him.

'Well, then,' says Alex, 'you'd better be! Have a good wash, shave the hair off. It'll grow through the scabs and give you hell, and then it'll cover up your big long word, but if that's what you want, I'll go to two-fifty a letter, that's twenty-five up front . . .'

A wedge goes in under the door. 'Ink,' Alex says, putting on his glasses, wire-framed NHS. 'Lie on the floor, we'll get intimate!' He squats to one side, leans in close; first there are a series of light marks as he measures the word out across Simon's chest, then the ballpoint presses into the newly exposed skin as it moves steadily around the shape of each letter, from right to left across Simon's chest. COURAGEOUS.

'Fits well,' Alex says. 'Look in the mirror, here.' The outline is faint and everything's reversed, seems fainter still in the small panel of polished steel. He checks it carefully. 'Hurry up,' Alex hisses. His Glasgow accent comes out thicker as he works and the point of his tongue sticks out between his lips. He's somehow warm and dangerous at the same time. The friend he almost killed ten years ago is in a wheelchair and still visits him. 'I'll do a few at a time,' he says. The pen moves minutely this way and that, pulling at the skin as he fills in the letters C, O, U, R . . . Then he sits back on his haunches.

'Look –' From a soft grey rag he unwraps a Walkman motor. 'My baby. See? I can go very even with this . . . plus, it's quick. Wake up your nerves, she will . . . Tense up, then you won't move, OK?' Alex bends close, holding the skin firmly with two fingers of his left hand. There's a deceptively gentle humming noise, then the needle bites, rapid and relentless. Simon gasps – he's almost forgotten what it's like, to be just feeling the needle dig in, not controlling it at the same time. He breathes steadily, imagines the pain as something he has to absorb through his skin, dissolve and incorporate. A good thing. Something he wants . . . Certainly it's better not to watch Alex's face: the tension round his eyes and the zeal in them, the wet tongue-tip between his teeth, the pores of his well-shaved skin, its growing dampness. Simon shuts his eyes and tries to follow the shape of the letters. Sweat runs down the curve of his ribs, around and under his back. When suddenly the buzzing of the motor stops, the pain continues, changes, grows even, as if what's already there expands to take up the available space.

'I should stop really, but what d'you want?'

'Finish it off,' Simon replies, one half of his chest liquid fire, the other blank . . . Well . . . ten letters instead of the usual four! Something different. Something to not forget, but also, something to grow into.

'Keep it clean,' Alex says. He rubs some vaseline over the word, then sticks a bit of torn sheet on top. 'Swelling should be down in a week or so.'

19

Then there's Lockerbie, 270 dead. Possibly a bomb. 'Puts all of us in the shade,' Jolly Roger next door opines; his enjoyment of the recent spate of bad news from the outside world is driving everyone mad. The air is, literally, thick: by Christmas Day the smell of hooch: sickly but sharp at the same time, has thickened, risen, filled every crevice and pocket of the confined, indoor space to the point where just walking around the landing might give you a hangover. Stolen sugar, yeast, tap-water, a sweatshirt chucked over the top to keep out dust . . . there are three buckets in cells on just Simon's landing, plus one in the cleaning cupboard and that's just the tip of the iceberg. Not that he touches the stuff himself, after he once saw someone carted off in the ambulance for drinking from a batch that turned to ethanol. The majority have been at it pretty solid since the screws v. cons game yesterday afternoon (actually, before, because, let's face it, it's only because of OK Simpson in goal and Simon himself scoring once that they managed a draw). Now, in the lunch queue, the fumes could spontaneously combust or at the very least make you throw up. Down at the servery Diesel, Hoskie, Q Tip and Co. are wearing plastic antlers as they dish up, watched by fifty-odd pairs of bloodshot eyes. They had better get it right because if some bastard thinks he's missed a sausage or hasn't got enough meat on his plate or pudding in his bowl, then whoosh, up it goes. The vegetables are another matter.

'Here, mate,' says Q Tip, as he grabs Simon's plate with one huge brown hand and with the other shovels on a double load of the Brussels sprouts, colour of snot, texture, no doubt, of rotting sponge and already more or less cold. 'Veggie-tarian, ain't you?'

'Great, ta,' Simon says. It's good he's only half there. The rest of him is spread between the Portakabins and West Cork, which he has looked up in the library atlas. He hopes it's a sunny, bright day over there, though the chances aren't good – all the place names on the map seemed to have water in them somewhere.

'Can you give me some *more* of those please?' he says to Q Tip.

'Boy, you want more?' Q Tip comes back. Q Tip is about seven foot and on a short fuse, but all the same Simon jerks his plate out of the way just as the spoon angles, thinking: Go on then, start something if you want, so long as I come out of it alive, a week or two in the block would be a blessing in disguise. The overcooked Brussels sprouts land damply on the floor, Twinkletoes Jones slips on one and crashes into Simon from behind, so the rest of the plate goes flying too.

'Call the ambulance!' Twinkle calls out in a falsetto, hamming it up to stop himself looking a fool – or maybe to save them all? There's a split second of laughter, loud but hollow, then shouting from the back to fucking move on, will you?

Grease has solidified over the entire replacement meal by the time Simon's back at his cell, where Jolly Roger, lugubriously hopeful, waits, leaning by the door. 'Join you?' he says, pulling himself up to his full six feet plus. He has sloping shoulders, pale skin, dark stubble and lank black hair, one eye that was lost in a fight and sewn shut. Simon shrugs.

'Seen you in the library,' Roger says settling himself cross-legged on the floor. 'I enjoy a good book myself. How's things?'

'Not bad,' Simon observes, from his position on the bed, tray across his lap. He accidentally puts one of the Brussels sprouts into his mouth and neither tastes it, nor feels its wet collapse. 'There's talk of me going on a course.' He's still only half there, and from a distance, these bizarre words sound almost natural.

'It's probably not worth it,' Roger tells him, mouth full.

One of the many annoying things about Roger is that he has a habit of making depressing statements like this in a bright, perky voice, as if he enjoyed them being that way. Bernie, Simon hopes and imagines, will have better company than this. She'll be listening and smiling, sitting among her brothers, sisters, aunts, uncles, some old lady in a wheelchair, all of them crowded round a huge mahogany table in a big dining room with French windows that look out towards the blustery sea . . . She's wearing a deep red chenille sweater-dress, close but not clinging, just like one he saw advertised in the *Mirror* magazine, tights, ankle boots and her silver pendant like a melted O . . . but no, come to think of it, he's getting it all wrong because now, at 11.45, she is maybe just coming in, perhaps with one of her brothers, from taking the dogs out.

'Anyway, what course?' Roger says. 'I've done 'em all.'

'I don't know,' Simon says. 'Some new thing.' The letters on his chest itch suddenly, and he fights the urge to rub at the scabs through his shirt.

'You're not some kind of *nonce*, are you?' Roger asks, half serious. 'They're always setting up new stuff for them, aren't they just, state of the art, but everyone knows none of it works . . . You know what I think?' Jolly Roger forks in the last of his grey turkey and pale-brown gravy, then climbs onto his own personal hobby horse: 'Us lifers should have the right to suicide. An injection, if you wanted it. An alternative –' as Roger waves his plastic fork, gravy lands on Simon's bed, 'to this.'

'You'd take it?' Simon says. Right now? he's thinking. Ireland is lost, he can't get back there with this cunt in his room.

'At times,' Roger says. 'If it had been there, I'd be gone by now. Less trouble for all concerned. Especially me.' *No, me.* 'Know what I mean?' Roger asks.

'No,' Simon says. If I did, he thinks, I'd fucking do it, not expect someone else to oblige . . . 'And listen, what's wrong with a shave and a shower,' he says, 'it might cheer you up.'

'You'll get there,' Roger tells him. 'You'll hit bottom. Then you'll know.'

'Oh yes? Piss off,' Simon puts his uneaten meal on the floor and leans back against the wall, closes his eyes briefly. He's going to take a breath in and then he'll open them wide and yell: 'Still here? Didn't I tell you to –'

'No harm in talking,' Roger tells him, mildly, before he can finish the breath, 'and look – company!' Simon opens his eyes to see Big T filling the doorway, the sheer bulk of him making the room seem even smaller. Even so, he's started to go to flab, Simon notes. Tev holds out the pint-sized blue plastic mug he's walked past the screws with.

'Real Smirnoff!' he announces, grinning at them both. 'Genuine Christmas cheer. On the house! . . . I've got the lot,' he continues, leaning in, 'weed, tabs, the absolute lot, even though that cow sent me nothing. So take some, go on, Christmas, you've gotta have a drink!' Wrong: I haven't gotta do anything, Simon thinks, but Tev is half way down the plughole and he can't be bothered to point it out in words . . . Plus, a drink, a real drink, might just take the edge off things, let him slip away again. He holds out his own plastic mug and Teverson tips in a good measure: vodka, and undiluted orange squash, fiery, sickly-sweet.

'Me too,' Jolly Roger says.

'Get lost,' Tev tells him.

'What about that spare pudding then?' Roger asks, scooping it up, shameless, as he gets up to go. Tev stumbles over – it's a matter of move along or have him in your lap, but given the state he's in, if Tev gets any ideas in his head (not that there looks to be room for them) he'll be easy enough to deal with. Roger has gone, so one down, one to go. It's noon, he'll be locked up again by eight.

'Cheers!' Teverson beams. He's pretending to be in a pub. Simon feels the alcohol burn its way to his stomach, descend, minutes later, like a soft fog inside his skull.

'Cheers!'

'Cheers . . .'

In West Cork, Bernie will be drinking dry sherry, say, in an antique crystal glass. Waterford. Or is it Waterville? She won't drink much. She likes to loosen up, but keep aware. A glass of red wine, maybe a brandy with the coffee at the end of the meal. For that, they'll move into tatty leather armchairs (like the one he once saw in Anthony's Antiques in Streatham, costing almost a grand) around the fire. Maybe they'll open their presents. Some little niece or nephew bringing them around. A gift for Bernie would have to be jewellery. A one-off piece made by some queer bloke in a tiny shop for two months' wages. Earrings, necklace, something for her hair. Bold shapes. Intimate gifts which you have to have the right to give. At any rate, there was nothing here that he could give her, and because of the timescale, nothing good enough to be got from outside. He had to choose from the selection of cards at the shop: Dutch snow scene, teddy bears or drunken reindeer. Seasons Greetings, Bernie, you deserve a break, Simon. Did she check her pigeonhole before she went? Will Bernie, at some point during the course of the day, even momentarily, think of him? His head swims as he gets to his feet.

'Do you mind?' he asks Teverson. 'I need to piss.'

'Give me a break!' Tev tells him, closing his eyes. 'I'm not looking.' He's lying chin on chest, eyes all but closed, body melted. All the same, Simon puts his cup on the floor and goes out, down the landing to the stalls where the usual amoniac reek of piss has been overwhelmed by that of hooch-induced vomit. He picks his way out, stops half way down the landing for some reason to look down over the rails and through the safety netting to the ground floor, where a few men mill about in the extra space there, smoking, going to or from the TV room, while others lounge in their doorways, looking on and waiting for this extra bit of association, irresistible, but not in the end a pleasure, to be called to its end. The lighting makes them look paler than they are, and at the same time shows up the stains and marks on clothing, walls and flooring alike, the scars and stubble, the fading professional tattoos and dark blue new ones, like his own, done inside. It's the first time in a very long while that he's looked at the place and the people in it, unprotected, as someone from outside might do. A world without colour, or softness or contact. I will get out of here, he tells himself – but thinking has no effect at all on what he sees around him, and he hurries back to B222, where at least he'll see less of it.

'What's this?' Teverson asks him as he re-enters the cell. The exercise book in Tev's hands is marked Property of Her Majesty's Prison Service, Do Not Remove, and he begins reading from it in a loud, carefully flat voice like some unwilling kid at school:

' "You are turning me inside out." '

'Give it here!' Simon tells him. 'I'll fucking kill you –'

'It fell out when I got the pillow to lean on,' Tev says, shrugging. ' "When I am with you I feel as if I can be the better part of me that has been hidden so long . . ." ' He spins the book across. 'That's good stuff,' he says. 'How much, to do one for me?' The page already torn out, balled in his hand, Simon grabs at Teverson, then punches him in the chest – it should hurt. But the big man's flesh is somehow disconnected, pickled in vodka, it doesn't react. 'Get out now!' he yells again, as Big T reaches for Simon's half-full cup of vodka, drains it, then rises to his feet, putting an arm out almost gracefully to steady himself.

'I'm off,' he says.

'Someone lock this fucking door!' Simon shouts after him, his whole body going into the shout, his skin red, the opening of his mouth pushing his eyes shut – for once, he's lucky: an elderly screw drafted in for the holidays, comes slowly along the landing, whistling 'Good King Wenceslas' between his teeth . . .

'Want locking up do you?' he asks. 'I'm your man. If I had my way,' he says, 'there'd be none of this neighbours stuff that goes on here. Recipe for disaster. In or out, either way, the door locked, better all round . . . that's how it used to be and ten to one it'll be that way again in a few years' time –'

The door shuts, not slammed, but metal on metal all the same. Simon's hands are shaking; he has to keep on the move. He straightens the bed, wipes off the gravy as best he can, washes, feels his heart gradually give up the battle to jump out of his chest. Around him, other doors are banging closed now. Then it's suddenly, achingly quiet, as if no one lived here at all.

What next? Really, there's only one thing. He pulls the little table out, squats by it, starts all over again, by hand, in the shadowy afternoon-dark of his cell:

You are turning me inside out.

When I am with you I feel as if I could become the best of me that has been hidden so long, and I burn with wanting to. I feel I could pass through the eye of a needle. In a low voice, he sounds out the words as he writes them, listening carefully. They seem true, but at the same time, utterly impossible. The room is six foot by eight foot by twelve foot high. She is with her family in a rambling mansion in West Cork . . . She did once say she admired him, but also he is a murderer, a man who killed a woman, a weirdo, albeit bright; callous, twat, cunt, et cetera.

All the same, Simon Austen can remember the feeling of Bernadette Nightingale next to him, when he sat with his head in his hands not daring to look up. Just a warmth, and then that slightest touch, her hand to his shoulder: how long did it last? Then, it was only part of what was happening, but now, in memory, it has somehow flooded and overwhelmed the whole scene . . . What is this? he's asked himself. 'Crap,' he has replied and of course he has also told himself the facts: 'She's a do-gooder. Barry with tits. Fucking paid for it, isn't she?' But, but, but – he answers, not with words but somehow with the whole of him: flesh, blood, ghost. It was perfect.

Love is the word he was following through in the Encyclopedia when Jolly Roger saw him in the library. Romantic love, it seems, thrives in hostile or inappropriate circumstances; to prefer them even. Its nature is to rise to the challenge of any interdiction. It seeks out someone who has promised themselves to someone else, or who is in a family at war with one's own, or who is cast by evil magic into the body of a hairy beast, or is a mortal, or a god, or locked in a tower and guarded by a witch. And also it seeks out opposites, the lost other half that makes a person whole – so there's hope: her water to his fire; her caring, his rage, his messed-up life, her proper one: chemistry.

It wasn't there before. He didn't love Amanda, he just liked her and envied her; he was scared of her too. He didn't know about love, didn't believe in it, just didn't understand that this thing existed, this transforming force presided over by a god called Eros, who disobeyed orders, shot himself in the foot by mistake, then said: Just believe me, don't look, and don't try to test it out . . .

If he had loved Amanda, perhaps everything would have come out different?

But now, with Bernadette:

I feel I could become the best of me that has been hidden so long, and I burn with wanting to. I feel I could pass through the eye of a needle. And I want to drive, to walk, to travel to the other side of the world with you. See glaciers, deserts, rainforest. I want to work for you. With you. I can learn whatever is necessary. Also, I want to hold you. I want you to touch my skin despite what is written there.

In B222, somewhere behind Simon's eyes, Bernadette Nightingale opens a box and takes out the neck ornament, half celtic, half modern, asymmetrical, the blue stone on one side, blood red on the other . . . He fastens the small chain and hook at the back of her neck. It's an act of sheer will, to overcome so many objections and obstacles, all the practicalities, the unknowns (in particular, does she have someone already?) but in imagination at least, he can do it.

I want to give you gifts.

I am terrified.

And this, he realises, is no longer a letter. It is something that he has to be able to actually say.

I want to be able to say all this to you, face to face.

On the first working day after the holiday, a letter comes from Tasmin. It can only be her, from the writing, but the postmark is different, somewhere in Oxfordshire. Maybe, he thinks, she's run away.

'I don't want this,' he tells Owens. 'It's a girl I wrote to by mistake.' But apparently they are legally obliged to give it to him. In his cell he turns the envelope, a cheap, thin envelope, different to those she used before, over and over in his hands, uncertain what exactly to do. Inside is probably a postcard, though he can't quite make out the image on the front, nor, however much he shifts the angle of it against the light, can he quite decipher the writing on the back.

They may be checking to see what he does, they may not; you can't tell. The point being, if he sends it back to the usual place, it might not get to her, someone else might open it or even if she *is* there her father could well find it first – so, she could be dropped right in it; he's not sure why it matters but he doesn't want that.

It's just a piece of paper, but he's sitting there with it in his hand like it was some kind of life or death thing and that, he suddenly finds himself thinking, is the trouble with letters: the way they have their own existence, independent of both writer and reader, the way they can continue to have an effect, even after you might have changed your mind, the way they follow you around like this. When you say something aloud, it's just the here and now, then it's gone, it's just a memory. Letters are evidence, lying there in the shoe box.

What happened to Vivienne Anne Whilden? he finds himself wondering. She probably kept on drinking, that's the truth of it.

He drops Tasmin's card, unopened, into the box: a kind of limbo. This way, he thinks, she gets to send it; I'm doing more or less what I said so they can't really go for me. Poor kid, he thinks, she ought to find something better to do. Then he puts the lid on the box and forgets both of them. He's way beyond all that.

20

Bernie is still getting out of her coat and this gives him a chance to look at her, which is more than usually good, since part of why he feels light-headed and almost sick is that he has been worried that he has somehow got her wrong, exaggerated her or even made her up completely . . . The rest of it is that he's determined to make his speech, to say it face to face. Not right away, but as soon as he can, once they have broken the ice. At some point she will ask if he's done any writing and perhaps he can say it then: *Bernie, I have to tell you that I think about you a lot. When I am with you I* – It's madness, like one of those crazy sports people take up: jumping off cliffs on elastic bands, scaling office blocks without a rope. But he will do it, out loud.

He watches her hang the coat on the chair, slip the keys in its pocket. Still standing, she opens the square-edged briefcase that's on her desk, pulls out various envelopes and papers.

'Sorry about all this,' she says, smiling at him. Her lips are darker: new lipstick. She's wearing a brown sweater he's seen before, a knitwear skirt and brand new ankle boots, several earrings at once, though for some reason, the rings on her fingers are gone. She sits down in the nearest of the two obliquely together chairs, gestures for him to do the same.

'Happy New Year. Best wishes for 1989,' he tells her.

'You too,' she says, taking the outstretched hand and clasping it briefly in both of hers. 'And I hope –'

'How did it go?' he interrupts, apologises for doing so, continues. 'How did it go, then, in Cork?'

'Oh, you know, family . . .' she says. 'But yes, overall very good. Well –' She glances down, shuffles through the papers in her lap. Her face seems somehow younger, a little fuller than before. There's a blush on her normally pale cheeks. She's had a break, he thinks, that's what it is.

'How was the weather there?' he asks.

'Quite fine on the day,' she tells him, still concentrating on the papers. She doesn't ask how it was here. She doesn't ask if he's done any more writing. 'Simon,' she says when she eventually looks up. 'There's good news. In fact, there seems to be quite a lot of it about, but let me tell you yours first –'

'Bernie –' he begins just as she hands him a couple of pages from the pile on her lap, the first headed in bold: Transfer of inmate AS2356768, Austen, Simon. '– Bernie, I –'

'It's an incredible opportunity,' she says, spreading her hands, as a child does to catch raindrops or snowflakes falling from the sky. 'You'll be in a group of up to eight, in a completely constructive, therapeutic regime, two years max, then back into the main system is the only downside. Groupwork, psychiatrist, work or education in the afternoon. Multidisciplinary. A modern building, good relationship with the local community, opportunities for charity work and so on. It'll be tough, but very constructive . . . They've worked for years to get this off the ground and it has just started last year. Lord knows how long it'll last in the current climate . . . Sorry,' she says. 'It must be an awful lot to take in. There's a whole pile of stuff here for you to read . . . But it's really so fortunate that this has happened. You could have waited a year, or for ever –' The silence that follows this is like glass between them, has to be almost literally broken.

'Where is Wentham?' he asks.

'On the east coast,' she says. 'I think it's north of –'

'I don't want to go,' he interrupts, glaring.

Her face softens, falls still as she says, 'It is what we have been talking about all along.'

'I don't want to go,' he repeats. 'Don't you *see*, Bernie?' he asks her, his voice suddenly hoarse, so that he has to stop and work his throat to clear it.

'I see you're getting very agitated,' she says, slowly, moving the remainder of the papers from her lap to the floor, but all the time looking at his face. 'Will you try to stay calm and tell me why?'

'Why do you think?' he barks back at her. 'I like it here, don't I? Just so fucking lovely, isn't it?' he says. Why did he think she was special? What the hell has happened? How has he ended up like this, tied in a mass of knots by some do-gooding social worker type, older than him anyhow? Why can't he find the switch to turn down the heat even though he really wants to? It's absolute shite – 'I like having these meetings –' he says and the effort of getting to the words stuck inside him makes him rise abruptly to his feet, so that she does too, bending as she does so to push the chair further back: she's making sure she can reach the panic button, red, mounted in a metal housing and screwed to the desk, which itself is bolted to the floor. One press on that button and twenty screws will be running across the yard; in ten seconds they'd be through the door and have him face down on the rough grey carpet tiles marked with Barry's and others' dropped cigarettes, his arm pulled up his back and probably out of its socket too.

'Don't!' he tells her, his eyes flicking between her right hand and her face, trying to judge: Will she? What will I do if she does? *Please*, he thinks, though he can't say it . . . She's frowning and there's a sliver of something new in her eyes, not fear so much as a different kind of alertness.

'If I think you're going to assault me, Simon, I will have no choice,' she tells him, her voice just a little slower and quieter than usual. 'Please step back.' It's true – somehow he's already leaned forward as if to catch her arm, to stop her from stopping him from telling her what he needs to say. Now that she's made him see himself he's frozen like a statue: it is only with a deliberate effort that he gets the muscles in his legs and torso to relax, to allow him to stand straight again. There's about four feet between the two of them.

'That's better,' she says, and breathes deeply. 'Now –' Now, he'll have to do it, or he never will.

'Bernie, listen. I think about you a lot –' he begins and for a moment, the words seem to carry him up and along. 'I've got to say this: when I'm with you – I feel as if you're turning me inside out. I feel as if I could become the best of me, all that has been hidden so long. Most of my life. And I want –' He pauses and lets his eyes take her in, standing there in front of him, the same person he always thought she was: utterly extraordinary, full of promise – but not, he can see from the warm but as ever curious look on her face, the sympathy there, the *distance*, not *in love* with him. She does not feel the same way. And she is Bernie: you absolutely can't make her do anything she doesn't want to do.

'I want all sorts of things,' he says, suddenly exhausted, 'but – you get the drift and I can tell it's a one-way street . . .' She doesn't deny it. His legs feel leaden and he sits down, exhausted, watches her gather up the papers that were scattered all over the office floor when he jumped up. I knew this all along, he tells himself, reaching to pick up a couple of pages that are close to his chair. One is labelled *Research at Wentham Special Unit for Violent Offenders*, another *Principles of Drama Therapy*. Drama therapy? Will they have him in a wig and tutu, then, or wrapped in a sheet with leaves on his head like those idiots that did the pantomime two years ago? What the hell. It'll be a relief, he thinks, as she hands the rest of the papers to him. Just to get away from this. Not to have to think about you any more.

'That's why I didn't want to go to fucking Wentham,' he tells her. 'You.'

'Well, first, thank you,' she says, simply, standing there in front of him empty-handed, ringless. Then she sits down, leans back in her own chair. 'You've cleared the air. These kind of circumstances,' she adds, 'throw up a lot of emotion, but I –'

'Don't tell me, I know, right!' he cuts in. 'You're married.'

'I do have a partner,' she says. 'We're very happy together.' The more she says, the stupider he feels. He wants out, is actually making moves to get up from the chair – but the thing is, she knows when to stop or change tack. She's always known that.

'That must have been difficult to say. But it cleared the air and stopped us ending up with a crisis . . .' That means she won't be writing him a bad report to go in his file. She won't be claiming he nearly grabbed her, pointing out that she felt threatened and that he is in her opinion still a danger to society, women in particular, et cetera . . . that's what she's telling him: she is giving him the benefit of the doubt.

'Actually, it was you that saved the day there,' he tells her.

'Both,' she replies.

He looks at the other stuff she has given him. There is a picture of the place on top of the pile of papers; it looks like low-slung, seventies comprehensive school, with what look like patterned breeze-blocks over the windows rather than bars. Underneath, it says again HMP Wentham Special Unit for Violent Offenders, then a lot of small type.

'I'll go, then,' he tells her, putting the sheaf of papers down on his lap, letting his eyes settle on her face, noticing all over again the lipstick, the way she looks younger than a few weeks before. *Woman with Good News*, he thinks.

'I think you should take it away and read through carefully, then talk it through with someone else before you sign the papers,' she's saying. 'Like my colleague Martin, he's very good. Plus, we have to get the Medical Officer to refer you.'

'No,' he tells her. 'It doesn't matter. I've gotta do something, haven't I? I'll sign it now, if you've got a pen.'

She gives him hers, a fancy marble-effect ballpoint with a gold clip, no cap, you have to click it on at the top. He goes over to her desk for something to lean on while he writes. It's at this point that he notices that the cable track leading up to the panic button is not quite long enough: there's a small gap between it and the metal housing and from that, a wire protrudes.

'It's not properly connected,' he tells her, putting his finger almost on the wire. 'You must get it fixed!' His name comes out too big for the space and nothing like any signature he's ever done before, but who cares, it's not as if anyone is going to accuse Bernadette Nightingale (her own name, he notices, an even worse scrawl) of forging it.

'Shake, then,' he says. She doesn't immediately take his hand. Her face looks different again, emptier, as if something private is taking place behind its smoothness. Standing there, hand out, one half of him wants to cry, the other to laugh. Any minute, the crying will win: something to do with being left out. With how very far he is beyond the pale, with the absurdity of it all . . . he tries to somehow freeze his own face.

'You've done a good job, thanks,' he tells her. She doesn't answer straight away. Just stands there and then suddenly, shockingly, she puts her hands over her face, fingers up, covering her forehead and eyes and presses them in hard – it makes him want to grab hold of her, pull her to him – and then what? But a second later the hands are back at her side and the old Bernie is back, eyes shining, head cocked just slightly to the left.

'Simon,' she says, taking his hand, squeezing, letting go. 'I believe you can make it through . . . And look, you do know you can make another appointment meanwhile, if you want to? I appreciate that right now you probably don't . . .'

By now, he's busy getting out of the door. 'Cheers!' he calls back at her as he tumbles half blind down the three little steps and waves at the shape of an officer waiting by the wing door, who beckons for him to walk across alone. Well, so long as nothing runs down his cheeks he'll be OK. It's a kind of blind tightrope walk.

'Tough as old nails, that one,' the man says as he locks the barred door between them. 'Mind you, she's got to be a lez, hasn't she?'

'Lunch,' he's told on the wing. 'Just get it, then get out of my way.' It's good to lie down.

'Work, Austen,' another screw says, then louder. 'W-O-R-K.' He's still lying on the bed without moving. The lunch tray is untouched on the floor beside him . . . because why had she taken off all her rings? he is wondering, did she just get up late, and forget, or what? And what the hell does *partner* mean? Could the idiot on the gate be right? What was that other 'good' news she implied but never told him? Where was she when her face emptied out, and again, just after, when she covered it up?

'Snowing,' the screw tells him. 'We need you. Come on, you'll get a coat out of it.'

Since he was last out, the ground has become lighter than the sky. A thin white film has fallen over the yard, begun to melt, then been covered over with fresh fall. He can feel, through the worn soles of his trainers, how treacherous it is. He heaves a sack of salt and grit into the barrow, splits it open and begins, as instructed, with the path from the gatehouse to the Governors' wing, clearing with the shovel first, then scattering a thick layer of the pinkish grey salty grit. He grows hot inside the coat and gloves, wet about the feet; the sky darkens. *Sun* headline, he thinks with the vestige of a grin: Callous Killer Falls for Lesbian PO . . . Bernadette Nightingale, he says to himself, in a different voice entirely. What's happened can't, he senses, be undone. Or *maybe* it could be, if he wanted to undo it badly enough, but that's it: he isn't sure that he does.

The Medical Officer approves. The Governor signs. Dickie Walters tells him he thought he'd never see the back of him, don't come back! He'll be leaving *soon*, though they won't tell him exactly *when*. Then, all of a sudden it's *now*.

Simon does not need a phone call to inform anyone of his moving at short notice. He packs his radio, typewriter, exercise books, yoga pamphlet and the Adidas box into a transparent plastic sack; he gives the end of his shaving foam and toothpaste to Jolly Roger. A couple of officers on the landing wish him the best, some of the men hanging around on the wing say, 'Cheers.' It feels as if he's leaving the place without a mark behind him and also as if he's already vanishing while he goes through the last motions of his departure, handing in his clothes, signing out his sealed property box. He follows Owens out to a small room and sits, locked there, to wait while Owens smokes and chats outside until they are ready to take him. Owens doesn't bother with the solid door, just the bars, but there's nothing but bricks to see from where Simon sits. The barred window, high up, casts a rectangle of dusty white light on the floor near his feet. As well as Owens's cigarette, Simon can smell engine oil and fuel from the vehicle yard beyond the window, and hear, from further away, a radio playing. He can't put a name to the song but it seems familiar, a woman's voice, strong and slow. He closes his eyes and imagines, as per Yoga for Beginners, that his head is painlessly suspended from a silken string that runs through the centre of the top of his skull, what was once the fontanelle, and his spine hangs beneath, the spaces between his vertebrae opening just a paper's width, a crack of light, as gravity pulls them down.

Outside, an engine cuts in then goes off again. Someone says, 'You must be joking!' Owens laughs, a car door opens and then slams shut. Footsteps. One way or another, I'm moving on, Simon tells himself. But still no one comes to get him and the fact is he's alone in a freezing room and his feet are getting cold. About twenty minutes pass. He thinks of other journeys: in a minibus, handcuffed to a bloke doing cold turkey. In the sweatbox, with its narrow cubicles and the dim light filtering through. He wonders how far he will get before he starts to feel sick. It always happens, something to do with sitting in the back or in the dark and not being able to see where you are going. The first time it happened was in that police van coming down from Whitby, straight after his arrest. One of them yelled at him when he asked for a stop, and then he had to sit with the windows wide open and his feet in the stuff for nearly two hours.

'I'm saying nothing!' he told them in London. 'I'm entitled to a solicitor!'

'Keep it simple,' the brief said when he arrived at last, a pudgy soft-looking guy with a bag full of plums in his mouth and hair that kept falling in his eyes. 'She told you she was seeing someone else, then you lost it. That's the important thing here . . . It's easier for people to understand.' Now, he's undone that bit of work and it seems that Bernadette Frigging Florence Nightingale, bless her, has sentenced him to spend the rest of his life understanding five minutes of the past. Well, cheers, Bernie!

A key chain rattles outside and then Owens steams in.

'Right then,' he says. 'Long day ahead of us.' An officer Simon doesn't know comes in behind Owens, locking up behind himself. Simon holds out his arms to be cuffed up, one to each of them. You can do it, he tells himself. Got to: your bluff's been called and you've got that damn word on you now, haven't you?

They make their way, an awkward threesome, to the cab and civvie driver waiting outside, ease into the back.

At any rate, he reminds himself, as the car door slams and the engine cuts in again, at any rate the chances are I won't be seeing fucking Teverson again! The car does a three-point turn, lurches forwards. It stops at the gatehouse for the final checks: someone opens the door, slams it again, bangs on the side. The inner gate closes behind them, the outer one opens. Then they're on the road, full speed ahead.

A

21

The door facing Simon is painted bright blue and the burnished aluminium plate fixed to it says Assessment. Just to the right-hand side of it are a tiny speaker and a button. His instructions are to simply press on the button and call out his name: the person inside will then just as simply let him in. Or so he's been told – along with the sudden increase in his freedom of movement, the simplicity of an action like this is both hard to believe in and unsettling if he does give it credence. All the same, there's no point in standing here reading the plate over and over again.

'Come on in, Simon,' a cheery voice booms out from the intercom as the door unlocks itself. There's a short corridor, more of a hallway, painted yellow and carpeted blue, with a framed print of a vase of angry-looking flowers. The owner of the booming voice pokes his head out from behind one of half a dozen doors. 'There you are!' he says. The hand he holds out to shake is big and hot, and overall, with his sandy hair and sideburns, his lumbering gait, brown sweater and brown suede shoes, he could be half animal, a bear or a lion, perhaps – at any rate, a creature ill-suited to the once-white lab coat he wears over his other clothes, unbuttoned, crumpled, too small for him. A selection of pens are clipped to the breast pocket. On the other side of the coat a label proclaims that he is Dr Martin Clarke. Simon is going to have a very busy day, he says when the greetings are over.

'How are you finding it so far? Big adjustment to make, no doubt? Come in here and take a pew . . .' Simon follows Dr Clarke to a large, airy room, furnished with blue easy chairs and a coffee table. There's a strong smell of oranges, as if someone had only minutes ago finished eating one.

'Everything we're going to do here,' Dr Clarke explains once they are seated, 'is about gathering information so we can build up a detailed picture . . .' Does Simon, he wants to know, have a good grasp of spoken and written language? Good. Is he in good health at present? Good. Any sexually transmitted diseases? Good. Not using any drugs?

'Whenever you feel ready,' he says, 'pop into the bathroom and do a urine sample in the container there, just for the record . . . Good, good, good . . .' Dr Clarke smiles, rubs his hands together and offers coffee, tea, water, chocolate biscuits. He goes next door to pour out the coffee, returns with a cup and saucer.

'And now,' he says, 'we might as well begin.' He shows Simon a booklet made up of A4 pages ringbound together. 'This is my baby!' he says. 'A short questionnaire, nothing to be worried about. No need to think about it too much. Off the top of your head is fine . . .' *Please answer ALL questions* is written on the front, *add any comments in the spaces beneath*. 'Let's go through it together,' Dr Clarke suggests.

'Were your parents married? Did they live together?'

'All that is in my file,' Simon says. 'I've been over it a hundred times.'

'Are you married or in a long-term relationship or have you been married or in a long-term relationship in the past?'

'No. Not really,' Simon says. Amanda probably should not count.

'Which, if any, of the following are you sexually attracted to?' Dr Martin asks, beaming. 'You can choose more than one option here, or none. Women, men, both women and men?'

'Women.'

'Just women?' Clarke asks, nodding encouragingly.

'Yes!'

'Are you additionally attracted to any of the following?' Dr Clarke pauses, leaving long spaces between the options that follow, as if to allow time for Simon to make up his mind. 'Female teenagers? Male teenagers? Male children? Female children? Infants of either gender?'

'What is this?'

'These questions are designed to cover everything. I have to ask them all . . . do you need me to repeat –'

'No,' Simon says. 'None of them!' He breathes out hard, tries to loosen the muscles in his arms and hands but there's no point, they tighten again straight away.

'Animals?' Clarke asks. 'Or any other variety of unusual stimulus?'

'What the fuck is going on here?' He must have been sent to the wrong place. This can't be what Bernie meant. It can't.

'Just answer yes or no,' Dr Clarke replies, smoothly. 'These are only questions, not accusations.'

'No, then.' Simon tells him. 'But if this place is full of people who fuck sheep, I'm out.' How, though? How do you get out of here? And how does it look on your records if you do? Supposing they don't agree to it?

'Which varieties of the sex act do you enjoy?' Simon gulps down his coffee, it's too hot, and some of it splashes on his shirt. He dabs at the stain with some tissues.

'Is there much more of this?' he asks.

'Simon,' Dr Clarke says, 'you seem very agitated. Would you like to talk about that or would you perhaps prefer to complete the questionnaire on your own?' Well, that one is pretty easy to answer with a yes.

'No sweat,' the doctor says, a phrase that seems bizarre coming from someone in a white coat obviously educated at a fancy school. 'Just make sure that at the end of each question, you read carefully where to go next. Give me a shout when you are through, and we'll check it over.' The doctor beams at Simon and ambles to the door, leaving it half way open behind him. Simon goes straight away to close it properly. Then, minutes later, he leaves his chair, opens it again and goes to the bathroom, where there's a Don't Die of Ignorance poster and a wicker basket full of condoms. He does the piss test into the plastic bottle, returns to the huge room, closes the door, sits down again. You don't have to do this, he reminds himself, sitting with the booklet on a clipboard on his knees. But then again, does he want to bottle out and go straight back to where he's come from? Does he want to tell Bernie he made a mistake? Suppose there's something in it? He sits for some time with his eyes shut, remembering yesterday's orientation talk: a *therapeutic unit*, the new intake were assured by a successful inmate from B wing, is *not* a mental hospital . . . *Tests* are not to catch you out but to obtain information which will be useful to you in your therapy. Some of the assessment will likely seem way out of order, the man said, but think carefully before you overreact . . . Simon breathes deeply a few times, opens his eyes and finds his place in the form.

Which of the varieties – these are just words, he tells himself, reading through the examples given. He circles female-to-male oral sex, which does interest him and might be OK, and intercourse, both man and woman on top. It doesn't mention *watching*. Next, it asks, *Have you ever paid for sexual services? How frequently?* The last time is what he remembers, how the girl lay down exactly how he wanted and did what he told her just fine until just before he was finished and then she started to squeeze him with the muscles inside her. 'What's the matter,' she said as he pulled out of her, too late, yelling. 'That was your free gift, handsome, why don't you relax!' He didn't go back and he won't be telling Dr Martin's form about that. Well, no harm was done, why should he?

Do you find it hard to talk about sex? Not easy.

Was sex discussed openly in your family or by adults in the place where you grew up? Was it ever explained to you at home or at school? What kind of a joke is that? *At what age would you say you fully understood sex in terms of what men and women do and how babies are made?* Three of the girls in Burnside got pregnant while he was there, two had terminations. Maybe there were more of those that he didn't know about.

At what age, Dr Clarke's baby asks him next, *did you have your first sexual experience?* What exactly is that supposed to mean? Simon gets up again and strides straight out to Dr Clarke's office opposite. The door is open, and the noise he can hear is a printer churning out a graph on continuous paper. The office too smells very strongly of oranges and the doctor, half hidden by an enormous computer screen, is reading a journal called *Research into Deviance*. He looks up, smiling.

'I was fucked in the arse in the kids' home, right?' Simon tells him. 'But I didn't like it, it hurt. I did it so that I wouldn't get beaten up. Is that a sexual experience?'

'I see, well, yes. I think so.'

'You should make it clearer, right?'

Somewhere between eleven and thirteen, he writes.

Who did you tell about this? No one. It wasn't a big deal, it could have been worse: say if it was the staff. The main kid who was doing it got moved on, it faded out.

Pornography? John Kingswell sometimes left it in the garage. He'd be about eight. What imagery did it include? *Women's bodies? Genitals? Heterosexual Intercourse? Coercion, Violence, Sado-masochism? Lesbian? Homosexual? Other?*

Women. Intercourse. Genitals. Women touching themselves. Putting things in. Offering it. Fascination. Fear. Curiosity – how do you get them to . . . He remembers the smell of engine oil.

'It's John's fault for having this muck in the first place, but if I find you in here again . . .' That's what Iris Kingswell said.

Finally, it's done: *age at time of first wet dream, masturbation, frequency of, duration, number of orgasms, recurring dreams, how do you rate yourself as a sexual partner*, the lot. He puts the pen in his back pocket, drops the form on Doctor Clarke's desk.

'Good, good, very good,' the doctor says, wiping his fingers on a tissue. How many oranges can a man eat in one morning? What kind of job is this man doing?

Back at the reception unit for lunch, they've kept Simon a plate of egg mayonnaise sandwiches because he missed the hot lunch. The food tastes unusually good, but there isn't enough of it. Everyone else is out playing football, but they want him straight back in Assessment after half an hour's break. He does some stretches, jogs on the spot. Well, hopefully, the worst is over.

★

'What do you call your penis?' Dr Clarke asks, as they settle down, this time in the office with the printer. Well, Simon thinks, here's a man who's got no small talk.

'I don't call it anything,' he says. 'D'you have a name for yours, then?'

'I mean, which word for it are you most comfortable with?' The next test, Clarke explains, is a physical one and will take place in the special diagnostic suite at the end of the hallway. He hands Simon a small piece of rubber tubing, made into a circle, attached to a wire. It's oddly heavy: a mercury filled measuring gauge, Dr Clarke explains, which will sit a third of the way up the penis and is sensitive to increases in girth. It's individually fitted. There is no possibility of electric shock.

'Once this is fitted, you'll view a variety of slides with sexual content and listen to some audio tape scenarios. The gauge will measure the strength of your response . . . and this information can be used to increase our understanding of your sexual drive in the context of the index offence. We try to make it as relaxing as we can. Any questions?' Yes, lots. Does everyone do this or have they just picked him? Suppose he don't get it up to any of it? Suppose, for some reason, he just reacts to everything? Could you turn out to be some kind of beast without knowing it and what happens if they find out? Suppose, he thinks, I refuse, what then? He can't get all that out, not even half of it.

'What happens,' he says, grinning, 'if I get a hard-on at a picture of a sheep's arse?'

Perhaps Dr Clarke has met this question before; in any case he smiles and says, 'Ah, yes, that would be very interesting! But of course we are really far more concerned with your response to women . . . Just sign here, to show that the procedure has been explained to you and that you give your consent . . .'

'Does everyone do this or is it just me?'

'It's perfectly routine,' Dr Clarke says, holding out the pen.

They walk to the end of the hallway, and enter another room, very warm, windowless, lit only by a standard lamp. Here, the smell is disinfectant. A skinny man comes out from behind a partition, turning on the main light as he does so and revealing that the room is painted baby pink, and that his white coat, in contrast to Dr Clarke's, is crisp and dazzling white. A reclining chair, covered in huge sheets of pale-blue paper towelling, sits on a square of plastic. There's a hand-wash basin, a towel rail, a potted plant.

'Julian,' says Dr Clarke, 'this is Simon. Simon, this is Dr Julian Bentley, who will administer the test. I'll leave you to sort things out . . .'

'Well,' says Julian Bentley, when he returns from closing the door Dr Clarke left ajar, 'first I do like clients to know how the room works. You can see, here, this is the screen – I'll pull it down. And here, attached to the chair, some headphones, for you to put on when I tell you to. I will be there, behind the partition, with the door closed. You'll notice the ceiling mirror up there, which is angled to allow me to observe your eye movements via the observation panel over there. I will check from time to time that you are actually watching the screen during the presentations . . .

'Well now . . . what else? The suite is fully insulated against sound. There's a two-way intercom, so you can talk to me if you need to, just your normal pitch of voice will be picked up easily . . . That, there in the partition, is the opening for the projector. OK so far?'

OK? Hardly. It's a kind of nightmare. But at least, Simon tells himself it is not Dr Clarke sitting behind the projectors and eating oranges at the same time. At least this man speaks in a steady, dullish kind of voice and doesn't constantly rub his hands together . . . All the same, he can feel his heart stepping up its beat. Fight or flight . . . He'd like to run away, or smash the place up; he can't. But you can stop this any time, he tells himself, you can. It's hard to believe.

'OK,' he says.

'We need to fit you first. It's easiest if you take your jeans and underwear right off and settle yourself there on the recliner. I'll just go and get some gauges . . .'

When he returns, Dr Bentley is wearing white latex gloves. He puts down a plastic box and a jar of disinfectant, casts a practised glance at Simon's genitals which, despite the warmth of the room, have never seemed smaller. He selects a gauge from the collection in the box, holding it by the wires as he immerses it in the disinfectant and jiggles it around.

'I like to reassure clients about hygiene!' He blots it dry and passes it over, using a piece of kitchen paper. 'If you could just . . .' He stares pointedly away for a minute or so. 'A little lower . . . yes, perfect. You're all set.' He connects the trailing wires, and – at last – turns off the bright overhead lights. The door in the partition closes behind him with a muffled click.

'Are you comfortable, Simon? Can you say something?'

'Oranges and lemons,' Simon says. The lights go out. A piece of strange, repetitive string music plays for a minute or two and then fades away. Suddenly, and three-quarters life-size, there's a naked boy maybe twelve years old, with an earring, holding his cock and grinning out of the wall at him: look at what I've got. The boy's face reminds Simon of someone he's met, whether it's the tilt of his head or the glint in his eyes, someone in a café, a playground somewhere – but before the name comes clear the boy vanishes, to be replaced by first a blank screen and near-total darkness than long-haired blonde with huge breasts, one leg raised on a low footstool, fingering herself. Simon studies her, the curves and the pink-nesses of her flesh, the way she's using her fingers. It's quite something – after all this time between pale-grey walls. Then Bentley whisks her away too and the next one has her hair messed up and a black eye, she's bruised all over and tied up, lying on the ground in some dark place, looking up scared – it reminds him all right and it goes on much too long, so he shuts his eyes even though he was told not to and counts to sixty. When he opens them, he is glad of the naked toddlers splashing at the edge of a municipal paddling pool, who are replaced by a couple fucking on a floor somewhere, him on top, her head thrown back, exposing her throat. Last of all there are two women, fondling each other's breasts and kissing, weird, but –

‘Now please put the earphones on. You are going to listen to some stories,’ says the doctor’s voice. ‘You can close your eyes now if you want.’

It’s over an hour later that the hiss in his ears stops, leaving a shocked silence behind. Simon lies on the recliner, sticky from his eventual success in response to the final request to make himself come, any way that works, because it would be very useful as a benchmark.

He’s exhausted, overwhelmed by the fantasy tour, by the plethora of taped voices – who were they all? – soft, harsh, male, female, wheedling, brutal, insinuating, lascivious by turns, who have whispered in his ears describing how he, that is Simon, likes teenage girls at the swimming baths, likes them best all fresh and clean and smooth, just before they turn into women, how he watches one in particular and then waits outside in his car, offers her a lift and then gets her to go down on him, or else how he watches from the garden while a woman slowly undresses in her bedroom with the curtains open. He has listened to a man telling him in a south London accent about sodomy in a men’s urinal from the point of view of a boy who just can’t get enough of it and he has also been told how he waits for the blonde, grabs hold of her and forces her down to the ground, slaps her face, tears her pants off, turns her over, she’s struggling but she can’t stop him, she’s screaming, you can hear it on the tape, she screams even more when in it goes in her –

The lights fade up again.

‘Well done. That’s great, Simon,’ Dr Julian Bentley’s voice informs him. ‘Please remove and disconnect the gauge then place it in the jar on the table to your left . . . When you’re dressed, please just dispose of the chair covering in the orange rubbish sack under the basin. Then wash and dry your hands . . . Thank you.’

The sack, Simon notices, is labelled hazardous waste.

22

In Wentham the officers lean in doorways, make eye contact, crack jokes, share pots of tea. You see the same ones on a regular basis and are encouraged to call them by their first names: Dave, Carl, Jimmy, Bryan, etc. The 'us and them mentality', is avoided. As for the rules, all infringements of them are punishable by expulsion and they are clear enough: no drugs, no alcohol, no violence, no self-harm; stay in your chair during group sessions unless directed otherwise, attend all sessions unless a doctor says you are sick, disclose everything relevant, tell the truth at all times.

Cell doors are unlocked from 7 a.m. to 9 p.m., and these cells on A wing are big, a good ten by nine. Simon's is freshly painted, cream, with a blue and green striped bedcover. There is a 16-inch TV, a desk for his typewriter to sit on and a chair, as well as the bed, on top of which he now lies, reading the leaflet entitled *What to Expect*. There is a built-in cupboard and, as you might expect in somewhere newly built, a sanitary unit . . . Simon has never actually stayed in a hotel, but he's fitted carpet in quite a few and this place almost puts him in mind of one. Not luxury, but commercial. It just needs some tiny soaps in a basket, an electric kettle, telephone and some sachets of coffee and tea by the bed, though the dark shapes of the concrete lattice on the other side of the window do break the atmosphere a bit. Beyond the screen, there's a glimpse of the courtyard garden: smallish shrubs, some large boulders, gravel, a stone-rimmed pond, bristling on one side with yellowing reeds and, in the centre, a fountain made from piled rocks – the slow, over-flowing rather than the spouting kind. There's a wooden bench beside the pond. Does anyone ever get to sit there? Access to the roof is barred with razor wire and there's a security gate to the right, by the wing entrance, so it should be possible, though so far Simon's seen only the gardener go in and remove some prunings . . . And the birds, of course, sparrows that drink the water and putter about in the reeds. Well, here he is. For better or for worse, they appear to have taken him on.

'You would appear to be heterosexually oriented,' Dr Clarke informs him at the end of the week, two cups of coffee steaming on the desk, 'neither heterosexual nor homosexual paedophilias are evident nor any attraction to violence during sex or as an arousing factor prior to sex. That's good, very good . . .' He leans back in the chair, continues: 'On the other hand – very interesting – you are erotophobic, seven on a scale up to ten. That is to say you are ambivalent about, or disliking of, sex and women, despite experiencing a normal-strength drive towards it and them. Also, you have strong voyeuristic tendencies, that is, you prefer to watch as opposed to engage directly in mutual activities. So I am recommending that you explore the reasons for this with your therapist and use a variety of reconditioning and other appropriate behaviour-modification techniques to make a more normal adjustment . . .' He signs the paper in front of him, smiles. 'Any questions?'

Is that, Simon thinks but does not ask, a *ph* and a single *t* in 'erotophobic'? Given that someone yesterday called him an introvert, he's collecting quite a few longish words. So, where's he going to fit them all in, let alone find the time to have them done? On his cock?

'What techniques?' he asks.

'Well,' Doctor Clarke explains, 'an orgasm is the reward that reinforces a particular action or fantasy in a self-perpetuating cycle, which must be broken.' *Broken?* What the hell are they going to do to him?

'It's quite simple,' Dr Clarke says. Once aroused, Simon might, for instance try to substitute an appropriate fantasy, such as a woman fondling him, or intercourse, and bring himself to orgasm. Over weeks, time spent with the new stimulus would increase and eventually this would –

'Turn me into a wanker?'

'– completely replace the original. We can work on this.' Now, Clarke says, they must move on to consider the results of the tests for aggression and impulse control . . . I suppose that means, Simon thinks, that it would be a bad moment for me to tip that metal bin full of coffee grounds and orange peel on top of your head? Who do you think I am? Or is it *what*?

On the wall opposite the door of the group room is a fake mirror, so that the wing psychiatrist can observe everything that takes place. There are seven of them in the group and they have to shake their hands and feet, then run, hop and crawl around the room without bumping into each other until told to freeze suddenly on the spot. They have to shout as loud as they can, trying to make the walls fall down, then whisper an important message, using only the word dustpan. They have to show, using no words at all, that they are happy, sad, furious, in love, dying for a pee; also they have to become dogs, swans, bees, ants, snakes . . . after which they take turns to fall backwards into the linked arms of the rest of the group. Well, it makes a change.

Now they're in the middle of the room, seated on a circle of ten chairs: the seven cons, plus Annie, who runs the drama bit, Greg from probation and David, who is an officer just completing his training to co-facilitate groups.

They have to say who they are.

David says he is a beginner. He's only twenty-four. He's as terrified as they are, or more, but glad to be out of the main system.

Annie tells them she has just returned from a holiday on a Greek island so she's not quite up to speed. She started her career in social work but left to do a Ph.D. in Drama Therapy . . . She's small, wiry, fit-looking, with a faint tan and bright, almost turquoise, blue eyes, very intense.

Greg, on the other hand, is half bald, worn-out-looking, which fits with the wife and three children, rare-breed sheep and an old farmhouse he renovates in his spare time. He has a beer gut, he sits in his chair with his legs straight out, his feet, ankles crossed, in battered old trainers. The rest of him leans back in the chair as far as he can go, slouching as if the group were all on TV and here he is watching it, a beer in his right hand and a cigarette in the left. But when he starts speaking his eyes brighten, his face wakes up.

'You've gotta do something that makes a difference, otherwise what's the point?' he says, lifting his hands briefly from the arms of the chair, then dropping again. 'Now you. Who are you? What're you here for?'

'Pass,' says a sallow man sitting obliquely opposite Greg, who spends most of the time staring at his own thin knees: Andy. Andy's shoulder-length hair is limp; two of his top front teeth are missing. He looks out of his depth, defeated. Next to him, Simon sits straight-backed and clean-shaven, neat in a fresh button-up shirt that he ironed this morning. He's telling himself he can do this, can't he? He knew it was coming. It said so in the handouts, which the rest of them probably haven't bothered to read: *The first stage is to acknowledge, without minimising it, the offence* . . . Well, that's a piece of piss after what he's been through in Assessment. Might as well get it over with, then.

'Simon Austen, serving life,' he announces and all of them, not just the staff but blanked-out Ian with his frizz of curls, Pete with the crew-cut and broken nose, Ray with the grey-streaked ponytail, cool, hard-faced Nick in his brand new clothes, chubby-cheeked Steve, even Andy, all of them are looking at him.

'I killed my girlfriend,' he adds. 'She wouldn't take out her contact lenses.' Words can't hurt you, not if you take charge of them.

'Man, that's no reason!' says Ray.

'I know that,' Simon says. 'That's why I'm here. What about you? Self-defence, was it?'

'Hold on,' Annie says. 'Can we stay with you? What was your victim's name?'

'Amanda,' he announces, coldly, thinking how Annie is absolutely nothing like Bernadette: she's sharp and hard, her voice is not sexy at all, plus the colour of her eyes can't be real. He adds, to prevent her asking him: 'I strangled her, but it didn't quite work, she choked to death . . . Well,' he looks round at them all, 'have I started the ball rolling here or not?'

No one replies. The silence stretches around them and the room they are sitting in – charcoal office carpet, the same blue armchairs as in the Assessment unit, nothing much else until you get to the abstract prints screwed to the wall and a stack of tables and spare chair cushions in the corner beside the coffee stuff – seems suddenly far too big.

'Aren't you going to do something, then?' Simon asks Greg.

'I can't make people open up,' Greg says. 'It's a choice.'

'Seems like we're going nowhere fast!' Simon tells him. He feels very alert, noticing everything he can, such as the slow, careful way the staff talk, and trying to get a grip on what's going on.

'Well, no,' Greg says. 'You've taken the first step, haven't you? This isn't something to rush. We are moving very slowly towards a clear, detailed account of the offence and then –'

'Actually, you're wearing contacts, aren't you?' Simon interrupts, cutting across to Annie.

'Yes,' she tells him. 'Is there a problem with that?' The air is thick with projections, transference, hostility, denial. They sit there, silent, breathing it in: two murderers, an armed robber, a rapist, a kidnapper who left his ex-wife locked in the trunk of a Vauxhall Cavalier, a paedophile, a man who says he is innocent of the fatal stabbing he's been sent down for. David, observing. Greg, beady-eyed. Annie, back here after two weeks gazing at the join between sea and sky.

Greg suggests that they begin with something relatively small, like where the offence took place. A car, Ray says, parked outside his ex's house . . . plus he had a good reason too, she wouldn't let him see his kid, what man could stand for that? The gents' toilet in Spangles, but it's not what you think, Nick tells them: he's straight as a die . . . St Mark's playing fields. A canal towpath . . .

'Nowhere,' the tall, thin man called Ian says. 'I didn't do it.'

'Party games?' Nick of the gents' toilet asks, when they have to stand up and take the ends of some bits of string that Annie holds bundled in her hand. 'Are we going to pin the tail on the donkey next? Got any sausage rolls and jellies?' They find their partner at the other end of the string and have to ask each other what happened in the place they've mentioned. Ian gets Annie.

'There's no point, anyway,' he says.

'The bloke had a gag on him,' Pete tells Simon, 'but he kept making noises in his throat.' Pete couldn't concentrate on breaking the safe lock so he hit him till he shut up. Then he set the place on fire behind him, but someone called the fire brigade.

'That it?'

'They said he had a heart attack, but like I say, he was OK in the end. He got good compensation.'

They report the other person's account back to the group without changing anything or leaving anything out. Simon reckons he's done a good job but Pete complains that the wrong impression is coming over.

'This is a waste of fucking time,' he says.

'Well, what else do you think we should be talking about here at the tax-payers' considerable expense?' Greg asks. 'Football? Fishing? Let's get on with it, please.'

David, the trainee, twists a tiny gold and diamond stud in his ear, anomalous with the uniform, but all the same, not actually forbidden. This, Simon thinks, is the blind leading the even blinder God knows where. At the end of the session he feels as if someone has drilled a hole in the top of his head and vacuumed his brains right out.

Dr Clarke explains how he will supply a brand new personal stereo for Simon to listen to some reconditioning tapes on.

Batteries will be supplied too. Are there any particular details Simon can give, to help make the tapes more effective? What kind of woman does Simon find attractive, for example? Skinny? Athletic? Plump? Statuesque? Petite?

Bernadette, Simon thinks. More than anything right now, he'd like to write to Bernadette. The fact is, she never did say anything about keeping in touch, though that could be an oversight and, of course, he could always just write c/o the prison: *Hey, did you know what you were getting me into here? Seriously*. Just saying that to her would surely make everything feel that bit easier. *Well, I'll just have to believe there's a method in this madness and take your word for it that it works!* And suppose she might even come and visit him, or promise to, when it's over? *I wonder, would you consider . . .* No. She told him no. She said she was happy with her partner. So no letters. This is the real world. Really? He asks himself. Shut up and stick it out, he replies.

'Not skinny,' he tells Dr Clarke. Blonde, brunette, redhead, Afro-Caribbean, Asian? the doctor wants to know, and are there any particular ways he likes to see a woman dressed?

'It depends on the person,' Simon tells Dr Clarke, after some thought, 'how the clothes look.' A good point, Clarke concedes. What about the scenario itself? Does Simon have any feeling as to where they might begin? Can they toss a few ideas around?'

'I don't think so,' Simon says.

'I'll just go through my files, then,' Dr Clarke decides. 'We'll fine tune it once there's something to go on. Well, well, good, then. We'll have it ready for you in a week or so. Anything else I can do for you? Another coffee? Orange? I'm going to have one.'

Meals are served in a dining room, eight big tables; one week you get the early serving, the next week the late. You sit wherever you want, any table, you can save a seat for someone, or submit to whosoever lands on you, in this case Nick.

'Total nut house, isn't it?' Nick opines from opposite.

'Right,' Simon says.

'Don't think I'll be sticking it out,' Nick says. 'Seen the shrink yet?'

'Clarke?' Simon asks.

'No, Mackenzie. Complete wind-up. Now –' Nick leans forwards over the table '– what do you think about a nice bit of a smoke, just to help get us through?' He mouths the words almost soundlessly, then grins, sucks in his breath, blows it slowly out.

'You've got the wrong person,' Simon tells him, forking in one of the slices of samosa that have been cooling down on his plate.

'That so?' Nick says, as a bloke, completely bald and clean-shaven, comes up and without saying anything, sits heavily down a couple of spaces away on their table. He's has a plump face, smallish nose and blobby mouth, plus no eyebrows or chin to speak of. On top of that there's a couple of rolls of fat at the back of his neck . . . Well, is it real? Or, talk about drugs, is there stuff in the water here? Or are they paying the bloke to give people a fright by going round and pretending to be some enormous great cock dressed in a shirt, hanging there over a plate of food? Or maybe most likely, Simon thinks, has he just already gone right over the edge?

23

Dr Mackenzie gets smoothly to his feet and reaches across the desk, holding out his hand to shake. He is about Simon's build and around the same age too – perhaps just a little older. He is immaculately dressed in expensive-looking, rather formal clothes – a waistcoat over his shirt, the jacket carefully arranged over the back of his chair. His hair is dark, closely cut; his glasses have thin golden frames.

'So,' says Simon, 'I get to meet the man behind the mirror?'

It seems worth comment: Mackenzie has, after all, been observing him for a good twelve hours prior to this appointment. It's not the normal way to start out, is it? But Mackenzie just says, 'We'll sit over there,' and points to the area by the window. As for the office, it is at least a normal room, with no machinery, mirrors, screens or computers of any kind. The windows would look out on the football pitch but the blinds are half closed so you just get a soft blur of light. The chairs they move into are soft, the same as those in the library, upholstered dark blue. There's a childish kind of picture on the wall, by an artist called Klee.

They sit down. Mackenzie says nothing. Been here, Simon thinks, done this . . . He's seen the list of letters after the man's name, he's got qualifications coming out of his ears. Even so, what he's thinking is: What gives you the right? But then again, what did the old-timer say in week one? You've got to be open to stuff that gets your rag up. So, he'll give it a try.

'I seem to be meeting a doctor a day at this point,' he says. Mackenzie nods.

'How does that feel?'

'I get the message I'm a weirdo, but that's not new.' Simon grins, but his hands are fisted. Another long silence follows.

'Well,' Simon says, deliberately stretching out his fingers, 'everyone seems to have their own agenda. One of them says he's going to give me wanking for homework . . . What's your line?'

Mackenzie considers, then says, 'I try to look at the broad picture. Listen, make interpretations, put the pieces together.' *After they've been taken apart?*

'What will we be doing here, then?' Simon asks. Talking, of course. About? Anything Simon wants to talk about.

'Well,' Simon says, 'suppose there's just nothing at all that comes to mind? Suppose there's a complete blank in that department?'

'You could start by telling me about your tattoos,' Mackenzie suggests. 'They're certainly saying a lot. You have some on your hands. Are there others? What do they mean to you?'

'They're words, all words,' Simon says. 'Judgements, if you like –' Like you'll be making, he thinks, but manages to hold it back.

But then Mackenzie says,

'So you think I will be making judgements?' And before he knows it Simon's said yes, of course you will! The fact is, he realises, that here they know how to stir you up so much that you have to talk, you need the release. Whether you want to or not, there's no way out of it. The man's got his rag up all right.

'Have you considered having the tattoos removed?'

'No,' Simon says. Despite the fact that they mark him out, that they draw attention to his past (what do you mean, past? Is it over yet?), despite all that, he hasn't ever considered removing them; on the contrary, there are quite a few more he'd like to add to the list.

'It seems like the least of my problems, actually,' he tells Dr Mackenzie, then wishes he hadn't.

'What are your more important problems then?'

'Relationships,' Simon tells him. 'Full stop, End Of Story.'

'What aspect of relationships?'

'All aspects.'

When he runs out of steam or goes up a cul de sac, Dr Mackenzie is always ready to throw him another line as in: 'That homework from Dr Clarke, then, can you explain what you feel about that?'

'I feel like a fucking animal!' Simon says. 'As in *dumb* and as in *beast*. I feel like I'm so bad I'm supposed to just let you doctors right inside the private parts of me, bringing along your drills and spanners, the manual you wrote . . . all in a day's work for the experts!' There's nothing that isn't supposed to be up for grabs, no bottom line and nothing he can do for himself, that's how he feels and basically, that's how it is. But he wishes he hadn't said any of it to the man sitting opposite him and he won't make that mistake again.

Simon lies down, as instructed, presses the silver button marked *play* and waits for a muffled click, the deepening voice of the tape's hiss. Someone draws breath, a man's voice says: 'You've had a couple of drinks in the pub and you meet up with a very attractive woman . . .' Who the hell does the voices on these tapes? It's not Clarke; it doesn't sound like Julian Bentley either. Some posh out-of-work actor type putting on a normal voice and going way over the top. He presses pause, and considers again, what exactly is *attractive*? Has he got a type? He certainly likes a woman to look like a woman, not a weight-lifter or a clothes hanger. Amanda was on the plump side, but other things about her, her uncertainties, the fact that she seemed willing to do things his way, were just as important. As regards Bernie, he thinks it's different again. The opposite from Amanda in many ways, but at the same time not dissimilar physically. It is impossible to separate her from her physical presence, her actions, words, silences. If he closes his eyes, he can still see and feel her, sitting opposite him in the stuffy Portakabin, getting to her feet . . . He opens his eyes again, turns the machine back on.

'She's wearing a very short skirt,' the voice says, 'and a clinging, low-cut top . . .' Bernie, of course, wouldn't. It would be nothing like that. He thinks again of their last meeting, when they stood opposite each other and he wanted to take hold of her but couldn't.

'You buy her a few drinks,' the tape says. 'She seems to really like you! She invites you back to her flat, close by . . . It's a nice place with rugs on the floor and low lighting . . . There's music playing . . .'

Simon stays in the Portakabin. We're both pretty wired up, he thinks. Bernie is standing there near the panic button and I'm a few feet away. I can see her breath go in and out . . . I say my piece, I tell her I could become the best of me that has been hidden so long, tell her I burn with wanting to . . . I tell her I want to touch her . . . I want to. She takes a step towards me –

'Now you've got your hand on her thigh, you lean in and kiss her . . . She starts to breathe hard. She opens her legs, she's desperate for it, you can feel under her panties if you want . . . her hand is feeling your cock, rubbing you in a special way . . . she unzips you . . .'

We hold each other. Simon tells himself instead. I feel her pressing against me. She's very warm. I want to slip my hand underneath her clothes, between where the sweater and the skirt join, there, reach in and touch the source of the heat, the smoothness of her skin, but I don't dare in case she doesn't mean this to be –

'Oh, man . . . it's just how you like it!'

'Get out of my head!' Simon rips the Walkman off, throws it against the wall.

And now Bernie says his name and rubs her cheek against his. Their lips touch; after the kiss, he cups his hand over her breasts, hears the sharp intake of her breath.

'Supper time!' The shout goes up, spoiling things completely: this is Wentham. Life sentence.

'Sorry,' he says to Bernie's lingering after-presence. What, he considers as he washes his hands, would the real woman think of what he's just done? If he asked her, 'Do you mind me doing this to you in my head?'

'I'm not keen,' is what he reckons she'd say. But she won't know, so does it matter? It bothers him but it doesn't feel like something he can discuss with Dr Mackenzie or Dr Clarke.

Perhaps the plastic the Walkman is made from is of special prison quality, because he notices as he leaves the room that there's a crack on the case but the tape is still turning round and round.

24

Small group is four mornings a week, which includes drama on Wednesdays, so like it or not, you get to know each other fast and you have to take it for granted that pots will be calling kettles black, but at least you're still allowed to say that here, eh? It seems that hardly any blacks sign themselves up for stuff like this; draw your own conclusions. And how many psychiatrists does it take to change a light bulb? And Doctor, Doctor –

'Point is,' Steve repeats, his eyes a-glitter, his cheeks flushed even pinker than usual, 'point is, everyone had a ride, the whole estate, it wasn't like she kept herself to herself and that's why I say it's right out of order, seven fuckin' years –' he looks around the circle to see if those who seem to be holding back on him have got it yet. 'A chronic whore, really chronic. It's just not the same, right?'

'Right,' a couple of them mutter into their hands. Nick, exuding the smells of soap and aftershave, grins from ear to ear. Yesterday he said he thought the whole place was right up its own arse, and what is happening now would, in his book, certainly seem to back that up.

'Well,' Ian comes in, his voice bright, chatty almost, 'look at it this way. You like bacon sandwiches, don't you, but it doesn't mean you have to eat them all the time –'

'Jewish, are you?' says Nick.

'I mean, she might like it a lot, but not right then or not with Steve,' Ian explains. Ian still maintains that he's innocent, convicted on the strength of an identity parade and some circumstantial evidence, of something he would never do. Some of them believe him, especially at moments like this, but that's irrelevant because he'll be ghosted out soon if he refuses to take responsibility for his offence. Catch two hundred and twenty two, he says.

Opposite Simon, Pete, the armed robber, sits arms folded, glaring at the floor. Whose side am I on, Simon asks himself. Where do I go? Because the way they have the say-so drives you mad, but maybe it just *seems* as if the females actually run the show? Maybe it's the other way around? Sometimes, at any rate.

'You've got a point,' he tells Ian.

'Listen,' Steve says, 'he's not on the planet and you're the weirdo who killed his girl because you couldn't put it in so –'

'Steve,' officer Dave intervenes, 'I'm going to have to stop you right there, because –'

'OK . . . *with respect* . . . with respect, what I'm saying is, it's not as if she was a *woman* like Annie –' He turns to her. 'She was a *slag*, right?' He isn't doing himself any favours and no one's rushing to back him up. Annie stares coolly back at him. She's trying to keep her face neutral, Simon thinks, but she hates him, she must do. It stands to reason she does, but she's got to hold it back, for professional reasons. 'A woman,' Steve continues, 'who wears a skirt up to here –' His eyes fastened to Annie's face, he gives himself a kind of karate chop, just below the genitals. 'Then she can't complain if people get the wrong impression, *that's* what I'm saying, Annie.' His face relaxes and he smiles at her, as if to say *problem solved*.

'You're saying that you got the wrong impression?' she asks. 'Before, you were saying that you thought it didn't matter so much that you raped Louise because she had sex with other men. Which is it, then?' She's handing him the rope to hang himself with, Simon thinks, that's what it is. Also, she's not frightened of words. He watches Steve bunch one hand into a fist, slam it into the palm of his other hand.

'Everyone knows what I mean!' he says. 'You're just too scared to back me up! Ask Susanna, she's on today, right? She'll give a straight answer.' The group votes unanimously in favour. Why not? At any rate, it'll be a diversion. Susanna, a prison officer who is married with three children, is deemed to be a representative of respectable womanhood. Annie's face is white and pinched, Greg drums his fingers on the arm of the chair as they all wait for Dave to bring her in. Steve puts out an extra chair, ceremoniously waves her into it when she arrives, explains all over again.

'Right?' he asks. 'Got it? There is a difference, got to be, stands to reason, hasn't there?'

'No,' Susanna says. 'In the past, I might have said yes to that, without thinking. But now I'd have to say no . . . Anyone should be able to choose who they get intimate with.' She gets up, smiling, her blonde curls catching the light around her head. 'Suppose,' she adds, 'you were in court, and the judge said, oh, he's done this kind of thing before, let's not bother with the trial . . .' She wears make-up and nail polish, plenty of rather delicate jewellery to offset the uniform. There's laughter as she leaves the room, all eyes on her until the door is closed.

'Just another fucking screw, that's all,' says Steve, as the tone sounds on the PA, indicating five minutes left to go.

'To be continued,' Andy mutters under his hand, which is his trick, to say nothing much until there's no time left, to seem to participate, without actually doing so.

At the end of the group they stand in a circle with their eyes closed and hold hands. Holding hands is weird enough to begin with and further complicated because, while these pairs of hands have done a host of ordinary and useful tasks like counting change, laying bricks, playing catch with a ball, mending a bicycle or picking up a fallen child, they have also committed awful, unwanted intimacies. Another thing is that right now Simon is standing opposite the fake mirror, with Doctor Mackenzie presumably sitting behind it, watching everyone but especially, he feels, him. Or maybe he isn't there and it's all just a con, you can't tell.

It's your best chance, he reminds himself. And the fact is that after a good group you do feel different. Take today as an example: you absolutely know why Steve doesn't want to see the writing on the wall. And somehow, even though he won't read it, you can, and you can say to him, 'Tough group, mate? Nice bit of self-control you did there, I thought you were going to lose it, but you didn't . . .' You can have a good idea of exactly where he's at, and even offer to make the bastard a cup of tea, if you feel like it.

Steve won't come out of his cell, so Simon offers the tea to Ray instead. Ray sits on the bed, while he's at the desk. Ray has had his pony tail cut off and he's bought some designer-effect jeans; he gulps the tea while it's still at boiling point and nods in the direction of the cracked Walkman parked on the window ledge.

'Don't use it,' Simon tells Ray. 'I'm just hanging on to the machine. Drove me mad. Besides, I'm not some fucking nonce, I just –'

'Me neither,' Ray cuts in. 'I just like to scare them out of their wits first! That's all!' He cracks his knuckles, grins. The scar on his jaw glows white. 'What did they dream up for you?' he asks. 'As for me, The Thunderstorm, I like that one. She's scared already, see? Or else there's this *other* bloke, right, that has scared her and then I come along . . .'

25

Simon is on the floor of his room, belly down, knees bent, the soles of his feet reaching back and up towards his head, his head thrown back towards his toes, his hands gripping his ankles: *The Bow*. For the first time ever since he took up yoga, he has an actual foam mat to lie on, blue, which he got from the catalogue for three weeks' money. It makes a big difference and he's going to get curtains next. Another thing that would really help would be access to the garden; he has written to the Governor about that. He keeps the typewriter out on the desk and the chair set on four blocks so as to obtain the ergonomically correct posture when he works because now, he's got a job. He only got the job after two hours of infuriating self-justification in a special meeting, but that's history now and it is his: editor of the newsletter, reporting to Phillipa from Education, which means: incite staff and residents to write articles, draw cartoons. Then tidy the stuff up, fill the gaps himself, put it all into the computer, arrange the pages . . .

Computer training is provided; the pay's bad but even so, he can't believe that no one else wanted to do it – that they'd rather trim the edges of the lawn, sweep the corridor or chop carrots when he can already see it in his mind's eye, the columns, the typeface, the headlines in bold: *Sorry, Sigmund! What Next?* A yoga column, perhaps . . . ? It's hard not to think about it, even right now when he should be emptying his mind. He shifts the grip on his ankles, deepens the stretch across his chest.

Editor is certainly up on CARPETT-FITTER, which is tattooed around his right buttock, the two *t*s on the carpet not his fault, but still . . . When there's time, maybe he'll have

EDITOR done underneath. A neat little asterisk in between . . . He relaxes, goes onto knees and hands, arches his back up, holds it, then kneels and bows, forehead to floor, inverted hands to feet.

There's a knock on the door.

'Post, Simon,' says officer Bryan. Simon grunts his thanks, stays with the position. Eventually he relaxes, and slides back and up into *Dog*, then down into *Float on Belly*, then it's a jump into *Dog*, back to *Belly*, head up and back, down, *Dog* again, jump . . . finally, up. His heart pounds from all the jumps and it's only when its slow again and he's finished the standing pose and the rest at the end that he goes to the office to collect the letter.

Inside the large, shiny-brown institutional envelope is a smaller cream one dated February 10th, from Tasmin. Who else? It's stiff and quite thick, probably a card, postmarked York. Bewildered, he examines it for a moment or two. It's like something from another world. He slips it into the shoe box and then turns his mind to the half-dozen eggs he purchased from the canteen and is planning to scramble for himself, Ray and Pete. Afterwards, seeing as for some reason bananas are not banned here, they will have banana custard, courtesy of Ray. A yellow meal. Then he'll read himself to sleep. Here, the library is open every day and there are soft chairs to sit in while you chose up to six books. In a row on the shelf above the desk he has his current selection: *Intermediate Yoga*, *Freud for Beginners*, *Smiley's People*, *The Paintings of Chaim Soutine*, *The Golden Notebook*.

'Tell me about watching,' Mackenzie says.

'Why don't you tell me? You do a lot of it,' Simon points out, and Mackenzie writes something, just one word, in his small leather-bound notebook, then underlines it. He's frowning when he looks up again.

'So what is it you think I am trying to do to you with my questions?'

'Make me hurt. Show me how bad I am?' Simon says. What

Mackenzie wants is for him to talk off the top of his head – keep going, get it off his chest and the right kind of thing that Mackenzie is after is bound to pop out . . . But if it does, what will he do with it? That's something Simon feels he's got to wonder about. He doesn't trust the man.

'What about the contact lenses, what is she going to see?' The questioning about the contact lenses is pretty much constant and it's not as if he doesn't know what Mackenzie is getting at there: he didn't like Amanda being able to see better in case she saw how scared he was and he didn't like her not doing what he told her to. He had to keep her under his thumb or else she'd have him under hers. Then she'd squash him like a beetle, wouldn't she? Annihilate him, if he let her. Because, basically, women don't like him, they piss off, and they're right, aren't they? Bernie was the exception, in a class of her own. Bernadette Nightingale is a kind of a saint with a body, and if he had met her earlier in life then things might have been different . . . that's how it seems, off the top of his head, but he doesn't say any of it. Of course, if Simon were to give in and talk more, the forty-minute appointments would pass more quickly, but mostly, he holds out. It seems safer that way.

'What are you frightened that I will see?' Mackenzie asks.

'Something that isn't there.'

'Have you thought about how you might safely have sexual relationships with women in the future?' That's a question and a half. Since he came to Wentham the past, which used not to exist, is getting blended into one with the present, but he's not really got any feeling at all for the third term, or how to get from here to there. What future? It's frightening.

'No, I haven't. What would you do, in my situation?' As ever, Max Mackenzie falls silent when Simon turns the question back like this. Not to answer is some kind of rule that he obviously thinks very important, though what harm would it do, for fuck's sake, if he knows, to tell? And if he doesn't know, what the hell is he doing here?

It's a wind-up, but one good thing is that at night, when

finally the talking stops, Simon falls into a pit of deep, dreamless sleep.

Greg is solid and very fair. Martin Clarke means well, despite his methods. As for Annie, Simon can't tell where she stands, nor what she makes of him: that's the problem he has with her. She sits there, group after group, tiny, upright in her chair, her white, bony hands loose in her lap. Could be a ballet dancer, perhaps, waiting to go on stage. Her face is calm and still; it gives virtually nothing away. Sometimes, he's sure she must be cracking up inside at the things the group say, such as in the workshop on Expectations of Women – where it turns out that most of them are wanting their clothes washed and their children raised by a totally faithful playboy centrefold constantly available for sex who knows when to keep her mouth shut and also when to disappear completely, who never interferes but understands them completely and forgives their sins – even then, Annie sits there, her hair in its elfin cut, her elaborate earrings hanging motionless from her ear lobes; she sits there like that, gets up now and then to write what they say on the white board and all you see is her eyebrows momentarily shooting up a few millimetres and then straight down again, or maybe her lips widen an even smaller amount and then she swallows and they relax again. What's she getting out of it? That's what he wants to know.

Outside of the group, he's noticed her chatting to Greg and other staff as they walk between the different parts of the institution, or along the gravelled walkway to the car park, and then she is quite different: her gestures free, exaggerated even; her head thrown back when she laughs. Clearly there are two Annies, and it looks like an us and them situation . . . So Simon waits until Greg and David have gone ahead and then he follows her out of the group room.

'Annie?' he calls out, 'I've got something to ask.' He stays a few paces away, careful not to go too close. She glances at her watch, a tiny golden thing that must be almost impossible to read. He smiles, shrugs.

'It's just that I've been wondering: what is it that makes a person work in a crazy place like this?' he tells her. 'Especially a woman,' he adds.

'Good question!' she says, and, to his amazement, returns his smile with a full-sized one of her own. 'But it would take more time than I have to answer it.' She settles the satchel she's wearing over one shoulder, raises her other hand in a kind of wave – any moment, she'll be on her way out of the door, and he doesn't want that yet.

'That's OK. I was wondering,' he says – the thought comes to him as he speaks, a complete gift – 'I was wondering, would you write about it for the magazine?'

'Write about why I do this crazy job?' she asks.

'Up to five hundred words,' he says.

'I'm very busy at the moment,' she tells him. 'It's something I've thought about a lot and it's a nice idea, but really –'

'It could be whenever you've got time,' he says. 'No deadline. I'll just fit it in. Getting things out of the staff is like getting blood out of a stone, but I want the magazine to have some depth, you see, and to get in something from a woman's point of view.'

'Oh, all right,' she tells him. 'I'll see what I can do.'

He can hardly believe it. Later, when he lies in his room thinking over the day's events, it seems clear that the Annie in the corridor is the real one, and the one in the group is a set of skills or techniques that she's learned. He doesn't like this: it seems as if she's got something over him, an unfair advantage. Of course, it's the same with Greg, no doubt, but it doesn't bother him so much in a man, women being as ever the issue here. Was it the same with Bernadette? He would hate to think of the warmth he felt from her being judiciously applied. No, he feels it really wasn't that way. She was a natural at what she did and didn't need techniques. She was a professional but at the same time, she was herself. That's why he trusted her and why, when in his imagination he allows the gap between them to close to nothing so that their flesh is pressed together, and he is breathing in the smell of her, it's all right. More than all right. Habit-forming, even.

He slips back into the Portakabin, the kiss; he feels all over again the ignition of his flesh, the sudden, overpowering wash of sensation. But this time, to his surprise, she pulls away, and says, 'Not here.' Fair comment, but here is all they've got! He eases up the thin sleeve of her sweater and strokes her forearm. She can feel it all over and through her and he can feel her feeling it; soon, they are kissing again, their hands inside each other's clothes, him pressing himself into her – but there are footsteps outside the Portakabin and she has to answer the knock on the door, because everyone knows they are in here. At the last minute before she opens it, she turns to him, flushed –

'Si?' yells officer Bryan. 'You coming to football practice or not?'

'No!' he shouts back.

'You're letting us down!'

Too bad. What was Bernadette going to say? He tried to find his way back, but it's gone. All gone. And, as he reminds himself as frequently as he can bear to, it was not her as such and neither was this madness his idea to start with.

An interesting thing, he thinks, is that the more she hesitates, the surer I am . . . Sometimes, it seems as if they, the probation officers and psychiatrists and so on, have been right about him all along, even *Barry*. On the other hand, sometimes not; and very often indeed it seems as if they don't know when to lay off, and one thing he's sure of is that he is keeping the imaginary Bernadette to himself.

'Look,' he tells Martin Clarke a few days later, having declined a visit to the media room, 'I didn't use the tape and there's no point in trying out a different scenario, I won't use that one either. I'd rather go solo with this. I am taking it on, but in my own way, all right?'

'Well, not really. It does rather defeat the object,' Dr Clarke tells him. 'We need to monitor and to measure progress. On the other hand . . . Hmm . . . Perhaps you can give me an account of what you are finding effective?'

'No,' Simon tells him. 'I can't. I'm telling you and it's up to you whether you believe me.'

'Can we work towards disclosure, perhaps in stages?'

'I don't think so.'

'Perhaps later?' Clarke suggests. Simon shrugs, smiles back, which might just be construed as suggesting the very faintest possibility of a 'yes'. You have to admire the man for his persistence, he thinks, but at the same time, if I give an inch, they'll be taking a mile, or ten.

'Aren't you encouraging us to see women as *sex-objects*?' he asks, keeping the smile fresh. 'Isn't there a danger we're all going to come out of here expecting them to behave like they do in our heads?' and at this, Martin Clarke puts down his pen, leans forwards.

'Interesting point!' he says. 'Yes. This is a matter for your group, really, but I can certainly say –' he pauses, to reach over to the side table to switch on the coffee machine '– I can certainly say that there was something in those heads already and what we're trying to do is see if it can be improved upon . . . of course, you've still got to learn to take no for an answer. Accepting the other person's will. Negotiation, all that . . .' He rubs his hands together, studies Simon with interest.

'Also,' Simon says, 'suppose real life doesn't ever live up to it, have you thought of that?'

'Do you mean,' Clarke says, 'that in that case it would be better to have nothing in your head so as to avoid the disappointment? I'm not sure about that.'

'I don't know,' Simon answers. 'I was just wondering about it.'

'Very interesting,' Clarke says. 'Want a coffee?'

In my case, Simon thinks, perhaps it doesn't matter, because real life is a very, very long way away. And another thing to remember is that even when Bernie is an illusion she is still herself; that's got to be true because just as in real life, he can't push her around. She surprises him and he even likes it.

'I won't this time, but thanks,' he says, getting to his feet and offering Dr Clarke his hand to shake.

'Two weeks' time,' Dr Clarke says. 'We'll discuss all this again.'

26

Detailed case conferences come around once every seven weeks, unless there's an emergency. The staff meet in Mackenzie's office; he gives a draft report then asks for their comments to include. What is said is recorded by the tiny Dictaphone that sits on Mackenzie's desk, then typed up by the secretary and distributed within a week.

'He finds emotion overwhelming or devastating in its consequences, so he tries to intuit things intellectually. At the same time to erect barriers which save him from fully experiencing them emotionally . . . or sexually,' Mackenzie says. The others consider, grunt, nod their agreement. 'Subconsciously, even consciously, he believes we want to hurt him or rather, to make him hurt –' Mackenzie pauses, gives a slight smile. 'Of course, there is a sense in which this is true: insight will inevitably be painful. These intuitions of his are conflated with the hurt he has suffered on his own account in terms of repeated rejection and maternal abandonment. That's the background, I think we're roughly agreed? Well, how do we find Simon here? What's he up to? Martin, would you like to fill the others in on what's been happening?'

'A slow start, admittedly,' Dr Clarke says, smiling affably round at the rest of them. 'Yes. Very slow, in fact. We're doing a lot of negotiation and there's something of a stalemate over his homework at present, but frankly it's not a surprise. Not in a case like this. I haven't given up hope. He's very articulate, intelligent. An interesting chap, I find . . .'

'Annie?'

Annie lights up before she answers; she and Greg both smoke, are constantly fighting it. Staff smoking is always commented on in the group meetings, so they try to avoid it, then chain-smoke when they can't be seen. Mackenzie, who jogs at lunchtime and doesn't smoke, gets up to open his window.

'Well, he's definitely the most attractive con we've had in here so far!' Annie says, just to see Mackenzie's jaw drop. Greg's face relaxes; Martin Clarke laughs aloud. 'Seriously,' she says, 'he's coasting along. He'd got a certain distance before he came, but I don't think he's been challenged yet. He likes it here. He's enjoying his editing role. He even got me to agree to write an article for the sodding magazine,' she adds.

'Really? Perhaps that should have been discussed?' Mackenzie says. 'What's it about?'

'Why I've ended up doing this weird job.'

'So he's looking to see what makes you tick,' says Greg, stretching out, hands behind head, click, click in his neck, 'that's for sure.'

'Anything new there?' she says.

'It could be he's making you undress while he just sits there in his leather armchair and watches,' Mackenzie points out. 'When did he ask?'

'After the group, in the corridor.' Annie colours, just a little, frowns. 'OK. Maybe,' she says. 'But it's a perfectly reasonable question after all.'

'Context,' Mackenzie tells her. 'Go over it, see what comes up.' His tone of voice suggests, without anything being said, that he is speaking not as part of the team, but as line manager.

'*And why have we ended up doing this weird job*?' Annie asks, rhetorically. They've been over it before. To make a difference and prove that things can be fixed, according to Greg. Out of curiosity, in Mackenzie's case. To be part of the force for good in the world, engaged in the patient work of making something out of the ruins violence leaves behind is Annie's line, or part of it.

'Some people like to be close to violence without actually getting hurt,' Mackenzie once pointed out to her.

'Someone has to do it!' Martin Clarke says with a grin and a quick rub of his hands.

'We're getting off the point,' Mackenzie says. 'I am certainly finding Austen extremely resistant and highly manipulative. Still, we know he has opened up before, to the duty probation officer often at his last institution. A very positive transference occurred. Unfortunately, he seems to be building this into a self-defeating mythology about an impossible object.' He smiles, waves one hand airily. 'Well, time will tell, but we definitely need to keep an eye on him.'

'I just wish we could have the meetings in the pub,' Greg says, clasping his hands above his head again and stretching his unwieldy body in a huge arc over the chair. It's after five, on a Friday afternoon. Just a few more minutes, and the staff will walk to the car park, climb into their vehicles and drive to their homes, to ordinary, insignificant arguments; children's laughter; the blessed babble of unexamined life.

27

Simon's eyebrows bunch over his eyes, which glint in the shadows beneath. His jaw tightly sprung, he speaks with unnatural clarity and more loudly than usual, as if to a group of deaf people: 'I am just doing my job! That's why I asked you! There is nothing else to it!' Behind him, pinned to the wall of the group room, is a circular diagram, laminated in plastic and labelled 'The Wheel'. A circle is divided into segments, coloured so that they fade into each other. 'Sad', 'Contemplative', 'Angry', 'Motivated', 'Active', 'Happy', the labels say. Various arrows suggest connections between the different states. Speech bubbles amplify the connection here and there: *Anger takes me away from my sadness and moves me into action. Action can create change or reinforce the way things are*. Often, as now, the diagram appears as an absurd kind of halo behind someone's head.

'You could've asked Greg, couldn't you? Or even Bryan or Dave or Derek here, they work here too,' says Ray. His new jeans are bedded in now and the pony tail is just a memory; he looks almost like some smart-arse superior type on the outside, though the gravel-pit voice gives him away. Nick grins, nods:

'A woman, see,' he says. 'A threat, so you've gotta get a handle. Know about her so that you can deal with her, that's what it looks like –'

'You're on to something, mate,' Steve tells Nick. 'And it takes one to know one doesn't it?'

'How are you feeling Simon?' Greg suddenly asks, so Simon spins around and tells him.

'Like I want to beat the lot of you to a pulp! So would you, mate! I am just trying to do a job. I want to do something constructive –' It's hard to stay in the chair, which is one of the rules: no violence or threats, no getting out of the chair, no leaving the group . . . Say what you want, but stay in that chair. He grips the edges of it, tries to relax his legs.

'You've been challenged. You're angry and you want to be violent . . . Let's look at this. What is it like physically, the way you're feeling now?' He glares back at Annie, who sits with her hands in her lap as usual, staring at him.

'Something wants to burst out of me and I'm having to hold it in, like pulling back some dog, some starved Rottweiler or Razorback or Alsatian, and it takes a lot of strength to keep it back, but also I'd quite like to see it go and I'm thinking –' he jabs his finger in Greg's direction '– if you push me one bit further I might just –'

'Who are you angry at?'

'You! Her! And you too, mate! The fucking lot of you! This fucking place!'

'Look,' Pete chips in, 'it's gotta be your mum, hasn't it?' He's absolutely serious, completely certain he's got it right. 'Dumped you, didn't she?' There they all are, idiots, remembering what he's told them, mauling it around, drawing half-baked fucking conclusions.

'Leave it out! She screwed up but she was just a no-hoper from the start. Will you listen to me –'

'When you get angry enough, Simon, you can kill someone,' Greg says. 'That's what happened to Amanda. That's why we want to know about you and getting angry . . . That's why we want to know about your feelings for Annie here. We want to find out how they might link up to –'

'Well both of their names begin with A, don't they?' he says. She's sitting there still, like a blank page. Oh, how he'd like to make her jump. 'They're both cunts, aren't they?' he says. They're all looking at him again, some of their faces have gone limp with shock, the others have tight grins. 'I've had it. I want out of this nuthouse –' He's on his feet now, looking round at the rest of them, to see who'll stop him if he makes a move. Everyone's frozen, looking back.

'Sit down,' Ray says. 'Get back in that chair, right? We're all in the same boat. Count to ten.'

'Simon,' Annie says. 'If you leave your chair without agreement, you will have to leave the programme.' It's a nursery school, that's what it is!

'I want to leave!' he tells them. Ian left two days ago, refusing to back down. The staff said they had no choice; he said he didn't either.

'You want to take me to bits,' he yells. 'Shake it around, throw most of it away, turn me into something else, like there's absolutely no fucking limits, well wouldn't you be angry, mate?' Greg nods, but doesn't reply. There's a silence, broken, eventually by the officer of the day, Bryan Mills.

'The thing is,' he suggests in a quiet, almost timid voice, 'when you're a danger to others, the way you are, you can't really complain, can you? I mean, I can see how you feel, but in the end it's just not reasonable to cling to your identity, is it?' He looks at Simon over the top of his glasses then takes them off and polishes them with a lens cloth.

'You're admitting it, are you?' Simon barks back at him.

'Plus, you've got to remember, mate,' says Ray, 'what's the alternative?' And then all of a sudden the stuffing's gone out of Simon. He reaches back and touches the arm of the chair. His shirt is wringing wet across the chest and under the arms. His hair's sticking to his head. His legs are shaking so hard that surely the others can see. But now they're in a group hug, half embrace, half scrum, people saying, 'Well done, mate.'

'Well,' Simon says, as the scrum eases apart, 'I'm a piece of shit, aren't I? Now you all know for sure.' He gives a hard laugh, grins around at them, sits down. Annie says, Good, they have opened up the discussion and she will write the article, but she doesn't appreciate being called a cunt, which suggests that women are no more than their private parts, viewed negatively at that.

'Sorry,' he tells her. 'It was a way of trying to cut you down to size.' There's a moment, then, when she drops her guard and laughs, along with the rest of them at the notion of cutting someone already so small *down to size.*

Afterwards, all he wants is to lie face down in his cream-painted cell, pull the covers over his head and sleep. But once he gets there, even though it's as quiet as it ever gets, with most of the others out on exercise, he can't do it. He's first freezing, then suddenly too hot. His body won't relax. He gets up and walks to the officer station.

'Can't sleep after all,' he says, declining a cup of tea, and Kevin Wilkes calls for someone to take him to the field. He joins in the end of a game of five-a-side, which doesn't feel exactly good, but it's better than being on his own.

On his return, there's a memo from the Deputy Governor, thanking him for his comments and saying that he is prepared to have the courtyard garden door opened in the afternoons, 2–4.30 p.m. for a trial period of two weeks with immediate effect. Simon goes straight round to test it.

The inner door is clipped back against the wall. The barred door hangs ajar and he pushes it aside, then steps through. He walks several times around the central area, which is paved in some kind of yellow and grey irregular-shaped stone, the same as the fountain is made from. If he peers hard through the vegetation, he can see into his own cell, and the others on that stretch of corridor. No one's in, but they might be. They might be lying on their beds with their eyes closed and their headsets on, or they might be looking right out at him sitting in the garden. Double goldfish bowl. Then again, what in this life here isn't? He stretches out on the wooden bench, which is still in the sun, closes his eyes and listens to the outside sounds, the fuss of the birds in the budding shrubs, the occasional splash of water on the rocks, the tiny breaths of wind that somehow find their way inside . . . It seems like a good place to think of Bernie.

They've had it with the Portakabin now. You could say that the world's their oyster, except that Simon hasn't in fact seen very much of it, not much, even, of England. So the way it goes is that he and Bernadette are in a street café in Covent Garden on a sunny day with a bit of a breeze, scudding clouds. They're holding hands, leaning close over the little wrought-iron table.

He sees her, real as anything, wearing her melted O pendant and one of the tight black dance tops they seem to go for now, with a loose, floaty blouse worn unbuttoned over it. Wind stirs in her hair. She's smiling and they are looking into each other's faces. And somehow they have got over the whole prison bit, just levitated him over the wall and through time without either of them ageing . . .

Her thumb caresses the back of his hand, feels its way along the bony ridges and dips beneath the skin. The inking still runs across his fingers, DUMB CUNT, and maybe he will get rid of that one day, but it will only be because *he* wants to; *she* doesn't mind at all. She turns his left hand over in hers, opens it, holds it in both of hers, looks a while, then strokes the thin skin of the wrist, circles the palm with her forefinger and, finally, bows her head to plant a kiss there in the middle of his palm. Her lips press, open slightly as she lets out the warmth of her breath. Her rich red-brown hair is pulled towards the knot at the back of her head, strands escape here and there and he wants to reach forward and set the rest of it free.

'Bernadette,' he says.

'Let's go home now,' she says and they walk away through the crowds in the street, his arm round her waist, her thumb hooked into the back pocket of his jeans.

'Si!' Pete yells at him through the door to the courtyard. 'You got it! Thumbs up!' Simon lies there, still as a stone, eyes closed. It's touch and go but the interruption closes over and then they're in a flat, somewhere he's seen in a magazine or a film, with thin-slatted Venetian blinds letting in stripes of light, an old-fashioned carved marble fireplace with an antique mirror above, an ornate plaster ceiling rose with a fancy modern chandelier hanging down. They are standing beneath the chandelier, standing close as she undoes the small buttons of his shirt, pushes it back over his shoulders. Courageous.

Bastard. Cunt. Then the belt buckle, more buttons on the fly, he's very hard and she presses his cock to his stomach as she eases the pants and underwear down with the other hand, now he has to step out of them, staggering a bit and there he is, heart in mouth, cock up, naked, standing opposite her.

It's unbearable, almost.

Touch me, Bernadette!

Lie down here.

And now they're both naked in a walled garden, lying on soft moss beneath the spreading branches of a tree, their hands on each other like this, like that, and she's moaning and the whole thing explodes.

Wonderful. Disgusting. Simon surfaces, alone, to the sounds of water near by and the birds.

Later he uses plastic hooks to hang the navy blue velour curtains that arrived yesterday from Argos; the cell becomes a room. The Saturday following, he watches aghast on his TV set as people are crushed to death in Hillsborough stadium; Monday, they do a group on it and decide to raise money for the victims' families. He's been in Wentham three and a half months.

28

Outside, the sky is a burning, beautiful blue; a shimmering haze has settled over the fields that lie beyond the walls. Inside, light plays in broken patterns on the wall opposite the window. Otherwise, it is just the same as any other day: the burn-marked carpet, the blue chairs, the low ceiling, some new wall charts.

'Still up for this?' asks Greg. He arrived late today because of a pile-up on the motorway and he smells faintly of soap, more strongly of sweat. His hand descends on Simon's shoulder as he asks. 'Ready?' Simon nods. He's bottled out twice already, though that doesn't matter, it's not a race. *You learn from other people on the way.*

'Susanna?'

'OK,' she says, brightly. 'All in a day's work.' She's abandoned her uniform in favour of pink and white trainers and her baggy grey tracksuit from home; this is the same outfit she wore a few weeks back when she took Belinda's role in the scene between Ray and his ex-wife: the bit when she came out of the double garage next to her house around lunchtime and Ray jumped on her.

Ray described the action he was carrying out in slow motion. He was supposed to say what came into his mind while he did it but at times he forgot to speak at all and seemed to be right back there in the garage, the car, the pub; his eyes had a flat kind of glare to them and his breath came in mean gasps even though the movements were slowed right down. Susanna had very little to say, just: 'Ray, Ray, please, why are you doing this, please, I beg you, stop!' The week before, Ray had told them everything he could remember about Belinda, her habits, routines and appearance and the things she had said to him, what he knew about her past. Then, in slow motion, Ray mimed the blows to Susanna's head while the others watched.

'She's not going anywhere, what are you trying to do when you hit her?' Simon asked.

'Scare her,' Ray told them, 'shut her up . . . hurt her.' He mimed putting on a gag, tying her up. He threw a blanket over her to simulate the trunk of the car, and sat down in front . . . A boiling hot day, he'd told them. Easy enough to imagine what it was like for Belinda in there, mile after mile in the stifling dark, not knowing when or how it would end . . . Afterwards, Susanna said she was worrying about the little boy, who was from before she went with Ray, and what would happen when she didn't pick him up from school. She was worrying about whether she would die and what would happen to him if she did. Ray sat on the chair pretending to drive.

'I'll take you to that empty farm house I know about and fuck you and give you something to cry about,' he said. He'd always said he wasn't intending to kill her but he admitted then that he was well out of control and it could have ended up that way, except that he ran out of fuel. He left the car all locked up in a lay-by, hitched a ride for himself, ended up in a pub, got pissed, passed out. Belinda was there another six hours before someone reported the vehicle and the police came. Not the kind of show you'd find in the West End . . . Ray talked afterwards of being in a dark place with no way out.

'Wasn't that Belinda?' Nick asked.

'Always ready with the smart comment, aren't you?' Simon told him.

'Why did you say that, Nick?' Annie asked. 'Was it to help, or was it to score a point?' E is for empathy: being able to suspend judgement and follow the other person's feelings. Even if they are Andy's.

'Go on then,' Greg said, when Ray refused to work with Andy. 'Just show me how you're better, exactly how what you did is not so bad. From whose point of view? Go on, I am genuinely interested.'

There will be no end, ever, to the questions asked. Simon's hands are damp with sweat.

'That's the door to the bathroom,' Simon explains to Susanna, 'Where you come in from just before. There would be another door at the back here, that's the door to the flat. This way,' he points, 'is the window.' His voice sounds bright and tinny, unlike itself. He carries a soft chair from the lounge area of the room where they usually sit, then one of the low tables. 'The TV,' he says, 'My chair.' Then he gets three more chairs and puts them next to each other for the sofa bed, to the right of the TV and the chair, but not obscuring the bathroom door. 'Over there where they all are is the fridge and electric ring,' he says. 'It's night time,' he adds. The others, Annie, the men with their old scars and new haircuts, sit in a loose line, legs akimbo, watching.

'So that's it. Still OK?' he asks Susanna.

'What did we say the fee was? OK, yes, I'm ready,' she says. So that's that: no last-minute reprieve. But with luck, might he still somehow be able to walk through this, immune?

'Come on then,' he says to her, aware of the mixture of smells that reach him when she's this close, make-up, perfume, cigarette smoke, breathmints, beneath them all, a woman's flesh. 'We'll go in.'

He mimes opening the door, she walks through. Anyway, she's nothing like Amanda actually was physically: quite short, but a size fourteen, a sixteen even. She often wore her clothes that bit too tight.

They stand close to the rest of the group as Simon mimes the business with the wine.

'Here – I got some of this in!' he says. *Henkell Trocken,* he suddenly remembers, catching a whiff of it, almost feeling the extra weight of the dark-green bottle as he mimes putting it down.

'Cheers!' she says. Her smile is different, more straightforward, not so shy in its beginnings as Amanda's was. But that doesn't matter, because he can feel now that the past has a life of its own. If it wants to come through, he realises, it will: a word, a gesture, even just the fact of them, man and woman, standing there.

Susanna mimes a sip or two of the drink, then looks at him, waiting. It's just how it was.

'Take all your things off,' he tells her. She goes to the area that's supposed to be the bathroom, turns her back to them and stands still, while Simon sits in the chair and pretends to watch TV.

'I'm in a good mood,' he says. 'I'm thinking about what she might look like and how she's going to really want me and how when she's gone I'll have a good time thinking it over –'

'Let's get this clear,' Pete interrupts, 'you won't fuck her but you'll wank afterwards?'

'Yes. I'm on edge because I do know this is a bit weird, what I'm doing, but on the other hand, right now, it works for me, she goes along with it and there doesn't seem to be any real harm in it.'

'I'm ready now,' Susanna announces. She stands by Simon, about four feet away, hands on hips. Perhaps the trick of this is that she doesn't relate to you as she knows you now, but according to what you were then? Is that how it works? It doesn't matter. He notices his heart gearing up. 'I'm excited,' she says, 'pretty happy. I feel kind of powerful. Sexy. Proud of myself. I look good.'

'Amanda didn't stand like that,' Simon says, turning away from her to look at the group: as a delay tactic it's pretty pathetic, but they let him get away with it.

'Hands just hanging down,' he says. Susanna goes back, walks in again.

'Don't my eyes look nice? I've got lenses! They're the new soft kind. I had to break them in but now I can wear them all day.'

'Simon?'

'Panic. I've lost the advantage. She's out of control and now she'll see me for what I am, she'll be off like that –'

'What's the poor cow got to do to show you she wants you?' crew-cut Pete cuts in.

'Keep going,' Annie says.

'What's the matter? Don't you like them, then?' When Susanna says that, Simon's skin tightens; the hairs on the back of his neck rise. He yells.

'No, they're shite! Take them out! Put your fucking glasses on or phone a cab and get out now!' He looks at Susanna looking back at him, and doesn't really know the difference: either she's gone back into then with him, else he's brought it with him into now, doesn't matter which.

'Why not just do what you're told?' he yells at her.

It's not in the script, but she answers, 'I'm me, not a bit of you!'

'Come on.' She steps forward, bends, and inch by inch, awkwardly, puts her hands in the air above Simon's shoulders then slides them down above his arms, still not touching. Her hands reach his.

'Get off! Get off!' he shouts. Susanna mimes the backwards fall, he follows it with a slow-motion kick. Did he actually do that or not? Or is he adding it in now? He can't be sure.

He's breathing hard as he sits down again. 'I'm turning the TV on now, really loud,' he reports. It was the news, he's pretty sure of that.

'Simon!' Out of the corner of his eye, Simon watches Susanna stand up, walk over and squat down in front of him.

'I won't lower myself. I won't wear glasses for you when I don't want to. I know I've got nice eyes. And if we two are getting nowhere, well, let me tell you, I –'

'Just get out of here!' Simon yells. The words were a message from some rapidly shrinking part of him that knew there must still be a way out of this. They meant: *if you don't, then I . . .* But she didn't realise that; she just didn't know how it was with him.

'I've been out with a bloke from the gym, a few times,' Susanna is saying. Amanda wanted him to see how it was for her; she wanted to communicate, to wake him up, to somehow make things work between them. He can see it. At the same time, his blood is boiling all over again. Look, he'd like to tell her, do this some other way, right?

'I'd much rather it was you, I really would.' Susanna buries her face in her hands. 'I really like you,' she says, 'but maybe you're just some kind of weirdo?' There's nothing from the group now. It's very quiet in the room as Simon jumps to his feet.

'Slow . . .' Annie warns.

'Now,' he says and by a kind of consent, they fall to the floor. He kneels over her. She puts her hands by her sides.

'Simon! Gently,' Susanna says, just as Amanda did. Her eyes are wide open, alert, studying him, and he could count each eyelash if he wanted to; the purplish skin of the lids, frosted with silvery make-up, the tiny capillaries in the bluish whites, the muddle of forest colours in the iris, finally, the pupil: a black hole with its own face in it. Amanda's eyes were brown, dark, simpler. He didn't see himself, not then.

As agreed before, he puts a small cushion on Susanna's upper chest, then places his hands on it, the thumbs above her collarbones, tense, but not squeezing. His arms begin to shake. Susanna shouts, 'No! No!' He sees her mouth, wide and huge, then he shuts his eyes. Susanna arches up, drums her legs on the floor; although he can't see the clock, Simon can feel the seconds passing in the darkness behind his eyes. To begin with they pass far more slowly than the drumming of her feet on the floor, then gradually it is not like that any more. Seventy, seventy-one, seventy-two . . . The seconds are even, equal, clean and will not be hurried. Each one of those seconds, he is beginning to understand, each one of that first minute's worth of seconds, back then, offered him a choice to let go. Now each one of them marks the possibility of doing something different, missed.

Susanna slows down her movements, then lies perfectly still. Simon opens his eyes and turns away from Susanna's face to meet the gaze of the others in the room. Andy is staring at his own feet but the rest of them are all looking right back at him.

He and Susanna get up, shake hands, remind each other who she is, and that this is now, not then; he thanks her.

'I'm beginning to think,' she says, 'that I've been murdered more times than I've had hot dinners!' They brush fluff from their clothes, then help move the blue chairs into a circle again. Susanna sits opposite him, like some twice-removed ghost, or the witness there never was, her legs crossed, her hands in her lap.

Simon? Annie asks. There's a great distance there. He did this, they did not. He's thinking, of course, about Amanda, how it could have been different. Couldn't he have just kept on telling her to go? She might not have. Well, then, so what, he had legs, didn't he! He could have left the bedsit himself, could have walked down the stairs through the big door with the spring attached that made it automatically slam behind, out into the street with the traffic still pulsing by and the drunks and down-and-outs sheltering in doorways . . . He could have gone to a club in Peckham or the late-night shop and got a can of beer. Even later on, at that moment when she said was he some kind of weirdo, he could still have sprung up, shouted anything he wanted but not stayed there, run out, straight down the stairs, kicked the wall, broken the glass in the door as he slammed it . . .

Who knows what would have happened to Amanda and to him if he had managed to do that? They still might have talked on the phone after, though if she had any sense she would have ended it and gone out with the other bloke, but at any rate, what happened would not have been exactly *this*: her dead, him sitting soaked in sweat with a half a dozen other killers, rapists and assorted low-lifes in a concrete bunker of a room.

No, it was before that. It was when she showed him the lenses. He should have done something different then.

'*Bit of a surprise. Take a while to get used to, Mandy.*'

'*They're lovely.*' Suppose he had said that? It's only when Greg hands him a box of tissues that he realises his face is wet.

Time's up. It's like diving: they've been down, now they must come up in stages, pausing to acclimatise. The men stretch, grimace, sigh. Everyone agrees Simon has shown some bottle. He's still very focused on himself, granted, but that's OK at this point.

'You did good, mate,' Ray tells him, clapping him across the shoulders. They're allowed off the chairs. Pete fills the electric kettle, throws teabags into the pot.

'Thing is,' he calls out to Simon, 'you can think of ways round it now, but you were a different kind of bastard back then, weren't you?'

But how? How much different, when he's just been right back there, back to the doing of it, felt the hairs rise on his neck?

29

He doesn't sleep well, loses weight, can't concentrate.

'Look. It's been interesting,' he tells Dr Clarke, 'but I've come to the end of the line with this sexual stuff.' He shrugs. 'Chuck me out if you want.' Clarke meets his eye then glances at the file on his desk. He suggests, after a moment or two, that Simon should take a break. They will get back to work in a month or so, when Simon is ready. They will make a fresh start. He writes a date for this in his diary and says he will send a reminder. At the door, he rests his huge paw on Simon's shoulder.

'Try to get things off your chest in the group,' he recommends. A good plan, perhaps, but the trouble with it is that, since the group on Amanda, Simon has been losing it with words, or with thinking: it's hard to know which. It is increasingly difficult to say what he means. Or maybe what he means is not good enough, is not worth saying? When he reads, sentences fight back against his understanding of them. Mainly he gives up; if he succeeds, he wonders why he bothered. He lies on the bed with his navy blue curtains closed, his eyes searching the shadowy corners of the room while his heart – the thing that keeps him alive whether he wants it to or not – pounds away in his chest.

He finds himself remembering Amanda all the time: things she said, jokes she made. She and her mum sitting on the patio to sunbathe with identical drinks and hats. The moment when she told him about the lenses.

Life goes on. Ray, his arms folded across his chest, his ankles crossed and his eyes screwed very tightly shut, tells the group about sleeping in the bathtub and being shut in the cellar. He has to tell it this way, he explains, so that he can't see people not believing him and taking the piss.

'But, Ray, if you look, you might see us believing you,' Annie suggests, her voice unusually soft. Ray shakes his head and starts to sob, still with his eyes shut. He refuses all comfort and asks if he can get onto the floor and curl up; they let him. It's as if he's turned into the child he used to be. Is it also because of the dark in the cellar that he must keep his eyes so tightly shut? Simon wants to ask Ray about this, but can't.

'Got any ideas?' Ray asks, when the storm has passed through him. He's still on the floor, although sitting up now, red-eyed, looking oddly young despite the lines and stubble on his face. 'Where do I go from here?'

'Very good question,' says Pete, who last week in drama spent forty-five minutes gagged and tied to a chair. Now, he cracks up, laughing: 'Look at it this way,' he tells Ray, it's just gotta get better, has it not?'

Another thing that's happened is that the figment of his imagination Simon called up after Bernadette has abandoned him. She has gone, leaving no message, no explanation and nothing to argue with, even if he wanted to. Seen him for what he is? Come to her senses? Got real? Well, good for her. So must he. He's having a rough patch.

'The fact is,' Simon tells Annie, 'you're on your own with it. You want to beg forgiveness, or you want to point the finger. But there's no one there to be begged or pointed at. You want someone to love you, no matter what, someone to hold your hand and say it will be all right but, not surprisingly, there isn't anyone for that either.'

'Yes. It's hard. Don't withdraw,' Annie advises, leaning forwards in her chair as if to bridge the gap. 'Whatever you do, keep communicating. Try to stay open.' She means well, he knows she cares and she is probably right. But he looks down at his hands, away from those huge eyes the colour of swimming pools.

'Don't forget, we're all in the same boat,' Ray points out, running a nicotine-stained forefinger along the scar on his jaw.

'You mustn't give up,' Greg insists. 'You owe it to yourself to keep on. And to the rest of us, come to that.'

'I'm finding it hard going,' he admits to Mackenzie.

'Well, yes.' Mackenzie, leans back in his chair. 'Yes: the past cannot be undone or be made to go away. Its consequences continue to exist and develop. Perhaps, under the circumstances it is normal, at some point, to experience despair?' Is this supposed to be helpful? It's hard to tell. A couple of minutes pass, during which Simon's eyes don't stray from Mackenzie's face. Then Mackenzie reminds Simon of the contract at Wentham: his despair can be spoken of, drawn, sung about, explored – but it must not be acted out. Suicide and self-harm are not options. Expulsion from the unit is the penalty for attempting either.

'Why?' Simon asks. 'Why aren't they options? Why drag it out?' He remembers Jolly Roger chewing his greasy bit of turkey and saying much the same thing. 'I've murdered a woman.' He checks this first point off on his forefinger, waits for some kind of acknowledgement. It doesn't come, so he continues: 'I can't undo it.' Another finger. 'Even if I did some wonderful heroic deed, would it help Amanda? Or Hazel and Tom or her brother for that matter . . . right? No easy solutions. Agreed. That makes three . . . Well then, Why? What's the point of me?' He slumps back, exhausted by the effort of so much speech. Of course, Mackenzie declines to answer; the two men sit facing each other in their identical chairs.

'Punishment?' Simon asks.

'Is that how you see it?' Mackenzie blinks, swallows. His face is calm. What's underneath? Where is the man? What matters to him? Why is he here?

'What's wrong with a fucking *answer*?' Simon asks. There's a kind of pain in his chest. He bends down, holds his head for a few seconds with his good hand as if shielding himself from a blow. Still no answer. Why doesn't Mackenzie *do* something? Simon unrolls himself, quits the session without offering a hand to shake, not banging the door behind him, but leaving it open, like another question mark.

'Simon!' Mackenzie calls after him, more than a trace of anger in his voice. 'This session is not finished!'

Simon calls Alan – the one who fell off a rock face and finally came back to work wearing a neck brace and using crutches – not a bad bloke, as it turned out.

'Can I talk to Bernadette Nightingale?' he asks. He's thought about this a lot: the next best thing to someone who loves you has got to be someone who you wish loved you even if they didn't, but who all the same did a bloody good job, and once touched you on the shoulder in a certain way that somehow opened everything up. Yes, as it happens, she is also someone whose image he's had sex with in his head, without her permission . . . Given that, could he still talk to her about this life and death stuff?

Yes. He's desperate, sense doesn't come into it. Could? Must.

'I don't know,' Alan says, slowly. 'But, you know, you definitely can talk to me. I'm booked to travel up and visit you the first Wednesday of next month. Do you want me to come sooner? I can, if you want.'

'She was very helpful before. Would *she* visit me? I mean, just the once?' It doesn't sound that unreasonable, now he's said it. 'It's important,' he adds.

'If you send me a letter, I'll forward it,' Alan tells him and it's good to have something to do, a step to take: *Dear Bernadette* – it keeps him going for over a fortnight, until he realises September is almost over and there's been no reply.

One afternoon Philippa from Education comes back into the computer room for a box of discs and finds Simon Austen is still there, staring at the exact same screen she left him with ninety minutes previously, when he outlined for her the magazine contents so far. Two short stories: one true, about a kid running away from home, doing drugs, going under; the other set in a different solar system, where they were doing fine until earthmen arrived and tried to set up a McDonald's franchise. Crossword, a pen-and-ink drawing of a rose, cartoon of the Governor finding a mouse in his soup, four poems, a ramble from the Governor about how proud he was of them all for June's fun sports events in aid of the children's play area in the visitor centre . . . At that point, Simon had just finished entering in a list of the runners' names and how much they each raised. He was just beginning the editorial.

Now, an hour and a half later, he seems still to be on the very same first sentence.

'Are you OK?' she asks. 'You're very pale.'

'Alive,' he points out.

'You're one up on me then,' she says, looking over his shoulder at the screen. 'What about your own pieces, then?'

'I haven't done anything yet. Maybe I won't.'

She pushes some papers aside and sits on a nearby table, a middle-aged woman with thinning salt and pepper hair and a twinkle in her eye.

'You must!' she tells him cheerfully, crossing her ankles. 'I tried the yoga tip last time. I got my feet right over, like it said. Getting them back was another matter – Jon nearly had to call an ambulance crew to get me out of it! Best laugh we'd had in ages!' He returns the smile, but there's no life in it. 'I liked that alphabet idea that you showed me, too,' she says. 'Done any more? Those little essays. A is for appetite, B is for beautiful . . .' Suddenly, he jerks up the T-shirt, exposing the flesh beneath and Bernie's word, COURAGEOUS.

'No touching, now,' he says. The torso he has revealed is muscled but slim, tanned. Her face flares up as she looks at him. From inside the curves of a C and an S his two nipples stare back at her like a pair of sad, puffy eyes.

'You can read me like a book!' he says. 'No offence,' he adds as he rolls the T-shirt down again. 'It's quite a word to live up to. Now I'm stuck on D.'

'Dogs?' Philippa suggests 'Dinner? Look, for heaven's sake

don't stay in here all day. There's no natural light, it'll only make you D-pressed. There, you smiled. Go out and play for a bit.'

After supper, Simon gets himself put on the evening-class list and goes back into Education. While nine guitars start tuning up next door and the pottery teacher slowly explains how to put a handle on to a mug, he opens up his alphabet file, erases the contents, starts over. He ignores the smell of re-re-rolled fag ends in a no-smoking zone, the temptations of the tea break, the terrible near-unison of the guitars and the broken voices singing along. Periodically, the computer interrupts its perpetual hiss and mutters to itself as he instructs it: save.

A, he types, is for answer. Perhaps there will be one. Perhaps not. Answers are shy beasts, terribly hard to find; it may be best not to even look for them. A is also for ambivalence, a word I learned here, and for art, a kind of communication to which some people dedicate their entire lives to the detriment of all else, a religion without a God (see G). Yes, I am A-voiding because more than anything A is for Amanda, who lived her whole life in the same house and liked to laugh and eat and drink and sunbathe in her parents' garden, who remembered everything that had ever happened to her and wanted the ordinary things of life, commitment, closeness, children, a future opening out into who knows what – but I, Simon Austen killed her in a bedsit in New Cross, September 2nd 1979.

B is for Bernadette, from West Cork. Bernadette knew, still knows even, how to handle me. I began to be different. It was like being turned inside out. It was frightening but delicious. I fell in love (see L). I wanted to deliver myself to her whole. But Bernadette did not fall in love with me, she already had that post filled. Dr Max Mackenzie tells me this was not a mature relationship. It was Bernadette who sent me here (see D).

C is for courage, from the French *cœur*, for heart. We see in others what is in fact our own but still I wanted what

Bernadette said and had it tattooed across my chest: an incitement to better things, though now I have lost sight of them.

D is for despair, a shorter word than desperation. It has none of the longer word's potential for dash and glamour. Despair just is and follows you like a great big dog that won't be shaken off. You have to remind yourself it is normal in these circumstances, and then try to forget it is there . . . If I receive any better advice, I'll pass it on next time.

E must be for escape: let me know if you succeed!

Fuck. If you are a man, this means to put your cock inside someone else and move about till you come: maybe both, but first and foremost, you. Also, and often at the same time, it means to humiliate, annihilate. I have discussed this with Max Mackenzie and got nowhere, but the point is, does he never use the word? You can end up feeling like shit but it's not as if I'm the only one.

G: guilt, the condition and the feeling of guilt are separate. You can hear the verdict, guilty, or even plead guilty, and live for years, even a whole life afterwards, without actually having the feeling of guilt. But should it come, you will know it. And G is also for God, who, his representatives say, made everything, and gave his only son as a sacrifice. The blood of this son washes away all our guilt. So, he has plenty of followers, in places like this (see E).

H is for Hazel, Amanda's mother, who used to make sure to have a cake made or bought when I was due to come around. Imagine.

Ice cream. Intimacy.

Justice.

K is for being k-nown. Here, everything has to be known, and you'd better like it, because it's good for you. Another few months in this place and maybe I'll be the psychological equivalent of a flasher, dropping my defences at every opportunity, letting it all hang out whether you want to know me or not?

L is for love, a mystery I stand at the edges of. And letter: I used to be good at them. But now:

Dear Bernadette, Alan suggested I write. I know it is a cheek to ask, but although I have made progress I am currently feeling very low. I feel it might help to talk things over with you, and if you were in a position to visit me here I would be delighted . . .

The best I could do! Crap! No wonder she hasn't replied. Forget the *talk*. It might help just to see her? It might not, but still I want to.

Dear Simon, a love letter would go, *Your eyes look strong and kind at the same time. Sad too. You are the most important person in my life. I trust you completely. I keep your photograph beside my bed and think about you before I go to sleep.*

Murderer.

N is for now: the present tense. I always used to hold that now was the best place to inhabit but since arriving in Wentham, I've lost the knack of staying there. Time is shapeless, flexible. The past floods in and fills us up. I even think sometimes of the distant future, when, depending on how all this goes, I may be allowed out.

Out! It's unimaginable. Out might as well be Mars, but the idea of it does make my heart beat faster all the same.

Please. Prison, aka the Wendy House, Clink, Bucket, Jug, Nick. A second home for some, an only home, even. A way of life. You see the visitors stiffen up as they cross the yard and you know they want to get back Out.

Q is for questions, such as:

But if I got out and there was to be a second chance, can you tell me what kind of life I might have?

What would I do, how would it be?

Do I want it?

Does it matter whether I do or not?

What the fuck? (see A, see F).

The Rs. Regret, remorse, rehabilitation: sufficient experience of the first two is an absolute requirement of the Review Board. How do they measure it? How do I? (See A).

Sex, see fuck. Self, the eye inside.

T, teachers. Ted Kennet. Tasmin. Typewriter. Trouble. Touch. Time.

University, where the clever people go.

V is for Vivienne Ann Whilden, who wanted Joseph Manderville to go to Barcelona with her. I'm still grateful.

Women (over half the human race): difficulties with, attraction to, fear of, rejection by, anger towards, ambivalence concerning, empathy with, cognitive issues relating to, as substitute mother figures, as fantasy objects, guilt feelings towards, ongoing. Also, words. They are failing me.

X marks the spot.

You, whoever you are. If you are. Still there? I can't finish this.

30

'What's going on?' Alan asks. He reaches into the bag slung over the side of his chair, brings out the Thermos, pours out the coffee – real, filtered coffee, black, strong, with plenty of brown sugar already stirred in. He unwraps a KitKat bar, breaks it in half, slides two fingers across to Simon, who nods his thanks, and then just sits, completely still, aware of the rich odours flooding the room. He wants the chocolate, the sweetness, the crunch of the wafer inside, but at the same time, he can't be bothered to pick it up, just as sometimes he wants to say something, but can't actually get his mouth to do the work.

'Look,' Alan says, 'you mustn't be too knocked back by Bernadette's response. She does have a couple of very good excuses, don't you think? Here, look, she sent this along.'

There, in the colour photograph which Alan puts on the table between them, is Bernadette as Simon has never seen her: her hair still dark chestnut but cut in a short, urchin cut, her eyes huge, darkly shadowed. She's wearing some kind of loose, shapeless white blouse. Her smile here is fuller and franker than the smiles he remembers and her breasts appear to have doubled in size. She holds one baby in the crook of her left arm, another nestled in her lap. One is dressed in white, one in blue, but otherwise they're identical.

Such darlings, it says in the letter. Her handwriting pelts across the page, leaning to the right. *It has taken a while to get over the operation and all this is new to me. I really don't think I can manage the trip, but please know that I wish you as ever, the very best, Bernadette.*

'They're moving back to Ireland, apparently,' Alan adds.

'Drink some coffee,' he suggests, and watches Simon obey. 'Mackenzie thinks you're engaged in attention-seeking behaviour,' he continues, 'and the trouble is, Simon, if you continue like this, they can't let you stay here, that's what they're telling me. And since talking is what goes on here and you've stopped doing it, I can see their point,' he says. 'It would be a real shame, you've made progress. What you want to hang on to is that lots of people have a real interest in you. Like me. I was concerned, I got out of bed and drove here today. I mean, it's a job, yes, but I was genuinely worried about you.' Alan checks over his shoulder where Simon appears to be looking: there's a notice pinned to the wall behind the table but the print is far too small for him to be actually reading it. 'Wakey wakey!' Alan says, rapping with his fingers on the table.

Simon shifts slightly in his chair, frowns. He brings up his hand and holds it out over the desk. Alan glares at the hand as if it were some kind of hallucination, clasps it dismissively, then finds that when he lets go, Simon does not. He re-engages, then after a moment manages to release himself. 'OK?' he says, pulling away.

'I know they don't like psychoactive medication here, but you've lost a lot of weight. It can't go on. Do you eat anything at all? Is it just depression? A hunger strike? A reaction to the work you've been doing? Are there things in your head that you are not saying? I guess I'm going to have to go and ask someone else, right?'

Physical work is the best thing. When the group is needed to cope with the first fall of leaves from the silver birches, oak and ornamental maples inside, from the tall beeches and sycamores that grow behind the perimeter fence, he's in there with the rest of them. The dry crunch of the leaves fills his head. Doggedly, he rakes, loads, shifts. They barrow the leaves into huge piles, supposedly to rot down and make a mulch, but unless it rains soon they'll pretty soon be blowing around again . . . The air is crisp enough to bite; it smells of apples and smoke. The sunlight is thickly yellow, as if making up for its weakness with a warmer tint and the men's shadows stretch long in front of them. Their breath steams; they try to blow rings with it, take their time, muck around. Andy lies in one of the piles and lets himself be buried in leaves, then springs out of the pile just as Pete tips his barrow up.

'Fucking leaves!' Pete says, once he's recovered. 'If I was in charge of this place I'd cut these trees down and save everyone's breath.' They try to score hits with handfuls of thrown leaves, which always fall short. When they go back in, Steve puts his arm across Simon's shoulders. 'OK mate? Give us a sign.'

'Leave that idiot alone!' Ray yells at him. 'Who cares if he talks or not? His life, isn't it? You're just playing his game.'

'Spot on!' Nick says, brushing fragments of leaf from his sweats.

Behind the gatehouse glass, an officer presses the button that opens the final door. Annie and Greg walk out either side of Alan. The sun has gone now, but even so, everyone feels the relief of being out.

'I think he wants to be held,' Annie says as they walk towards the car park. 'Literally, I mean. He's suffering. If he asked, we could do it. In the group. But you can't just grab hold of a man like that, well, in my position, I can't, but I wish somebody would.'

In the courtyard Simon is settled on the bench, head back, eyes closed, his face to the square of yellow tinged sky. From deep in the wing, he can hear the preparations for serving the evening meal. Voices, laughter, the clatter of dropped saucepan lids. TV news and advertisement jingles blare out from Pete's room.

An officer takes a few steps into the courtyard, stops. 'I'll give you five minutes to get in for supper, OK now?' It's David, the bloke with the earring. Simon keeps his eyes closed and he keeps them that way even after he hears the first strange noise, a faint dry creak above him, and feels the disturbed air whisk past his cheek. But when two distinct, faint splashes reach him, he opens up: there's a tall, hunched bird standing just a couple of feet away in the pool closest to the reeds. Its long legs are yellow, the rest of it grey and black and white, and seems for a moment almost as big as he is, like some strange kind of alien in a suit. Its neck stretches up, bearing the small, sharp head aloft and a pair of sharp yellow ringed eyes scan the water close by. The beak is long and pointed. Slowly, the bird raises one foot and then slips it down into the water again, this time without any noise at all. You're fishing, he thinks, just as David comes back in, crunching efficiently over the stones, rattling his keys. The bird twists its neck 180 degrees and glares at them both for a moment, utters a low, angry shriek before taking a few clumsy steps and then hauling itself up and out of the courtyard, its neck neatly folded down.

'Mr Heron a mate of yours, then?' David asks.' Come on now, I've got to lock this up.' Simon levers himself from the bench, then buckles and falls to his knees.

'I thought he was going to say something,' David reports to the orderlies who are carrying Simon to the hospital on a stretcher. They pause, while he unlocks a pair of doors. 'But then he dropped. I did more or less catch him.'

'Horrible colour, isn't he?' comments one of the orderlies. 'People say white as a sheet, but it's not the kind of sheet you'd want to lie on.' It's sweltering in the hospital wing and the lighting is very bright. They get him half undressed and onto a bed. 'What the hell's he got written on him?' says the talkative orderly. 'Put a decent woman off, that.'

'Get some fluids into him,' the doctor orders. Simon's eyelids glide halfway up and he looks out, unseeing or uncaring. 'Bed rest. Three meals a day,' the doctor says, adding over his shoulder as he walks away: 'snacks, vitamin pills.'

'Soon fix you up!' the orderly adds, supplying the bedside manner. The three of them gaze at the man on the bed in front of them, the vivid white skin, tight over bones that are beginning to show through too much; the words, all but the one, inscribed in uneven, makeshift letters. David pulls the covers up and goes to write an incident report.

31

He dozes in a blur of white noise (no radios allowed) and wakes up only to eat. Two days later, he's back on the wing. They could have transferred him to a special observation cell, but then again, it might have set him back. He is driving everyone right up the creek, David tells him, and if he goes on like this he'll have to go, but they, or some of them, want to give him a chance.

Saturday on the wing is too noisy and distracting for sleep. He tries to settle down with a book and the TV on without the sound but people keep coming by to look at him, to crack a joke and try to catch him out: 'Back from the dead, eh? Better here, is it?' It's like some kind of fairy story, in which the king offers a prize to the man who can make his daughter smile. They come from far and wide to take their chance: 'Did you get a new tongue sewn in then? Did they give you dog or cat?' 'What kind of dumb bastard are you, then? Ha! All right, mate, just joking! Good to have you back on board ship again . . .' He gives out a few smiles. He's definitely getting stronger. Even though he turns down football practice, he could have almost done it. Later, when these idiots give up on him, he might try some stretches, a couple of easy poses, things he hasn't done for weeks, even months. And surely, at some time not too far away, he'll start talking again. It'll come back.

Meanwhile, pictures flicker on the TV screen: an old black-and-white movie from the forties, women in tight skirts and elaborate blouses, shoulder-length, curled hair that doesn't move with the rest of them. Men in suits, the bad guy smoking in his dressing gown. Then, the ads, saturated with colour. Washing powder, shampoo, banks, an amazing black horse galloping across apple-green fields. News: Princess Diana and Aids. An IRA bomb in a barracks in Kent. He keeps the sound just below properly audible, a murmur, punctuated with strains of music.

'You had me worried, all right.' David leans in the doorway. 'You went down like a pack of cards.' He walks over and crouches down beside the bed. 'This came while you were on your rest cure,' he says, proffering a large brown envelope. Inside it are a picture postcard and another, smaller envelope, flecked pale blue on white. Simon nods and tucks both items into the back of the book he can't get started on. 'Thanks' would help him out right now and bring things to a close, but he can't quite rise to it.

'Someone's taken the trouble,' David says, 'Read it. See what she's got to say. Go on.' Simon's inner voice is out of practice too, or else it would be saying something like 'Bollocks.'

Ten o'clock comes, then eleven; he can't sleep, probably because he's been doing nothing for days. It's very windy outside, the kind of wind you can not just hear but almost feel, pushing against the walls, getting worse, rather than better, making it impossible to concentrate. He closes *The Savage God*, and the letter and card fall out, so he picks them up and looks over the card again. It's a picture of some jungle; rising out of it is a stepped building made from greyish stone. A string of tiny people in bright clothes are on their way up to its flat summit. He admires the sheer density of the palm trees surrounding the building, the bright blue sky. It's like something in a film . . . Fancy just up and going to a place like that! He turns it over. There's a stamp with some bald bloke on, MEXICO, and the postmark says August 13th. Mexico? What's T for trouble doing there? And before Simon knows it, he's reading.

Stunning place – huge fruit and palm trees, fat white lizards running on the ceilings. It seems harmless enough and he closes his eyes a moment to picture what she describes. There wasn't even an envelope, he rationalises, it was right there for anyone to see, so he might as well continue. *Really gross insects that take off in front of you like jump jets, straight up, as big as lobsters, brilliant like butterflies. Am here with Mum, her new partner Leo, my friend Jo, wish I could show it to you! Miles of fantastic beach! Jo and I nearly got drowned, Tasmin.*

Who is Jo? Simon registers a twinge of curiosity, along with a faint feeling of pleasure that things seem to have turned around for Tasmin. So, he thinks, End of Story. Good. Outside, the wind drops for a moment, then roars again. He opens the curtains and watches for a few moments the agitated shrubbery in the courtyard and then it is only at the last moment, when he goes to file both items in the shoe box he keeps on his desk, that he notices on the top left corner of the blue-flecked envelope, written in neat capital letters, the word EMERGENCY.

Hang on! Something inside him says. He hears, but all the same, takes the letter back to the bed, sits down, unaware, now, of the storm outside. He reaches in, takes the letter out. He holds it, still folded for a moment or two. *Emergency*, he tells the warning voice. How can I ignore that? Even now he could still turn back, but he won't, because, he realises, this feeling of stepping into another world, the whisper of a voice coming from elsewhere, even if it is an emergency, is just exactly what he wants:

> Simon, Like I said before, I am very sorry about what my dad did. I know it's hard for you to reply to me, and maybe you can't? Maybe they don't even give you these letters, but I think even just knowing you *might* be there reading this will make me feel as if I am not so alone trying to work out what to do. The thing is, I am pregnant & have got to make up my mind what to do for the best.

Christ! The word leaps from his mouth and into the cell, surprising him.

I got pregnant the same day I last wrote to you! Also on that same day Jo and I nearly drowned because we went out beyond the waves and there was an undertow. No one could hear us, we swam for our lives and we made it. Then at night we had dinner and afterwards in the dark I was sitting at this table that was literally on a platform right over the creek with the forest all around watching the giant moths and writing cards. The owner of the place, Manuel, came back and sat down next to me. He asked could I hear the sea and I stopped very still to listen, and he kissed me. I ended up going into a spare studio with him. The sexual part of this was really incredible, nothing like it was with the boys I did it with when I was in that phase a while back. And I liked him because he had made the place so beautiful. Now I hate him but I don't want that to get in the way, do you understand? He said there had been a wonderful thing between us. He said he and his girlfriends were free with each other and lived for the moment . . . I know this was a load of shit but there was still this kind of magnetism between us, and you could hear the sea now and all the animals rustling outside, it was fantastic, so I ignored that feeling and we did it again and fell asleep. When I woke up, he'd gone and later, he just treated me like any other guest. Maybe you think I'm a real idiot.

'You are a rich girl,' he told me when I phoned the hotel from England. 'You can pay to make your life how you want it.' I just hung up.

I've done the test three times. I don't want to destroy a baby just because I'm afraid of what people might think of me or say but even though I am fifteen now I don't know if I am really mature enough to look after a baby properly. People say it ruins your life, but then my life seems already a bit of a mess and I haven't got any definite plans except to travel and maybe a baby could just come along with me? But maybe I would just get stressed out. I don't know what to do for the best. I am writing because even though you only wrote to me a few times (please believe me how sorry I am that I did lie to you about my age), I trusted you straight away and there is no one else who can help me decide because Aunt Jay would have to tell Mum and Dad and I don't have many friends except Jo and she just panics. So I will wait as long as I can, in case I hear from you. Please write back.

He checks the postmark: almost a month has passed since she sent it, from Edinburgh, on September 15th. August 12th was the day of the postcard, the night it happened. If, that is, it happened: remember, he tells himself, she lied before. It's a definite possibility.

He stands in the cell a few moments, listening to the wind. He's alert, feeling clearer-headed than he has for weeks. Obviously, he needs to get the whole picture. He gathers the unread letters, arranges them in chronological order. The first, almost incoherent, was a note inside a Christmas card, sent from Oxford: she was very sorry about what had happened and would wait for him to be ready to be with her. She was in a prison just like him, but she was determined to escape . . .

Then, a brief scrawl saying just that she was on the run, from Edinburgh, and offering best wishes. In April, a long letter folded inside a greetings card, sent from York. It explains in detail how she had spent three months in a private mental hospital full of messed-up rich kids and detoxing junkies, walked out, got caught two weeks later, taken paracetamol of all dumb things, but had her stomach pumped in time. Back home, her father let slip that he had read her letters, which led to a big family row. Her mum, Olivia, walked out. Since then, she has been going to a fancy co-ed boarding school, *expensive but still much cheaper than the loony bin*! Olivia visited her there in a new car and announced that her father had already moved to Manhattan – new job, new wife to be; she was going to get the Chiswick house but wanted it completely remodelled.

I'll be grown up by the time they sort themselves out. For now, I'm staying with my Aunt Jay in York. Actually, I like her. She and I agree nether of them are honest with each other, and for sure, neither of them know what Love *is* and meanwhile, I just got my hair done in this really great asymmetrical cut and I came off the anti-depressants after I read about them being addictive and actually stopping you from dealing with your real problems, so I think I'm doing pretty well considering, my hands still shake a bit sometimes but it's really OK. Mum keeps my money topped up. I can get whatever I want from the university library, where Jay works. I'm reading this amazing book called *Freedom*, about how there are infinite possibilities. But Freedom is, actually, commitment which most people don't realise. Jay says I should decide what to go for at university. But I'm not interested. You can always read the books . . . I want to travel, I mean, *really* travel. See things as they are.

He looks at the card, a large abstract of circles in red and ochre and black. He quite likes it and finds he can easily imagine her taking her time to choose it in some art gallery shop, then moving over to the queue at the till, turning heads as she goes: in his mind, a tall, white-faced girl with jet black hair in a space-age cut, enormous grubby jeans belted around her waist, like all the kids on TV are wearing now, plus maybe a bright orange loose-knit sweater, blue eyes, long fingers. A girl-woman, pregnant, just as Bernie must have been the last time he saw her for real, when they stood opposite each other, not touching, and decided he would come here.

So, he decides, she's not lying. Where does that leave him? Amanda, Vivienne, Tasmin, Bernadette – he feels as if they are all of them waiting, watching to see what he will do, as if this were some kind of test. Doing *nothing* isn't actually possible. He pulls the blanket over, turns out the light, hears the cover on the viewing slot on his door click open, click shut.

32

'Planning on talking, are you?' Johnny Lyndon asks, as Simon signs his name in the register.

'Thanks,' Simon replies, as he pockets the green phone card in its transparent plastic sleeve. The voice that comes out is a little quieter than before, but perfectly serviceable.

In the queue, he has plenty more time to think the call over. The thing about phoning is that it's immediate; also, it isn't writing a letter, which is what he agreed not to do. All the same, it is a crazy thing to be doing, unpredictable, distracting, not to speak of the fact that someone in an office somewhere might well be listening in and even if not it's probably being taped. But is there any alternative? File the letter and try to forget it? Get Alan over to talk it through, and you're talking a week, plus what does he know anyhow? This is an *emergency*. It's the weekend; so with any luck she will be at the aunt's house.

'Go to the Citizens' Advice,' the man currently on the phone is shouting into the handset. 'I'll call you tomorrow. Keep safe now . . .'

Simon has given up his turn twice so as to be last in line with no one listening in, but now he slides the card into its slot and presses out the long sequence of number keys. It rings five times and then a woman's voice says, 'Jay here.' She sounds so crisp and so close that it's shocking and for a split second, his mouth almost balks at the job.

'Afternoon. I'm trying to get hold of Tasmin.' He coughs into his hand. 'Is she around?' If not, he'll promise to call back. He'll say he's an old friend and please to tell her he called.

'Just a minute.' The receiver goes down.

'Who is it?' another voice, softer, younger, asks as the line explodes into life again.

'Tasmin?'

'Yes. Who – ?' Her voice is slow, with plenty of inflection. The accent's very posh. It feels as if her lips are right next to his ear.

'This is Simon,' he tells her. She must be able to hear his heart crashing about in his chest.

'You *phoned*?'

'I just got your letter,' he says. 'The Mexican bloke was a bit of a bastard, eh?' He lets the words stand unmodified, even though they make him squirm. He shuts his eyes. It's possible to imagine that they are standing each side of a thin partition; they could even be standing in the same blacked-out room. 'You OK?' he asks.

'It's been driving me cra-azy. I feel better now, though.' She lowers her voice to a half-whisper. 'I can't get over that you've called. It's just the most amazing thing! But I did know there was this connection between us. I was sure you didn't want to cut off like that just because –' She sucks in a breath. 'Oh – sorry,' she says, 'I'm going to cry –'

'We haven't got long,' he says, ignoring the way her voice loses itself in a gasp, the swallowing sounds, sniffs. Again he checks the corridor both ways: no one.

'Look, I'm in a different place, they forward stuff but it takes time. So I've just read your letter. I wasn't going to, but I opened it because it said *emergency*. I agreed I wouldn't write, but because you put that, *emergency*, I've phoned, OK?'

'I feel so alone,' she says.

'Tasmin,' he interrupts, used now, to saying the fancy-sounding name, 'you've got a problem, right? You asked about what to do, right?' He glances over his shoulder again. 'I can't tell you what's best to do. I can't even tell you what I'd do because I'm not you. I'm not even a woman, right?' She cuts in, something about he's been through a lot and how much she values his opinion. He ignores it, presses on:

'Look: this is from the horse's mouth: my mum couldn't

cope and the outcome wasn't good for either of us. She killed herself when I was small. I've ended up here, OK, I'm right now, maybe making a bit of sense of things, but someone else is dead, right? See what I'm driving at?'

'Well,' she says 'I think –' He interrupts again.

'Second, well, OK, if you lived in village in the jungle you'd have three by now, but you don't. You've had an easy life. It'll be hard to be on call 24/7 and all that. You probably are too young. That's just an opinion, because you asked. I could be wrong.'

There's a pause. She says absolutely nothing, makes no sound of any kind, then suddenly tells him: 'I've already got a bit of a tummy, you know. No one notices because I'm so skinny to start with but –'

'I've said what I can,' he tells her. 'And, you need to find someone out there to talk to . . .' He hears her sigh.

'I do really like you, Simon,' she tells him. 'Will you call me again? Or can I call you?'

'No!' he says. 'I'm in a special unit, doing therapy. I'm supposed to be honest about everything. Just like you recommended! Well, sometimes I think it is a waste of time, but maybe I'm getting a result. I don't want to mess things up.' She considers a while.

'Don't you want to know what I decide?' she asks.

'No,' Simon tells her. 'No. it's got to be End of Story, Tasmin.' His new voice is that bit gentler than the old one but even so, she bursts into tears again. It's a fact that women do cry a lot, he reminds himself. It doesn't mean they'll kill themselves. Ten minutes later they can feel fine, better for it. All the same, he can't leave things like this, feels he's got to give her something more. What?

'Look, it doesn't matter what you choose,' he says, his voice full of a sudden, desperate energy that comes from some place he doesn't know about. 'Whatever it is, stick to it, stick up for it. You can't know what's right, but whatever you do, it's yours. Tasmin? You there?'

'Yes,' she says. She's crying up there in York and down here on the east coast his shirt is soaked: sweat not tears, but for a moment you could be fooled about that. It's too much. He's done his best, hasn't he? He didn't ask for this, for fuck's sake!

'I'm going,' he tells her. 'Best of luck, now.' It's as Simon hangs up that Nick passes, wearing his latest designer sweat pants and shower shoes, carrying a not-bad-looking towel and a bottle of fancy shower gel.

'Well!' he says with a grin. 'Gotcha! It's not you can't talk, just you won't talk to *us* eh?'

'Emergency,' Simon says, trying to stare the other man out. At the same time, he's thinking, suppose she goes and does something stupid? Should he ring her back and say, don't? But then –

'Don't tell *me* about your girlfriend that you never had before,' Nick says, as he sets off, again whistling between his teeth. 'Group business, ain't it?' Simon thinks briefly of the blurry, drugged-up peace that swaddled him in the hospital wing, but it's too late for that. He's gone and done something and now he'll be in it up to his neck.

33

'I don't feel safe. Not if there are important things I don't know about someone and where he's coming from –' Nick makes a brief gesture, both hands fisted to his heart.

'Bollocks!' says Steve.

'Safe?' Simon yells. 'Where's that idea coming from? Who *ever* feels *Safe*? Am I supposed to feel *safe* right now?

'It said *emergency*.' He looks round at the rest of them, their hunched shoulders, fisted hands, their legs akimbo, or wound round chair legs, or thrust out ahead, their feet tapping the floor; their necks bent at odd angles, their tight jaws . . . today everyone is sallow and hollow-eyed except for Nick, whose eyes glitter with excitement, or, the rumour is, smack smuggled in by his sister on her monthly visit . . . But surely it's obvious, surely they can all see his point?

'I was going to tell you all along,' he tells them, an almost, a *possible* truth, who knows, he might have, probably would have, except that he hadn't got so far as working it out before Nick came up on him like that, so his hand was forced and now he's gone the whole fucking way, told them all about it, and why. Mistake. 'But,' he repeats, 'because of that, the word *emergency*, I had to act.'

'That's where you went wrong, mate,' Pete tells him, jabbing the air with his blunt, nail-bitten forefinger. '*Impulsive*, see. Not good.' He grins, creases forming in the stubble around his mouth. 'All the same, it's not drugs, violence or sex is it? It's a *phone call*! So we're not talking chuck-out, just making sense of what's going on with our editor here, right?'

'*Nothing* is going on!' Simon says. 'Is it my fault she wrote to me after she was told not to? Is it my fault she got knocked up? What would you lot have done?' No one answers this.

'Not been exactly *transparent*, have you?' Nick says 'Because what *is* this about getting the letters and just *not reading* them? Do you think we're morons? How are we to know you haven't been on the blower to this underage girl every single day? I mean, we've gotta ask, haven't we? What else aren't you telling us? With respect.'

'Has anyone *ever* seen me on that fucking phone?' Simon says. Stay in the chair, he reminds himself, gripping the edge of it, keep going. They'll see it in the end . . .

Ray grinds out his roll-up, surveys the room. 'Sounds like he did a good job. Plus it got him out of his dumb thing, which was a wind-up. Why can't we leave it at that, or do you have another agenda here Nick – like you need to be top of the class, or something?'

'Top of the *grass*,' Steve suggests.

'Is this payback for that warning you had? Or do you want Si out of the way because he's on your case? With respect . . . Because the rest of us just want to get on with what we're here for, right?'

'Well . . . can't we just –' Andy comes through after trying to get a word in for the past ten minutes, 'can't we just say: idiot, you should have told someone, don't do it again?'

'Well,' officer David gathers himself up and turns to Simon, 'maybe, but we do have to work from a position of trust here. So is there anything else we should know, Simon?'

It actually doesn't occur to Simon as he glares around at the room that there is anything else he could add.

'What more do you want? A blood sample? There's others that would be better used on, let me tell you,' he says, and the room goes quiet, alert; everyone sits that bit straighter in their chairs.

'Is that an accusation, Simon?' Greg asks 'Are you saying that someone here is using drugs? Please be specific.'

'I'm saying, it might not be a bad idea to do a test.' Oh, it's familiar, this feeling of going for broke, familiar, and exhilarating at the same time . . . Who knows how many of them are having a little smoke or dipping the tips of their tongues into whatever it is that Nick's sister brings? Maybe everyone's in on it and they'll all hate him now, but why not go the whole way, seeing as he's started? He looks Greg right in the eye.

When they all rush over to the tea urn, Simon stays put, sits in the empty circle, grafted to the chair. He sees Nick coming over to him, carrying his mug. Simon's foot is stuck out and he decides that he'll just leave it there, and that since Nick isn't looking down there's a good chance he'll trip.

'You cunt,' Nick yells, saving himself just from hitting the floor, but not from the coffee. 'The bastard tripped me!' Hot liquid steams from his legs and crotch. Simon gets to his feet, just in case. 'You should look where you're going,' he says. Oh, he's really done it now: Nick's ripping his pants down, got to get cold water on it, he says, and then the rest of them are sent off to exercise with the promise of a special meeting in the morning.

'Look,' Mackenzie says on the telephone to Greg, 'we have to take this very seriously. None of this stuff about the girl was disclosed. I've looked and there's just a very brief reference in his file to a discussion with the Governor at the last institution after a complaint was made by the girl's father. It's been overlooked.'

'All the same, he's not here for molesting teenagers,' Greg points out.

'He's here for murdering a shy twenty-year-old girl who still lived with her parents . . . Don't you think she could be described as rather child-like?' Mackenzie suggests. 'Why shouldn't he move in that direction? A vulnerable girl like Tasmin could be very attractive to someone who needs to have the upper hand. I think we all have to agree about that. A relationship like this could well start off in a benevolent, rescuing form, but later, it might begin to follow old patterns. This has to be taken very seriously indeed.'

★

After lunch, they turn over his cell. They're polite about it and do a tidy job, purposeful, no dogs, no taking the bed to bits or throwing stuff around. Derek stands next to him while David and Johnny Lyndon look inside his books, confiscate the shoe box full of letters, two exercise books, some papers to do with the magazine, and the typewriter.

'Those letters, I want them back. They're not even just mine. They belong to the people that wrote them too, it's their privacy as well, isn't it?'

'Yes, well,' Derek says soothingly. His greying hair has been cut to within a couple of millimetres of its existence. He peers at Simon through new bifocals. 'I see the point you're making. But mail can be read at any time, you know.' Simon insists on being taken to the office to fill in an application.

'I want to see Welfare. And I want to see the Governor, like *now*,' he says, filling out his name and number in capitals. His voice echoes in the unusually quiet corridor. Nature of complaint? Lack of fairness, he writes. 'How long will this take?' he asks. Well, it could be a couple of days or it could be a week. *A week?*

In fact, it's half an hour later at 3 p.m. They call it a conference, and it takes place in one of the rooms on the therapy wing. His box of letters is on the table. Everyone's read them. Everybody knows how he pretended to be someone else and how many times he wrote the letters to get them right. Max Mackenzie, Greg and David, who ran the morning meeting, plus Annie, a probation officer from Welfare and the Governor, Mr Honeywell.

'It's clear enough from what she says herself that she wasn't getting any answers from you. That's not the point.' Mr Honeywell looks weary, his greying hair smoothed to the sides of his head shines in the fluorescent glare; his jacket is undone, his collar and tie have been loosened, his body slumps in the chair. 'The point here is that we have a rule of full disclosure. We're supposed to know about all of your outside contacts. These other letters –' He waves at the box. 'Clearly there was in the past a breach of prison rules, not to speak of wilful deception – and now you have kept it to yourself and acted deviously and impulsively, not consulting any of the team. Then, of course, there is the incident with Nick Berryman.'

'Nick Berryman hates my guts and is trying to get me out of here,' Simon states. 'OK, I shouldn't have left my foot out, but that's the score.'

'Dr Mackenzie has some very serious concerns. We have to ask, is this the best place for you?' Mr Honeywell says. 'We don't like to use conventional discipline tools here in the unit, so if you behave in a way that warrants them . . .' He sighs. 'Maybe someone else can get the message across better than I can?'

'Simon,' Annie says, in perfect Barry-speak, 'it's not about the rights and wrongs of the call, it's about whether you can show us that you can hold back on your first response to a situation, reflect, ask for advice.' They're all staring at him like he was some really dumb kid in a class, but all their lives depended on him doing one thing right for once. Whereas the fact is, there's just one of him and he has to get his point across to a whole class of dumb kids.

'You're telling me I was supposed to show her letter around, explain it all, get it voted on . . . or talk to some stranger from Welfare about it, or get hold of Alan, wait *even longer*, till he could come and visit?'

'Why not? And have you asked yourself why did you find this appeal so irresistible?' Mackenzie asks. Just those few words from him are enough to make Simon lose control of his voice, make it come out in something like a growl.

'It was already a *month* late!'

'Why assume we would have stopped you?' Annie asks, her turquoise eyes drilling into him.

'This is doing my head in,' he tells her, shaking his head, looking away. 'Did you do the piss test yet?' he asks. No one answers. Two wrongs don't make a right, etc.

'I am available this afternoon,' Mackenzie says. 'If you'd like to explore this.' Like hell! Instead, he sits in his room looking out through the window at the pond, thinking how he hates it at Wentham, how basically they are brainwashing him and he's supposed to abandon every last shred of himself and be rebuilt according someone else's plan and not one of them would stand for it if they had to stand in his shoes . . .

He remembers the feeling after the phone call: a satisfaction because he did what she asked of him, pure and simple. It wasn't like Vivienne and Joseph Manderville, where he shot himself in the foot by being someone else. It was different again to talking with Bernadette, because it wasn't about his problems and he wasn't the one being helped. It was her, and he did his absolute best, under the circumstances, right? Annie might be right that now he's contacted her, Tasmin may not leave him alone. Could be a problem. But there's nothing he did that strikes him as *wrong*. They're all talking arse, right up the bum-tree; if that's how it is, if they want to believe someone like Nick over him, well, they're idiots, right? And he'd be better off elsewhere, some normal nick where you just go head down and plod through your time, just keep *saying* you're sorry instead of having to feel every bit of it for real all the time and be turned inside out and try to actually do different . . . Why push against the tide? Why be messed up some well-meaning but half-trained psychobabbling idiots with their own problems plus a load of other offenders including nonces and a good sprinkling of actual die-hard psychos?

Just as he's almost convinced himself, some other part of him thinks: it's different here, isn't it, though? It's something new. Maybe I've started to move along.

Well you can keep on *moving along*! he tells himself. No problem there! You've got the plan and the tools now, haven't you? You know the books, they're all in the library. You know a bit about yourself, your *id* and your *ego*, your *introversion*, *voyeurism* and *erotophobia*, your *lack of attachment* and *stunted emotional growth*, your *buried needs for affection and connection* and *desire for total dependence masquerading as the complete opposite*.

You've got a grip on that little lot, haven't you now? So you won't slip back. Actually, you don't need this place. You can work something out. Alan will help and you'll get on just fine that way . . . Plus, if you leave now you won't have to go through that pure bullshit meeting tomorrow, forty cons watching you justify sticking your foot out in front of Nick, yakking on about whether it was *actual violence* or not.

Why let the lying bastard squeeze me out?

Why let him force you to stay?

It's too much. He thinks back again to the phone call, goes over it phrase by phrase, remembers the swooping of her voice, the posh vowels, how she started to sob.

'It doesn't matter what you choose, just stick with it,' he said to her. So, he tells himself: you, you too, just choose, then get on with it. He looks at the pond, which reflects an evenly grey sky, blank, unhelpful, from which, long weeks ago, the heron descended . . . He can't decide.

'Got a coin you can toss for me?' he asks officer Derek, who does the job, lifts his hand to reveal: tails. He's going, then. 'Thanks, mate,' he says. The door closes. A great heaviness falls over him, like a cloak of lead.

'I'll stay,' he decides.

In the morning thirty-eight men, all the groups in the wing, are crowded into the biggest room.

'This place is shite,' Nick snarls. 'It's full of beasts and pillow-biters, drama queens, a real man can't stick it here!' The test was positive and two others from one of the other small groups have attempted to avoid punishment by admitting in advance of tests to sampling what he had.

'That test was fixed,' Nick says. 'People here want me out of the way because I tell it how it is . . .' But he's had his chances and the focus of the meeting has shifted completely. Simon makes an apology for sticking out his foot, and that's that . . . Nick's gone the next day. It's enough to make you think that some old man in the sky is lending a helping hand, that justice actually exists.

'You think so?' Ray tells Simon. 'Don't ever forget, you've made an enemy and until he drives someone to kill him, he's still around. And also, don't ever forget, this place isn't the real world.' That's true, but Simon's on a roll and even forty-five minutes with Mackenzie can't bring him down.

Does he have anything to say about the letters? He most certainly doesn't like them being read, they're personal. What was he trying to achieve when he wrote them? He was trying to have relationships with women. Why did he have to assume an other identity in order to do that? Isn't it obvious? No, he won't spell it out. No, he doesn't intend telling the group about that side of things. Because it's irrelevant. He doesn't do letters any more, it turned out to be more trouble than it was worth. He just wants his letters back is all. Why? He just wants to have them. Because they were sent to him. Does he read them often? Never.

'What do you think will happen if you continue to refuse to co-operate?' Mackenzie asks. The two of them sit for some time in a heavy silence, during which Simon finds himself thinking how Mackenzie just never gives a millimetre and how the only time he has ever given him a straight answer to a straight question was that one time when he said despair was normal. He has never been keen on the man, but now it's getting serious. The feeling of disliking him is like having a burden to carry. A stone, a rock – about the size of a human head. Maybe bigger, even. Its weight surprises him. He has to cart it up here with him every time and sit it on the table between them. Still, it's only once a fortnight and just about another eight minutes to go. He shifts in the chair, drums his fingers on its arm.

'I do co-operate,' he says. 'It's just that you and I don't get on.'

'Think about it,' Mackenzie says. 'If you were me, what would you do?' So he doesn't. Can't. Won't.

34

'Let me tell you why this is going to be a waste of time,' Simon tells them all. 'One, because I know I can stop it any time. Two, I can never feel it as big as it was. Three, we're leaving out the *pain*, for chrissake . . . I blotched it, it *hurt*.' He sits still, but his arms and hands slice the air in sharp gestures, a kind of angry ballet. 'And – four – this whole thing is sick: who do we think they are, trying to get inside some poor woman's head even when she's dead?' The rest of the group stare back at him, watching as much as listening. He's sitting there in just a pair of boxers, because that's what they agreed. It does make a difference. He can feel the air on his skin and he knows everyone is reading him. Outside, it's a day of spasmodic winds and blustery rain, the bare trees outside whipping in the wind then freezing suddenly still.

'It's going to be me, not her, isn't it?' he says. 'Because you can't actually get inside someone, can you? Even if they are there to help. When you communicate, you guess someone is feeling something, you check it out, they come back to you, you listen, et cetera, but with this, it's just going to be fantasy, isn't it? You can't get it right when someone is not there to correct you, when they are *dead*.' His hands meet in front then move apart to suggest a horizontal line. 'Is that the point? Are you just trying to show me that she's dead? Because I know that already . . . You can't force me to do this.'

'No,' Grey says, 'we can't.'

'So?' Annie asks.

'I'm scared,' Simon admits, because now, after all this time, he knows where she's coming from when she asks him something like that: it's an invitation. She wants to rebuild something out of what's been destroyed. It's a huge and probably impossible project, a team effort; it might take more than one generation: that's what she said in her article. 'What I said is true,' he says, 'but yes, I'm scared. Bear it in mind, will you?' He rises suddenly to his feet, carries his chair over to where it is needed.

If Nick hadn't gone, Simon thinks suddenly, sod's law would have put him sitting right in that chair where Ray is right now. A blessing to count, though Ray did ask if he could smoke, so now a thin, blue-grey plume unwinds itself slowly up from Ray's right hand. He's not actually dragging on the thing, it just hangs there between two nicotine-stained fingers. He narrows his eyes as he says:

'Take those out or get out of here.' Simon steps forward touches Ray's shoulders. Ray exhales, glares at him.

'Get off!' Ray shouts. 'Get off!' He does anger well: it's a release for him, he's said, it's a bottomless pit, he can always find more: white-knuckled fists, burning eyes, clenched teeth, tight jaw, the genuine article. With Ray bearing down on you, you wouldn't move to save your life; you'd know it was, basically, over.

'Now!' Ray yells, as he springs up, his face beaded with sweat. 'Fall!' he yells. Simon goes down, Ray throws himself back in the chair, gripping its arms, his eyes drilling into the space ahead of him where the TV was. Silence compacts the room. Simon wants to stay where he is, he wants to get out of the rest of it. You were right, Amanda, he thinks, but why did you pick this moment to have it all out and say your piece?

No reply. She did it, is all. He pushes up onto his hands and knees, crawls over to where Ray sits. When Amanda did this, her cheeks and mouth were loose with shock and her eyes would not leave his face, they were huge and dark, hurt one moment, furious the next. Not afraid, though. Proud, in fact. He forces himself to say her words.

'I won't lower myself. I won't wear glasses for you when I

don't want to. I've got nice eyes. And if this thing is going nowhere, well, I do get –'

'Just fuck off out of here, you cunt!' Ray barks, spinning round. But Amanda continued; so must he.

'I've been out with a bloke from the gym, just a few times – but we haven't done anything, really we haven't . . . I'm just saying this, because I'd much rather it was you, I really would –' Simon reaches his hand out towards Ray. The gesture takes him further than the words: what it is to want someone else to understand, to see who you are.

'Get off me!'

They're on to the floor, it's slow-mo, symbolic stuff now. Ray doesn't put weight on him, or hold him down; he has a rubber quoit as a prop, something to grip. Something in Simon gives a sick lurch when he looks up at Ray, whose face is a grid of lines, unseeing, apparently unhearing, who spits his breath in and out between bared and gritted teeth. The sweat runs off him and falls on Simon's chest.

Simon beats his arms and legs on the floor. 'No! I'm not going to let you! No! Get off. Help! Save me!' he finds himself yelling. 'Let me go. You don't mean it. It doesn't have to be like this. I'm sorry . . . I love you. Please! I'll do anything, I'll go away please, please –'

No one's coming, he thinks.

'Open your eyes, you sick bastard, open them!' he yells. The room swallows the sounds, not the hint of an echo. 'Help me, someone!'

They were at the extreme ends of the same event. Where their skins touched, it felt opposite. His numb, hers agonised . . . It was the inverse of intimacy. There must have been a moment when she knew it was useless. *This is it. No one can hear. I can't win. I'm going to die like this . . .*

'Mum! Help me, Mum!' he shouts. Then he turns his head towards the group, what he can mainly see is boots and trainers, chair legs. The rough carpeting grazes his cheek.

'I've had enough,' he says. 'Please, I want to stop.'

⋆

Ray climbs off, helps Simon up; they stand apart for a moment.

'Did I do good?' Ray asks. The scar on his jaw is livid, his eyes glitter still. 'Did I scare you, eh?' He holds out an arm for Simon to steady himself on as he climbs into his jeans.

'Well, I'm pretty sure I would have stopped, if she'd said all that!' Simon says as he takes his place in the circle. A few of the others pull quick grins, but Annie's voice is brittle:

'Since you were asphyxiating her,' she says. 'She couldn't say anything at all!'

'Give him a break!' Ray says. It's true that Simon is shaking, vibrating really, especially his legs, if he tries to change their position at all. But all the same, he doesn't want defending, he wants Annie to continue, to bludgeon him (physically even) or failing that with the hardest words she has: as if she could in that way pay him back for the other woman's suffering, imagined, real, both, doubled, it's immaterial. But Annie inclines her head; stops. Her small, bony hands lie upturned in her lap; she won't give him what he wants. Outside, the trees toss and jerk, but in the room, for a moment or two, everyone sits absolutely still.

He knows the whole story of his life has led him to this: a shadowy, concrete bunker of a room, on a winter afternoon, these companions, witnesses, the saintly and the awful alike. Led is too mild a word. Pursued? Propelled? Driven? In any case it has caught up with him now but instead of frightening him to the death, it has climbed, somehow, inside of him.

He can't say any of this and Annie doesn't make him try. They shake out their arms and legs. They do breathing exercises. You can hear the tick of the electric clock on the wall, and the wind outside.

35

Simon sits opposite Alan, pushed back in his chair, one foot up on the other knee, head to one side, waiting. He's relaxed, although perhaps there is also a hint of a challenge in his gaze: *Can you believe this? Here I am.*

'Like I said, I've come for your advice.' He gestures at the envelope on the table between them. 'It's something like myself and Bernadette, but the other way around. I can see how it is for her, and I can see why Bernadette said no. But I don't want to upset her.' Alan unfolds the letter, scans through it, noticing the quality of the paper and the large, confident writing as much as the contents. Of course, everyone on the staff already knows the letter has arrived, and what is in it; Alan already knows what he will offer to do.

Three days later a taxi takes him from the station at York through Walmgate, out of the city for a few minutes, then left through a tangle of residential streets, red brick and old roofing slate, heavy in the rain.

The house is in a cul-de-sac. It's three storeys high, semi-detached. There are a few steps up to the door. He pushes the hair back from his face and presses the bell; a tall, elegantly dressed woman in her forties comes almost immediately to the door.

'Alan Wishart,' he says. 'Good of you to meet like this.' He sits for a few minutes alone in a high-ceilinged room, painted dove-grey with white mouldings and an enormous intricate ceiling rose.

'You can imagine!' Jay says, as she puts down the tea-tray. 'First I discover she is pregnant, and now it seems she's bent on writing letters to a dangerous criminal . . . Perhaps it's lucky I never had children of my own!'

He returns her smile, fills her in on the letters, Tasmin's lie about her age.

'The school threw her out,' she tells him in turn. 'I've had to get a private tutor. She might just get some of her exams in before the due date, if she can concentrate. She's determined to have the baby . . . and I can understand it, actually. Her father won't talk to her. They both work all hours, write me cheques, arrive, depart . . . My sister says she can't cope with her own life – as if this wasn't part of it! I'm getting used to the idea of being a granny for a while,' she tells him. 'And now that I've met you I can say yes, do please talk to her about this man. That's her, coming in now.'

Tasmin enters the room carrying a bunch of red tulips and a canvas bag full of books. She looks at least eighteen, maybe twenty, is tall and pale like her aunt, who leaves the room once the introductions are done, so as to give at least the illusion of privacy. Alan takes in Tasmin's flawless skin, her generous lips, shiny with gloss. Her breasts and the bump are showing under a loosely knitted sweater, worn over old black leggings and a T-shirt. She leans back in one of the old armchairs and waits for him to explain his business. Her eyes don't leave his face; she's quite something, he thinks.

'Simon's life is complicated enough,' he tells her. 'He is doing intensive therapy. He has to go over and over the past, consider his motives all the time in great detail and try to set up new patterns of behaviour.'

'I always knew he had to do that,' she tells him. Alan notices some old scars across her wrists, but she strikes him as remarkably self-possessed, intrigued by his presence, rather than defensive.

'Also, Tasmin, you should know that the crime he committed is a very serious one.'

'He told me that,' she says. 'How do I know he wanted you to come?' she asks.

'I guess you'll just have to take my word for it,' he says.

'I believe he did say, when he telephoned, that he wanted it to end?' He's relieved that she doesn't deny this. 'It doesn't help him to have this going on. As regards your last letter, he definitely does not want a visit. Of course, it's pretty much impossible for us to *stop* you writing . . . we're just *asking*. If the letters keep coming, I suppose I will just have to advise him to send them straight back. But why would you write to him if he doesn't want you to?' She looks quickly down into her tea.

'I really like him,' she says, when she's recovered herself. 'I think he's a very special person.'

'You'll be very busy with your baby soon,' he points out. 'He's in there, locked up. Can we agree to let this drop?'

'Will you tell him he can always come and see me, when he gets out,' she says. 'Will you do that?' It's not the perfect thing to do, he knows, but because he wants a result, Alan doesn't actually say *no*. Instead, he smiles at Tasmin, reaches forwards over the untouched tea things and holds out his hand – recognising, just before Tasmin decides to slip her hand into his, that the gesture he is performing, the manner and timing of it, is something he has learned from Simon himself.

Jay, who must have been listening at the door, chooses this moment to come back in the room. She bends over the back of her niece's chair and whispers something in the girl's ear. Tasmin gives a small smile.

'We're going out now,' she announces. 'What was your name again?' she asks, as she gets to her feet. 'Alan Wishart,' she repeats. 'Thank you, Alan,' she says, as if he were the cleaner being paid off at the end of the day.

'What was she like?' Simon asks Alan. He finds himself suddenly wanting Tasmin, now that she's gone. 'Did she decide what to do?' But of course, it's impossible.

'We agreed to let this rest,' Alan points out.

'Was she OK?' Simon asks.

Alan finds himself offering a quick smile and an infinitesimal nod of his head as he continues, smoothly: 'Now that's over with, how do you feel about summing up progress and setting some goals for the next year? There are some areas which Dr Mackenzie, in particular, feels we have to address . . .'

The fact is, it's not just the end of a year but also the end of a decade – and, out there in the world beyond the wire, of an era. On his in-cell TV Simon watches crowds surge through the gates of the Berlin Wall, hack at the concrete with hammers, stones, whatever they've got. Out there, collective liberation is in the air. Here in Wentham they have to set goals and wait their turns, but it is possible at least to feel the beginnings of a connection to the outside world and not just because of having the TV sets. The staff, who move daily between the two worlds, bring the smell of outside in the fibres of their clothes and the feel of it in their jokes and stories, their complaints about the poll tax, mortgage payments and the state of the roads.

He's looking at at least another six years. It could be eight, ten; the thing is to keep busy. He gets the December issue of the magazine done. It's not bad at all and includes yoga tip no. 3 and the first three letters of Austen's Alphabet: A for artists, B for busted, C for Christmas, all with a humorous touch. The Christmas Revue is to take place on the 22nd; Simon is in charge of the microphones and sound system and teaching people to use them correctly. The group's party: juice, sausage rolls, celery sticks, vol-au-vents, grapes, cheese, juice, lemonade is on the 23rd. Meanwhile, he has purchased a pack of cards – robins and snow – and sent them, with personalised messages, jokes, thanks and new year's wishes to all the staff, even Max Mackenzie. In that case, though, he merely signed the card and included a word-processed note explaining his feeling that they are on a hiding to nothing. He pointed out that he didn't like Annie at first, but now has an enormous amount of respect for her; that he thinks Martin Clarke is a decent, good-hearted bloke despite it all, but as for himself and Mackenzie, they just haven't budged. It's stalemate, oil and water, they don't get on and never will. Maybe they could give themselves a break this year? Isn't there someone else he could be assigned to?

It's worth a try, because number one: he's not ever going to trust the man any further than he could throw him, and number two: he's not going back into the media room to be wired up and monitored.

As for the group, everyone gets a card but he takes particular trouble over the message for Ray, because they are friends of a sort, and for Andy, because maybe no one else will bother with him. Also, he pays Andy a week's money in tobacco to make him up a one-off greetings card. The design was Simon's own idea: two champagne flutes, full to the brim; a tiny, pudgy hand clutching each stem. It's turned out well enough, though the border of holly leaves and berries is heavy, almost funerary, and would look much better with some variety of colour, but Andy only does monochrome; he uses the finest possible fine liner to suggest the outlines, then fills in the shadows with meticulous cross hatchings, tiny dots or parallel lines. He works in a kind of trance while he does it, bent over the page, listening to spacey music, his cigarettes burning to nothing in the ash tray.

The writing inside Simon does for himself with a felt-tipped calligraphy pen from the canteen, £2.50. What with the outsize envelope and the cartridge paper at ninety pence a sheet the whole thing is pricey, but hasn't that always been my way? he jokes to himself. No expense spared in the mail department. He rules faint pencil lines, finds the centre, measures out letters and spaces to either side, outlines the writing in pencil first. Only when it's absolutely even does he ink it in:

Double Congratulations

&

Merry Christmas!

Underneath, he writes with a normal fine-liner: To Bernadette Nightingale and her family, with warmest regards, from Simon Austen. After some thought, he decides against a P.S. to the effect that he is doing all right, that he nearly left, but will stick it out now. There is plenty he could say: he would like to try and describe to Bernadette the feeling he has had, not all the time, but often since he took Amanda's part, of his life being somehow returned to him – a mixed blessing, certainly, because it is an unlovely, struggling, kicking, biting thing, but all the same, his to take on, guide, provide for. He'd like to say something of the feeling of that, of the way it changes things, of the way in which Amanda has returned to his dreams, not terrifying as she used to be, not striding along the wing calling out his name, but sitting quietly in the chair at his desk, sad and bewildered, wearing the turquoise tracksuit he first saw her in. He'd like to write to her about this, and about the odd warmth he was able to feel for a teenage girl he'd never met. But it might not come out right and once he started, it would be hard to know where to stop.

There are no groups over the holiday. In the visits room a variety of tattooed Santas hand out lollipops and promises to the kids; inter-wing football matches take place in the mornings. On Christmas Day it goes 4–3 to B wing. No one's drunk or hungover and it's a cold, piercingly bright day.

Ray is out of sorts. Christmas is a gigantic con, he says. The snowy stuff and the baby in Jerusalem, how's it supposed to link up? The God-squad just took advantage, is all. And what are people with no fucking family supposed to do? Sit there singing carols and wait to be given a packet of crisps? Stop belly-aching, for a start, Simon says. The fact is he's on some kind of high. He feels excited and it's not just by the game and the goal he scored. It's more than that: another year is almost gone and he has a real sense of the passing of time, progress, possibilities, however remote.

After lunch some of them go to sleep, others read or watch TV in their rooms, or else stand hopefully in the phone queue. The rest drift into the recreation room. Susanna is on daytime duty, with a plate of mince pies she has bought in. But hasn't she got a home to go to? they ask, Who's going to cook that goose and boil that pudding? One of the others, someone without a family, should have taken the shift, opines Pete. Soon he's pretty steamed up about it, but given the season, no one bothers to point out that his own wife is having to run the show on her own for the sixth year in a row.

'Thanks, but I signed up for it,' Susanna tells them, then chooses a pie for herself and bites delicately into it. Roots are showing in the blonde of her hair, but she has done her nails in a Christmassy red.

'She just can't leave us alone,' someone says.

'We need the money,' she explains. 'Mark was made redundant last month. Five mouths to feed, all that.'

'Well, then, thank God us bastards are here, for you to earn a living off,' the joker comes back at her.

'Bless you,' she says, dusting crumbs from her finger-tips. They offer to be good, if she'd like to sneak off home? Simon's laughing with the rest, and at the same time, remembering what she did for him, months ago. This, he thinks, and the thought itself has an amusing edge, this is the best place I've been.

36

The meeting is in the new Lifer Governor's office. The room is hot and cramped, but coffee in cups with saucers and a plate of Walker's shortcake biscuits have been laid on. There's a big No Smoking sign on the wall. Beverly has only been in the new post for six weeks, and says she wants to take a very hands-on approach. Her desk is against the wall to make more space; she has the file out on her lap. Mackenzie comes in last. He removes his jacket and hooks it over the back of his chair, loosens his tie before he takes his place. He looks pale.

'Well, then. *Simon* . . .' he says, looking around at the rest of them. 'This has been on my mind for some time.'

'What did you get in your card?' Greg asks. He is supposed to be off sick with flu but he came in especially for the afternoon's special case conference. He has a day's stubble on his chin, circles under his eyes. 'We were just comparing notes. He told Annie that –'

'Actually,' Mackenzie says, 'we'd better get down to business.'

'He put in a good effort doing the sounds for the Christmas play, didn't he?' Beverly says brightly. She's boney-thin, her hair cut short. A frail gold crucifix glints in the modest v of her blouse. 'Apparently he's never done anything like that before. And the magazine, of course, he is doing a fantastic job there . . .'

Mackenzie picks a piece of a paper out of the file on his lap.

'Simon says he has no intention of completing the behavioural modification programme, is that correct, Alan?'

'Well, yes, that's what he said,' Alan confirms, 'but aside from that, I've got to say I feel he's made such *huge* progress, and if we keep the pressure up, well, he might come round. This meeting came as a complete shock to me because I've actually been hoping we'd plan a progressive move from here in a few months' time. I'd say we should start to look forwards to a successful review and open conditions within five years.' Mackenzie's eyebrows shoot up.

'In therapy, he always resists, massively resists,' Annie comments. She looks tinier than ever in an oversized cable-knit sweater. 'But then, suddenly, he really goes for it. He comes round in the end. It's as if those are two sides of the same coin . . . you really have to give space to the resistance, that's what I've found. Working with him can be very satisfying – and moving too . . . though yes, of course, Max, he experiences a lot of anxiety, and has some compulsive behaviours, and, as you've pointed out before, there are still some issues which –'

'Indeed!' says Mackenzie. 'To my knowledge, the sexual element of the offence hasn't been addressed *at all*. Martin?'

'Well, not significantly,' Dr Clarke admits. He's taken off his lab coat but still looks somehow out of place in this small, crowded room. 'We negotiated a break and it went on longer than I expected. But we have had some very interesting discussions. On the purely cognitive level there's certainly been progress.'

Mackenzie closes the folder again, tosses it on to the low table in front of him.

'Am I really the only one to think something is seriously wrong here?' he asks. 'We flag up a major contributing factor to a very serious offence, we put it down explicitly as something to be addressed. The client completely avoids addressing it, just bows out of that bit of the programme for almost a year, and we, or most of us, let him? I think we should be asking ourselves some very serious questions here. I'd say the work of the unit and the role we hope to have in the wider system is on the line. I think we have a problem.' In the silence that follows this, he looks carefully at everyone in the room. Beverly, sitting serene and upright to his left, gives one of her occasional nods.

'There are about a hundred and twenty problems walking around in here,' Annie says.

'Our role is to solve problems,' Mackenzie says simply, 'or admit it when we can't.'

'What about with yourself, Dr Mackenzie?' David puts in, his voice a shade or two higher than usual. He flushes, fights the urge to play with his ear stud. 'It must be hard to go into that sexual stuff in a group, especially with a woman there too, mustn't it? I mean, none of them do that very much, do they? Has he talked it over, one to one, with you?'

'I've given him every opportunity to do that,' Mackenzie says. 'I have frequently suggested to him that the ability to establish a mutually satisfying heterosexual relationship is what he must work towards. He says that he thinks the opportunities here are poor, which, while momentarily amusing, shows how little he is prepared to engage with this, a crucial risk factor, or to engage with the opportunities there are. Recently he told me, 'If I could get intimate enough with you to address this stuff, then I wouldn't have the problem, would I?' On the other hand, he'll spend an entire session arguing that there might be a limit to how much someone could change, and isn't it valid, therefore, to look at the best way for him to live, given the kind of person he is –'

'You know, I do find all that very interesting,' Clarke says, rubbing his hands together and looking round to see if anyone agrees. 'He's got a mind of his own, that's for sure.'

'Max, all of them do this kind of thing!' Annie says. 'All of them avoid things and see what they can get away with. I'd do the same, wouldn't you?' Everyone looks back at Mackenzie.

'Granted,' he says. 'But I think you are losing sight of our ultimate concern, something I certainly have to put first: the safety of the public. I hope I don't need to remind anyone here the consequences of us making bad judgements.' Everyone knows he is referring to the Somers case of some months back: a man was released by another institution into the community because everyone thought the job was done. Three weeks later someone was dead.

'Simon is highly intelligent,' Mackenzie points out. 'All of them try to get away with things, but he often succeeds. For example, we know that he succeeded in convincing some lonely woman he somehow smuggled letters out to that he was a middle-aged man who looked after his mother until she died . . . and he succeeded in getting a vulnerable girl to fall for him –'

'He invited me to intervene, there!' Alan cuts in. 'It was successfully resolved.'

'You resolved it for him.'

'He could hardly do it for himself!'

'He's certainly very bright,' Greg puts in, considering. 'He'll argue the hind leg off a donkey, just for the sake of it . . .'

'Can't we look at what he *has* done?' Annie says. 'He's taken on responsibility for what he did, quite a lot of it. You've observed yourself how he has been in the role plays.' The room falls silent: surely Mackenzie is not going to say that this (and therefore the drama programme itself) counts for nothing, or else that Simon is faking it but has Annie fooled? If he does say either of those things, Annie will have to stop herself from walking out, or yelling at him. But actually, he doesn't:

'Yes,' Mackenzie agrees, smiling at her. 'Good work has been done there. But we have a multidisciplinary approach and that is not all that's required of him here. It's my role to take an overview.' Mackenzie sighs, gestures at the file.

'Surely,' Annie suggests, 'changes in other areas will have some impact on his sexuality? On his ability to surrender emotionally?' The room tries this on for size.

'Yes,' Alan says, 'with respect, Max, that's what I think too.' Mackenzie looks slowly around at his colleagues. His cool grey eyes show, if anything, a trace of sadness as he gathers his thoughts together.

'Simon,' he points out, after a moment or two, 'is very good at getting people on his side. He has you driving over here every month, Alan, when you don't have to; he has Dr Clarke making a special case, abandoning his programme and losing valuable data; he has the entire wing giving him a second chance when he technically speaking breaks the No Violence rule. He even has the Governor so charmed that he lets him into a garden that was previously deemed to be a possible escape route . . . In my judgement, what he is doing, time and time again, is very skilfully protecting the core of his offending behaviour: by paying lip service to the values of the institution and being open to other, lesser, changes, he – or shall I say that part of him that lies at the core of the offending behaviour – hopes to distract us from what he is *not* prepared to do.'

It's true, at least, that everyone can remember letting Simon get away with some little thing or another, or wanting to, and Mackenzie, seeing that they are listening now, picks up his cup and takes a few sips of tea, waits while what he has said sinks in.

'It's quite possible that what we have here is a personality disorder that has slipped through our screening process . . . The sooner we tackle it the better,' Mackenzie continues, 'If we keep him on here, we're tacitly giving him a stamp of approval and we're denying a place to someone who might benefit.'

'You want to ghost him?' Annie turns to face Mackenzie full on, her lips parted, her eyes huge. 'Get him here, open him up, get him to admit he has problems with rejection, then fire him?'

'I see you are very involved,' McKenzie says. 'Presumably you'll discuss that in supervision.'

'I can't believe it,' Annie says.

'I've given this a great deal of thought and nothing I've heard here today makes me want to reconsider my clinical opinion. It will leave us with two rather small groups, and we can look at amalgamating them and starting a new intake. Of course, I'd like consensus on this, but if it can't be had, then I do have to do what I think is in the interests of the public and the community here.'

Afterwards, Annie and Greg go to the pub – a characterless place, smelling of fried food and smoke, but conveniently situated on a corner just before their separate ways home. He buys the drinks, red wine and a pint, she goes to the machine for cigarettes. They sit opposite each other, light up.

'How's Juliette and the sprogs, then?' she asks, as she raises her glass.

'Pretty good,' he tells her. She nods, drinks again, shunts her coaster around. The silence grows.

'We win some, we lose some,' he suggests. 'He may have a point.'

'He's wrong!' she snaps back at him. 'I know he is making a mistake. Leaving Simon aside, this will cause trouble here for weeks,' she says. 'Here we go!' she gasps, banging the flat of her hand on the table, then her face convulses. She rests her head on the table and weeps. When the worst is over, she dabs at her eyes with an old tissue from the bottom of her bag.

'What a way to start the new year. How can you be so calm about it? What can we do?' she asks, calmer herself after another swallow of wine. 'Resign? Why the hell isn't the decision-making democratic? We get the men to vote on every little thing?'

'Responsibility. He who theoretically carries the can. And he's *objective*,' Greg says, deadpan. 'We're not. Especially not you.'

'That's fair to say,' she grins at him, pink-eyed, and he reaches over the table and takes her hand in his.

'It's why you're good at what you do,' he says as he lets go.

'Max and Simon are two of a kind,' she tells him. 'They bring out the worst in each other.'

Later, in the windswept car park, they hug as usual, but instead of pulling away she reaches up and takes a kiss, her fingers spread wide to cup the back of her colleague's head, as if to keep him there.

'Oh, no,' he says at the end of it, stepping back.

'Time I got myself a life?' she suggests, opening the door of her car, slipping in. 'A little private practice, an outdoorsy hobby or two, meet new people . . . Hmm. I know. Well, good night.'

*

It's a cold, crisp night, the sky studded with stars. The two vehicles nudge out onto the A road, leaving the place behind them as they accelerate oppositely towards their respective homes, hers a fixed-up terrace with white walls, wood floors, thick rugs, original artworks on the walls; his a far larger, less convenient property, full of children, the baby Chloe, all their mess.

In Wentham, boilers pour out heat, night and day. Even when someone turns a thermostat to nil, heat still seeps through from the other rooms and the corridors. Here and there, a window standing ajar admits in a blade of cold air, just for a moment sharp as ice, then melted, lost. The corridor is bright, shadowless. In the darkened rooms to either side, the men sleep. Simon's blue velour curtains are closed against the yellow lights that shine on outside, where the courtyard pond skins with ice, the reeds crisp with frost. He's lying on his side, one arm tucked under his head and Bryan, on the return leg of his inspection, pauses a moment to lift the observation panel and study him before turning back to the office and his computer magazine; he'll be glad to get off shift.

It's still dark outside at six, when they unlock his door. The main light goes on, flooding the small room. Two go in, three wait outside, just in case. Johnny Lyndon squats down beside the bed.

'Simon, hey, Simon, lad, wakey, wakey.' He turns away from his visitors, and drills his head deep into the pillow. Someone shakes him. 'Come on, mate, it's morning.' Now he's sitting bolt upright, blinking at the light, trying to make sense of Johnny Lyndon standing there.

'What the fuck!'

'Time for a move. Your carriage is waiting . . . Best pack up quietly, now.'

'Why? What's going on?' Simon takes in that there are three more uniformed men waiting outside.

'No idea,' Johnny Lyndon says. 'We've just got a job to do and let's do it quietly, eh? . . . Right, now –'

'No,' he says. 'Alan said he would get me a C cat from here. This must be a mistake.'

'We don't know the reasons,' Mike Barnes says, flatly, from his position at the door. 'It's not in our hands. And life isn't always fair . . . Maybe it'll make sense later on. Are you going to pack up now, Simon? Want help with these curtains of yours?' Simon pushes his covers off and stands up. His jeans are over the back of the chair and he climbs into them.

'That's it,' Johnny says softly, unrolling a couple of large transparent bags. Mick goes over to the window and begins to unhook the curtains. Simon puts on his sweatshirt, his shoes . . . It's impossible. It's real.

'No!' he says. 'I've been here nearly a year. If I'm going, I want to be told why.'

'There's quite enough of us to pick you up and take you, son,' Johnny points out. 'But we don't want to do it that way.'

'And if I'm going, I want to fucking well say goodbye!' Simon shouts, at which point Johnny Lyndon gestures to the rest. Mike Barnes drops the curtain he's folding and the others rush in. Once someone's got hold of his right leg, the rest follows easily. They grab a limb each. Simon's off the floor, twisting and shouting, but all he can do is make it more difficult.

'I'm ghosted –' he yells. 'Ray! Andy!' Then Johnny Lyndon jams the corner of a towel in his mouth, so all he can do is gag, sweat pouring off his face and they make for the door. So he can't say: What's going to happen to my stuff? Those books? My typewriter and the box of letters that was confiscated? The photo of Bernie and her twins? He can't turn round, to get a last look.

37

Once they're off the wing, he stops struggling. They sit him down in an office and take stock. If he stays quiet, he can go escorted in a minicab, otherwise it's the sweat box. Guess which they'd rather . . . Simon shrugs. He's blank, emptied out by his rage. Everything has been wiped out. Nothing matters. Nothing will ever matter again. There's a kind of safety in it, almost. But then Johnny Lyndon calls reception to request the cab and while he's waiting for a reply, Mike turns to Simon:

'By the way,' he says. 'We saw Dave as he went off shift, he said to tell you don't let this knock you back, and all the best, that's what he said.' Simon folds up in his chair and sobs like a baby.

'You want to get that right out of your system before you get to where you're going,' Lyndon says.

When the cab comes, Lyndon sits next to the driver. In the back, Mike is on one side, cuffed and discreetly chained to Simon; Bill, likewise, on the other; both of them are large men and their legs and shoulders press into his. Apparently, it'll be a couple of hours. On the way back, the officers will stop for a pub lunch, so they're in a fine mood.

The sun's just up and the bare, chocolate-coloured fields are steaming slightly by the time the car sets off. Flocks of grey birds rise from the ground as they pass, settle again in a different field. You can see why they put on the chains: at a moment like this, if it were possible to just open the door and jump, roll, run, off into another life, even for a couple of hours, then you would.

I don't get to finish anything! Simon thinks, looking out. I didn't do everything they told me; I didn't swallow it all, hook, line and sinker, but didn't I go quite a way? The roads widen. They turn off into a service station just before the motorway and Johnny Lyndon brings everyone Styrofoam cups of coffee and microwaved bacon sandwiches.

'Sorry, mate, forgot you were a vegetable . . . You really are best off out of it,' he tells Simon as he hands the stuff over. 'Those nine-to-fiveing shrinks and social workers are all the same, mess you around and make life difficult for everyone. If I had my way, I'd sack the lot. Cut staffing by half and get the place running on proper lines. Save the tax-payer a bloody fortune.'

Maybe.

They head south. The motorway is six lanes of solid metal and it feels like they're doing 80 m.p.h., though he can't see the speedo. The feeling of wanting to escape is gone; now it's a matter of wanting to live. He eats the sandwich, tunes out their talk and peers at the people in other cars, the signs telling everyone where to go, how to navigate the hugeness of the outside world. Wentham soon begins to seem less real, like some other reality you might reach through a manhole or trap door . . . Eventually they peel off into an urban hinterland of ring roads, industrial estates and tatty ethnic restaurants. Finally, they arrive.

Shower. Body search. Property. He grabs his books as they cascade out of the plastic sack. Everything's mixed together, trainers, notepads, Walkman, radio, curtains – Curtains have to go in stored property, they're not allowed in cells here, it's a fire and suicide risk . . . Don't argue, the man says. What about the confiscated shoe box, the typewriter, when it comes?

'What d'you think?' the officer snaps back at him. 'It's a metal object! Kill someone if you threw it at them, couldn't it? Or it could be turned into three dozen very sharp little knives . . . I don't give a flying fuck what they did somewhere else! Waste your time applying if you want but there's no chance. You'd be better off trying to make a new one out of lolly sticks.'

He's back in Victoria's architecture again: brick walls, metal landings and stairs. Distant windows high up at the end of the wing admit a dusty light that filters down, mingling with the ghostly flicker from fluorescent tubes and the scuffed blue-grey of the walls. The officer follows right behind him, close enough to hear his breath. The inmates are locked down but you can tell they're there: the place stinks of old sweat, blocked toilets, unwashed laundry, damp mortar, leftovers, drains. Tough, Simon tells himself, you've been spoiled, haven't you? He won't notice it after a day or so . . . Likewise, the lack of colour. But the crackling of aggression in the air, that electricity that impregnates every space and charges every surface, which makes a man's fists automatically clench, that won't be so easy to ignore. He walks as tall as he can, the bag of gear bumping on his back. The bedroll is under his free arm, the cutlery bowl and mug in his hand.

'Right, in there, Austen,' the screw says, and he walks in, knowing the door will crash behind him, the key turn in the lock.

It's dirty. And one reason for the stench here is obvious: a lidless bucket stands at the end of the bed, emptied, but not cleaned. He dumps the bedding and bag, climbs on the bed to look out. The window faces east and is already open as far as it can go. There is tarmac as far as the wall, which is topped generously with coiled razor wire. A high fence, also topped with razor wire runs about six feet in front of the wall. Beyond, he can make out a distant urban sprawl: hilly streets of smallish terraced buildings, a pall of smoke drifting in from the left. But it's good to be alone at last. He lets go of the window bars, climbs down and sits on the mattress.

What can you say? Half of them here are two'd up. It's a pit, a dumping ground, worst place he's been so far. Thanks a lot! He thinks at the walls, which stare back at him, blank, insulting. *Did someone tell you life was fair?* He can almost hear the exasperated voice of the first person to tell him that: Helen, one of the social workers at Burnside. He told her where to get off, but she was right, of course. Things happen. You're chucked out: not so bad, though, compared to being murdered. Maybe he is a piece of shit or maybe they fucked up big time. So what, he tells himself, you're here now, and you've got to work out how to survive.

He wants to hit the walls. He can imagine going berserk, hitting out until they lock him in some hole of a punishment cell, hitting out again when they finally open up the door. Plenty go that way. He can imagine it. He can imagine it so well that his nails are cutting grooves into the palms of his hands. But something in him won't let him do it. Instead, he gulps in air, sends it hissing out between his teeth. No: he did get somewhere and they won't wipe him out, he decides. It's not going to be the end of the story. Annie said that often; she always pulled them up when the phrase trotted out: 'No, there *isn't* an end to the story,' she'd say. 'There's always something you can do.' And Bernadette gave him the C word, there, under his clothes. The fact is, you've got to admit that women seem to know what you need to live and they want to pass it on: these words are resources, hang on to them. Even Tasmin, just a kid, didn't she write to him that a person rebuilt from the ruins could be stronger than before? It's in the letters somewhere, if he ever gets them back. When. He's going to make sure of it and he's going to stick up for himself. He'll get himself out of this hole, the shortest possible way.

Slowly, Simon wills his fisted hands to uncurl and relax to the point that he can use them. He makes the bed, then lies down and sleeps, dreamless, until the din of unlocking brings him back to where he is, the familiar over-strenuous pounding of his heart in his chest. Think of it as a bad dream, he instructs himself. You'll wake up. But then, you've got to laugh, because to cap it all he's in the supper queue and finds himself three behind someone who looks just like Teverson, and when the man turns to make his way back to the cells, he realises it is the actual bastard himself, just the same except for a touch of white mixed in with the ginger bristles on his scalp and jaw and some deeper lines around the too-blue eyes.

'Android, back from the funny farm!' Tev says. 'How long is it?' It's not long enough, Simon thinks.

'Weren't you going to be out by now?' he asks.

'Job I got set up for when I was on parole went pear-shaped.' Simon shrugs, turns away as Tev claps him across the back.

Here, you're either locked in your cell or you're locked out of it. No in between, no messing around. When Association comes, Simon goes to the other side of the showers, where there's an unlocked area smelling of unrinsed cloths and weak disinfectant. He swirls the pail clean in the butler sink, leaves it to drain, pick up later; there's nothing to wash or dry your hands with. But it's done, first things first. Next thing is to put in an application to see Alan. Get him on the phone.

'Look, don't come near me, don't bother, I'm just passing through,' he tells Teverson who seems to spend most of his life on the landing, with a mop and bucket propped up near by, or else smoking and talking in a low voice to a bunch of hard cases in the cleaning bay. None of the screws ever tell him to work. The story is that he is getting *married* in a few weeks' time, but they won't let him out for it so he is bringing the whole business in, cake, buffet, suits, flowers, the lot. 'Name of Carmel. Half his age. Sexy or what?' a stunted-looking bloke called Ratty tells Simon. 'Legs up to here and the rest of it. A mate bought her on a visit to cheer him up and that was that.' It's impossible to believe. Almost.

'I didn't agree with it,' Alan tells him, the two of them sitting in a cell that has been converted into a miniature office for the use of visiting professionals. 'I wasn't the only one either. I made my feelings very clear and I've made a note of it in the file. And now, I really, really don't want you to throw the baby out with the bathwater. I want to help you make sense of this.' Alan looks exhausted, grey. Simon's sitting straight back in his chair, hands loose on his thighs.

'Can you get me out of here?' Simon asks.

'I'll do what I can.'

There's 23-hour lockup on the weekends, also for days every time there's any kind of incident, such as someone has their arse cut open to get a charger of drugs out, or gets stabbed for debts. So there's more and more lockup, more people losing it, imploding, wrecking cells. The alarm bell goes off every other day. The place is like a pressure cooker or a village on the edge of a volcano, except that the volcano is them too, they're all inside of it, driving it up to the boil. Monday, everyone comes out desperate, ready to batter someone with a chair or some batteries in a sock: chicken and egg, hopeless case thereof, and one of the worst places in the civilised world to be.

It's going to be months, not weeks, Alan says. But Simon does get an interview in Education. Education is down in the basement, with no windows at all. As you go in, there's a mural of gaudy tropical fish with a candy-pink octopus lurking in the corner. After that, it's grey again.

'Quite apart from the pressure of numbers, we don't have anything on site here to offer that you haven't already done,' the pale, blond man down there tells him. So what? He'll do it again, while he's waiting to get out of here. But instead, the bloke there gives him the Open University prospectus to look through. He reads it during the lockdowns. He studies information on the Access Course, and the options thereafter: Linguistics, Philosophy, History of Art, Languages, Literature, Politics, Media Studies, History, Sociology, Biology, Geography, Psychology, combinations thereof. You get videoed TV course units to watch, books and materials, which might be paid for by a special grant. A tutor writes you reports on your work, within ten days of receiving it. He could eventually be allowed to attend one of the special seminars. Which course is for you? the brochure asks. Any! All! Using the script he used to call Dead Normal, Simon completes the application for the

Access Course; the grant forms too. Education have not done many of these, but the pale man, Martin, can't see why it shouldn't go through.

H is for hope. Don't do too much of it, mind.

The answer comes in just over two weeks: yes. A starter pack will be on its way as soon as the cheque from the charity has arrived and been cleared. 'Glad to be able to help,' Martin says. 'We can get you some computer time down here once the stuff arrives.' So he's set up. It'll keep him going while he's in this hell hole, and he can just take it along with him when he goes . . . He shakes Martin's hand in front of the mural and he can feel both the threat of tears and the grin stretched across his face, it almost hurts, but he can't turn it off.

He emerges from the basement to find that things are just getting back to normal on the wing after another incident. Officers stride about, unlocking doors for lunch. Teverson is back in his usual spot, face like thunder.

'Look,' he says, barring Simon's path, 'you've gotta help.'

'Well, no,' Simon replies, which should have been 'Fuck off' or 'You deaf or what?' but it is hard to be fierce while walking on air, dreaming of brand new books and golden spires, the smile still lurking on his face.

'It'll be worth your while,' Teverson says.

'I've got everything I need.'

'I'll swap that bucket of yours for a new one.' Teverson says. 'There's one in the cupboard, right now. It's yours, just to listen, right?' Just to listen? Nothing will get the smell of other's men's shit out of the bucket he has, so Simon follows Teverson to the cleaner's bay. Teverson picks up the bucket, yellow: pristine, with matching lid. He demonstrates the fit, hands it over. Then he bars the way out of the cleaning bay.

'I've been through three best men, already!' he says. 'Tony got ghosted, the next bloke went on some sodding course, and now Bates has just got himself fourteen days in the cage for threatening a screw. It's next week and I've paid for it all, can't get a cent back. What I'm saying is, how about fifteen quid – actual money? Make sure I'm together, be sweet to everyone on the day?' He's standing there with the bucket and Teverson has got him by the shoulder and is grinning from ear to ear as if there was nothing at all weird about asking someone he's ripped off, fucked up the arse and insulted to take on such a role . . . it's so awful, it's funny and Simon feels as if his face has fallen off.

'Eh?' Tev prompts. 'I don't want some runt with the sleeves folded up, or a fat bastard with the waist undone, see? You're the exact right size for the suit I've got.' Simon laughs out loud; Tev lets go of the shoulder and sticks out his hand to shake. 'I'll fill in the application.' He has the form in his pocket, ready. 'You just sign it, OK? I'll pay when it comes through.'

'No,' Simon says. 'I don't want your cash.' He gives himself a moment, but the decision is made. 'I'll do it for the hell of it, but I don't want your cash.'

'Rock solid, mate,' T tells him. Well, he's not worn a suit before. He's never been to a wedding.

38

'Very smart. Now come along,' Sykes tells Simon, who has been waiting for some time, standing up so as not to crease the hired suit, grey wool with tiny flecks of blue in it, Italian, apparently. There's a yellow carnation and a bit of fern tucked into his lapel.

'Where's T?'

'Pissing around,' Sykes says. 'He had the DTs this morning and cut himself shaving, so he wants to check in first aid to see if there's some plastic skin . . . wants you to welcome them all. If he don't hurry up, maybe you can marry her instead.'

For a minute or two, he's the only person here other than Sykes, rattling his keys over by the door. It's a big room with a high ceiling. Compared to normal, an immensity of space. The windows are fifteen feet up and barred, but there's a lot of light and a royal blue carpet. Set obliquely at the front is the registrar's table with some flowers and two chairs to either side of it. More chairs with Wentham-blue padded seats are set out in two blocks of rows of three with an aisle between. There are flowers on the trestle table at the far end, next to the cake, and he goes up close to have a real look: all different types of them, yellow and white and cream with some powdery green stuff thrown in. Things he doesn't know the name of, but not daffodils, that's for sure.

The outer doors shoot their locks. There's a clatter of heels on the hallway lino. Sour-faced Bremman brings in the bride and her party. She's tall, wearing a short-skirted cream suit, heels to match, and a hat with an itsy bit of netting over the top part of her face. Add to this a bunch of cream and yellow flowers in her hand, unblemished skin that's got a dash of coffee to it, and enormous light brown eyes under arched brows. In her wake, a shorter, plumper version that must be her mum, four other older women, a few younger ones, one couple, and a middle-aged black man who is Carmel's uncle, attending because her father is set against the wedding and won't come. The bridesmaid, seven or eight, carries her own flowers, a miniature version of Carmel's. All of the visitors are dressed up, jewellery, hats, nail polish, tie, shoeshine, scent. It's a spectacle all right, like being in a play, and Simon's pleased he took the job on.

'Simon Austen,' he explains, as he steps forward, holding out his hand, 'the new best man. Best he could find! Tev, I mean Malcolm, is on his way. Make yourselves comfortable,' he tells them, after the hand-shaking is done. 'Why not make sure of your seats at the front?' Most of the relatives obediently go and sit, all in a bunch to one side, but Carmel and her mum stay up, walk together slowly around the room, inspecting it. Then they come over to Simon. What are you doing here? is all he can think, I mean, given you could have anyone? But it's not his business is it? Go with the flow.

'Don't worry,' he says, laughing unnecessarily, 'Don't worry. He'll be along soon.'

Harrison, C wing Governor, comes in, peering through his glasses to see what's what. He too shakes Carmel's hand, and, to Simon's mind, lingers over it. There's dandruff on the shoulders of his jacket.

'Your husband-to-be is on his way,' he says. 'The registrar was stuck in traffic, but I'm pleased to say that she has just arrived at the gates . . . Sorry for the delay. We're doing our best here.' He goes to the door to crack a joke with Sykes. The registrar and her assistant enter next, smiling, open their briefcases and start to set things out on the table at the front. Carmel sits down on a back-row seat, takes out a mirror to check her perfect face and re-apply lipstick from a shiny gold tube, 'Just one thing missing now . . .' she comments, blotting her lips. 'So long as he comes,' she adds, shooting Simon a glance through her lashes. Her voice is a bit rough; she's from Leeds, he guesses, or Manchester. Maybe she is twenty-two, twenty-five at the most. She could be on the cover of *Vogue*, something like that. 'A year ago, I'd never have guessed I'd be doing something like this,' she says. 'But now, if he stood me up, I'd be gutted. I don't think I'd get over it.' Her mother, standing behind her, gives her shoulder a gentle pat.

'Don't worry about that,' Simon says. 'He never stops talking about you.'

'Really?' she says.

'Straight up,' he tells her. Where does this stuff come from? TV? And where on earth is Teverson? How long can it take to patch up a shaving cut? What would happen if he didn't come? Anything's possible . . . He smiles at Carmel as encouragingly as he can.

'Thanks. You're a good mate, I can tell,' she tells him. 'D'you want to know something, Simon?' she says. 'I've got a real thing for beat-up-looking older men, so I fancied Tev from the start. But I had my doubts, like, Hey girl, what are you getting into?' She gestures around her. 'I definitely did have doubts. What made me know I was doing the right thing was this letter he wrote me. Here . . .' She opens her bag again, puts away the make-up, brings out an envelope, flattens the letter on her knee. She looks up at him again, her face breaking into a wide, even-toothed smile, then reads aloud:

'"Carmel, when I am with you I feel as if I could become the best of me that has been hidden so long. I burn with wanting you. I feel I could pass through the eye of a needle." Isn't that just so beautiful?' she says. Then, suddenly embarrassed, she looks down at her fingernails.

'A man who wrote that has got to have some bit of good in him,' her mother adds. Simon can remember, clear as yesterday, coming back to find Teverson pawing his book and reading out those very words, which were written for Bernadette. He can remember sitting in his cell, writing them. How they seemed to burst out of him. How scared of them he was. He wanted to say them aloud, and he did. But it didn't work out.

Now Carmel's mother is telling him about some poem Malcolm sent Carmel on Valentine's Day, no doubt nicked from someone else too, or copied from a book, and he's thinking, or trying to: Well, it's made someone happy, hasn't it? Does it matter that she thinks the wrong man wrote them? His heart is crashing in his chest: Yes! It matters to him. It ought to matter to her. And the rest of what he knows about Teverson ought to matter too, but of course he can't tell her. She doesn't know him from Adam and even if he did say something, she'd likely not believe him . . . So Simon finds himself nodding and saying, distractedly, 'Yeah, too right . . .' as finally, the bastard himself comes in, takes Carmel's hands and kisses her heavily on each cheek: the same for her mother. Why should he get away with it? Why? Simon thinks, as T waves his greetings at the other guests. Then he grabs hold of Simon's arm.

'Not bad suits, eh, Android?' Simon eyes him, noticing that T has done what he threatened, shaved off all his hair to get rid of the white bits. There's a Band-Aid, on the back of his head, where it went wrong. And his eyes are red-rimmed, they shine too much, the pupils have shrunk to dots . . . No wonder, Simon thinks, you tried to pay me for this. He says nothing.

'Got the rings, love?' Tev asks Carmen. 'Sweet . . . How do I look?' Simon leans in close as if to brush a hair from the bridegroom's shoulder.

'That letter you wrote to her! –' he says, and knows, immediately that he should wait.

'What letter? What shit's this?' Tev says, as the door creaks open and six cons, all in suits or dress jackets with white T-shirts under them, file in. *Get a grip*, Simon tells himself.

'Let's begin,' the Governor booms out.

'Please be seated,' says the registrar.

'What?' Tev asks Si.

'Forget it,' Simon says. 'Later.'

'Sit down, Austen,' Sykes calls out.

His seat is at the front. He goes to it and sits, clenched,

through the walk Teverson and Carmel make, arms linked, between the two blocks of chairs, through the preliminaries – the pleasant grey-haired woman talking about how happy it makes her that even in circumstances such as these, two people can find each other, et cetera, et cetera, and that perhaps they stand as good a chance as any of making a relationship that lasts . . . Now, she says, let's begin . . .

So, this is how it goes, Simon thinks, this is the way the world spins. Not that he'd want *this*, not this exactly . . . but someone who said *yes*. Who? *Why?*

Teverson, his hand clenched around Carmel's long fingers, turns for a moment to shoot a laser-eyed glare back at Simon: You dare fuck this up for me mate and you're dead, it means to say. Then he turns back to start on his lines. He clears his throat, declares:

'I, Malcolm Teverson, know of no legal reason why I . . .' The shuffling, coughing and finger-drumming stop. A backdrop of silence falls into the big room so that it's possible to hear the speakers inhale at the beginning of each phrase.

'I, Carmel Rose Summers take you Malcolm Teverson to be my lawful wedded husband. Please wear this ring in symbol of our union.' The room is still silent as the couple lean forwards and sign the register. Then they stand. The women's eyes from one side of the room, the men's from the other, watch the kiss that follows; hands on, deep, and as long as they can get away with. The willowy girl, the stocky, shaven-headed man, Beauty and the Beast. Tev holds her tight, one hand on the curve of her buttock, pulling her on to him. Her skirt rides up. The disposable camera that was finally allowed in flashes a few times, and when they pull apart there's clapping and stamping from the men, hands full of confetti from the family side. Teverson, his arm still around Carmel, punches the air – another flash. Everyone gets up, mills around. Carmel is flushed. She kisses her mother, hugs the little girl and gives her the bouquet to hold.

'We only have another twenty minutes or so,' the Governor warns. Beaver from the kitchen whisks the covers from the food. There are paper cups to be filled with sparkling Ribena or lemonade and to help keep his lid on, Simon applies himself to the task. Beaver touts the tray of drinks around. Cigarettes are lit; Teverson introduces the outside and inside groups to each other: May, this is Sparks. Hodge. Ben, good mate of mine . . .' Despite everything, there's a buzz, the smell of smoke, flowers, food and too much aftershave.

Well, Simon thinks, A being for absurd, he might just as well go through with what he's supposed to do.

'Excuse me ladies and gentlemen –' the room falls quiet. 'There's no time for speeches, but we must have a toast. Big T and Carmel – good luck to you both.' It comes out like a curse, but no one seems to notice.

'Here, here!' More flashes. He notices, in the dazzle and the din of the salutations, that Carmel is leaning into Teverson, whispering something. He's frowning but grabs her face in his hands and kisses her briefly. Moments later, the cake is moved to the front of the table. The Governor hands over a knife, which once used, he takes back again and has sent straight back to a place of safe-keeping. Another photo. Five minutes left. There won't be time to eat the food.

'Come on, Gov,' Tev suggests, 'give us another ten minutes.'

'It would be a nice gesture,' Carmel's mother says.

'Staffing dictates what we can do here, I'm afraid.'

'No one's going to miss those two,' Tev points out, gesturing to the door where Sykes and Adams wait.

'We'll have to wind up now.' The Governor insists. Carmel starts crying. Teverson gets to leave the room last. The rest of them wait about five minutes for him at the first gate. 'I told Harrison I want that food served up on my landing at supper time. I fucking paid for it,' he tells everyone as he comes through.

'Too right.'

'The suit,' Teverson says to Simon. 'I want it back.'

'Come and get it then,' Simon tells him. He takes the thing straight off, thinking now if he pissed on it, or ripped the pockets off, T would be liable and that would be a start, just a start. But actually, it's easier to think once he's got the thing off. Straight away he feels a bit calmer. He puts it properly on the hanger with the plastic cover. No need to go apeshit, he tells himself. No need to revert to type. Wait a day or two, then have it out with him. Tell him he's got to tell *her*. In Wentham, of course, there'd have been a group meeting, but here, it's down to him.

It's only hours later that he passes Teverson, who is coming back from the servery with a tray of stew and rice and a slice of wedding cake.

'Look,' Teverson says, 'you can't nick words and who gives a fuck what *you* wrote . . . You're a fucking nonce!' he yells, throws the tray, lashes out at Simon, who dodges to the side, misses most of it. Might just have a chance of getting T to fall if he comes again but someone else grabs him from behind, then Tev knees him in the balls.

'Get him in the bay!' Simon struggles but soon three of them have got him face down in the cleaning bay with a sock full of batteries crashing down on his head and back. They tie his legs together and his arms behind his back. For a second he can just hear breathing, his, theirs. He rears up, Tev kicks, he careens backwards and his head crashes into the doorway. The world vanishes in starry darkness.

He comes to alone with his mouth, throat and chest ablaze with a searing new pain. He tries to call out but he can't; he sets himself to getting up and crawling out of the door, fails.

Doors crash home on the landing. A light goes on in the cleaning bay, blinding him. An officer yells something into the landing, blows his whistle then starts tugging at Simon's bindings.

'What the fuck?' the man says, grabbing a plastic bottle from the floor. 'Bleach? Water!' There are more of them now. They heft him up with his face over the concrete sink, the tap full on.

'Drink it!' They splash the stuff over him. 'Get a cup someone!' He drinks, throws up, passes out again.

C

39

Pain is an animal; it lives in his throat, chest and gut. Deep inside, invisible and untouchable, it devours him in order to keep itself alive; threatens, always, to grow. It's in him as he lies between white, starched sheets and he watches, as from a distance, the doctor carefully write something on a clipboard, then attach it to the bottom of the bed.

'Don't try to talk,' warns the doctor: a very young-looking man with paper-white skin and a bottlebrush haircut. 'The broken ribs, fractured arm and bruising to the head, that's all routine . . . As for the bleach, you're lucky,' he says. 'The right action was taken, you'll be OK. Damage to the throat and oesophagus and vocal chords should heal, given time, well, more or less, though there could be some scarring around the mouth . . .' Meanwhile, the doctor explains, it's going to hurt and there's a risk of infection, hence the drip, containing not just electrolyte and pain relief but antibiotics as well. 'As I said,' the doctor concludes, 'try not to talk. Your officer is outside.' It would not have occurred to Simon to try to talk. He frowns, and nods imperceptibly to show he has heard, closes his eyes. He tries to turn over, and realises that it is not only the drip that is restraining him; he is also chained to the end of the bed.

Some time later the same doctor visits again, wearing a fresh, impossibly white coat.

'They say they want you out of here,' he announces, 'but I'm insisting on seeing progress first – under the circumstances I'm just not confident of the care you'll get elsewhere.' One moment, someone can want to kill you; the next, there's another person who is bothered not just that you live, but exactly how well you are going to be looked after, who sends a sweet redhead nurse to give you an injection and persuade you to try a chalky kind of drink. He can't swallow.

'You're lucky,' she says (funny how everyone can see it except him), while she shows him how to use the remote for the TV and radio, how to make the bed tilt up and down. 'You're lucky, because these new rooms with the wallpaper and decent curtains – normally they are just for private admissions or overspill from maternity. You'll be feeling better quite soon,' she adds. 'Rest.'

Some more time passes, and then a prison officer opens the door.

'Look, mate,' he says, 'it's boiling in here but I'm doing my back in out there in that corridor and now you've woken up, so I'd better come in and sit in this easy chair you've got. Name's Bill Evans.' He waits momentarily for a reply, then shifts the upholstered chair nearer to the bed, hangs his jacket on the back of it and hands Simon a rolled-up copy of the *Express*.

'Not so bad in here, is it?' he says, eyeing the TV remote on the bedside cabinet. 'You were damn lucky,' he says. 'Just after they got you out, all hell broke loose. Full-scale riot. There's still men on the roof. Loads of injuries, one bloke, prisoner, in intensive care. Thrown off the landing, fell three floors. Officers drafted in from all over, like fucking Northern Ireland it is in there. Massive overtime. Lots of us drafted in.'

Later, they watch the news. A solemn-faced reporter reads out a list of demands, which include an end to 23-hour lockup and slopping out, and the removal of 'animals' from the wings. Police and fire engines are gathered around the perimeter, he reports, but they can't get in because of the hail of roof tiles and other missiles from above. The female newscaster calls it a siege. The screen shows a view of the prison from the air, one of the accommodation wings half gutted by fire, smoke still rising . . . In terms of the physical structure, it's not exactly something to feel sorry about. But then the camera pulls in a little closer, trying to show the half a dozen masked men hurling tiles down from one of the roofs. Simon can't be sure, but the way one of them stands puts him in mind of Teverson – and, right or wrong, he can't be looking at it any more.

'Yes, we're both well out of it,' Bill Evans comments as the screen dwindles to nothing. Simon writes PISS on the edge of the newspaper and the pair of them make their way slowly to the bathroom, Evans steering the drip.

A male and a female police officer visit. They take their hats off, sit next to the bed and enquire as to Simon's health. The assault, they say, was a serious matter, possibly beyond the scope of internal discipline procedures. Charges may be considered, though there are always problems gaining sufficient evidence, getting witnesses and so on, in cases like this . . . still, they might give it a go. Who were the assailants? Can he remember? *Remember?* But still, you have to weigh it up. What would T get? What would he do after he got it? Is it worth Simon's while, to be known for the rest of a life sentence as a grass, utterly beyond the pale? To be waiting for the comeuppance, even when – if ever – he gets released? He shrugs, writes, 'I will think about it,' in the woman's notebook; they leave him a number to call.

'Well,' Alan says, on the phone at the end of the week, 'you don't seem to need us lot at all do you? There was me and the duty probation officer both bashing out a letter a week and you've managed to get out of there all on your own!'

'Where are they going to send me next?' Simon asks. Every word hurts and they are barely audible. Another officer, Hedges, less well-meaning than Evans, stands a few feet away, attached by a long chain and taking full advantage of the lack of No Smoking signs.

'You know I can't tell you that, but obviously, wherever it is, you'll be in the hospital to start with, so I think you've fallen on your feet.'

'Don't make me laugh,' Simon whispers back.

*

'My cell is about half this size,' he tells the nurse, Rosemary, as she writes her final figures onto the chart for him to take with him.

'Sssh!' she says.

'And the staff aren't so nice,' he adds. It sounds creepy in the whisper, but he might as well say it, it's true. He's managed to drink a small liquid meal – agonising, but without too many medical ill effects – so that means that he is on his way, travelling this time in an ambulance. Another stroke of luck? he thinks at first, but then it turns out that there aren't any windows.

The new place is clean and quiet: a whitewashed room, high windows with curved tops. There are three proper hospital beds in the ward, a TV showing some soap without the sound on. Simon gets the bed near the door. Someone wearing a dark purple tracksuit is sitting on top of the bed at the far end: a fleshy-faced bloke, obviously queer, with a lot of long, blond-streaked hair brushed back from his face. He looks up from reading a magazine and says, 'Hi!'

Simon nods, waits while the doctor, a grim ex-army type, looks him over. Apparently his temperature is too high, which might mean an infection setting in: well, so what! Might make a change. He's getting impatient for the next dose of pain relief and breathes a sigh of relief when the doctor goes to get it.

'He's not supposed to talk, Vic,' the orderly who followed them in says to the bloke in the tracksuit. 'Hurt his throat.'

'That's no good!' Vic says, in a flat, rather soft voice. 'I've been going stir crazy this past two weeks, all on my lonesome in here all day long.'

'Not long now, Vic,' says the orderly. He's a stunted, lop-sided man, almost bald, but bright-eyed and clearly, Simon thinks, up to something or another with the queer. The pair of them had better leave him alone.

Once he's had the shot and the medication has shunted the pain somewhat to one side, Simon finds himself wondering about his property, all of it, the odd bunch of things that he has kept since he came inside: his mother's letter, the watch, the typewriter, the shoe box, the few books he's hung on to. Will it catch up with him? More importantly, what about the papers to do with his Access Course and the grant, the prospectuses and course outline, any mail to do with all that which might have arrived for him since he left . . . Did it get shifted out of his cell before the rioting broke out? Was it burned? If not, have they kept it safe and will they send it quickly on after him? He can see the answer to that one being no, no and no. So, if it has been lost, did Martin in Education keep a copy? He tries to remember whether what he himself had was the original or not, but then again, that's pointless, because Education might very well have been burned down as well.

'What's the matter?' Vic says. He's standing there at the end of Simon's bed, carrying a pale blue bathrobe and a fistful of toiletries. Christ! Simon thinks, glaring at him, noticing how, without knowing it, his whole body has stiffened up like a board, and at the same time, how very clear Vic's blue-grey eyes are. Bizarre. He lets out a hiss of breath.

'If you've got a problem, you press that buzzer and get them in to sort it out,' Vic tells him. 'It's what they are here for, so long as it's legal and decent, that is. I've been here in this hospital longer than you'd think possible and I've got them pretty much trained. Especially Brian. Want me to do it for you?' Simon shakes his head. He raises his eyebrows then draws a square of paper with his forefinger and mimes writing on it.

'That's just what I mean,' Vic tells Simon, reaching to press the buzzer by Simon's bed. 'Pen and paper, please,' he tells the orderly. 'It hurts him to talk, Brian, so he's got to write things down, hasn't he?'

'One good thing: you can have a *bath* here,' he adds when Brian has gone. 'A good soak.'

The air in the ward fills with steam from the bathroom. After twenty minutes or so a notebook and pencil arrive.

I need to see Welfare urgently, Simon writes, *or to call my Home Probation Officer, because I am registered to begin an Open University course and I am concerned that the paperwork will have been mislaid at my last institution; also I want to make sure that the course materials which have been paid for get to me as soon as possible. Thank you, Austen (AS2356768).*

Vic returns, wet-haired and enveloped in the baby-blue bathrobe. Also, Simon notices, there's a strong smell in the room now, half edible, vaguely animal, not quite floral – Vic has obviously put something in his bath, or maybe it's a special shampoo he has for that hair-do of his? Pleasant enough, if you like that kind of thing. But.

'Done? You'd better let me see,' Vic says, sitting on the edge of the empty bed that's between their two. That's as far as you come, right? Simon thinks at him, although the fact is that Vic is tending to amuse him rather than drive him mad. Perhaps it's a week's worth of drugs. He allows the other man to take the notepad and read.

'Good,' he pronounces. 'Well written. Very clear, polite. Stands a chance.' Carefully, Vic tears the page out, then gets up and presses the buzzer again.

'Right,' Brian says, accepting the request, with the suggestion of a bow. 'Anything else?'

'He needs a result by the end of tomorrow,' Vic tells him. 'It's really stressing him out, Brian.'

'So,' Vic sits down again on the spare bed, his neatly crossed legs poking out of the ludicrous bathrobe, a smile on his face. 'I still don't know what your name is.'

'Simon –'

'Don't talk,' Vic says. 'Use the notebook! What is it you want to study, then?'

Not sure, Simon writes. *Introductory Module first. Then Philosophy*? he continues, acutely aware of the possibility of making a spelling mistake, which he somehow thinks Vic will spot, *Literature*? *Social Sciences*? *History*? *Linguistics*? *You can mix them up. I need to have something interesting to think about.* Vic nods emphatically as he reads the note.

'Got a long stretch?' he asks. 'Lifer?' Simon nods for the second time. There's not much you can say to that, and anyway, he's wiped. He writes *tired*, then puts the notepad down, begins to make the series of moves required for him to get out of bed and make a trip to the bathroom.

'Can I help?' Vic asks, but Simon shakes his head.

'Are you a morning person?' Vic asks him, around nine-thirty the next day, just as the medication is wearing off. He shakes his head; Vic returns to the magazine he is reading, then, around ten, puts his trainers on and goes out to find Brian.

'Any news on that request of Simon's?' he hears him ask.

'*It's the weekend!*' Brian says. 'Just relax, will you?' Vic pads back in again, relays the information, plugs earphones into his Walkman. He keeps them on while he eats his lunch and it's late afternoon before he tries again: an offer to play cards. Simon nods, struggles upright and watches the other man deal.

'So what happened to you?' Vic asks. *Ingested bleach*, Simon writes.

'Suicide?' No, Simon indicates.

'A good thing,' Vic says, selecting his cards. 'There's something about suicides that makes me want to take them by the scruff of the neck and shake . . .' Victor frowns, sets down a jack of hearts, collects Simon's ten.

'Good to have some company at last,' he says.

We can get on OK like this, Simon writes, underlining the last two words. He means: *Keep your distance*. Vic smiles.

'Fine. Anyway, I'm leaving soon,' he says. 'Just tell me if you need anything.'

The last shot of the day is at five. Simon's done for by seven, shifts the pillows with his good arm, caterpillars down in the bed.

On the third day, Vic comes back in early from exercise. It's lucky that Simon has only had a strip wash and kept his pants on, but all the same he finds himself having to explain his tattoos to Victor: *A collection*, he writes. *Nouns. Adjectives. Some of the words people have used to describe me.*

'May I?' Vic asks, before he comes close enough to read

them all. He does it in silence, then sits down on the middle bed again. *Cheer up!* Simon tells him with the notepad. *It's no big deal.*

'You're cold,' Vic comments eventually. 'Brian!' he yells. 'How do you suppose,' he says when the orderly comes in, 'that a man with broken ribs and a cast on his arm is supposed to get dressed?' Brian shrugs.

'I'm not a nurse,' he points out. 'The care bear is off having a smoke, he won't be long.'

'But Simon doesn't want me doing it and you haven't exactly got anything else vital to do, have you?' All three of them laugh. It's something else, Simon thinks, the way Vic can say something like that, straight, and not end up with his nose spread across his face.

That last night Simon is almost asleep when Vic returns, humming under his breath, from his bath. Simon hears him put the toiletries down on his shelf, then pack them carefully into the special bag he keeps them in. Then he combs his hair. There's the sound of the big holdall he has over there being zipped and unzipped. Finally, some messing around with his many bottles of pills. What's actually the matter with him? Simon wonders irritably. Could it be AIDS, HIV, whatever they call it? There's a poster about it in the toilet. It's got to be a possibility, but the fact is, Vic actually seems pretty healthy. And certainly not tired: Simon hears more zippering, the rustle of paper, deep breaths, a little laugh. It's like having a man-sized hamster in the room and he might as well admit it that he's lost it as far as sleep goes. He heaves himself up again. Vic has the bag on his bed and is clearly in the process of packing and repacking it.

'Sorry,' he says, glancing over his shoulder then turning back to finish the packing as he speaks. 'I want to make sure everything is ready for the morning. I'm off out! So you'll have some peace and quiet, then.' He zips up the bag, stows it next to the bed, crouches down, unzips it again. 'I've been in this hospital for nine months and most of that time I've been the only one. Mind you,' he adds, standing up and turning to face Simon again, 'I've had a lot of visitors.' He is smiling broadly and oblivious, to begin with, of the gape of his bathrobe, which reveals, worn beneath, a floral nightdress in pale blue, cream and black with lacy trim, and beneath that, the oddest thing of all, a plump, smooth suggestion of actual breasts.

'What the fuck?' Simon forgets to whisper and finds tears of pain in his eyes.

'Oh, hell,' says Vic, covering up, then holding the dressing gown tightly closed. 'Look, that wasn't on purpose. It's purely for my own benefit . . . I just thought, on the last night . . . Well – it doesn't matter, really, does it?' he says, sitting on his bed. 'If it's a problem for you, I'm sorry.'

Simon studies Vic, as if mesmerised. He sees that there's a delicate sheen of some kind of cream or oil applied to his face and neck, but also, a faint dark shadow around the jaw. The calves that poke out of the bottom of the bathrobe are, he realises, hairless. When Vic sits, Simon notices, he sits shoulders down, with his ankles crossed and his hands in his lap.

'I can tell you now,' Vic says. 'It really doesn't matter: I'm in the process of gender reassignment. A sex change. I'm becoming Charlotte.' He reaches for a couple of pots of pills that are next to his bed, shakes them. 'Hormones,' he says. 'You have to do two years of it, before they'll consider you for surgery. Then the waiting list, unless you can go private. Which is why I did what I did, which is beside the point now . . . I was well on the way when they got me, and what did they do? They put me in dispersal with about a hundred of the worst-looking men I've ever seen, and pulled the plug on my prescriptions! Even though the offence was related to what I'm going through, it took me two months to convince them all this was real and they had to do something about it. I got my medication back and my solicitor got me out of there and in here as a stop-gap. We've been fighting ever since for me to go in a woman's prison but everything is just so incredibly slow . . . All I can say at the end of nine months is I've made a start on it, and it'll be easier for the next person. Meanwhile this –' Vic gestures at their shared surroundings '– is the best they came up with.

They did warn me to be discreet. I'm sorry,' he repeats, 'if I've shocked you.'

Simon is still staring. There's something about Victor, sitting there fifteen feet away, the soft skin, the big bones, sturdy feet, the disproportionate beginnings of breasts – he is so utterly half and half. A person stranded, in their own body, between one thing and the next . . . It's a story you could tell, Simon thinks if you had someone to tell it to, but meanwhile he can't think what to say and Vic reaches again to the bedside shelf, tugs a tissue from a pastel-patterned cube sitting there. He hides his face in his hands, starts to cry.

'Oh,' he says, 'I could have done without this.' The crying makes his voice higher, but at the same time he uncrosses his legs and the whole of his posture regresses, subtly, to something not male as such, but certainly less womanly. Just desperate. It's like a group, but there's only the two of them.

'Look,' Simon whispers, 'you're out. You've made it.' Vic rubs his face with his hands, takes in a huge, shuddering breath.

'Yes,' he says.' Good night, then, Simon.' He stands up, removes and folds his bathrobe, exposing the entirety of the nightdress, then opens his bed and climbs in.

'Brian!' he shouts. 'Lights off, please!'

A couple of minutes later the main lights are cut, and with them the annoying buzzing sound that pervades the place all day. The shapes of everything in the room are still visible, though, and it seems to Simon that he lies awake most of the night, amazed, sipping water from his mug and listening to Victor's breathing shift and change.

In the morning Simon is woken by the doctor, who doesn't look down his throat at all, but talks about getting him back in circulation and decides to halve the dose of pain relief: 'Let's see what happens, eh?' Pretty obvious, Simon thinks, but perhaps there's something I'm missing here?

Vic's bed is empty. While he spoons in the strawberry-flavoured soupy stuff he gets to eat, Simon hears him, splashing about in the bathroom across the corridor, then chatting to

Brian and an officer in the lobby. He is expecting some kind of show when Vic comes in to collect his bag, but nothing could have prepared him for what actually walks into the room: Vic is wearing tightly belted black jeans and a paisley blouse, his hair is up in a knot at the back, a few carefully arranged wisps hanging down at the sides. He has applied a pearlised lipstick, and is suddenly possessed of smooth, even-looking facial skin with just the faintest bit of blush applied on the cheekbones, the suggestion of some shadowing beneath them. The face is all there; the rest, not quite. But if you didn't know?

Vic smiles, extends his hand. It's soft and warm, the nails filed and varnished to match his lips. Simon takes it.

'Good luck, Vic.'

'Charlotte,' Vic says.

'Charlotte, then.' Even on the face, things do look a bit dodgier from close up. The make-up's an inch thick.

'Don't let them grind you down.' Victor-becoming-Charlotte kisses his own hand, blows it in Simon's direction then picks up his bag and walks out. From the bed, Simon hears the unlocking of the hospital wing door, an officer saying, 'Fuck me!' and the sound of Vic's heels on the linoleum dwindling into nothing.

After all that, his throat hurts. He squirts it liberally with the antibiotic and anaesthetic spray they gave him at the proper hospital. At noon, the pain has got beyond what he can bear. He reaches up and presses the buzzer. Waits. Has to do it three times before Brian comes.

40

Joanne, one of the probation officers from Welfare, sits in a bucket chair next to his bed. She is stick-thin, with limp brown hair cut short. But her manner is very animated and she makes good use of her hands as she speaks. Well, she explains, opening one hand, the fingers spread in his direction, well, where he is going to once he's discharged from the hospital is, basically, an entire wing of men under rule 43 . . . Both hands are now involved in a complicated dance. Sex offenders? Yes, she tells him. Sex offenders, along with a few men with bad debts, or vendettas against them: inmates who, one way or another, need protection from others in the general prison population. Given what happened, he is now deemed to be in that category . . . The hands flutter to rest in her lap and she watches him carefully as she suggests: 'Why not give it a try, before you get upset about it? Putting a lot of people together like this means they can have their own facilities, and a better regime than if there were just a few of them dotted around . . .'

He'll think about that later. He'll get Alan to sort it out. Meanwhile: 'Has anyone got my course materials?' he says as loudly as he can, then fumbles with the lid of his throat spray. It's run out.

Well, Joanne tells him, hand to heart, his course materials *were* lost for a while but now a new set have definitely been issued. Somehow the change of address didn't get through and then, when it did, he had to be assigned to a new regional centre, but the pack has now been sent out, definitely.

'First- or second-class post?'

Well, actually, she doesn't know about that. It might be

another three or four days before they arrive, then they have to go through the system, so Monday, perhaps. He will be able to have computer time and access to a member of Education staff. Someone will write a note of explanation to his tutor if necessary, he mustn't worry about that . . .

'I should have done the introductory exercise and sent my first essay in by now!' he tells her.

Fine: as she said, it will be done. Joanne's hands rest again in her lap. At this point, her main concern, she says, is his health. Prisons are not good places to be sick. She thinks a dietician ought to be brought in.

Simon shakes his head. 'Course materials, please,' he whisper-shouts at her, leaning back in the pillows. Though later, when he goes to the bathroom for a shave, he can see what she means. There's not much of him left.

The ward is quiet without Vic. It's a matter of passing time. Simon borrows something by J. G. Ballard from the library trolley and he has Brian's newspaper every day. Monday does come, eventually, but there are no course materials. It is when Simon reaches for his notebook to start drafting a complaint that he realises with an almost physical shock that someone else has been there. Someone has written him a message on the inside of the back cover: *If you want to write*, it says, *I'll answer. Nothing heavy, mind you. Friends. Charlotte Adams.*

It can only have happened while he slept. First thing in the morning, Vic must have come quietly over and picked up the book. Quite a liberty, but at the same time, the idea of it, the picture of himself on his back with his mouth open, Vic still wearing that nightie of his perhaps, or else dressed in the paisley blouse, brings a smile to his lips.

The address, care of a Mrs Adams, is in Brighton. Simon can remember Brighton, from a trip there with the Burnside kids. He remembers a bright, busy place, shops, hordes of people, light on the water, the crashing of waves and the squealing of gulls. He and a couple of other kids spent hours on the amusement pier, and then traipsed up the beaches, climbing breakwaters and daring each other to run along them. They tried to cut back by road, got distracted; the minibus had to be held back and everyone else got to have a fish and chip supper while they waited. He liked Brighton.

But basically, he's not interested. Why on earth would he write to someone way out there on some kind of a limb who isn't actually a woman? It could be catching, for all he knows . . . Besides, personal letters are a thing of the past, so far as he's concerned. He completes his complaint about the course materials, tears out the page, shuts the notebook and tries to read.

It's not easy. Vivienne, Tasmin, the women, he finds himself thinking, all that effort, the excitement of studying their words and sometimes feeling he knew something about them or seeing them in his head: it all came to nothing, except for the vaguest sense, again only occasional, of being, as they say, 'in touch'. Not quite nothing: he remembers Tasmin sobbing down the phone at him, a real person risen out of the page and refusing to go away, and of course then he must remember Amanda too, it all goes back to there, to her very similar refusal to be ignored. Perfectly reasonable: but will he ever really know how to deal with it? Writing letters can be dangerous, can lead to places you'd never choose.

On the other hand, he's been asked, person to person, by someone he already knows, to write. OK: it's a weird person, but all the same there's a knowing and there's an asking. He, or she, has read what's on his skin. Watched him eat a yoghurt with a plastic teaspoon . . . Before, that would have been a disadvantage, but now there seems to be a kind of promise there: something that keeps bringing him back, between his brief incursions into a story in which men fly aeroplanes around an empty swimming pool, back to the idea that he might just do it, he might just write to Victor-becoming-Charlotte. He could at least see how it feels.

I hope things are going well for you now that you don't have the penal system to contend with on top of everything else. I would be interested to hear more about what it is you are going through.

The words come easily. It's somehow simpler than before. The confusion he feels over the name, Charlotte, will disappear with practice; the matter of he or she only arises in his own head.

I must admit that what you told me was pretty mind-blowing. Then you left, and now, I am still here, sitting up in this bed in a place you are probably trying to forget, and I am curious about you. At Wentham, where I was last year, we did a lot of group therapy. I sometimes thought they wanted to take me to bits and make a new person out of them, and I hated it, even though I knew there was a lot wrong with me, but here you are, doing the same sort of thing, on purpose! I suppose you must be absolutely sure, or else you wouldn't be doing it. As for me, I'm trying to eat my way out of here so I can get some exercise. My course materials are supposed to come soon, I'll be a happier camper then. I'm keeping this short as you must be very busy. Please don't feel obliged to reply.

Aware of the instructions he was given: nothing *heavy*, he decides against a P.S. to the effect that Brian is missing Charlotte. Missing, even someone else's missing that might or might not be his by association, is definitely *heavy*. Of course, it's true that the room does seem empty, without the larger-than-life, double-named, floral nightie-wearing, bell-pushing person whom it tried, and failed, to contain. Someone who asked for the impossible and now seems well on the way to getting it.

'Did you know?' Simon asks, gesturing with a sideways nod of his head at the far side of the room. For a moment it seems as if Vic has left behind him not only a message, but an after-image of himself sitting in his pale-blue dressing gown on the empty bed.

'Know what?' Brian counters, deadpan, and clearly Simon's

requests – for notepaper, stamps, pens and the like – just don't hit the spot.

The course materials finally arrive in a large cardboard box which contains, amidst a sea of styrofoam worms, a fistful of pamphlets and information sheets, a plastic wallet full of A4-sized paper with carbons attached, two ring binders, three normal-sized text books, two cassette tapes and another, larger book, called *Starting to Study*.

Brian looks on, uncomprehending, as Simon unpacks it all. 'That's it?' he asks. '*That's* what you wanted?'

An essay, *Starting to Study* informs Simon, should have an introduction, stating the area of enquiry, a central section in which the argument is developed by means of examples and quotations, and a conclusion, which reminds the reader of the initial proposition and summarises the argument(s). Quotations from books must include the full title, author, edition and page number; periodicals must be cited by means of title, year and serial number. Essays are written to a set length and sticking to this is an important discipline . . .

Starting to Study is a triple-sized paperback, printed on thick, glossy paper with a column of text down the right side of the page. Occasional illustrations and acres of white space are to the left: are you supposed to leave it like that, or write in it? When the book is opened, ink fumes gush from the pages, fill his lungs and head, then vanish, volatile, intoxicating, new. Towards the end of *How to Study* is the list of questions he will later on choose from, many of them followed by the word *Discuss*, which, like its sister *Consider*, means that you need not come to an absolutely firm conclusion. What is an individual? *Discuss*. What do we mean by society? *Discuss*. *Discuss* the term *anomie*. What do we mean by 'rights'? *Discuss*. Using two or more examples, discuss the idea of works of art having a purpose or function . . .

The way things are expressed gets right up his nose: *Will take me time to get used to*, is the way he puts it in the introductory letter to his tutor, Michael Barnes Ph.D. but basically, he's on cloud nine. First of all, he must do exercise 1, on how to summarise what you have read. He'll need a bigger dictionary. More books. A *highlighter pen*, whatever that is.

'How long are you going to be in here?' Brian asks. 'We're going to have to come to some kind of arrangement, if you're going to keep wanting things.'

41

The stationery Charlotte uses is smooth, ivory-coloured; the handwriting has generous loops on the *y*s *g*s, *h*s and so on; it shows no signs of haste or excessive pressure on the page. There's just Simon's name, then a dash. No dear, no yours sincerely, best wishes, certainly not any love at the end. Conversational.

> Obliged is not something I do! I like to communicate, I have lots of friends. You struck me as unusually open-minded when you were put on the spot, and since I have no intention to live a lie, I really need that kind of person in my life. When I meet one, I try to keep in touch (and vice versa with the opposite). But at this point I am not always in the mood to sit down and write, so don't worry if sometimes I take a while to get back to you.

Open-minded? Well, Simon thinks, that's something new.

> You did look very rough when I saw you. I do hope they give you something decent now that you can eat, though from my experience there, I suspect not. As for me, my dose has gone up and I'm having to go on a diet, very boring but necessary to get the proper shape. You were right, I have been super-busy, what with celebrating, seeing my doctor, social worker, etc., shopping for some decent outfits, and finding somewhere of my own to live. Mum is very sweet but the two of us in the same small place is a recipe for disaster: hard for her to realise that while I may be in a changing body, I have not gone back to being fifteen! Of

course, she has had to put up with a lot and I'm lucky that she has.

It's not open-mindedness as such, Simon decides, because it's not as if he had found himself next to some queer that might have jumped on him. It's something else. Because it's nothing to do with him, he can be more curious than he might have been otherwise.

The new address above is from the first of May. Soon, I'll be even busier fixing it up. What I've got is a sweet little first-floor flat, walking distance to town, but very run-down. Also, I have to find work and this isn't going to be easy, given what I did to the Abbey National: I don't think I told you but I had a good job there. I was really sick of the wait and it seemed to me that they could easily afford £15,000. I do regret it, not only because we all have to be patient for what we want, etc., and because they were actually very decent to me beforehand, but also because it now turns out that the nine months I spent inside might not count, for some reason, towards the time I've spent living as a woman. I have to test myself by living 'as a woman' for about two years. I had already done a year when I was arrested. So I'm fighting it, of course.

There's a lot to explain if you're new to it, and Simon, I get sick of going over this again and again. It can make me feel very tense and it is all a means to an end as far as I'm concerned. The social part of being a woman comes very naturally to me; I have always been this way inside. What I have to go through physically is to make the outer reality match the inner one. Hormones are taking me a good part of the way and they make me feel so good it's almost like being stoned. I'm finishing off the electrolysis. Then, when they are sure that I can cope, the surgery: it probably sounds impossible to you but I've met many people who have had it done. You couldn't tell the difference and after that I will live a full life and there aren't words to express how desperate I am for that to happen. I enclose a couple of photocopies that will give you more detail. My experience is very like Angela's in the second article. I knew things were wrong from when I was small. So no, this is not at all a matter of being made into someone else, but of finally becoming me.

Charlotte.

By now, Simon has quite enough writing to do. Too much, even. So, why is he wasting his time on this, reading about androgen and oestrogen, et cetera? Is it because what he has got here is a person, neither woman nor man, but something more basic, something underlying, glimpsed by accident, impossible to forget? The real thing? He doesn't know and thinks he is probably on a hiding to nothing. But still, for now, he continues.

I have been moved onto the wing. The cell is clean, etc. There are some very unpleasant people here, but they mainly keep themselves to themselves. I feel OK but have to be very careful what I eat. I am studying a book by someone called Durkheim, who says, among other things, crime is normal and useful. Interesting! My tutor tells me I have to slow down, break things into smaller parts and focus more, instead of trying to get everything I can think of crammed in at once. How? He did send examples so I hope to work out what he is getting at.

Work is the main blot on the horizon. We all have to put time in at the laundry. Not good physically: a hot, dim dirty-looking place. You've got about forty of these outsized grey machines, washers and dryers. There's a constant churning noise from the machines and extractors. The air is full of damp fluff which sticks in the hairs of your nose. Sheets, pillowcases, tablecloths, shirts, jeans, mail and diplomatic bags, washers, drier, pressing, folding and packing . . . This week I'm pressing sheets: a pair of you take turns to remove the sheet from the wheeled bin that comes from the drier; between you, you spread it on the board, then both pull down the top half. Steam gushes around the edges. Then open, wait a second, fold, press again. A monkey could do it, so at least I get a bit of time to think, except that I've been put with a bloke who couldn't stop talking if you put a gun to his head.

You tell me I'm open-minded. I'm flattered, and will try to live up to the impression you have of me. I might even add it to my collection: do you remember? The words on my skin. Mind you, it would have to be a DIY job, because I am certainly not letting any of this lot in here anywhere near me.

Thank you for the articles you sent. I have read them all. It is scary stuff, but also amazing that you will have all that done and then come out of hospital after just a week.

How can you be sure? Suppose, afterwards, you realised it was a mistake? He doesn't dare to ask that. There are other things to be said.

It is good to be trusted with knowing all this and I admire your spirit and determination, Charlotte. It takes some bottle to go through with something as drastic as this.

The letter goes off, unsealed, for the censor to gawp at, but really, he doesn't think about that very much any more. He has a ring binder for his university assignments, another for his tutor's replies. He has various exercise books, Property of HM Prison Service, DO NOT REMOVE, for his notes on different subjects. In one of these he has started the list of words he hasn't got around to getting inked: *introvert, heterosexual, erotophobic, nonce, open-minded* – it's all rather like the Golden fucking Notebook, which drove him mad at the time he read it, but there you are. The letters from Charlotte will be kept in a new box, because even though he did get the old Adidas box back, it was broken at the corners, so he put an elastic band round it and started over. And another thing: he just writes and sends the thing off and he doesn't keep copies of his own letters this time around. It's all different.

Simon,

Let me know if I can help getting you books. I go to town most days. Things are good. I am on a bit of a roller-coaster and very dependent on how people see me when I am out, but overall I am making quite a bit of progress on all fronts, including a very boring computer course (but at least it is free). If I pass, Tony, a friend of a friend, says he will give me a job.

I do know that this is a huge thing to be doing, but at the same time the surgical side of things, which everyone including me focuses on too much, is only part of it. It's like a door that I am going through, at the end of a long journey. I like to think that it is still me that is on both sides of the door. But perhaps I won't know until it's done.

I know if it was an operation for reasons of illness, I would be terrified about the physical side of things and all that might go wrong, but as it is I am looking forward to it, and assume that everything will be fine. My only regret is that I have to be put to sleep and just lie there, that I can't do it myself. My friends from the support group think I am crazy to say this, but maybe you will understand.

I now have my appointment to meet the surgeon. I hope I like him. Again, since it is a kind of birth, I wish it would be a woman, but there are only men doing it at the moment. Really, I am just lucky to be born at a time when it can happen at all.

I enclose some photos so that you can see who you are writing to.

The photos aren't there, of course; he has to apply for them and wait. Receiving them, he feels a kind of dread and can't look straight away. Finally he sees that the Victor-becoming-Charlotte in the photograph is sitting at a wrought-iron table in a garden wearing a forties kind of dress with a wide belt and heeled sandals. The pose is slightly twisted, to accent the waist. The earrings and necklace match. Victor has almost gone, but all the same, Simon can still see traces of the person he met in the hospital. And yes, he can just about follow the idea of going through a door at the end of a journey. It's all right, it's not his business, so be it . . . *No*: it's utterly mad! Skin from the penis is used to make the inside of the vaginal opening. The glans penis is integrated into the clitoris. To create a fully realistic effect, the outer vaginal lips make use of follicle-bearing skin from the scrotal area . . . What can you say to someone who wants to do that?

> The lounge in your flat looks quite something, especially the curtains on those big sash windows. Also the polished wooden floors and rugs. Are they Indian or something? It looks very warm. You don't see colours like that in here, as you know. As for the picture of you, Charlotte, well, it must suit you out there.
>
> The news here is that yesterday I had an interview with a Mr O'Hara from the Parole Board. According to Alan, and Joanne, Mr O'Hara will make some kind of report on me, which, along with all the other reports, including Alan's – which he says is very positive – will be sent to the Board. Maybe I can write something myself too. Then some time soon (they don't give you a date) the Board will read it all and decide whether or not I can move to a lower-security classification. Well, if I did, quite apart from getting out of the ★★★★ing laundry, and having a few more freedoms, then the next time they reviewed me, they might look towards release. Having said that, it all seems rather remote.

Impossible. *Terrifying* . . .

> I'll probably get knocked back. I know for a fact that there's a psychiatrist who has given me a very poor report. And the fact is that actually I'm pretty happy here, what with the course and your letters to open the world up a bit. So, as

long as I can keep studying, I don't mind too much how it turns out.

I am glad to hear that you will meet the specialist.

And also, not glad: the truth is that the more Simon thinks about Victor's transformation the more it worries him. The medical procedures, the risks of anaesthetic and so on: as a one-off, that's life, it's nothing. Squeamishness he'll eventually be able to put aside. But when Victor has become Charlotte, will she stop writing to him? Too busy, too happy, to bother? Or will these letters somehow become more difficult for Simon to write, when something more like a real woman is opening them? Or will he be writing to someone he doesn't know at all, instead of just someone he hardly knows? Will he, Simon, lose interest, once things are resolved? After all, he has problems with women. Ambivalence, fear, anger, small things like that.

I must admit, though, it is a bit like you are going off into outer space. What do your friends say about it? Good, that you can talk to people who have been through it already. What are your plans for afterwards?

Simon –

Yesterday I finished the electrolysis on my face! It's rather swollen today but once the skin has settled down I am going to be able to use much less make-up and already, in the last stages of it, I have been noticing how much less unwelcome scrutiny I get when close up. Most days, I feel completely confident with strangers. My bubble doesn't get burst and I can't tell you what that is like! So, after the session I went out and spent £100 in Monsoon, a silk skirt, and a blouse for Mum as well.

Simon is struggling with his letter to the Parole Board when he receives this and really, he thinks, it's enough to make you weep. The contrast. The innocence.

I know it must be almost impossible to imagine the pleasure of this kind of thing and I don't underestimate how baffling this must be for some of the people who know me, or rather who knew Vic. I've lost some of his friends, gained others of my own. I may lose some of those again, once I'm through, and start over with some new ones. Of course, I hate to lose anyone, but that's how it is.

Simon, I want to clear something up. I appreciate your encouragement and support and there was definitely some kind of spark between us, wasn't there? But I wouldn't want there to be any hint of romantic feelings. I'm just not ready for that kind of thing at the moment, and after my operation, well – to be honest, after going through all that I'm going to want someone who is there, physically. I'm a very sensuous woman and that will be important to me. Also, as far as you and I are concerned, there's a lot we don't know about each other. Hopefully, after the operation, we can do something about that. Meanwhile, I know I am horribly self-obsessed!

I will let you have the clinic details nearer the time. Thinking of you. Keep in touch.

Romantic feelings? Spark? What exactly, is she saying here: is it what she seems to be saying, or the opposite of what she seems to be saying? Is she trying to put ideas in his head? In any case, she is a man . . . It's confusing enough that he decides to get a second opinion, or as much of one as he can without handing the letter over. He brings the photograph along with him, though.

'Look, you may well be way out of your depth here,' Joanne tells him, her hands signalling wildly. 'I mean, if someone is going through a change like that, you can't know where you are. You can't be sure what she wants you for, can you? Or how long any state of mind will last. I mean, the goal posts can move at any time. So, try to keep a distance, is what I'd advise.'

'Well, I suppose I'm safe enough, in here,' he tells her, deadpan. She misses the joke, offers to get him some other pen friends, via the Prison Reform Trust. They are really interesting people from all walks of life, and, of course, vetted to some extent as to their motivation.

'Maybe,' he says. But not yet.

Dear Charlotte,

Thank you for being so clear. Even if you were to have those kinds of feelings for me, I suspect my past would put you off, once you knew the details of my offence. I have had considerable problems relating to women.

Just to reassure you I do not have those kind of feelings you mentioned. I am struck by you as a person and find what you say very interesting and that is what is important to me.

Who is this I am writing to? he thinks, momentarily horrified, as he studies the photograph again, seeing at the same time Charlotte, the man in the hospital bed and the amazing hybrid creature he became. It's heavy. On the other hand, *Introduction to the Social Sciences* seems pretty straightforward.

Dear Simon,

An excellent piece of work. The points you make about the theory of *anomie* with regard to the goals of individuals in contemporary society are both insightful and well expressed. You have made very good use of examples, and likewise your choice of quotations is apt and well referenced. Smaller points are marked on the text.

Should you eventually choose a Social Sciences degree, which I feel you would be very capable of, I would be delighted to work with you again.

He tapes Michael Barnes' letter to the wall above his desk, and next to it, the photograph of Victor-becoming-Charlotte.

Simon,

Details of how to contact me after the op are on the card.

What can I say? I feel quite tearful, now that it's happening. Partly they are happy tears but also they are for Victor, who very soon will be gone for good. I am glad, but at the same time I was used to him and I will be so new, and all on my own, somehow. I'll miss him. You'll think I'm mad but on Friday I had a goodbye party for what's left of him! Over forty people came. It was pretty outrageous.

It's nothing, and it's everything. I'm like the mother at my own wedding. It's being born all over again into new flesh. I'm scared of the pain now but everyone says it isn't so very bad. My friend Diane is going with me.

Wish me luck.

Charlotte.

At work, he's still pressing sheets and still with motor-mouthed Keith. Apparently he does a good job.

'Like I told you,' Keith says, 'I got the home leave OK and I took the coach to London, Stubby, you know Stubby Yates? He'd set me up to collect some stuff, a big order, from someone he knew and the idea was I could collect, then get back north to see my mates, then shove it where the sun don't shine on my way back in, right?' He wipes sweat from his forehead with his sleeve. 'You listening?' he asks. Simon grins and shrugs; the steam hisses again and Keith gets into his stride, explaining how the contact didn't have the stuff and the contact went off home and he waited and he waited all night in some club for it to materialise, drinking Tangos until he pissed orange, and then gave up, got on a coach and went home, up north, where it turned out they were all either dead or inside except for one bloke, and he'd moved. Then, when he eventually found the place, the bloke wasn't there and his girlfriend was in tears, said that he'd just stolen her cash and gone to Wolverhampton.

'Wolver-fucking-hampton!' Keith relives the moment, watches, as if it's nothing to do with him, while Simon stacks a folded sheet on the outgoing trolley, reaches down into the bin for a fresh one.

'So I get a sawn-off, liberate a motor, drive there, right? I find the place straight off. I kick down the back door. Boom! I storm right in waving the sawn-off, yelling, You Bastard! And it turns out to be the complete wrong house, just this bog-standard family, two kids, nicely turned out, all sat round the table having roast chicken for lunch. I yell, Sorry! run straight out, but they call the cops, there's helicopters, the lot . . . I was almost glad when they got the cuffs on me. The only thing you can say is, I was so busy I kept off the drink, eh, mate?

Simon loads another sheet into the cart.

'But I've wrecked my parole and got all these new charges, plus Stubby's out to get me because I owed him, and that's why I've had to come in here on the Rule, see, even though the company's bad. Yourself not included mate. You're the one that got bleach down his throat, isn't that you? Me, I'd've messed the place up, taken a few with me. I'm a man of action. Plus, I like to talk.'

'Feel free,' Simon says. Any moment, the bell will go off. It's Friday: he gets computer time after lunch. Over the weekend, he'll read *What is Philosophy?* Tuesday, Charlotte has her operation. He's already sent a card. Wednesday, he'll call the hospital.

'Bit of a dreamer, aren't you?' says Keith.

42

His back turned to the corridor, his head under the perspex dome, Simon leans on one hand, elbow locked, into the wall of the booth. Cheery string music, intended to distract waiting callers from the passing of time, follows the receptionist's instruction to *hold, please*. Nonetheless, the units on Simon's phone card are steadily devoured; good, then, that he guessed this might happen and managed to get hold of an extra one just in case . . . The music stops and a woman's voice says: 'Hello, Simon!' The voice swoops downwards on the second syllable of hello, then rises again – not quite so far – at the end of his name and this, he assumes, must be Diane, the friend Charlotte said would accompany her to the hospital.

'Can I speak to Charlotte?' he asks.

'Speaking!' the woman on the other end of the line says, releasing a few small bubbles of laughter. 'It's me! How do I sound?' She sounds, this time, definitely flirtatious and his own voice needs a good cough to clear the way for it to emerge.

'Great!' he says. 'You sound happy. Congratulations.'

'It's just wonderful,' she tells him. 'No pain at all! I'm doing really well. Everyone here has been fantastic.' It is a completely different person he is talking to, no doubt about that. He feels a kind of panic, his mouth dry, heart racing suddenly in his chest. He leans closer into the wall.

'I've got to say, this is really weird!' he tells her.

'Yes!' Charlotte says, enthusiastically. 'You're meeting me for the first time. And likewise for me, except that Victor remembered you and I've got the rights to his memories. I've *inherited* them!'

What do you say to *that*?

'Oh – it looks like I got a good report,' he tells her. 'From the Parole Board. I'm moving soon.' That is *fantastic*, she tells him. She knew it would be a good year! It has been such a lovely surprise to get his call – but right now, she has to go and have what she calls 'some yucky medical stuff' done.

'Do let's keep in touch,' she says.

There are just a couple of units left on the second card. He puts it in his pocket, walks down the grey linoleum corridor to the deathly fug of the TV room, the screen there, two feet across, the colours all tuned up to their maximum, a kind of radioactive effect. He stands by the door looking in: there they all are, hunched and stocky, grizzled, stringy, clean-shaven, avuncular, the child molesters, pornographers and rapists of this world, a few real sadists thrown in . . . The local news is on. Something about a toddler being rescued from an abandoned well after being missing for three days. It's amazing what can happen out there, in the world. Even in here: one bloke's face is streaming with tears, as he watches the interview with the kid's ecstatic parents. And he, Simon, can't help thinking about it: a man he met has turned into a woman with an extraordinary, trapeze act of a laugh. You can't say life is entirely dull.

But neither is it straightforward: the Parole Board's official letter turns out to be more complicated than expected. On the one hand, he can move on, but on the other: *It was felt that good progress has been made in terms of coming to terms with the offence, although you have not yet given adequate attention to addressing some of the behaviours contributing to it, which the Board considers should be a prerequisite for any further recategorisation.*

Alan visits him to discuss his feelings about this, which are not good. At the same time, he has to write an essay of two thousand words entitled 'How do we know we exist?' and mid-way through it he is moved, by sweatbox, to the new place. It's modern, just four storeys high, built in acrid yellow, knife-edged brickwork. There's an excellent gym, but not much in the way of gardens.

He sends Charlotte the new address, along with a brief note

to say that he hopes she is having a good time but he doesn't hold out much hope, because as far as personal letters go, nothing has come for over a month. It's the end of it, he supposes. Very likely it – he – has served his purpose. Perhaps Charlotte wants to start over, with no one knowing the way she was before? He could understand that, but it would be nice to be *told*.

> You must be wondering where I got to! Yes, I am having the best of times. Stitches are a thing of the past, and I must say, now that the icing is on the cake, I look good! Plus, it all seems to be *working*! So, I'm getting to know myself. My confidence is so much better. The result is, I have been a bit hyperactive and find it rather hard to say no to anything because absolutely everything is so much more fun now. I have been out most nights, meeting just loads of new people in the last two weeks but I am really going to have to be more sensible soon. Everyone is telling me to slow down, I've got the rest of my life, but that's only half true, isn't it? After you're forty or forty-five, the action is bound to diminish, even if it doesn't completely stop . . . Plus, of course, most people go a bit wild at first. When I start my new job soon I will have to get up bright and early again, so I guess they have got a point. It's in a company that makes and distributes games, it'll be word-processing mainly and making arrangements, etc. My boss, Tony, seems pretty reasonable. Quite good-looking. Very girly job, which is nice in a way, but I expect I'll get bored. It'll do for now. Once I've been working for a while, I'll be able to afford a holiday, so there's the plus side. How's things, Simon? I hope life is treating you well too?

Simon hesitates to say that no, actually, it's a bitch right now – but on the other hand, he has a feeling that if he doesn't tell at least some of the truth, there's no real point to any of this and it could end up the way Vivienne Anne Whilden did, or worse. Charlotte may be a good-time girl, he reasons, but she's said herself that she did inherit Vic's memories, which must include plenty of less-than-perfect moments.

> I hope you'll forgive the frankness, Charlotte, but I need to get this off my chest. I am getting very distracted at the moment because I've had this meeting with Alan, who says I have to come up with some kind of plan for the rest of my sentence. The Board did give me my move to here, but they made it clear that further progress would be dependent on me addressing outstanding issues that have been flagged up. So I asked him how, exactly? Then he tells me they are now beginning to run these special training courses, somewhat along the lines of one of the treatments at Wentham, where I was until a year ago. I got thrown out of there, partly, I'm sure, because I wouldn't go along with one of these courses. He says, there's a new thing starting now, would I consider another go at it, a module, all on its own, lasting just four months or so. So I told him I'd rather be shot in the head. Alan said sorry, he knew I'd feel like that, but there isn't another option . . . I'll wait until there is, I told him. Not his fault, but I had a go at him and I feel bad about that. Plus, right now, I am really struggling with the Introduction to Philosophy. I don't mind reading about it, but writing the arguments out in essay form, where you have to define every single word as if people hadn't been using them since the year dot: it's a real wind-up when you just want to get on and say what you mean but never end up getting there at all and forgetting what it was. Well, Charlotte that is how it is for me right now, I hope this is not too heavy. I can say I am putting weight back on and managing to keep on track with my yoga and aerobic fitness, so that is something at least. Also, as you can see, I have got my typewriter back. Well, don't wear yourself out, forty-five is a long way off.
>
> Simon.

How old is she, actually? Back in the hospital, he would have put Vic the man at a little younger than himself: twenty-eight perhaps. In the photograph, half-way to her current state, made-up, she looks both younger and older. The face is younger, but the dress doesn't work . . . In any case, weeks pass, and she doesn't write back, whereas the Introduction to Philosophy tutor sends a typed letter telling him that he has done quite well but needs to develop greater patience in following through and testing the stages of an argument. He is welcome to take the subject further, but it is one in which temperament is as important as intelligence and it doesn't suit everyone. Right. End of Story, then. He might as well start reading for Literature and chooses *The Plague* because it's shorter than *Tess of the D'Urbervilles*.

I just can't seem to sit down and write a proper letter these days, but I do want to keep in touch. So here's an idea: how about I come up and see you one Saturday, if you have a visiting order to spare? Of course, you might not. But my thinking is that it is time you knew who you are writing to! Plus I might be able to cheer you up. It's not that far and I've got a new car. I'm doing lots of visiting.

News: On top of everything else, I have had my first romance and I've done a photo shoot for a magazine article about gender dysphoria! I got a free Sassoon hair-styling session and had to pose in a whole range of outfits: work, party, beach – should get some nice pictures out of it.

I've included my home number, so, if you want, you can give me a ring to arrange a time. Charlotte.

It's good to hear that voice again, warm and liquid, sliding down and rushing up, appearing, suddenly, around corners. Why speak in a monotone, when you can do all this? Why stick to just the words, when you can make them into music? Why not throw in a whole lot of soft exclamations, fragments of laughter? He appreciates it a lot, though at the same time, he makes no concessions to it, resolutely chats to her as if she were a man.

'I'm not busy. Take your pick,' he tells her.

'Mmm . . . Actually, I might bring Diane,' she tells him.

'Bring Diane? Why?'

'Why not?' she asks.

'It's not a zoo, Charlotte.'

'Someone to talk to on the drive,' she says. 'And she's nice, you'll like her.'

Why not? Why not sit down at a visits room table with two ex-men? Plus, of course, it's not been expressed as a choice. Probably she just wants to be sure he doesn't get any ideas. This way it's not too intimate.

'All right,' he tells her. 'Bring whoever you like, Charlotte.'

Naked to the waist, Simon spreads the washcloth, hot as he can stand it, over his face. COURAGEOUS is written backwards in the mirror and WASTEOFSPACE runs up the side of his spine, ATHREATTOWOMEN up the other. On one shoulder blade it says STUPID, on the other BRIGHT. Just below the hairline on his neck, in tiny capitals BASTARD; CALLOUS wraps around one bicep, MURDERER around the other. Bernie's word, across his chest, has the largest, neatest lettering. The rest depend on who did them for tidiness and spacing. Across his back, just above the waistline, it says ARROGANT. The rest, the job titles on his right buttock, the other recently added Wentham words on his upper right thigh, are covered by a nearly-new pair of prison-issue jeans with most of the colour still in. Across from the washrooms, behind him, is his cell, where a clean shirt lies ready on the bed. The mirror clouds over, he wipes it, applies foam to his face. He's so nervous he feels sick. There's only so much you can do about looking presentable. It's not that. It's what are they going to say, face to face? Just what can you say, in what amounts to public, to a person who has just had their genitals remodelled? What is Charlotte – not knowing anything above the basics of what you've done to get in here – going to say to him? And what kind of idiot would agree to a thing like this? Getting dressed, Simon's fingers are so cold that he fumbles doing his shirt buttons up, and has to go back to the washroom to soak his hands in a basin of warm water.

It's unusually bright in the Social Visits Centre: a row of windows look out on some bushes and flowerbeds, and there are two large skylights high up in the sloping ceiling. The room is already half-full, the warm air thick with the hum of voices. The tables and chairs are packed in close, with just a small area set aside for kids to play with some toy cars and teddy bears from a plastic bin. Officers stand at the edges of the room and one of the others who are patrolling between the rows of tables takes Simon over to a seat by the window. The two brightly dressed women sitting there stand up and then it's all a blur: she takes hold of his shoulders puts her cheek to his and kisses the air to either side. No one female-looking has touched him like this for over a decade, and his heart is doing panic-stricken overtime even while the smell of her perfume takes him momentarily back to Vic's baths in the hospital, but things move inevitably on: he's shaking hands with Diane now and the officer tells them to settle themselves quickly down at the table, please.

He looks from one to the other. Charlotte is both uncannily familiar and utterly strange. She sits with one hand on the table, her large grey eyes looking back at him, amused, from beneath eyebrows plucked to a perfect curve.

'Under the circumstances,' she tells him, 'it's OK to stare.' He does. She has blonder hair than he remembers, full of different gradations of colour and looking as if every hair has been individually polished to a shine. She's wearing a black top that's stretched tight over what are definitely breasts, a fuchsia shirt, with pearly buttons, unfastened, over it. Diane, a small woman with a helmet of tightly permed curls, is wearing a floral print dress and, he notices distractedly, a wedding ring.

'Well,' Diane says cheerfully, gesturing around the room, 'it could be worse.'

'Thanks for coming,' he says. 'How was the drive?'

'OK. You're looking better than when I last saw you,' Charlotte tells him.

'You too!'

'It sounded as if you needed cheering up.'

'It's gone off the boil now,' he says. 'I'm OK. What's going for you then, out there? Is it as good as you thought?'

'It's better,' Charlotte says. While Diane nods and smiles and offers the occasional prompt, she tells him a long story about how she met a man called Boris at a bookshop in her lunch break and he turned up outside her office at the end of the day, and they went for dinner together. It lasted for five weeks, with a couple of weekends away, he had a Porsche, and she liked it at first, but then she'd had enough of him; he was trying to take her life over. Plus, in physical terms it wasn't a perfect match, he was rather on the fat side and not prepared to do anything about it – after all, why cast pearls before swine? She tells him how her mother is beginning to enjoy having a daughter, and shows him the engraved pendant she gave Charlotte after the operation . . .

Men can be very irritating, she tells him, with Tony, her boss, as prime example. She does an imitation of him pretending he hasn't just changed his mind, forgotten something or made a huge error of judgement. Then, she describes a pottery figure she bought to go on the coffee table in her living room, he's seen the table, she thinks. It's a nude woman, lying on her side with a baby curled up in the crook of her arm – quite realistic, but simple. It must be fantastic to have a baby, she says, but after all, not all women do it.

'Not all women even want to,' Diane says, firmly.

'I'd like to be able to make things, things like that statue I bought, for myself,' Charlotte says. 'Maybe I'll take a class – sculpture, pottery – come September. Are you in any way artistic?'

He tells her no, but explains that there is a painter he remembers quite liking, though, a Spanish artist, Pendez. A lot of art strikes him as a bit hard to get the point of. Like philosophy! But he likes to study. He likes reading. He couldn't actually read, when he came into the system. Now, he's thinking he'll end up with a Social Sciences degree or even Anthropology, perhaps. Maybe some History or Literature thrown in.

'It passes the time better than anything else,' he says. His hands are sweating. It's a big effort not to gaze over their shoulders or down at the table while he speaks. What else is there to say? Ninety-five per cent of his life seems unsuitable for a conversation like this. Things are grinding to a halt when Diane, who has been sitting there with a benign, half-interested expression on her face, suddenly asks:

'How long do you still have to do? Or shouldn't I ask that?' He shrugs.

'I don't know. In theory it could be, say five or six, or eight, more. But honest-to-God, I don't think I'm ever coming out. Basically, I can't be released unless I do that course I told you about. And I know it's bollocks.'

'You did tell me,' Charlotte says, 'but I don't understand. Why on earth wouldn't you do a course, any course, if it helped you to get out of here?'

'It's hard to explain,' he says.

They both sit there, waiting.

Get off my fucking back! he thinks.

'Five minutes!' Calls out one of the screws standing by the door.

'There's no time,' he says. 'Let's stop talking about this. Tell me, where are you going after this? What car is it you've got, Charlotte? I see you in a BMW. Open top. A silver one.' She laughs.

'If only!'

They're about to go. He thinks how they'll probably be splitting their sides laughing at him as they drive off in the car to do their bit of shopping and sightseeing. Or saying what a creep he was, weird, poor you, Charlotte, fancy being stuck in a room with that! The fact is, he's wasted the visit and he'll probably never see them again.

'Look, the trouble is,' he says at the last moment, 'I feel like a fucking Martian!'

'Oh, Simon,' Charlotte says, leaning over the table. 'I know that one. I know it well . . . You have to push it aside.'

'That's it now, ladies and gents!'

They stand up, reach across the table, do the cheek-to-cheek thing again, the soft, hairless skin, the perfume, it's all there.

'Call,' she says, 'or write. Whatever.' He walks over to the inmate exit without looking back, working hard, already, to expunge the whole thing from his memory. End of Story. End of. End.

He starts on some of the supplementary reading: another one by the same Camus bloke called *The Outsider*, which is about a murder, but he can't work that one out, there's something missing and one thing's for sure, the bloke in it wouldn't do well in the group at Wentham. He orders some books about Camus from the interlibrary loans and whatever else happens, it's good to know that there will be enough books in the world to keep him busy until he dies.

Charlotte sends a card. Perhaps, she suggests, it was insensitive of her to bring someone else along. She's sorry. Can they start again?

He doesn't answer it for almost ten days. And then he doesn't call, but writes.

> I enjoyed meeting you and hearing what had been going on but talking about my sentence is not easy and while there was nothing wrong with Diane *per se*, it probably didn't help having her there. Also, I am not sure why you want to visit me, and that makes me tense. You can't be that desperate for friends, I'm inclined to think. I've got the impression you have a lot of them. If you were trying to make up for not having time to write letters any more, don't. I wish you all the best. Simon.

It's not exactly a welcoming letter, but by a kind of sleight of hand he allows himself to include the visiting order, intended as an option, only. Then he blots the whole thing out so successfully that he's caught out completely when the call comes: Austen! Visitor! He is miles away, shaved, albeit hours ago, but with nothing to put on but a shirt with a rip on the front as if someone's been stabbed in the thing.

She is there at the same table, next to the row of houseplants by the window, her hair up, wearing black jeans and a tight lilac top with a scoop neck, hoop earrings, lipstick. She's half-smiling as she looks around at the people deep in their conversations at the other tables in the room. If she catches someone's eye, she smiles, maybe gives a little nod. She doesn't see him coming until he is quite close up.

'Hello, there,' she says, standing up for the air-kissing ritual. 'I was just thinking you were going to stand me up!' He grins back at her.

'I was busy,' he says, 'reading.'

'I've been thinking,' Charlotte says and, he is beginning to realise, one of the things about Charlotte is that she can listen innocuously, or chit-chat for five minutes about someone she has met or about decorating a bathroom, and then catch her breath, allow a short pause and suddenly shift gears: 'I've been thinking, you've got a very unusual face. Some women have a thing for men in prison, don't they? But I'm not like that. I'm the complete opposite. Though I suppose,' she says, with another shifting of gears, 'that really, I should ask you to tell me a bit more about how come you got here?' He's sitting opposite, watching her closely. His hands rest on the table, fingers interlinked: DCUUMNBT.

'How much more?' he asks her.

'Just a bit.' He remembers Tasmin, years ago now: *tell me everything*. This is more realistic. Yes, he tells her. He will. Meanwhile, he asks her to tell him about Brighton, and she describes sitting on the little square of roof garden she has attached to her flat, with the grey-and-white gulls wheeling and quarrelling overhead, the smell of the sea fighting with the traffic fumes.

To begin with, he types later that week, sitting at the small table in his cell,

> To begin with, I knew I had done something terrible but I just blotted the whole thing out. I thought I had screwed up and would have to start all over again but I didn't have any idea how, I couldn't take advice and I didn't want to look back. After about seven years of this I came to the point of admitting outright that the reason for the killing was more 'intimate' than had emerged in court.

Phrases he wrote for the Parole Board present themselves as needed and the letter comes surprisingly easily, so long as he pushes away thoughts of Charlotte sitting in her roof garden or sprawled on the sofa in her red sitting room to read it. The fact is, he realises, I am writing about the past.

> I wanted to be in charge of everything that happened between us, including in a sexual sense. I didn't want her to have any autonomy but she had started to stand up for herself; I was terrified and angry that was what led me to murder her. It was as a result of my admitting this to myself and others that I agreed to go to the therapeutic unit at Wentham, where I was very often put in a position to appreciate the link between feelings of panic and my own violent response when I feel my control of a situation being eroded. I was also able to understand more fully the extent of the suffering I inflicted on Amanda at the end and how, even before that, I treated her as if she was a video and I had the remote, not as a person, even though I liked her.

At the end of it, he feels calm and empty, almost light-headed, though perhaps that is because they've just repainted the cells and the smell lingers, despite the open window. It is possible that Charlotte will read what he's written and then withdraw, as Vivienne did, or just vanish – but, he reasons, if so, best get it over with. Adopting a business-like tone, he calls her two days before the next possible visit, to check that she received his letter and whether or not she is coming to see him.

'Yes,' she says, 'I would tell you if I wasn't.' Though this is probably true, he can't quite be sure.

43

The visitors in their sundresses and bright, sleeveless tops are like clouds of butterflies, sipping at the sugary, fluorescent orange juice the volunteers serve, warm, in styrofoam cups. Most of the other inmates are wearing singlets and shorts.

'So,' Charlotte says, setting down her cup and shifting gear, 'you've had this problem with women and what I still want to know is, why is it you won't do the course that they want you to do?' That's another thing he notices about her: she doesn't care what the conventions are, has no interest in the fact that she, the visitor is there to cheer him, the inmate, up, and is not supposed to ask this kind of thing. Of course she doesn't.

'I mean,' she says, 'it doesn't add up.'

'The course,' he explains, 'basically, it's for sex offenders proper. It's very practical . . . There was a sexual element in what I did but the point is, I've already tried what they're offering and I know. Take it from me.' He wants, he says, to spare her the details – at which point Charlotte bursts out laughing, and it feels as if the whole of the room has gone quiet, wanting to know what on earth the joke could be that produced such a sound. He glares at her across the table.

'Sorry,' she says, as the hum of conversation closes over them again. 'But actually, I'm pretty easy with details. If you think about it, I've had to tell an awful lot of strangers how I knew I should have had a vagina and couldn't be happy without one. I'm hard to shock.' She sits there, dressed in a skirt and a short-sleeved, scoop-necked blouse with lace trim, a cascade of beads around her neck, her legs crossed, and says that. There's nothing she won't say if she sees a need, even here, right in the visits room of a men's prison. He stares at her.

'Wasn't that Vic?' he asks. Charlotte shrugs, nods.

'So?' Well, she's asked for it.

'They put a measuring gauge round your cock,' he says. 'You look at pictures. They measure what's going on. Then you have to work out tending-to-the-normal storylines and masturbate about them for homework. Or you put in the correct fantasy right at the end, and gradually work back from there. They test you to see.'

'Does it work?' she asks, sipping again at the fluorescent juice, dabbing her lips with a tissue.

'Well, maybe,' he tells her. 'I got quite a way with it, but I couldn't discuss it with the doctors the way they wanted, so they threw me out . . . I've been there,' he tells her, drying the palms of his hands on his jeans.

'It's a hoop,' she says.

'Yes.' They agree, then. Perhaps, he hopes, they can move on now?

'So: you jump through it,' she tells him. 'Four months is nothing. If you remember, I had to do two years for my final hoop.'

'The point is,' he tells her, 'I did do it. In a way. But I picked someone to think about, someone I cared for, but who wouldn't have liked it. Someone I fell for, but she already had a partner. Right? It did work, but I couldn't discuss it – her – with the doctor. I can't go through it again. OK?'

'How did you know if this person minded or not?' Charlotte asks. 'Did you ask her? Would she ever have found out, anyway? Who was she?' she stares at him, then tosses her head. 'Don't people do this to each other all the time, for heaven's sake?' she says.

He doesn't answer. Puts his elbows on the table, his face in his hands. There's about ten minutes of this to go.

'If you want something,' Charlotte tells him, pushing stray strands of hair from her face, 'you just do what it takes. You keep going back. You find a way.' She leans across the table, sending her earrings into a paroxysm of motion. He can see her bra strap on one side of the blouse, the dark dusting of grape-coloured shadow on her eyelid, the slow beginning of a smile.

'Do it again,' she says, adding: 'So what? Four months. You could use me, if you want.' *What*? It's his turn, now, to laugh, but his laughter is more of a gut-punched gasp; the room doesn't stop talking, doesn't hear him at all.

'Charlotte!' he says. She's back on her side of the table now, looking him up and down as if waiting for a perfectly ordinary decision. Not long ago, she was telling him not to get romantic feelings, now she suggests he wank over her. 'Drop this,' he says.

'Why not?' she says. 'So long as it's nothing nasty. I wouldn't mind. Actually, I'd like it. Maybe I could give you some ideas.'

'Stop it!' Rage washes through him. Then it's suddenly gone. They're still sitting there in their chairs.

'Maybe I wouldn't be good enough?' she says. *No. Yes. Maybe.*

'You don't know what you're talking about. It's very confusing,' he tells her.

'It is,' she says. She takes hold of the hand he has on the table, reaches out for the other one. Waits, insistent, until he gives it her. Her thumbs nestle in his palms. Big hands, but soft-skinned, each nail filed perfect. He looks down at them, feels slightly sick. It's unreal.

'I'm still finding out what I want,' she says. 'This part of me has been on ice for so long. I'm a terrible flirt. I love the excitement, when you meet someone – I know I'm attractive – it's fantastic, being a woman, the way you can reel a man in . . . But I can see – I'm already beginning to feel, I want more than this . . . As well, I mean. Not instead . . . First the fling, the passion, and then, gradually, it turns into something else – but with the men I've met so far, well, there's nowhere else to go, really . . . I know I'm all over the place. Sorry,' she says, releasing his hands and hunting in her skirt pocket for a tissue. 'Are we still friends?' she asks, and he ends up saying *yes*.

The thing about Charlotte is that she is just utterly impossible and in a category of her own. And to think about her sexually, Simon decides, you would start with what just happened, with two pairs of hands holding each other over a table, and go on from there. You'd stay in the present tense and only much later, when you had made something real, would you be able to go gradually back to the past, to think how you both got to be here, where you came from, and what it all amounted to. *How do you know that?* The philosophy tutor would ask. Well, he doesn't know how he knows, and now he's going to forget it, fast.

At the next visit, Charlotte asks politely about his course and the training he is doing for the print shop. She outlines her dissatisfactions with her job, describes her aerobics class, discusses at length whether she should join a gym and gets him to promise to write out some exercises for her to do.

The visit after that, she asks if next time she can bring Gavin along with her.

'Gavin?'

'I really want you to like him,' she says.

Gavin owns a restaurant. He sits there with his hand on her leg, wearing his fancy clothes and a suntan, every little thing he has *designed*, and looks around the room like an ambassador from a superior race. He wants people to notice him, and see what he's got. Charlotte, Simon thinks, is part of that. She's wearing a short skirt and sheer tights, has her hair down and blow-dried in a way that makes her look completely different. She's quieter than usual, tries all the time to get Simon to talk to Gavin about being in prison, what the regime is like and so on. It's a complete wind-up and he tells her so on the phone afterwards.

'I'm seeing a lot of him,' she says.

'He's not right for you,' he finds himself telling her.

He would know that, would he? He does.

Gavin accepts her completely, she informs him. They are going on holiday together in a few weeks' time. She won't have time to visit until afterwards, but she'll keep in touch, right?

Right.

He gets a postcard from Italy. It won't last, he thinks. He's a prick and she's all over the place, that's what it is. She's trying to prove herself and her desires are limitless, she'll crash and fall, cut her hopes down to size, sob on Diane's shoulder, start over. That's how it's bound to be.

But what is it to him, really? Just a bit of interest, though he has to admit, he does miss Charlotte's visits, the forty minutes a fortnight when, relatively speaking, anything can happen. At the beginning of September, he phones her at the flat and, waiting for her to answer, is gripped with the fear that she will have moved, that perhaps she never returned from Italy, and that it really is the end of it all, whatever it was . . .

The voice that eventually answers is subdued, less musical than he remembers. She'll visit soon, she says, once she's more on top of things.

'You've lost weight,' he tells her, not approvingly. She talks of being exhausted, hints at humiliations and insults from Gavin. She cries, apologises because he's surely got problems of his own; he takes hold of her hand and he tells her she just made a mistake, and a pretty small one at that, it's not the end of the world. After this, they take care to avoid sore spots for a while and start to write again, in between the visits. Accounts of their daily lives. His reading: *the most miserable book I have read so far, almost seven hundred pages long. It is incredible to think of him sitting down and writing it and not topping himself.* Her thoughts as to what her situation is, as to the kind of woman Victor has become: *they are right, in the end, we are a kind of woman, but we aren't the same . . .*

Periodically, there is a man in Charlotte's life for a few weeks or months; of these, she brings along Paul, a humourless computer fanatic, and Tom, a college lecturer, quite interesting to talk to but far too old and, it turns out, married.

'You need to watch out,' he tells her at the end of Tom. 'The world is full of bastards, I should know.'

'Tell me about it,' she says. 'I wish I'd been warned that it's only the locked-up ones that have time to talk and be interested. But there's no point in waiting for you, is there!' They both laugh, but she seems angry too, with herself as much as anything. The volume of communication shrinks, just as suddenly revives. A year passes. He starts the degree.

Alan has been promoted. He's had a too-short haircut, looks older. A brand new, square-edged briefcase sits on the spare chair beside him. He says he has come to tell Simon something, something he technically speaking doesn't even have to inform Simon of, but which he has decided to pass on, because he thinks Simon deserves to know and he will be able to deal with it . . . However, he wants to stress that Simon doesn't have to respond to what he is going to tell him, not at all, in any way.

Right.

Alan looks down at the table top as if something was written there in tiny print, up again, smiles, but it's obvious he's not feeling particularly happy.

It must be Tasmin, Simon thinks, because Tasmin always comes out of the blue, when you're not expecting her and she must be eighteen by now, old enough to do what she wants. He hasn't forgotten her, so she probably still remembers him.

'Tasmin? No,' Alan tells him. 'It's more serious than that. Probation have received a letter from Amanda's mother, Hazel Brooks, which she wants you to read.'

Simon hears, somewhere in the back of his head, the noise of the wing, a door slamming behind him. *In there, you. This is a one-way street.* What the hell can she want with him? Why now? He watches Alan reach forwards, unscrew the cup of the thermos on the table, remove the lid, pour.

'You're not in any way obliged to read it. If you want to, you may do so, that's what I want to make clear.' The letter can't be in any way circulated. It is between the two of them, with Alan as a kind of intermediary. If he wants to read it, then it will be a matter of them sitting side by side at the table, or in the same room, at least. They will have to commit to discussing it thoroughly afterwards.

'Look,' Alan repeats, 'no one is going to think badly of you if you say no.'

'I don't have an agenda here,' Alan says. 'I just felt you should have the choice.' Is choice necessarily a good thing? *Discuss*. Once there was the prison wall. There was the world of the wronged, and the world of the perpetrators, each protected from the other. Now, a communication, negotiated, inspected, unwrapped, sampled, discussed, is passing with tortuous slowness and many conditions from one side to the other. Towards the other: it has not yet arrived. Not quite. 'There really is no rush,' Alan says, breaking the long silence between them just before it becomes impossible. How, Simon thinks, can he not read what Hazel wants him to read? How long can he sit on that decision? The letter, he supposes, is right there, waiting, in the new briefcase with its brass clasps and combination lock.

It's word-processed and printed out on a dot matrix printer. The first thing about it is that he knows what it must have cost her to do, to pick these words and type them out, read them back to herself, decide. The second and by far the worst thing about the letter is its gentleness and the chatty, informal way Hazel expresses herself, which somehow puts Simon in mind of Amanda. Even a remark as to how once Hazel wanted nothing more than for Simon to die in pain too and even now, she would tear him to bits herself, if she thought it would do any good – even that is expressed as if she were talking to another bit of him, which would understand.

> You remember my husband Tom? He always said it was a fault of mine, to want to see the best in everyone. But it was more than just seeing the best. Terrible as it is to admit now, Simon, I liked you. I thought you two would make a go of

it and I was happy for her. That's the truth. Ever since, I have had to ask myself what was wrong with me that I didn't see, that I encouraged her in this, had no suspicions, no idea, failed her . . .

Then there are questions she wants answers to. A list of them. And finally, a request to meet him.

I used to think that if I had magic powers I'd use them to bring Mandy back to life or else, second best, just to wipe out her pain at the end of it . . . But seeing as neither of those has been given to me, if I could choose to talk to someone about all this, someone who might answer my questions, then it would be you.

'Read it as many times as you want,' Alan says. *Want*? 'Take time to think about whether you can make a response at all, and if so, what form it might take.

'Hazel knows there is no structure for this, that it will drag on and could come to nothing,' Alan says. 'It's important that you consider yourself here, Simon.'

He calls Charlotte straight afterwards, feeling faint from the shock of it. He's glad to be able to hear her stirring sweetener into her tea, her radio muttering in the background.

'Why on earth would she want to meet you? What could the point of it be?' Charlotte says, 'What bad timing.'

'I'm not sure. Her husband died recently.'

'Don't!' she tells him. 'They shouldn't even put you in this position! It's already messing you up, I can hear it in your voice.'

Hazel, he explains, used to kiss Amanda goodbye, put her hand on Simon's shoulder as they went out of the door. 'Have a good time.' She used to offer him tea and cake, while Amanda finished getting ready upstairs. She was always trying to get him to call her Hazel, not Mrs Brooks. She was like an older, plumper Amanda to look at, but socially the opposite.

Not a bit shy. Once, he bought an offcut from work, and carpeted the bathroom for her.

'That was you, then,' Charlotte tells him. 'You are a different Simon now.'

He's older, for sure. He's thirty-four next birthday and has been serving his sentence for twelve years and six months, plus the nine months four days on remand, which makes thirteen years and three months, give or take, since he killed Amanda. Outside, Thatcher's finally gone. He learned the alphabet. Now he's started a Social Science degree. As for relationships, he started out pretending to be someone else, was beaten at his own game by Tasmin, fell for Bernadette. Now he has an extraordinary visitor who tells him he is attractive and makes jokes about waiting for him: he has learned some things, you can say that, but nothing that's any use in dealing with the contents of Hazel's letter or the request she makes at the end of it.

Can he just put it on hold? Can he say that he can't think about it properly right now because he has to finish an essay? It's going to be assessed and he needs to do a good job. And also he is feeling stressed because Charlotte is infatuated with Kevin, a photographer she linked up with in some kind of club, and she insists on bringing him for a visit.

Kevin has longish, unmoving wavy hair and beady, reptilian eyes, he sits with his hands shoved deep into the pockets of his jacket and mutters about what a wonderful subject Charlotte is and how he would love to take Simon's photograph too, if it could somehow be arranged. A double portrait, perhaps . . . It's a real effort not to yell at Kevin to go fuck himself but Simon manages to just look through him, as if he hadn't spoken.

'Why are you always so uptight?' Charlotte asks.

'Look,' he tells her, 'just come on your own from now on, will you?'

44

He's the last one in. They do the air-kissing thing; mechanically, he notices a new hair ornament, the smells of warm skin, foundation and face powder, perfume.

'Hi, there,' Charlotte says as they slip into their chairs. 'I was just thinking you were going to stand me up!' He tries a smile, doesn't do well.

'The drive?' he asks.

'So-so,' she says, pushing some stray hairs behind her ears. 'I got off early, but you just can't beat the traffic on the M25 . . .'

'You're not listening,' she tells him a while later. 'I'm not going to talk if you're not listening.'

Actually, he can hear what she is saying perfectly well: she's had a bad week, scraped the car, and she's really had it with Tony at work . . . But at the same time, he can more or less hear Hazel's voice, speaking the words she wrote over two months ago now. Mandy was such a lovely girl, she tells him, and if he didn't love her, then why did he not leave her to find someone else? Why did he have to make her suffer? It breaks her heart, Hazel says, to know that Mandy was alone with her fear, her body closing down on her.

'What's going on?' Charlotte asks.

'The letter,' he tells her. 'I think about it more and more.'

'I wish you hadn't read it,' Charlotte says.

'I had to,' he says, shrugging. It's true, though, that at the same time, he too wishes that he had not. Could forget it. Could unread.

'Now,' Charlotte says, 'I imagine you are feeling: how can you not meet her?' He shrugs, nods: yes, that's it, more or less.

'Think this through,' Charlotte tells him. 'Do you want to show her how sorry you are?' she asks. 'To apologise?'

'Apologise?' He spits the word straight back at her. Apologise? Get out his remorse like it's a pet mouse he keeps in his pocket? 'I'd be embarrassed to apologise,' he tells her. 'It's not like he farted during dinner or dropped her best plate. Sorry, Hazel, I wish I hadn't . . .' How wrong can you be? His eyes bore into Charlotte across the table, but she ignores it, continues as if she has a list to get through.

'Are you hoping that Hazel might forgive you?'

'Why the hell should she?' Isn't it more likely that she'll hate him even more for what he did? And as for whether he is hoping to feel less guilty afterwards, that too is more likely to be the exact opposite, isn't it? So, what is this?

'Do you,' he asks, 'enjoy playing shrink?'

'Hey, back down,' Charlotte tells him. 'I'm only trying to understand what's in it for you.' Her huge eyes, shadowed in complex variations of pewter and plum, go momentarily hard.

'Sorry,' he says. 'I don't know what's in it for me.' It's unreal. Too real.

Charlotte has taken his hand in hers. She's rubbing the back of it, over and over the same place. At first he's so remote from her, from the room even, that he can't actually feel it, and then, suddenly, it irritates him. He puts his other hand on top to still the movement, then takes them both back.

'Are you expecting to feel better afterwards?' Charlotte's voice is low. 'I mean, when this woman whose daughter you murdered sits with you in a room and tells you how it's been for her, are you going to feel better or worse?'

There's a long silence between them. He is aware of her still looking at him, of his hands, of the pattern on the table and the muddle of voices in the room, the smells of smoke and perfume. A baby sitting on its dad's lap two tables away is crying, outraged. You can see the mother wants it back, but he keeps holding on, trying this and that. Some other kids are playing with toy cars on the mats in the corner.

He is aware that he has, at last, decided to say 'yes' to Hazel's request and that the reason is not just guilt, though it's there, of course. It's something to do with knowing that where it went wrong was the lenses; that when Amanda stood there in front of him 'yes' or even 'maybe' would have saved them both.

'There would be counselling before,' he tells Charlotte. 'There'd be other people there,' he tells her, 'to mediate. If it did something for her,' he says, 'if she got something off her chest, then it might make me feel a bit better.' There's something wrong with this, he knows, but he can't put his finger on it.

'She might feel a whole lot worse,' Charlotte says, her voice still low, her face set. 'As for what you told me before, about how she feels she should have known and been able to stop it, she doesn't need *you* to say she couldn't have. Anyone can tell her that . . . What bothers me is that if you do this it could set you right back and who knows where you'll end up. Then at the end of it, you'll still have your hoop to jump through, they've told you that. Simon, don't. Say no.'

Next to them, the man reluctantly gives the baby back to its mother and immediately, the crying stops.

'Don't you want to get out?' Charlotte asks. She just doesn't understand! 'You know you could get out of here, live a life, if you put yourself to it. It drives me mad,' she tells him. 'You don't seem to want to!' Simon glares at her across the table, aware suddenly of all her imperfections, the strong jaw, the over-use of make-up, especially blusher on the cheekbones, to distract from it; the skin-tight tops; the whole me-first way of thinking and the way she assumes she can have a valid opinion about anything when the fact is she herself is a total mess anyway.

'You don't know what you're talking about!' he tells her. More than anything, he'd like to go back to his cell and lie down. But she's not having it:

'No?' she comes back at him. 'I haven't killed anyone, if that's what you mean, but I have been alive for twenty-nine years and I can tell you, this is not something you can make better.' She just doesn't know when to stop and that is a thing about women, they just never seem to know when to stop. Who the hell do you think you are? he thinks. How dare *you* tell *me* –

'You're alive, aren't you?' she's saying. 'You can fill your life with something else, *as well*, can't you?' You stupid cunt, he's thinking, what's it to you? His hands are fisted and he's going to stop this right now.

'Listen –' he barks at her. But still Charlotte doesn't stop; she puts both her perfectly manicured hands flat on the table, leans forward a little.

'No,' she says, 'you listen to *me*, Simon Austen. I can tell you for free that the interesting thing isn't what you did but what you do *next*.'

'I – don't – know –' he belts the words out one at a time, so loud that his face and throat hurt, likewise, differently, his balled hands and rigid shoulders. 'I – don't – know – what – I – do – next!' The room empties of sound. Two officers descend on them.

'Sorry,' Charlotte tries, faking a smile even though she is swallowing back tears. 'It's all right really. Please.' It doesn't work, of course, and Simon is glad to stand up and be taken away. Glad? Well, he needs the movement but not the glimpse of her he has, still at the table by the window, a broad-shouldered blonde, head in hands, sobbing while an officer waits awkwardly near by.

In the cell, he punches the wall. The walls are well used to such attacks, were built with them in mind. They don't care. He punches the wall again. Pain shoots down his arm. The room has never seemed so small. When the hand won't take any more, he sits down, breathing hard.

Charlotte! How come he's let himself come to be mixed up with a disaster zone like her, set himself up for all this extra grief? Didn't he always know that visits were more trouble than they were worth? How is it she can't see how awful she's being? Why doesn't she understand that she can't know about this? That she should back him up, or keep right out of it.

Can't she see how she is just making it worse, putting more pressure on when he is already feeling like he could burst into a million pieces? Why is she letting him down, now, of all times? It's never going to be the same for him as it is for anyone else – why can't she see it? What he did is never going to go away. He can't have a fucking operation, right?

Blood oozes from the chipped knuckles on his hand. They're swelling up. He's got to get all this over to her, he thinks. How things are. That living includes this. You go along nicely and then wham. It's part of him. She's just got to accept it.

He lies down. Closes his eyes. Breathes, in and out until he can no longer hear the blood rushing in his ears. Then he tries to imagine what his life would be like without her. Suppose that name wasn't in his head any more.

Of course, he thinks, the fact is, Charlotte hasn't *got to* do anything. Won't. Charlotte won't ever do anything she doesn't want to do, or not for long. Only as an experiment. And the fact is, she didn't actually say that the past would go away. She said that it *wouldn't* and then she said: 'You can fill your life with something else as well.' That's what she actually said. The fact is, if you look at it straight on, she's not so very far out, but she's in there fighting him for something and they have just had a row. A *blazing* row.

He lies there on the bed, exhausted now, and says the words aloud: *a blazing row.* It's a fucking miracle! First, no one's been hit. Or died, for that matter. Second, there's this to consider: when she said, Don't you want to get out of here?, was she saying also that she wanted him to? Was she saying, despite him being how he is, she would really like to see what it was like, with him out of here? That they might, for instance, sit across each other at a table in a pub or restaurant? Drive somewhere, lie on their backs on a sunny hillside? Forget. Turn on to their sides, face to face, close?

You can't be sure, Joanne said, over a year ago now, what she wants you for.

She wants him to get out. That's something.

And third, he wants it too. It? To find out. To see. He wants to tell her that just as much as he wants to tell her all over again that he can never put the past behind him. That he has to respond to Hazel's request. Will she help him? Let him, any-way? Yes, he will do the fucking course! He'll jump hoops! But there will never be a line drawn. He'll be released, eventually, but never actually free. Does she understand this?

He's shaking a bit. There's the photograph of Charlotte, fixed above the table. There's notepaper, envelopes. In a letter, you can get it all down, everything; you can say exactly what you want. But a letter won't get there until Tuesday at the earliest. There's a phone card in his back pocket. He can use it at 6 p.m. tonight, so long as she is at home. If she isn't, he'll worry; he'll be there until he gets an answer. Finally, he'll hear her voice.

'Are you OK? Look,' he'll say, 'I'm sorry, Charlotte. This is difficult, Charlotte—'

Afterword & Thanks

Over a decade ago, I spent a year working as Writer in Residence at HMP Nottingham. During this time and afterwards, I visited a number of other men's prisons in the UK. My observations of these various institutions do of course inform *Alphabet*, but it is important to make clear that, just like the characters, the institutions and regimes described in the book are entirely fictional. They are, I hope, plausible for the time, but not intended to represent any particular prison or treatment programme within it.

It is never possible to remember or to fit everyone who has helped in the writing of a book into the acknowledgements. In the past I have allowed this to prevent me from even trying. In this case, it is even more difficult than usual, since some of those who have helped are out of touch, may not want to be mentioned, could be living outside again with new names, and so on. However, this makes the list shorter and perversely, I will try this time.

For invaluable help, direct or indirect, in researching and writing *Alphabet* I am particularly indebted to the following people and groups, although of course, my mistakes are very much my own: Wendy Silberman; Maggy Topley; Erwin James (author of *A Life Inside*); the Prison Reform Trust; the *Prison Service Journal*; many of the inmates and staff, especially those in Education at HMP Nottingham; Angela Devlin (author of *Cell Mates, Soul Mates*); David Wilson; Hazel Banks; Christopher Russell; David Cooke; Neil Blacklock; Lesley Moreland (for her book *An Ordinary Murder*); Ursula Smartt (for her book *Grendon Tales*); Waterside Press (for its excellent range of publications on crime and punishment in the

UK); the late Tony Parker (for his interviews in *Life after Life* and *The Frying Pan*). A special mention goes to the Arts Council of Great Britain, who many years ago granted me a writer's bursary for this project, and to Bobbi and Gordon Ruckle, who built me an office so that I could finally get to grips with it.

The most heartfelt thanks of all goes to Richard Steel, for his encouragement and support. More encouragement and thought-provoking responses to early drafts came from my writing friends, especially Vicky Grut and Helen Heffernan; from my agent, Lesley Shaw, and my tactful but ruthless editor, Helen Garnons-Williams. Without all of you I would not have finished what I began.